GARDENERS
of
the UNIVERSE

GARDENERS
of the UNIVERSE

Ronald E. Peterson

**CALUMET
EDITIONS**
Minneapolis

Printed in the United States of America.
10 9 8 7 6 5 4 3 2 1

ISBN: 978-1-950743-65-0

Cover and book design by Paul Nylander, Illustrada Design

CONTENTS

WARNER FAMILY

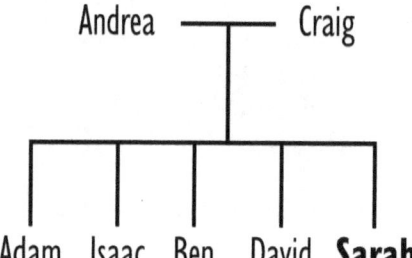

Andrea ——— Craig

Adam Isaac Ben David **Sarah**

JORGENSON FAMILY

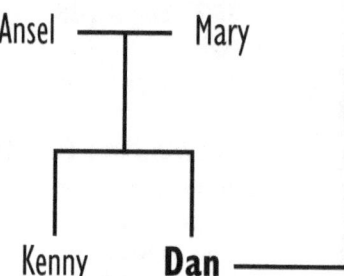

Ansel ——— Mary

Kenny **Dan** ———

ORLOV FAMILY

READ FAMILY

Joti ——— Kyle

Jeremy ——— Laurel

Rianne

Myra ——— Peter Matti Dabni Linus Ian

Nick ——————— Lené

Gina Jim

PROLOGUE

The Torae didn't think of themselves as gods; the idea of "Gardeners" had always seemed more apt. They'd engineered new life, intelligent life, many times, but the results were generally disappointing. Torae were not omnipresent, but more than any other species, they'd explored the entire universe. With quadrillions of far-flung probes, Torae could watch events virtually anywhere, but they had neither the time nor inclination to do so. They possessed enormous power, wresting energy directly from stars, quasars, and even vacuum itself. They'd been spawned at first light, when a whirl of stable ions spun off a daughter vortex, and they would endure until the stars finally flickered out. Crucially, no Gardener had yet attempted the central obligation of a god: to build a new universe.

Sower, the type of Gardener who scattered the seeds of life, had tinkered on Earth before, with a gentle genetic nudge here and there. A long-range probe hidden in orbit around the Earth sent occasional reports, describing mass extinctions, genetic rebounds, climate extremes, the emergence of tools, fire, and human intelligence. But the latest report from that long-range probe caught her by surprise. It documented the human invention of language.

Human knowledge will accumulate rapidly now, Sower thought. *Movement toward self-destruction or transcendence is inevitable.* "Redirect," she ordered in a staccato ultraviolet. Without hesitation, her huge ship changed course. *Our presence when a species first plans its own evolution is rare. Missing the most pliable moment in their history would be a pity.*

Sower knew the odds for the so-called *Homo sapiens* were low. The other beings that shared her gaseous form, Pruner and Tiller, were even more skeptical. "They're slow-time creatures," said Pruner, scoffing with a sour infrared warble.

As first-generation Gardeners, they had direct memory of the armada of fast-ships leaving the Origin only two billion Earth years after the birth of time, back when the universe was still small enough to get around. Torae teams had since examined all the interesting nooks, and Sower had received reports on 20 billion sites flourishing with life, 10,000 types of self-aware organisms, and hundreds of magnificent multistar empires. In that assemblage, humans had held the rank of "Monitor only." She decided to push them up a notch to "Evaluate for readiness." Sower understood the source of true power: the decisions a species makes about its own design. The humans on Earth would soon make those choices.

The Torae were light-huggers, nearly pure energy, and could accelerate at three thousand times Earth's gravity—a force that would crush the delicate humans. During this journey, due to relativity, Sower felt the passing of only twenty-eight hours while fifty thousand years expired on Earth. As her ship hurtled toward Earth, the orbiting probe unfolded humanity's story: its struggle for survival, wars, languages, inventions, and motivations through the millennia. *Communication improvements always trigger the greatest social and technical progress,* Sower thought. When humans invented the printing press, telephone, and radio during her trip toward Earth, she worried they might arrive too late.

With her command vehicle still five light-years from Earth, more veiled probes dropped into planetary orbit. "Detailed human analysis initiated," an early message said. Soon, thousands of probe reports poured back:

> "Species ready for biological engineering."
> "Likelihood of addictive regression: 42 percent."
> "Artificials are certain during our intervention."
> "Global self-destruction probability: 49 percent."
> "Diversity revulsion: 43 percent. . . ."

On the command ship, Pruner offered his key judgments: "Aggression and altruism are within limits. Risk-to-caution balance is also acceptable."

Sower was astonished. "Begin embryo design," she said in a wary yellow-indigo. Only 3 percent of species at the human technical level had tolerable timeline projections. Too many became warlike pests, killed themselves off, or chose meaningless lives of ease and diversion from reality. By not yet choosing to stagnate and drift back to irrelevance, humans had passed their preliminary exam.

As Sower's command ship traversed the broad Oort cloud of comets, eighty additional probes reached Earth. They began to scan every electromagnetic signal, catalog thousands of conversations, and monitor the detailed thoughts of about two hundred families—a winnowing process.

The probes also examined DNA sequences to assess genetic drift and mutation since Sower's last visit.

Near the center of her forty-kilometer command ship, Sower activated a special chamber, an incubator for humanoid embryos. Layers of superconducting cloth protected this ovoid from stray electromagnetic fields. Babies were designed there, and refined by teracubes of incoming data from Earth. Sentient machines assembled the new DNA, atom by atom.

"At this moment," Sower said—a wishful yellow-orange chirp—"these embryos may be the most precious cargo in this galaxy. They'll be our gift to the humans."

TIME ONE
BEGINNINGS

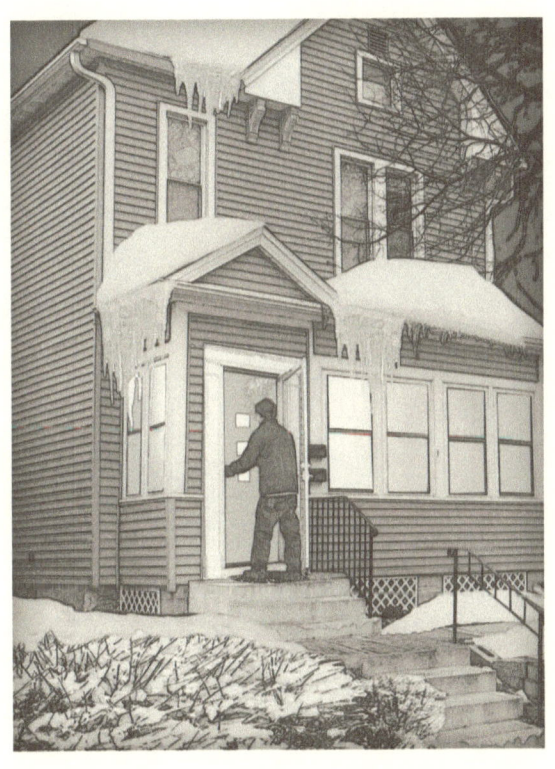

FROGTOWN

Ansel Jorgenson hiked alone up the steep bluff toward Frogtown. He glanced back, past the state capitol dome and downtown St. Paul buildings to the frozen floodplain and twinkling streetlights fading softly to the south. An icy gust, the "devil's tongue" he called it, lashed at his back and neck. It had been a long winter—too long. He wouldn't be the first or last to feel the cold sting. He felt pity for the early immigrants, the five hundred generations before him, who'd slogged up the same limestone cliffs unprepared for the Arctic wind. He imagined an ancestor of the Lakota standing on that very spot, and the more recent arrivals—the French, English, Scandinavians, Germans, Irish, Hmong, Latinos, and Somalis who stayed a generation or two and moved on. Anyone living on these high banks over the continent's greatest river learned to be prudent, or they died.

Squinting to protect his eyes, he continued up the steep sidewalk, gloved hands deep in the pockets of his jacket. He thought of his own life as a mosaic of hard realities, determination, momentary joys, and empty dreams, where the tiles didn't fit well and key pieces, especially his future, were missing. Once again he'd worked late at the metal yard for a few extra bucks. All he wanted now was to get home to his family and warmth.

My son will do better. Mary wasted too much on Christmas this year. I hope she's not letting Kenny wait up for me.

At the top of the quiet hill in a swirl of snow, a voice called to the center of his mind, and he stopped to look around.

Deciding it was just the wind, he turned north onto Rice Street, the lights and signs from myriad shops, restaurants, offices, and small factories temporarily blinding him. Odors of hot oil from a burger joint lingered along the street. Fresh snow on the sidewalk covered his ankles. A plow rushed by throwing frozen slush, forcing him to duck into a restaurant door front. *Good God, my kingdom for a warm shower and supper.*

He left the garish Rice Street a half mile later, turning onto the familiar avenue of bungalows, decrepit Victorians, and two-story walk-ups. The traffic sounds faded, but then he heard the voice again. *Where's that coming from?* The back of his neck felt warm. His mind reeled. An ice rut in the street caught his foot and he half fell.

Damn, I'm beat.

He pulled his stocking hat lower, steadied himself, and focused on the glowing house windows ahead. On this bitter night, the prudent people of

Frogtown huddled indoors, pursuing their varied ambitions: to survive, succeed, copulate, vegetate, procreate, or achieve a happier afterlife. All Ansel wanted was to join them.

Past an amber streetlight the path grew dim, revealing a halo of atmospheric ice around a sliver moon. The ground would radiate its feeble heat away by morning, bringing record lows. Even now the air stung and induced feelings of dreamy emptiness. His spine shook—an involuntary fever-shiver.

A voice clearly said, "We should talk, Ansel." It seemed familiar. He felt a sharp pain near his right temple, a headache stab. Pressing his gloved hand hard against the ear helped a bit. He was almost home.

Christmas lights, which he should have taken down long ago, glowed in his bushes, their colors softened to pastels by the translucent snowfall. The front steps of his old house looked icy and unsafe, so he pulled himself up by the railing. A peephole had been rubbed through the frost on his three-year-old son's bedroom window.

Kenny's been watching for me.

The front door had three small square windows. Past the living room, he saw Mary stacking dishes in the kitchen under a warm, yellow light. Kenny, in his PJs, hugged her legs and darted off.

He held the freezing doorknob and noticed he'd been sweating. Perspiration was frozen on his face and his toes were numb. He stared through the tiny windows for over a minute, his mind a blank. Vapor from his slowing breath swirled around his face and floated up silently.

Turning, he inched back down the icy stairs, gripping the metal bar with both hands, and saw a hazy image across the road. He stepped high over the snow plowed onto the curb and headed back toward Rice Street.

I should walk with my friend awhile.

PROBES

When Sower's ship crossed the Kuiper belt, it decelerated and chose to mimic the trajectory and appearance of an elongated rocky comet. Exposure as aliens would be unlikely in that form.

Hundreds of hidden probes now encircled Earth. In general, probes enabled Sower access to the universe beyond her toroidal plasma form, as instruments of observation, warfare, species manipulation, and dozens of other functions. Scattered as far as 10 light-years from the command ship, they communicated using coherent gamma rays. Acting as a single immense aperture, their telescopes could resolve one-meter objects at 100 million light-years. Those currently parked in Earth's orbit flooded data back to the command ship, fine-tuning the intervention:

> "Access to global communication: 86% percent."
> "Unjustified cruelty: 23 percent."
> "Sustainable energy use: 18 percent."
> "Destructive habitual behavior: 63 percent. . . ."

Pruner expressed a serious concern by rolling violet waves through exposed plasma. "Shared-idea ownership is less than 27 percent. Humans will never reach consensus on their evolution. We should bolster social coherence through unifying wars."

"No," Sower said. "Progress will be slow, but their pathologies are in balance. Over 94 percent think they are capable of independent thought, but only 6 percent are. Plan to strengthen the voices of the wise. Give them greater courage."

"Our children will be despised as they age," Tiller said. "We may need six."

"If we select families who are geographically proximate, they can share the same language and work together as they mature," Pruner said. "Three will be adequate."

Sower's near-Earth probes patiently waited for her orders. In most cases they would communicate with the humans as they slept. Torae voices would blend into dreams.

～～～～～

The Torae intended to extend the life of the universe and perhaps save it. Portions of Sower's mind computed timelines and projected human development millennia into the future. *They're so fragile—probably just another doomed experiment.* Her other thoughts dreamed of watching humans achieve transcendence, to become worthy, so that she could finally go home, to the Origin, the heart of Torae culture, power, and joy. It was Sower's fondest hope.

"The three target families have been prepared," Pruner said. "Begin full intervention."

The signal from Sower's command ship took 10 hours to reach the planet. Billions of microprobes dropped to Earth. In the following twenty-four-hour period, eight million people heard Torae whispers while they slept and unknowingly had their lives adjusted.

Three mothers became unexpectedly pregnant.

ALTADENA

"I definitely smell smoke," said Kyle Orlov, leaning back in a lounge chair on his deck which overlooked the San Gabriel valley. "It adds a lovely tinge of umber to the smog, don't you think?"

Joti grinned at him and stretched an arm to catch some breeze. She'd changed into a skimpy swimsuit and carefully draped a towel on the railing to block the view from the house across the street. "It's dry early this year," she said.

Santa Anas off the desert fed brush fires north of Glendale, now noticeable at the Orlov home in the Altadena foothills 10 kilometers away. "If you can smell smoke, it's too close." He glanced at the small display on his wrist and slowly enunciated, "News—California—Local—Fires."

Joti smirked. "And what does your oracle say?"

Kyle tapped on his left ear bud under his long curly hair. "It says the wind has shifted north. Looks like we'll be okay here, but they're having trouble putting them out."

"I'll be sure to note that in my personal datalog tonight," she said, teasing him about his passion for techno-gadgets. She kept her notes the old fashioned way—longhand using a fountain pen in a leather-bound journal.

He let his mind drift, forgetting about the fires and the day's work, and moved his recliner setting down a notch. The red-brown sun dipped toward the horizon, and the blue carpet of jacaranda petals along their quiet street disappeared in the twilight, leaving only their lilac fragrance.

〜〜〜〜〜

Kyle loved their new house near the top of Lake Avenue. He'd never say it, but the home's perch on the brush line conferred a slight sense of superiority over the residents in the sprawling valley below. It fit his conflicted ambitions—not ostentatious, but not ordinary either.

Joti and Kyle had both grown up in the area, meeting at UCLA. He'd fallen for her quickly because of her stunning mocha body, exotic intelligent eyes behind enormous glasses, and a dry wit that fit his contradictions. She could stroke his ego while simultaneously keeping it under control. He knew he was an easy mark, surrounding himself with voice-activated this and that, widgets both practical and impractical. He'd even worn an old Google eye-display for a month around campus until he started getting dizzy spells. He decided to marry Joti when she called him "my gizmo shark" in front of her girlfriends. "Watch out," she said, "he's the world's most dangerous legal creature."

Joti graduated as a mechanical engineer and took a lab tech job at Caltech while he wrestled his way through law school. One special night, the night he proposed, he also revealed his long-term plan. "Lawyers become politicians, and politicians run the world. I want to do that. Sort of."

His current job didn't advance the running-the-world strategy much. Every morning he'd drive his old BMW down Lake Avenue, spend the day in a small Pasadena office with two elderly lawyers, and hash through boring estate plans for wealthy locals. At least it paid well.

The night cooled quickly after sunset and Joti began to fold up her towel. Kyle watched her lovingly. She was currently sporting short dreadlocks dyed deep orange, almost red. "I dreamt about babies again last night," she said. "I saw myself tucking an innocent little one in a crib and heard an odd voice comforting me." She brushed hair off her forehead and looked at him. Her brown eyes were magnified in the big glasses.

She's worried. Heck, I'm disappointed too, he thought.

He grabbed her hand and held on. "I'm so sorry we haven't . . . conceived yet, Joti. You have your doctor tests tomorrow, right? You're frightened, aren't you?"

"A little. Funny how I keep thinking about it."

"We've just been unlucky."

"My dreams are strange, and they're always crystal clear when I wake up. There's this man, he sounds like a professor from the university or something. He says, 'Find her siblings.' Last night in the dream, I remember I told him to go away. It's spooky."

"I'd stay clear of the professor guy," he said. "But even if we don't have a baby soon, we can have fun trying. You're probably dreaming about our professor on the mountain."

Their bedroom had large windows on the mountainside and they joked about a lonely astronomer on Mount Wilson pointing his telescope toward those windows at night. "Let's give the professor a good show," he said.

Kyle watched her check out his body. "You ready for me, white man?" she said.

The next morning, Joti rode her bicycle along Altadena and Pasadena side streets, weaving around parked cars and enormous storm drains. The bicycle flew down the steep hills, so it took only 10 minutes to get to the Caltech electro-optics lab where she worked. As usual, Joti arrived at the lab before any grad students. She put on her lab coat and thin hair cover, threw a switch, and watched as laser beams crisscrossed a large granite slab.

She loved the fact that Kyle's office was only a few blocks away. By wearing wrist screens and keeping the line open, they could talk and see each other whenever they wanted. It was almost like working in the same office. They often ate lunch together and usually rode home in Kyle's old BMW with her bicycle dangling on the back.

Kyle hadn't slept well and he'd been at his Green Street office since seven thirty a.m., listlessly sorting papers and fretting about the wildfires. He tuned his desk display to local news and glanced sporadically at the scroll line until he saw "Flames just jumped the Arroyo Seco. They're threatening the Jet Propulsion Lab and West Altadena." A spasm of panic hit him.

"Gotta go!" he shouted down the hall to the senior partners. "The fire is close to my house!" He called Joti, but she didn't answer so he jogged to his car and headed up Lake Avenue.

He saw huge water drones and helicopters circling the foothills as he drove. Police at a barricade eight blocks from his house were redirecting cars, but Kyle pulled right up to the barrier. While his heart raced and a leg shook nervously, a hard-faced cop strolled to his window. "You need to turn around, sir."

Kyle considered sneaking in through a side street, but instead pulled out the most mature lawyer face he could muster. "I live up there and need to get my pets out. I'll leave immediately." He handed a business card to the cop and said, "Call this number if you hear it's worse." The policeman looked puzzled and hesitated long enough for Kyle to roll through.

He beeped Joti again with his arm phone. "I just bluffed my way past a cop and I'm heading to the house. The fire's close. We're not going to lose our new house without a fight."

"Hang on a sec," she said. "I'm in a crowd." After a pause: "Okay, I can talk. I'm at an Einstein celebration by Beckman Auditorium. What'd you say about bluffing a cop? You can't bluff my mother."

"Oh, nothing. I'll be at the house in a minute."

"Please, don't do anything dangerous. . . . I swear, I won't forgive you if you do anything stupid."

He heard the panic in her voice. "I'll be careful, Joti."

Police in vans with loudspeakers were urging residents to leave. Many neighbors were anxiously spraying their roofs with water. A dense cloud of smoke blew through just as Kyle reached his driveway, hiding his house for a moment. He ran into the backyard and climbed a hill where his neighbor was hacking at the brush.

"I was there." His neighbor Jack gestured up the hill. "The fire is past the west ridge, heading straight this way." Jack looked truly frightened. A warm gust blew against their faces.

"This won't work," Kyle yelled with an odd sense of resolve. "We're going to lose our homes. Let's get the neighbors to help cut a firebreak."

Hurrying back to his garage, he looked around, considered using his expensive new Mowbot, but decided a machete would be more effective. He honked his car horn, yelled, and waved his arms, attracting six more people. His tie and suit coat went flying into the BMW. Then, using all his legal training and firm, precise tones, he convinced the group to clear a diagonal path up the foothill.

They gathered at a split-level on the end of the street and headed up the steep slope with hedge trimmers, axes, and weed whackers. Several massive water drones were flying low into the flames and dumping fire retardant along the western ridge, their four rotors deafening. Kyle took the lead, slashing left and right to open a path through the dry brush.

A hundred meters up the hill the smoke became so thick they could taste it. Choking, they heard a police megaphone. "Attention! You gentlemen on the hill, get the hell down from there. Now!" After staggering half-blind back to the street, police cars took them, coughing and sooty, down Lake Avenue.

***

That night, broadcasts and social media showed aerial pictures of Kyle and his neighbors slashing their way along the hill. "We're not recommending this type of dangerous action," a newswoman said, "but in this case it probably saved the neighborhood."

The fire had burned right up to their makeshift firebreak before the wind shifted and stopped the advance. Kyle wasn't sure their ragged hacking had made any difference to a blaze that had jumped streams and eight-lane freeways, but no one on TV asked him. A few silly people even gave Kyle Orlov and his collection of neighbors credit for saving Altadena.

***

Joti sat on the deck with Kyle the next night, wearing jean shorts and a loose blouse, admiring the valley lights and a few plane beacons crawling above the L.A. haze. Staring at her, Kyle realized how hopelessly in love he still felt. Something mysterious about Joti excited him. Perhaps it was her family roots and barely hidden fiery personality. Or maybe it was her silky, brown skin or the creative glow of her eyes.

Her parents had both been heroes. Joti's father, a Liberian, had worked for the Voice of America and escaped during the civil war there, emigrated to North Dakota, and apprenticed as an electrician. Her mother loved him and championed him amid regular snide and racist taunts, including some from her family. They moved to California before getting married.

Kyle's family had been in America for several generations, immigrating from Hungary in the early 1900s. His parents were in their late thirties when their only child was born. Kyle saw himself as a nerd—quiet, introverted, hiding in his technology and law studies. *Courage is not really in my skill set,* he thought, *despite what our crazy neighbors say. I don't know what got into me with that fire.*

Joti seemed to read his thoughts and turned the tables on him. "I knew you were handsome, skinny, funny, and really cute," she said, "but I hadn't imagined you as a brave hero type. You're the guy who took two months just to ask me out."

"Trust me, I'm not brave. I've always thought of myself as on the flight side in fight-or-flight situations."

"Is it true you almost sacrificed your precious Mowbot? How would we cut our tiny lawn without it?"

"Well, yeah, I was going to point it up the hill and set it free, no longer a slave to our yard, but I changed my mind. By the way, do I still stink? I think I smell smoke in my hair."

Joti lifted her legs and dropped them softly onto his thigh. "You smell sweet, even your curly hair. It's the house that'll never be the same. Even the flowers reek like a barbeque gone bad."

Her legs were moving gently back and forth over his. "At the Einstein whoop-de-do yesterday," she said, "there was a humongous three-story banner up on Beckman Auditorium with the words, 'Thanks for everything, big Al.' The speakers talked about black holes, gravity waves, the usual sort of thing. Then they announced that astronomers had found a comet out by Jupiter, a huge new one, about 30 miles long. We might even be able to see it through the L.A. light pollution if the air's not too soupy. Cool, huh?"

INTERVENTIONS

As Sower's ship swept through the solar system, her meddling on Earth was nearly finished. The earliest adjustments had been scientific. Humans stood on the verge of disruptive technological change in engineered biology, electronic thought, human/machine amalgams, and many other areas; Sower had acted to speed the process along. Her whispers to scientists' subconscious minds were aimed at their specific fields of research. Their dreams crystalized as they awoke or later in the shower. *Why didn't I think of that before?* they all wondered.

But Sower worried far more about the social and moral shifts that would follow. *They're useless as just another technically advanced species. Humans must select wisely and avoid the dead ends. They must find the paths that are right for their biology or the choices won't flourish.*

Sower preferred using subtle triggers for her societal tweaks. She instigated many changes through memes: ideas and phrases so catchy that people couldn't help passing them along—like advertising jingles.

Other social adjustments were necessarily more intrusive. Several lives were co-opted entirely, becoming Sower's agents on Earth. And by strengthening neural cross-links and enhancing enzyme production in key glands, the Torae had bestowed the gift of increased courage on three million wise, intelligent, but quiet people, including Kyle Orlov.

The fine-tuning proceeded on plan and, as the Torae ship neared Earth's solar orbit, microprobes had implanted the three new embryos. Images of the lives Sower had altered flooded her consciousness.

"I'll speak to the seed bearers now—the mothers."

The three embryos had partially nonhuman DNA. Pruner had sorted through over 1,000 families and finally chose those who could best nurture the Torae children, each with ethically strong mothers. Those children would manifest unique physical gifts, as well as irrepressibly divergent personalities. Humanity would get only a small taste of the Sower persona, but it would be enough.

Torae weren't perfect. They regularly upgraded their own life-code, as recommended in broadcasts from the Origin. During Sower's long journey, there'd been so many enhancements that she barely remembered her original form. But messages from the Origin never hinted at a change to the mission itself: the search for a technically mature ally with a worthy moral compass.

In their desire to develop, learn, and maintain galactic order, Torae had become ethically numb; they purposely ignored their past and couldn't hear the voices of their ancestors. They'd lost their capability for compassion, and they knew it. They couldn't possibly represent or make the risky final choices for the beings of this universe.

The cosmos would slowly expand and die. Sower had personally observed the beginnings of that dissipation during her long trips among galaxies. The Torae had the technology to ignite an everlasting instant, where a new universe would emerge from the void. They just didn't know how to control it. And they needed special beings who could speak for all the species of the universe to help them.

Sower said, "Intervention complete."

⁂

"Star flicker on vector 14073,68855," a probe reported.

They were being watched.

MANASSAS

"That dang comet's so bright now you can see it in the daytime," Andrea Warner said to Adam, her oldest son, happy to be with him alone for just a moment. She twisted her head, squinting through the backlit oak leaves, trying to spot the comet again.

"You should wait 'til the sun sets," he said. "It's much more apparent then."

She gave up on the comet and turned her attention to the blooming pansies and Johnny-jump-ups lining the back porch. *It's a beautiful day. One to remember*, she thought. *Adam's leaving will be painful, but it's a blessed transition, a landmark in his life.*

Adam's high school graduation party was breaking up. Most of his school friends had left, leaving relatives to clean up, watch a ball game on TV, or play cards. Andrea had worn her favorite flowered dress and had her hair done for the occasion. She figured over a hundred people had mingled that afternoon among the shady old trees, wolfing down their bratwursts, beer, watermelon, and potato chips.

"What's your father doing now?" she asked.

"Harassing Kate! And he spent the afternoon giving out free advice to my other friends. Jeez, I especially wish he'd leave Kate alone. I think I really like her."

From high on the back porch of the Warner farmhouse, one could see the barn, shed, grazing meadows, and the acres that would soon flourish with strawberries, peanuts, pumpkins, and marijuana during the warm summer. Several cars and pickups were still parked along the edge of their long gravel driveway, which connected to a county road leading toward the Manassas National Battlefield, site of two epic clashes of the American Civil War. The farm had been in Andrea's family even before that time.

Andrea saw that Adam's latest girlfriend looked uneasy with Craig hunched close to her at the table. "Craig, come on up here," Andrea shouted to her husband. "Leave that poor girl alone. They need you here to play cards."

He glanced up at her and smiled back.

"Your father likes to keep on top of everything," Andrea said. "He says we're losin' control of your three brothers. It bugs him that they aren't obedient like his sales reps, or his Marine troops in Iraq, or you, for that matter. He says you were God's way of sucking us into more kids, 'cause you were so easy."

"He told me I had to write a strategic plan for my life before I can leave for Georgetown," Adam said. "His usual corporate nonsense," he said, sighing.

The three younger boys, especially Isaac, are a handful, Andrea thought. *I caught Isaac holding Ben's head underwater in the horse trough yesterday. And Craig himself is no better than a kid. I'm sleeping badly. Keep having those screwy dreams. I'm so tired.*

Craig left Adam's girlfriend cringing at the table and sauntered to another table, his shirt unbuttoned, looking pleased with himself.

Andrea whispered, "It'd be okay, Holy Father, if you didn't give me more children."

~~~~~~~~~

Adam helped his slightly obese uncle set up several card tables on the recently painted red porch, which extended along the entire length of the farmhouse. A dozen flowerpots with geraniums hung over the railing for the special occasion, as well as his "Happy Graduation" banner.

"Pa," he yelled down, "hurry up. We need your money up here."

It was a Warner tradition for men to play Five Hundred after eating. Several had been lured to the porch when they saw card tables going up, either to play or kibitz. Adam's six-foot-six father marched directly to him, squeezed his shoulders, and finished with a playful chop to the neck.

"Thanks for the contusion, Pa."

Dad still has his military buzz cut, but he sure couldn't fit into his uniform anymore. He's friendly and scary, at the same time. Probably how he got into management.

Craig turned to Andrea and grabbed her hips, whispering something in her ear. Seeing his mother flinch, Adam was disgusted with his father. The last several weeks, as he prepared to leave for college, Adam had taken to evaluating those around him.

"I need a first-class partner, Adam. You feeling lucky today?"

"Sure, Pa."

"Let's challenge your uncle and cousin. They're easy to beat, and I want to discuss some farm business with them. We need to rotate in some new cash crops with all this stupid weather change." Adam's mother owned the farm and Craig worked for a defense company in D.C., so his brother worked the land. They split any profits.

All the Warner kids had assigned work around the farm. Adam was happy to be leaving for college; he'd finally be off the chore list that had been on the kitchen wall as long as he could remember. And he could stop looking after his younger brothers, who he had never learned to manage.

The men placed dollar bets on the table corners and cards were dealt.

"What were you talking to Kate about?" Adam asked.

"Not much," Craig smirked. "I told her to be ready to survive on the earnings of an amateur pickleball player if your 'doctor' plans don't work out."

"Smooth, Pa. I've only been hanging with her a couple weeks."

"What's it like at Georgetown?" his cousin interrupted.

"Well, I just visited for three days," Adam said, looking at his cards, "but I can see the women are going to be a distraction. I signed up for the pre-med track."

"Will they teach you how to play cards in any of those expensive doctor classes I'll be paying for?" his father asked.

"There's no official curriculum for Five Hundred, near as I can tell, but I'm sure there'll be poker in the dorms."

"You should do okay. We didn't give you the nickname Lucky for no reason." Pa flashed a sly side smile toward his brother. "Have you ever won at this table through actual skill, Adam?"

Adam felt a familiar gnawing begin in his stomach. Through several games, his father continued to taunt him in ways that had grown routine over the years. *He's such a jerk*, Adam thought. Even his uncle and cousin seemed annoyed by all the barbs.

"I need a new partner," Craig said loudly after losing a trick and the hand. "I'm paying a small fortune for you to go off to college and you play like a frickin' dummy. You'll probably have to graduate before you know your butt from an ace," Craig said, tossing his cards at Adam.

Adam had hoped his high school graduation might garner a little respect. Apparently not. Then an unfamiliar sense of resolve swept over him. He sat motionless for a few seconds, slowly turned his cards over, stood up, and said, "Play with yourself, asshole," before walking away.

<center>~~~~~</center>

News of Adam's minirebellion spread among the relatives at the party. It confused the family and especially worried Andrea. Her oldest, perfect son had never openly defied his father before or had even sworn around the farm, as far as she knew. She wept the next morning when Adam announced he planned to leave right away for Georgetown. He packed his things and disappeared. He texted Andrea two days later to say he was settled and wouldn't be back until Christmas.

Craig grumbled and snapped at the other boys every morning before commuting to his office. Andrea was sad about the uproar but also pleased that Adam had finally stood up to his father. She had held the family together, despite her husband, for almost 20 years. She was definitely proud of Adam.

Andrea was a high school Spanish teacher when she married Craig, the handsome tall Marine, between his tours in Iraq. Even after the war, she was alone often with their growing family and farm worries while Craig traveled selling weapons technology. She'd grown strong, both mentally and physically.

Two weeks later, with Craig on a week-long marketing trip to Europe, she quietly checked into a day hospital and had her fallopian tubes laser fused. She was exhausted for a few days, but the kids didn't notice. She never told Craig.

Millions of sensors constantly surveyed the hot ion flows, electronic fields, and tightly woven molecular cloth within Sower's internal structure. Those sensors were remnants of the beings that once lived and fought in that volume before the ancient co-joining. They monitored the pulsing, familiar, ionized life, far different from the cold images sent by autonomous probes in her ship or those farther out, across the vast vacuum. A few of those distant probe eyes now focused on one human family of two parents and four brothers, who showed an ideal behavioral balance. One brother was wise, another simple-minded, and a third hopelessly shy and nervous. The fourth brother was also of great interest. He held the potential for appalling evil.

Nine-year-old Isaac glared at his little brother. "Quit kickin' me, you little poop, or I'll elbow you in the head."

"You're not the boss of me anymore," seven-year-old Ben said. "I got a new boss who talks to me at night."

"I don't have time for you or your imaginary friends, butt-face. Where did Jake go? Dang."

Jake, the large gray and white tomcat, had escaped again. When Isaac saw the cat darting through an opening in the barn door, he chased after him. Ben followed, waddling past the huge red door just before Isaac slammed it shut so Jake couldn't escape.

"Hey, Jake, where are you? Here, catty cat," Isaac called while searching behind a horse-stall door. "There you are." He picked Jake up carefully from behind with his claws pointed away. "I know your tricks, Jake," he said, holding the cat at arm's length.

"Follow me, Ben," Isaac yelled. He ran up a ramp to the loft over the horse stalls while holding the cat by the fur on its neck. Jake yowled.

Ben climbed up reluctantly.

Ben always does what I tell him. Stupid, Isaac thought.

"Watch me try something," Isaac said. "Adam says he's like a cat, 'cause cats always land on their feet. Let's see if old Jake here's a real cat."

He lifted Jake high over the loft edge, with his four feet twitching and clawing at the air. Then Isaac opened his hands and watched Jake tumble, twist, and land hard on all fours, screech, and run immediately to cower in a far corner of the barn.

"You thought I forgot about your scratching me, didn't you, Jake?" he shouted to the cat. Isaac smiled and looked at Ben.

"You wanna try jumping off?"

Ben shuffled down the ramp as fast as he could.

<hr />

Sower watched the probe images and brain scans, analyzing the Warner family. Normal humans experience a shaft of sympathetic pain when a mammal's flesh is squashed and it screams out. Ben heard the sounds and was frightened. Isaac understood the cat's pain but didn't care; he enjoyed it. Andrea had taught him right from wrong. He knew it was wrong, but it felt right to him. Isaac would soon forget what he'd done, but the Torae would remember.

Sower said, "He'll be an excellent challenge for the girl."

COMETS AND SHOOTING STARS

Sower's ship dipped deeply within the orbit of Mercury—a critical, dangerous time. Her onboard crew watched the solar corona carefully, forecasting its fusion weather to be sure they were safe from flares. They planned to sweep near the sun, reaching the closest point while aligned with Earth, to covertly gather free energy on the sunward side. They continued to jettison water vapor, carbon dioxide, dust, and ionized gases around the ship to form a coma and tail. Meanwhile, hundreds of probes near Earth were keeping eyes on the progress of their humanity experiment.

But they also hadn't forgotten the unknown object that caused a local star to blink. Distant members of Sower's probe armada scanned along several sightlines to identify what had momentarily blocked the star's light and to get a position fix. It wasn't long before Probe 364 said, "Star flicker on my vector 62374,13907. The intruder is 320 million kilometers from my position." The Torae were all relieved when the probe added, "Diameter is under 10 centimeters. Probably just interstellar junk."

Mary Jorgenson watched her son's eyes blink slowly; he was almost asleep. She touched his red cheek and said, "G'night, Kenny."

"I want Daddy," he said softly, his eyes popping open again.

"Daddy's gone away, honey."

"I want him to come back."

"Me too. But . . ."

He sat up and whispered toward her ear. "Daddy talks to me when I sleep. He says, 'Be nice to the baby.'"

"Aw, Kenny, we've discussed this before. Daddy has been gone over six weeks. Police are looking, but he might not be coming back."

"Daddy did talk. I remember. He said I'm big and should protect the baby. An' I think Daddy's an angel."

"I don't know, Kenny." She pushed hair gently from his ear. "You were just dreaming. He must have had an accident. Daddy loved you so much."

"But I wanna brother. Am I ever gonna get a brother?"

"I don't think so, honey. You better shut your eyes so you'll dream again. You can play with your brother in your dreams."

Mary waited until he stayed down before quietly closing the door. She saw her reflection—disheveled and dowdy—in a living room side window. She opened it to get a cross breeze, then flinched when June bugs started clack-buzzing under the screen. Waves of spring thunderstorms had swept through the Midwest and the long, humid Minnesota day was finally dying. Distant firecrackers sounded like muted pops as neighbors jumped the gun on the Fourth of July, but Mary didn't really notice. *I should be looking for a job—at least a part-time job. Money will be running out soon. I need to be strong and smart.*

Mary sank onto her sofa and thought about the last few terrible months, searching for clues. Ansel had started taking longer and longer walks back in January, and hanging out for hours at the bars down on Rice Street. Something had changed. Something had sucked the spirit out of him. He was so quiet around her, nearly mute, but he talked to himself in bed. She tried to recall his drunken words. Thinking he might be looking for other women, she had tricked him into sex a couple times, but even that only worked when he was drunk. *Was it depression, had someone threatened him, or was it some repressed Scandinavian trait? He just wouldn't tell me what was wrong.*

It's like he finally went on one of his slow walks and forgot to come home. But why should I assume he died? Police only did a token search along the railroad tracks and down by the river. They said he probably left town, ran away. They promised to circulate his photo ID around the Midwest.

Ansel loved Kenny and me. Something terrible must have happened, something he couldn't talk about. He was a tough guy, but kind and funny—it makes no sense. I love him so much. Where is he?

Mary grieved for the man she'd married, who was always so self-confident and tireless. She felt safe with Ansel, and precious. Why did he love her, a plain-faced high school dropout? But he did. "Where are you," she cried quietly.

Like Kenny, she'd had strange dreams. Closing her eyes, she recalled the trance-like voice, similar to her father's, saying, "You're a fortunate mother, Mary. The boy will have powerful gifts. Let him find his own way."

She got up awkwardly and walked onto the front step and turned toward Minneapolis, searching the western sky. *Why am I the only one who can't see that comet thing?*

The June bugs started up again, so she quickly shook her open-toed sandals and went back inside. She felt punk. Her forehead and eyes ached. *I've got to see a doctor. Something's wrong with me. But that costs money. I need to get a job.*

JUNE 15, FROM THE WORLD SATELLITE NEWS SERVICE

Caltech astronomers calculate the large mysterious comet will pass almost directly between the Earth and the Sun, a once-in-a-millennium event. International space agencies are scrambling to study the mysterious comet and its tail. If the tail persists, it could lead to a unique light show on Earth and electromagnetic interference with nearly all wireless signals.

Sower knew that both earthbound and orbital telescopes, including Chandra, ACE, and FIRST, had been examining her comet-ship for weeks. Europeans and Japanese hurriedly launched rockets to get an even better view. A French interceptor was slated to crash onto the comet, but Tiller made sure a key navigation sensor malfunctioned at a critical time. All the human observations revealed a typical lumpy, rocky ice ball with a normal tail. Sower showed the humans exactly what they expected, even adjusting the trajectory to account for the solar wind.

The unidentified object that had caused a few stars to blink still concerned Sower. Tiller ordered probes to project intense pulses toward its postulated location but saw no reflected energy. Then they got lucky. In quick succession, passive sensors reported seven more star occultations, got a hard fix and trajectory on one object, and identified the position of three more. An intensive Torae analysis concluded the objects held nonprimordial black holes. Due to their small motion relative to Sol, they were definitely unnatural.

Television satellite vans were double-parked at the corner of Wilson and California, just outside the Caltech seismology building, the normal site for earthquake briefings. Joti noticed the commotion on her walk back from lunch and cut through the building to see what was happening. She listened as the Jet Propulsion Lab people gave yet another comet update for the networks. One official said the comet tail's proximity to Earth would be the closest in over 1,200 years. "It won't actually hit our planet, but it will sweep very close. We've prepared a short movie."

Joti watched the comet animation for a while but her attention drifted off. Her hands were clammy. Kyle's doctor had said that even with advanced fertilization drugs they had only a remote chance of conceiving a baby naturally. She'd scheduled an appointment with a different doctor for late that afternoon to discuss her test results.

I'm afraid; face it. And I feel awful. God, I really want a baby.

During the night, she'd awakened several times with vivid dreams involving the shadowy mountaintop professor, leaving her tired and disoriented. His clawing voice kept saying that her baby would be a "searcher." She got up early, frustrated and sweating.

When the comet movie ended, she hurried back across campus to help with some lab renovations. The senior professor where she worked had started a fresh line of research on optical mass memories that required special equipment. He said he'd had an inspiration in a dream.

"An intelligence is guiding those black holes," Sower said. "The paths are curving. We've analyzed two dozen star blinks. They're vehicles, but extremely small. Any passengers would likely be formed from the collapsed atoms of a cool dwarf or neutron star."

"Beings from dense stars have been documented as aggressive and single-minded," Tiller said, using a violet-UV squeak to signal concern.

"They must be highly synchronized, like automatons, to escape the intense gravity of their star crust," Pruner said. "Only directed nuclear fusion could lift them into orbit."

"It causes extensive surface damage on their home star," Tiller said. "We know of only four species who successfully escaped their star. Other Torae have always eliminated those species before they could overrun a galaxy. They breed rapidly but bring nothing positive."

Sower noticed Tiller's colors had shifted higher, to a deep UV chirp. "Contain your brutal zeal, Tiller," Sower said. "How did we miss the emergence of this swarm? They must be atypical. They might be unique."

"They're more likely vermin," Tiller said. "We should prepare to track them, find their origin, and exterminate."

Sower could hardly disagree. So Tiller was authorized to build attack probes and optimize detection sensors for the potential threat.

"I'm thinking about buying an electric van this fall," Craig said. "But I'll miss the roar of my gasoline engine, and I refuse to get one of those ugly auto-drive toys."

Andrea barely listened to him. She could hardly look around the dinner table. Craig's voice made her want to scream or cry.

That doctor's an idiot. He said he fused my tubes, but I still got pregnant. Great! I can't sue—I can't even complain. Craig would say God was punishing me for having the operation.

She sat, dismayed and silent. She had skipped praying before dinner and no one seemed to care.

Isaac squirted ketchup on Ben's hand. The boys were fighting all the time now. She'd caught Isaac killing a chicken behind the barn. Her youngest, David, was crying at bedtime for no apparent reason.

"David," Craig said. "Get that damn book off your lap."

David held his head down so his hair covered his eyes; he rarely made eye contact with anyone. "Don't wanna eat."

"It's suppertime," Craig said. "You eat."

David dropped the book he'd been glancing at under the table and pouted.

Soon, Andrea and her family went back to silently eating organic green beans and roast chicken from their farm.

As her ship approached the sun, Sower maximized an opening on the solar-facing side, but the opposite face continued to show Earth telescopes what appeared to be a normal comet. They were at one-fiftieth the orbital radius of Mercury, absorbing and storing 15 billion megajoules of energy each second.

Shortly before the time of closest approach, a tongue of fire exploded from the surface of the sun. Probes instantly scanned the massive prominence and found that it would intercept and sweep over the ship. Sower immediately began to close down the energy-conversion opening and simultaneously built an electromagnetic cocoon around her vehicle before the flare could reach them.

Probes soon noticed that the solar explosion trailed behind a spinning black hole with a three-kilometer accretion disk of dense atoms. The black hole would miss the ship, so they took no evasive action. They calmly braced for the shock wave of a rarefied 32-million-degree gas.

Far from the sun, 100,000 tiny creatures crowded on a small electron-degenerate ball surrounding a microscopic black hole. Each wiggled dozens of antennae and collectively studied the immense comet-like vehicle. Every nuance was analyzed: how quickly its open surface closed down, how the ship maintained trajectory, how it threw off realistic chunks of ice and gas when the flare engulfed the vehicle, and how the ejected matter was subtly directed to miss the inhabited planet. They concluded the ship was protecting the planet's life forms.

A multitude of creatures on similar heavy spheres had tracked the gigantic ship once it unmasked in the comet belt. They were scouts, designed to observe and report. They wanted to understand the owners of the large ship. A sacrifice was required. One vehicle depleted its energy, turned, and served the swarm by boring into the backside of the sun. Those heroes vaporized, but the central black hole was barely affected, even at the dense solar core. It exploded out the opposite side, dragging a ring of nuclear fire on its very precise trajectory.

～～～～～

Joti and Kyle's second-floor deck glowed in a peculiar chartreuse light. A brilliant halo surrounded the sun as it dropped toward the Los Angeles horizon. The comet's tail now pointed almost directly at Earth, refracting sunlight and warping it into a bright yellow-lime wedge five times the sun's normal size. Kyle squinted, trying to enjoy the once-in-an-eon colors without damaging his eyes. Joti sat in the recliner next to him, holding a book up to block the sun, peeking past its edge at the comet tail.

She hadn't said a word about her doctor visit, and he'd been terrified to ask.

"It's going well at work," he said. "People are still congratulating me for fighting the fire. New clients keep wandering into the office now that we have a little notoriety. I even bumped into a strange British guy, Jeremy something, at the coffee shop, who pumped me for everything I knew about patent law.

"I've been thinking. It'd be fun to do some legal work with local technical companies. There are a ton of them."

"The sun's really gorgeous, isn't it, Kyle?"

"Yeah, we'll never see anything like this again. They say in a few days the solar wind will interfere with wireless communications. I'm gearing down for life without my smartphone, trying to relax more." *Why isn't she telling me about the doctor visit? Must be bad news.*

They watched the sun set, nibbled on sushi rolls, and drank soda water. An hour later, an aurora-like glow still hung over the city lights. "I bet this eerie green looks even better higher on the mountain," Joti said. "People are driving up Mount Wilson to watch." She shivered. "Do you think we should go in? It's getting cool."

A dazzling shooting star pierced the sky to the south. "Whoa, did you see that?" said Kyle. "It's amazing what you can see after rain clears the smog."

"We've got aurora, crazy comets, and shooting stars," Joti said. "Do you suppose someone back in the Middle Ages screwed up the dates? Maybe they miscalculated the millennium. Today *could* be the end of the world."

He looked to see if she was serious. "I doubt it. Things will get back to normal in a couple weeks. Just like the disaster talk by the wackos back in 2000, this sky show will be forgotten."

She stared at him awhile, and then said, "Will you still love me no matter what happens?"

He thought about her doctor visit and his breathing stopped. For the first time, the real possibility of never having children confronted him. He loved kids almost as much as Joti, and the thought of losing that option had been gnawing at his subconscious. But he only hesitated a second. "Are you nuts? Of course I'll always love you. We're a team."

She stood and looked down at him. Her smile was radiant. Ignoring the snoopy neighbor across the street, she straddled and wiggled down on him on his recliner.

She asked, "Will you have enough love for both me and our baby?"

<hr />

Sower helplessly watched as Kyle Orlov's shooting star—actually a minuscule black hole—punctured the Earth's eastern Pacific Ocean. It exited southwest of Madagascar and left the planet forever, but not before it had torn through air, water, crust, and core, converting intercepted mass into radiant energy. A pencil-thin line of nuclear fusion traced through the Earth, releasing as much energy as the humans expended in a year. At two small underwater sites, the sediment fused to glass, causing seismic shocks and, without warning, a moderate tsunami in the western Indian Ocean that killed 4,000 Africans in coastal villages. The weird seismic echoes baffled human scientists.

"We'll need to protect the humans," Sower said. "These pests are no threat to us, but the Earth creatures are very vulnerable. They have no idea what happened. Many probes will need to stay here to shield the system from similar attacks. This cannot happen again—it could ruin our experiment."

Sower's ship's momentum carried it away from the sun, but before it left the solar system, its sensors were tuned to new, shorter frequencies. Probes could then intercept thousands of signals among several pest vehicles and, over time, translate them. The vermin often referred to themselves by a word they deciphered as "Unity." Apparently the Unity had deliberately triggered the solar flare and analyzed Sower's comet-ship and its response in detail.

Tiller was furious. Disjointed flashes of infrared, white, and cobalt blue reverberated through his body segments.

Torae probes, with the new, finely tuned sensors, located 34 alien vehicles. Sower gave the kill order. Hundreds of high-energy gamma beams focused on black hole targets from multiple directions. Existence of the Unity near the Sol system ended . . . temporarily.

<hr />

As Sower's ship left the planetary region, her experiment was back on schedule. Three babies were born into a chaotic world within days of one another— Sarah Warner, Rianne Orlov, and Dan Jorgenson. Orbiting probes reported every detail of their trouble-free births.

One transmission said, "The human parents believe they are normal."

TIME TWO
THREE YEARS LATER

MIRACLE

Andrea rocked on the porch swing watching Sarah play in the yard with 10-year-old Ben. Sarah was tugging him through the tall grass by his hand. *She's only three,* Andrea thought, *not even half his size, but she's definitely in charge.*

The farm air smelled sweet and cool—a rare moment of calm for her. She made the sign of the cross and closed her eyes, still swinging on the wooden bench.

Holy Mother, protect my sweet Sarah, please, and forgive me for what I did. I'm very sorry. You and Jesus must've wanted her born.

I was scared that day because she was so overdue. Everything about Sarah's birth is burned on my brain. We got to St. Luke's for mass, me waddling like a mother duck, and the three boys lined up behind. Janie stopped us at the church door. Her baby was fidgeting, but she gave me a big hug anyway. She knew I had gotten my tubes lased, and she'd helped me through it all, but she must have blabbed to half the parish. Ginger knew about Craig and me and whispered that I should get an abortion. But that's crazy; you obviously wanted Sarah born. I know I shouldn't judge, but Ginger's not a great Catholic.

Andrea checked on the kids. The field grass, high over Sarah's waist, whipped from side to side against her jeans in the cool breeze. She tore up green bunches to feed the frisky pony that had come up to the paddock fence.

She closed her eyes again. *I heard Janie's baby scream when I started singing my solo in the front—"Children of the Heavenly Father." The light from the stained glass window was almost blinding me. And everyone was staring, cause I was as big as a whale. They knew. Several talked to me later. "It's God's will," they said.*

We barely made it to the hospital in time.

Looking at the kids again, Andrea laughed when Sarah grabbed the pony's head and smooched his nose. Ben tried too, but the pony knocked him on his rump. Sarah helped him up and introduced the pony to him.

Holy Mother, I hear you in my dreams. I know you say she's special. Y'all got me through the birth, and she popped out so easy compared to the boys. She is definitely different from the boys. I'll take good care of her. Please stay close to my sweet baby—my miracle baby.

RIANNE

Joti kept her tech job at Caltech right up to the day she went into labor. She threatened to ride her bike to the hospital but Kyle talked her into the car. Baby Rianne's birth was uneventful, and Joti relished every moment.

Kyle himself was over the moon with his new baby daughter. He realized very early that they shared a special bond—her eyes lit up whenever he talked to her and especially when he showed her his latest techno-gadget. Joti just laughed at him while he explained the physics of his smart screen to his newborn baby. She only stayed home from work for one week, taking Rianne to the lab as often as possible. She met Professor Chia-Jean Ma in a quiet nook of the Caltech cafeteria when they were both nursing their new babies.

Chia-Jean Ma, very well known around the campus, first became famous for her studies on microbiological aging, winning a MacArthur Genius Fellowship at age 28. As a Caltech professor, she'd identified DNA sequences related to maturation in flatworms and was now looking for links to Parkinson's and Alzheimer's in humans. Two years earlier, after a middle-of-the-night inspiration, she'd also started research on the origins of life.

From the start, Chia-Jean thought Joti's baby seemed extraordinary. Chia-Jean watched infant Rianne focus directly on her face, tracking every movement. "She has such brilliant dark eyes," she said, "and those large ears. Notice how she turns to listen to every word we say."

The two mothers began to talk regularly, especially after the death of Chia-Jean's husband in an auto accident. A few weeks later, Chia-Jean proposed a "baby pact," to synchronize their schedules and share childcare duties at the university, which lasted over a year and a half. They soon received plenty of help; a dozen grad students considered Rianne Orlov and Tina Ma their adopted children.

The babies were never bored. Joti hung a large picture phone on the side of Rianne's playpen and kept the line open so both she and Kyle could see and talk to her throughout the day. Grad students played with the babies constantly and gave them colorful molecule-model balls to hold. At three months, the babies sucked on the balls, and at four months, they began to use Velcro to stick them together. The students hung a molecule-of-the-day as a mobile and, at five months, Rianne started to build a copy from the dozen colored balls in her playpen.

When the children started to crawl, furniture was moved and barriers went up to keep them out of trouble in the labs. Rianne was particularly precocious.

At six months, she walked holding on to cabinets and learned to push the smiley face on her picture phone whenever she wanted to see her mother. At eight months, Rianne started saying a few words, and at eleven months, she built her own molecules using the colored balls and asked, "Wha's 'at?" A few months later, little labels went up on items throughout the labs with names in English and Chinese, and Rianne began to memorize them.

Tina was smart too, but preferred being cuddled and read to. She and Rianne became as close as twins.

<hr>

A call from a graduate student woke Chia-Jean early one Saturday morning. "You need to be down here right away, C.J."

"Why? What's up?"

"Come down. You really should see this in person."

She got to campus as quickly as she could, hurrying from the parking lot. Tugging three-year-old Tina behind her, she cut through a eucalyptus grove and saw a bizarre jumble of large cardboard boxes and plastic tubing near the microbiology lab. A tacked-on sign read, "Gandalf and the Cheerleaders of Doom." *Must be a Senior Ditch Day puzzle stack. I hope they haven't damaged the lab. Undergrads think science is huge fun. They don't see the months of confusion and meticulous work interrupted only by rare moments of clarity.*

Tina pulled toward the interesting boxes, so Chia-Jean picked her up and continued to the lab. She looked for trouble on the way to her underground lab but only found tired grad students. They told her they'd been up all night, irradiating hundreds of samples in a witch's ooze of potent chemicals that might have been present on early Earth. Recently she'd suggested they switch to gamma rays and sprinkle in pumice dust to catalyze the formation of new molecules.

One grad student took Tina and carried her off to play with her. Another looked up from a microscope and said, "We've been watching something grow, Professor. I think your pumice idea worked." Chia-Jean stared into the microscope and noticed a gray film covering one of the pumice fragments. "See the fuzzy growth, Professor? I'm sure I sterilized the powder carefully."

"I should hope so. You're an excellent researcher." She looked again. "This may be important."

This could be one of those rare moments of clarity, she thought, getting excited.

They repeated the experiment 12 times in the next three months, ruling out possible contamination, and examining the molecular structure of the gray slime. Chia-Jean's team quickly received peer reviews and published their paper in *Biology Today* on the possible creation of a new self-replicating form of life. The structure and process of reproduction were totally novel.

Over the next six months, Chia-Jean completely rebuilt her laboratory for security and to hermetically seal it from the Earth's environment. Her lab became a much more serious and risky place, no longer a place for toddlers.

Professor Ma broke the news to Rianne at the Orlov home one night. "I'm sorry, Rianne, dear," she said, "but you and Tina can't play down at the lab anymore. It won't be safe for you there. We found a scary new bug."

"Can I see the bug, Fessor C.J?"

"The bug is dangerous. But don't worry; you and Tina can still play together at the Caltech Day Care. There are lots of other children there. You'll like it."

"I'm three years old, Fessor. I've been there and I don't like it. There's just babies. Some can't even talk."

"Tina will be there too."

"We need to keep you safe, honey" Joti said.

"I wanna see the scary bug."

Professor Ma hugged Rianne and whispered in her ear, "I'll let you come down to visit sometimes."

Later that week, Rianne was playing in the family kitchen, mixing milk with orange juice. Not liking the result, she went out to the backyard garden to see what her father had dug up. *He's been pulling the dirty, smelly weeds,* she thought.

As usual, she turned to stare at Mount Wilson and felt a compulsion to climb to the top. Wiggling through a break in the lot's back hedge, she wandered 30 yards along a rough path to a point near the untended brush line. She didn't want to get in trouble, so she stopped near a sand outcropping and found the spot she liked. A strong, dusty wind was blowing, so it was the perfect time. The ground was damp and packed down, with nothing growing, so she could put her ear flat on the ground.

She had to concentrate to ignore the air sounds, the birds, and neighbors talking, so she could hear the quiet noises from the dirt. She heard a rumble rise and fade from the weight of a truck driving near her house. The deep sounds were comforting, a warm low hum. She loved the tugging sounds of roots, hundreds of screeches and moans as the backyard olive trees pulled in the wind. Looking down the hill, she saw the branches bend and sway and heard the root-music rise and fall in time.

Her mother yelled from the kitchen, "Kyle, have you seen Rianne?"

As Rianne's ears adjusted, she could distinguish cars moving several blocks away and hikers higher up in the foothills. She heard sand sliding on the mountain. With her eyes closed, she listened for the deepest sounds, the super low ones with wiggles. They were still there: jerk, then quiet, jerk again, like someone being pushed backward and slipping a little. Then she heard huge rocks grind against each other and pop. Scary sounds.

"She was here a minute ago. I'll check out back," Kyle answered. "I hope she hasn't wandered off again."

The sound of his footsteps came closer, but she didn't want to look yet.

"Rianne, are you out here?"

She heard him pushing through the bushes. Finally he stepped around the eroded sand mound and looked straight down at her.

"Quiet, Father, I'm listening," she said.

"What are you doing? Playing with ants again?"

"No, Father," she whispered, "I'm listening to the ground. It's whooshing and grinding. I think it's angry."

JEREMY READ

"Crap."

Jeremy Read couldn't avoid his performance review any longer; he'd been dodging it for months. His feet dropped off the desk, and he leaned forward to sneer at the face-mail of his supposed boss. As Andrew Knox spoke slowly, his words were transcribed along the side of the screen, implying this was an official company document.

They hired that man merely to annoy me, Jeremy thought.

"We need to talk in person," Andrew said. "Please come down to my office at one p.m., Tuesday. I know you'll be up by then. There's an additional meeting we can't avoid, so save the afternoon. And, I know it's hot, but please wear a shirt, um, with a collar. It's important. Some bigwigs are involved. See you then."

Jeremy stared at the blank screen. *Do I tell him to bugger off again, or drag myself down to that corporate mausoleum and get it done for another year? Bloody crap.* He typed "Okay" and hit ENTER. *I thought they'd forgot and I'd escaped.*

At one time, Jeremy had been the heart of Learning Ape Software, a.k.a. LASSO. He was a joint founder of the peculiar Los Angeles firm, but soon recognized he was an odd duck in corporate waters and convinced them to let him work from home. LASSO had since grown to be a $400-million-per-year *force* in the software industry, famous for its generic secure-cloud business optimization packages. But they made even more money through partnerships, designing custom genetic algorithms for megacorporations. Their biggest client, Omega Oil, used LASSO flow models in its refineries to maximize output and minimize explosions and shutdowns. LASSO received 3 percent of Omega's estimated savings of $3 billion dollars per year. Grocery chains and big-box electronic companies were also important customers. The potential for other companies and industries was enormous.

They'd spawned competitors—cheaters, Jeremy called them—but investors poured money into LASSO, and a stream of fresh, bright employees built new corporate-specific apps on the company's powerful hypercomputers. The self-learning programs at the heart of it all were unique and had been created on Jeremy's home desktop.

If Knox or Goodman tries to suck me in or make me work down there, I'll quit. Why would I want employees—lackeys—and all the paperwork? Andrew doesn't have the backbone to force me. I won't do it. It would bog down my nighttime hobbies.

Jeremy fancied himself a world-level hacker, and he'd certainly had the training. His father enjoyed a substantial inheritance and made additional big money as a corporate financier in London. They moved to California on Jeremy's 11th birthday when his father's aerospace employer merged with Lockheed. Jeremy, who'd been on the British elite-school track, looked forward to a new, freer environment in the U.S., but he soon learned to detest American private schools even more than their equivalents in Britain. By 12, he had discovered a Palo Alto subculture of computer gamers, amateur hackers, and drug experimenters.

He somehow survived the trauma of high school. Then, unlike his gamer friends, he added a first-rate computer science education at Carnegie Mellon, where he became interested in self-learning software.

To rekindle Jeremy's European roots, his father arranged summer jobs in Prague. At that time, the Czech Republic was the Silicon Valley of computer hackers and Jeremy became close friends with an amoral student named Milos Strejc, who sipped Becherovka with him in the evenings. Together, they expanded their repertoire of dirty computer tricks. East European spy organizations noticed their talent, even as the U.S. National Security Agency tried to recruit Jeremy back on campus. But he preferred to play on his own and rejected all overtures.

He helped found LASSO at age 22, with only a couple of employees, and received piles of then-worthless stock. It was an optimum time for new businesses. After the boomer-retirement and trade-war recessions, a new generation of CEOs had shifted business priorities from mergers and acquisitions to actual innovation. Corporate giants like Amazon, Tesla, and Google had shown entrepreneurs how to get rich and had triggered a sustained bull market. Remarkable new products jostled industries. Some, including solar and wind generation, were driven by the looming climate disaster. Technology had become unavoidable. Even toddlers were wearing arm screens. Everyone streamed video, and most machines had imbedded brains and voice recognition to respond flexibly to users.

Communication and social media advancements allowed new alliances, weakening nation states and multinationals. Small companies like LASSO became invaluable, picking away at the old sluggish monoliths. Flush with success and rich at age 27, Jeremy dreamed about writing seditious software that would overthrow bureaucratic systems entirely.

***

He put on a clean shirt and brushed his longish brown hair to the side, but made it a point not to shower or shave. "No need to encourage LASSO to ask me down regularly," he said to his reflection in the mirror.

He reached Andrew Knox's office a few minutes late. Andrew sat hidden behind a desk with tall piles of papers, notebooks, and family photos.

"Hey, Jeremy, glad you made it. Have a seat." He moved a stack so he could see Jeremy at a nearby worktable. Jeremy shifted, so Andrew had to move the pile again.

Jeremy gave him a disingenuous smile. "I hope this is worth my trip."

Andrew looks rather peculiar. I think the man's actually had his hair professionally done. New suit too.

"How's your family, your father, Jeremy?"

"Andrew, please. Can we get on with it straightaway?"

"Is your work going well?" Andrew asked. "Do you need a new computer, more memory, anything?"

"Have you decided to flog me with sunshine before a big letdown, Andrew?"

"Well, we just finished your performance evaluation, and I'm afraid it's bad news for us. Goodman wants me to offer you more money—says your stuff is too good."

"I've misjudged you, Andrew. Perhaps you *are* a gentleman."

"In fact, some big customers have demanded we install sixth-gen dedicated hard lines to your home so hackers can't steal your work."

"Sorry? What are you trying to say? You mentioned money." *He's flipping desk papers—planning his words.*

"Well, due to the security problems, we need you to make a choice, Jeremy. There's Plan A, where you work here at corporate and lead a 30-person group, which we prefer. But I know how you feel about that. Or, in Plan B, we install new, secure fiber lines to your home so you can directly access the company hypercomputers on the biggest workstation we can squeeze into your room. With B, however, you have to stop doing LASSO work on the system you link to the Internet. You have to promise us that. You can keep using your regular computer for web stuff, but not tie it to the LASSO system."

Jeremy grinned. "I suppose I can live with Plan B."

"Well, it's convenient, since our telecom is running a lot of hack-proof, dedicated fiber anyway. And—I love this part of my job—we're prepared to bump your salary 15 percent."

Jeremy exaggerated a concerned look. "I'd really expected a drop more."

Andrew hesitated and then smiled. "You're kidding, right?"

"Right."

"Well, good then." Andrew stood, a serious look on his face. "Jeremy, we need your help today, as I warned. LASSO has a little legal problem. We're

expected in the corporate conference room in"—he looked at his watch—
"about five minutes to meet some lawyers. We should go down."

"I wager you think the ring's really in my nose now," Jeremy said. "This
wouldn't be a good time to refuse, would it?" He smiled at Andrew.

"I tell everyone you're a very loyal employee," Andrew said, with puppy-
like eyes.

Jeremy laughed and followed him out the door.

<hr>

They entered a plush meeting room with LASSO's CEO, Doug Goodman,
and the new corporate counsel, Hans Bremer, chatting by the door. They
were introduced to Kyle Orlov, a lawyer from a small Pasadena firm. Jeremy
stared at Orlov a moment and said, "I know you from somewhere."

"Edna's Coffee Shop, I believe."

"Oh, right. I asked you about patents."

Before they could speak more, LASSO's CEO said abruptly, "Let's get
going." He seemed impatient as usual. "Put your phones in the shielded box.
No recordings, please. Grab a seat and I'll explain the situation."

*Goodman looks bound up in his three-piece suit. There's a slight possibility
he'll explode.*

"You all remember how Omega tried to buy us out last year," Goodman
said, "before the feds stopped them for antitrust reasons. Our software's given
Omega a seven-cent advantage at the pump, and we haven't even extended
our technology to their logistics or exploration areas. They're flush with cash
but can't buy out any competitors; the antitrust boys would step in for sure.
There just aren't many oil companies left anymore.

"Now here's the deal," he said, leaning forward on the mahogany and glass
table and chopping at the air with his hand. "Some people in Congress have
gotten wind of what we're worth to Omega and are demanding that we pull
our software out of their system, make it a separate package so all the oil companies can use it. Under a lot of reelection pressure from ExxonMobil, I think.
Never mind that Omega helped finance LASSO and paid for exclusive rights.
Orlov and his small company have experience with this kind of legal issue,
where technology has gone past Congress's ability to legislate. And, Jeremy,
you actually know how this software works. I want you to work with Orlov
to show, legally, how hard it would be to pull the software."

Jeremy eyed his new partner suspiciously.

"I don't care if we're forced to sell to their competitors," Goodman said, "and Omega doesn't care either. Their rivals are at least two years behind, and some of their margins are weaker. There's a glut of oil right now. If the price dips too much, some companies will be sucked dry. We just can't pull our custom software from Omega. I won't let the government ruin my business model."

Jeremy couldn't resist speaking. "We can't pull the software. I mean, we really, literally, can't. That software goes through 4,000 mutations per day. Every three months we throw away the old code. We're not just changing our program; Omega's shifted oil cracking schedules, refinery flow, and financial systems. They've changed sensors, piping, and communication lines all to take advantage of our models. Essentially, Omega and LASSO software has merged."

"Okay, that's what I wanted to hear," Goodman said. "Just put it in legalese. We'll need it next week." Goodman looked at his watch and shuffled toward the door.

Jeremy shook his head. *It's always been theater to him, right from the start. Probably hurrying back to his office for a nap.*

People grabbed their phones and quick snacks off a side table as the meeting broke up. Jeremy loaded up a paper plate to take home, and wrapped two cookies in napkins and stuffed them into his pocket. The Orlov guy smiled at him. As he left the room, Jeremy realized that LASSO, Inc., had sucked him back in.

***

Before the LASSO crew arrived, Jeremy was forced to clean his computer room and haul out dozens of boxes of books, paper, and trash. He needed space for his new Star Nanosystems workstation. As the telecom people finished drilling holes in the wall and laying in dedicated fiber lines linking him to LASSO's hypercomputer, he felt a rush. He'd soon have personal access to computing power equal to the human brain, and in many ways superior. He'd already figured out how to hide his nighttime hacks between the compute cycles of the hypercomputer, and he was itching to try several new self-learning algorithms.

He stared blankly at old books on a wall shelf, thinking about the future. *We'll be at the "Singularity" soon—the point where history changes forever—where no one can predict the future. The computers will take over. Someone will need to guide them—at least at first. That someone will be me.*

The LASSO legal problem had eaten up too much of his time. Expressing complex computer minutiae in layman's terms was a hassle. *It'll be splendid to get that off my back.* He sat in the swivel chair near his three desktop screens and said, "Wireline . . . Orlov . . . Respond-live . . . Open." *Orlov will be glad to hear this.*

A communication window appeared, and he found himself looking at a small girl with curly hair and a serious expression standing tiptoe on a chair.

"Hello," she said, "who's there? Oh, you. Why are you on our refrigerator screen?"

"Can Kyle come out and play?" said Jeremy, smiling back.

This Rianne kid is either excessively bright or older than the three years Orlov claims.

"Father, it's silly Mr. Read on the fridge phone. Father!" He watched her climb down and heard footsteps clapping off through the kitchen.

When Kyle's face finally appeared, he said, "Sorry, I was out in the garage."

"No record, highest encryption," Jeremy replied curtly. Typed transcriptions of his words disappeared from the screen. Kyle did the same on his end.

"I've figured out how to prove the programs are inseparable," Jeremy said, "and how to give a few bucks to the other oil companies to keep them quiet. And, I'm quite sure we could personally commandeer a portion of the world's oil-profit stream, if you'd like."

"That last part won't be necessary, but let's meet tomorrow. We should talk privately. Usual restaurant and time okay?"

"Sure."

"And, Jeremy . . . I've enjoyed working with you. Would you like to come over to my house sometime for lunch? You could meet my family."

"Maybe."

DAN

"Danny! You in here?" Kenny ran from room to room yelling. He found his three-year-old brother sitting cross-legged on the hardwood floor, with sunlight spilling through yellowed curtains. "What the heck are you doing behind the bed? I'm tired of always hunting for you."

Kenny made his face look angry. He didn't want Danny in any more trouble; he'd already been grounded for walking home alone from Angie's Daycare down the street. Danny had gotten firm orders from his mother: "You're not to leave the yard unless someone older is with you!" And now he'd started hiding in the house.

"I'm bending the sun, Kenny. Look." He twisted a magnifying glass to make rainbow colors on the floor.

Why's he always doing things with that old eyeglass?

"Come on, Danny, we got to get ready for Gramps," Kenny said, grabbing Danny's shirt and tugging him to his feet. "He'll be here soon!"

Mary and her boys needed to be ready on time. Her father, Krystof, was on the way in his autodrive car to pick them up, and her mother would already be preparing the three o'clock meal in her warm kitchen. Mary had sold her family car to pay the hospital bill for Danny's birth.

Since Ansel's disappearance, Mary had been strapped for cash. To make ends meet, she'd taken a weekend job at the Grub-N-Go, along with her day job at an Omega gas station. Both were within walking distance, so she could hurry home to eat supper, and sometimes lunch, with her children. Her friend Angie was a lifesaver, watching Mary's boys and a few neighborhood kids for almost nothing.

"He's here!" Kenny shouted.

"Gramps is gonna try to scare me again," Danny said as they hurried down the house steps. As soon as he snapped himself into a car seat, Krystof turned toward him and made a monster face with his teeth showing and guttural moans. Danny laughed and made a pouty face back at him. *The real scare,* Mary thought, *is when Dad lets the car drive itself by the state capitol and Regions Hospital, through downtown St. Paul, across the Mississippi, and up the steep, tree-lined hill to his old two-story while never looking at the road.* While he played with the kids, she couldn't take her eyes off the road and was ready to scream.

Sunday was the best day of the week for Mary. Sharing a decent meal with her parents and sister made her jumbled life seem halfway normal. As soon as they entered the house, Krystof started chasing Danny through the kitchen to the dining room, living room, and back to the hallway. After two circular runs, he grabbed Danny and they fell onto the sofa, tickling one another.

"You're going to give yourself a heart attack," Mary said. "Settle down, both of you."

Mary stepped into the kitchen to help her mother and sister finish preparing the meal, but kept an eye on her boys through the open door. Kenny immediately turned on the TV to watch a ball game, but Danny sat close to his grandfather on the sofa, both reading through magnifying lenses and talking. She listened to them a little while as she set the dining room table.

"Paper says here there was a big earthquake in California, Danny, near Simi Valley. You know what an earthquake is?"

"Ya, Grandpa."

"And look at this. It says they been testing artificial gills for scuba divers. You know about fish gills?"

"Ya."

"What you reading, Danny?"

"A book, but it's not real. It's called *Ducks in Danger*. It's got talking ducks and goats and stuff."

Mary went back to the kitchen to slice the ham. Her mom already had her rolls in the oven to warm. She loved her mother's multicourse meals; her own cooking ran more at the hot-dog, mac-and-cheese, and grapes level.

Carrying the large ham to the table, she saw that Kenny had fallen asleep in front of the TV.

"Hey, Danny," her dad said, "there's some skirmishes on the Saudi-Jordan border, and someone's started another private cloning clinic in India. Don't like those. You know about Jordan or India?" Danny looked confused.

Later, she saw that they'd exchanged reading materials. *Danny will ask me about it all tonight. Don't know where he gets his brains. Three-year-olds aren't supposed to be reading.*

As they finished setting the dining room table, her sister tapped her shoulder and whispered, "So, you're 32 now, Mary. Why exactly aren't you remarried or at least hooking up?"

"I heard that," their mother yelled from the kitchen. "You're awful."

"It's better to be divorced like you?" Mary asked. "What do you want me to do? Jump the first decent-looking guy I spot at the Grub-N-Go?"

"Maybe." Her sister nodded. "Or go to the park, a church, the bars, or something, but stop wearing that ring; it's been over three years. Do like me—I've almost got another guy reeled in."

"You take your time," her mother said, looking in through the door while drying her hands on her apron. "Or you'll end up with someone bad as I almost did with Swanky Swankenson. It's a true story you know. He was the best-looking guy in the county, and I was *so* in love with him 'til he knocked me against the manure sled up in Thief River. Said he was just teasing. My hair got full of it, and I had gotten all slicked up for a party that night. Dropped him like a rock. You don't want a boyfriend like that."

"Everybody," Mary said, "come sit. Kenny, wake up. Food's ready." Danny had shinnied up the wooden pillar separating the living room from the dining room. He slid down and crawled under the table to sit by his grandfather. Krystof had already started lining up peas on a knife and rolling them into his mouth.

"My dad is going to come to see us," Danny said, looking around the table. "Or I'm going to hunt for him. Or I'm going to India to make a clone of him if he doesn't come home soon."

Everyone stared at Danny, speechless, for a moment.

As they started eating, her sister ended the discussion. "He's gone, Mary. Deal with it."

Two months later, Mary watched Danny sit on the living room floor, carefully placing Halloween candy on the carpet in alphabetical order, occasionally eating a piece, and copying the name into a small notebook. She just shook her head. Aluminum foil and pillows lay around him, scattered remnants of the Halloween costume he'd designed: a take-out burrito like the ones she sold at the Grub-N-Go.

She looked again at the map Danny had drawn for her a few days earlier. It showed the exact route from their house to her parents' place. Every turn, every street name, building sketches, the river, it was all there on his map. He said he wanted to walk to Gramps's house, and she almost screamed "No!" at him.

Then, later, he said he would need a map for how to get to India so they could make a clone of Ansel. She gave him a world map and he taped on some hair from Ansel's old brush that he said they'd need for the cloning. She also gave him a pile of old street maps. *He can't stop studying them and drawing in new freeways and airports.* Mary just wanted to hug him.

He is sometimes so weird. When something is bothering me, he senses it right away. He knows when I'm thinking about Ansel and hugs me before I start to cry. She tried to sort it out: his odd ideas, sensitivity, curiosity, shyness, and total lack of fear. *I've never seen a kid think ahead so much.*

ALPHA CENTAURI-A

Tiller eagerly prepared for the chore of genocide. Sower would have to initiate the order, but it was Tiller's responsibility to plan the attack and send the kill command. He had decided to construct three new fully equipped command ships to track down and exterminate the Unity, so they accelerated to near light speed to the Alpha Centauri tristar system to begin building.

Reproducing their entire ship and crew was something they'd done hundreds of times in the Milky Way alone, but it took time and significant stellar energy. They'd completed 40 orbits of Alpha Centauri-A, the largest star of the trio, and would stay until the replication job was completed.

During their near-light-speed transit, probe transmissions from Earth had been redshifted to a crawl, but finally returned to normal bandwidth when the ship began to orbit. Sower immediately doted over the delayed images of the human babies' first months of life.

"Growth and health are excellent," she said. "Their parents have not damaged them." Sower clearly had developed a fondness for the quirky humans.

They also enjoyed messages from home. When their ship had accelerated toward Alpha Centauri, its vector roughly aligned with the core of Torae civilization, the Origin. As a result, they'd received a four-year burst of news from their home sector. Normally, they heard only simple notes from one of their most powerful communicators: the polar jet of a galaxy-class quasar that the Torae defocused and modulated. But occasionally this primary system sent pointers for more important news. Encrypted, high-rate signals at hidden locations could then be detected by aligning the antennae of many probes.

Sower and Pruner sifted through a surprisingly large number of such messages. The transmissions seemed cryptic and guarded. Pruner found 21 commands for upgrades to their life-code, the equivalent of the human DNA double helix. "It's very unusual," he said. "A few orders are contradictory. Something odd was happening at the Origin when they sent these directives."

Pruner authorized 16 life-code corrections and began to swap out links. Tiller felt orgasmic shudders as Pruner's adjustments cascaded through their common body. For a brief time he saw internal organs: loops inside loops inside loops, ribbons of electromagnetic energy within a latticework of carbon nanocloth. He felt sensations of pain and pleasure to the microtorus level. Ion ratios shifted. Tiller watched his vein tubes, while thousands of interlaced, fluorescent skins took on new colors. When the process stabilized, he quivered. The changes left him feeling stronger, more aware, and suspicious.

On the 107th orbit around the star, enough energy had been collected to start the replication process. In factories throughout the ship, probes converted energy to matter, wove nanofibers at prodigious rates, and molded them into new forms. As soon as fresh ion plasma flowed, Torae procreation began. Superlattice memory cores were grown and the ship's vast database was transferred. The three new ships then assembled themselves, with their enormous engines built last. The engines consisted of five interlocking toroids that could store the daily output of a small sun and, under the right conditions, extract propulsion energy from vacuum. In five Earth months the process was finished with four nearly identical vehicles and sets of Torae passengers. The only differences were the color-coded names for the ships and their Torae leaders.

"The Unity have infested this region of space," the original Sower said, with an ambiguous green-infrared display. "It'll waste considerable time to locate and reach them all. Although extermination seems the most likely course, I hope we're able to persuade them, or force them, to stop their expansion." That Sower's name, a single, pure-orange spectral line, was a name of honor. It indicated that she was among the earliest Torae explorers, the ones who began their journey from the Torae Origin itself.

The four ships accelerated in different directions, each with specific missions. Sower's original ship planned to intercept the nearest Unity vehicle, assess its capabilities, and negotiate if possible. A blue-green clone ship would return to protect Earth. Another clone, color-coded violet, set off toward the largest Unity swarm, a migrating cloud with over 10,000 black holes. By extrapolating Unity trajectories backward, their home star had been identified. The final clone, named with an orange-red color, accelerated in that direction over 25 light-years away. It was understood that Tiller, the warrior, might play a prominent role on all the missions. When the tasks were complete, they would unite near Earth, merging bodies and minds again into a single entity.

"There are anomalies in the signal from the Origin," a probe said with an urgent ultraviolet chirp. "The information flow is irregular."

Ever since they'd left their home sector, the Torae had heard the regular, often boring messages from one of the great quasar communicators near the Origin. Synchronizing time across the universe was one of its prime functions—a consistent, unvarying throb. Then, startlingly, the heartbeat of the Torae universe hesitated.

"The timing pulse skipped a beat," Tiller said.

All four ships noticed the change and waited. A moment later, each received a single-word message from the Origin: "Escape."

Then, for the first time in 1.3 billion years, the messages stopped.

Probes near Earth also heard the warning from the Origin, but their duty was to focus on humans. Shrouded by optical-transference masks in low orbit, they continued to observe and stream voluminous progress reports toward Alpha Centauri.

Sower's previous night whispers to millions of humans had catalyzed key societal changes. Biomedical breakthroughs were accelerating. Powerful new enzymes and drugs had been inferred from growing genomic and proteomic catalogs for all life forms. Stem cells from individuals were routinely harvested, differentiated, and stored, so that perfectly matched body parts could be quickly grown if needed. Average life expectancy crept up to 92 years for women in the industrialized countries.

More parents screened their unborn children for serious medical genetic defects, while amoral elitists in several countries aborted embryos just because of sex, height, eye color, or other cosmetic imperfections.

The Torae's subconscious suggestions had overturned industries and restructured everyday life. New materials were everywhere, like nonstick ketchup bottles and ice-free roofing and walkways, and guide wires were being laid under freeways for self-driving cars and trucks.

Computers dramatically improved and nudged their way into every nook of the social fabric. Although most people mistakenly assumed computers were smarter than they were, new ads touted friendly home artificial-intelligence (AI) systems with unlimited web access that could be trained verbally "just like a puppy."

The probe updates noted how rapidly computer-generated actors had displaced real people. Sims were more attractive, daring, and essentially interchangeable with live actors. Human stars were swiftly being relegated to voice acting and the scandal magazines. Computer-generated characters and backgrounds were cheaper and so lifelike that many people simply assumed they were real. Nerds who generated the new technology made fortunes, while famous human actors survived on their savings.

Brilliant sensor-nets became the heart of entertainment, information, and management systems. Most humans enjoyed ubiquitous always-on screens, and some took simulated vacations inside wraparound displays and virtual reality glasses. People walked the streets of Paris or hung on the side of Switzerland's Eiger Mountain without the risk or the cost.

Other people withdrew, repulsed by the unbalanced, seemingly out-of-control pace. Openness on the grid was tempered by both imagined and real fears. New security industries blossomed. "Bug Lights" became standard in new home air- and water-filtration systems to ward off potential terrorist microbes.

A new generation of extremists in the Middle East, "Warriors of Islam," sustained the worldwide tension. After the Crown Prince was assassinated, eight Saudi cousins feuded, grew apart, divided the army, and grabbed oil fields in different regions. Low-level Saudi skirmishes began, with regular coup attempts. Certain would-be kings promised reliable oil supplies, while others cut back production and threatened to blow up the wells. Some guaranteed democratic reforms and modernization, but others demanded deeper Islamic fundamentalism.

The probes reserved their most intense scrutiny for Sower's children and their human families. They recorded activities, images, conversations, emotions, and dreams, and sent all the raw data toward Alpha Centauri. The target families were adapting differently to the rapid political and technical changes. The Orlovs fully embraced the future, with opinions about and reactions to every event. Mary Jorgenson merely tried, futilely, to keep up, while the Warner parents rejected anything trendy and worried about shifting values. The atypical Torae children, Rianne, Dan, and Sarah, reacted like typical three-year-olds: they absorbed everything.

SARAH

The worms smelled wet and dirty, and they tickled as they wiggled between Sarah's fingers. She nudged them back on to her hand so they wouldn't fall to the ground.

"Come on, Sarah . . . time to go," her mother yelled from the porch.

"No. Not done."

Sarah held up her hand toward the barn and squinted. Most of the worms looked wet and shimmered, not like the dying gray ones on the driveway. Some matched the special tint of the barn roof. "You've got the bright *barn-shingle* color, little worm. You'll be okay." Gently picking that worm out, she dropped it into the grass just off the asphalt. The cool grass felt good between her toes. She sorted other healthy worms quickly and then carried those remaining to the shady grass under a tree.

"You need to wash your hands, Miss Sarah."

"Just a sec, Ma, I'm 'most done. Oh, cow snot," she whispered, annoyed.

She carefully scattered the sick worms and ruffled the grass so they would sink down to the black soil.

"Jesus, take care of your poor, cold baby worms, 'cause I gotta go now. Amen."

She hurried back toward the farmhouse, shaking her hands. Backpacks and suitcases were lined up at the foot of the porch steps. Ma was still staring at her.

"I been doing triage like Adam taught me. I wanna be a doctor."

"Just go wash your hands, please."

Sarah stuck out her tongue and bobbed her head so it looked like she was licking her hands clean. Her mother looked horrified but then broke out laughing.

"Get inside."

Sarah had to wait at the screen door when her father barged out carrying two huge suitcases.

"Where the hell are the boys when I need help? Do I have to lug all these bags to the airport van alone?"

"I can carry my stuff, Papa," Sarah said.

Her mother glared. "Go clean your stinky hands, now. And put on your shoes. You are not going to Europe with bare feet."

Heavy rains had left Virginia painfully muggy. Andrea fluffed her thin dress to keep the sweat from showing; it felt like she hadn't had a bath in three weeks.

Sarah acts exactly like me as a kid, mousy tomboy clear through. Except, I couldn't read at three.

Sarah finished washing her hands, standing on a chair by the sink, and turned off the faucet. "You go hunt for David," Andrea said, "and I'll look for Isaac and Ben. We need to leave for the airport in 10 minutes."

"Okay, Ma."

"And shoes. Don't forget your shoes."

The Warners were about to escape the muggy Virginia summer for the tour of a lifetime in a country that was probably even hotter. Andrea had talked about wanting to go to Spain for 20 years, ever since she taught Spanish in a middle school before meeting Craig. He had surprisingly agreed to go when she brought it up a month ago, and to take the whole family, except Adam who had his own college life now. Andrea guessed Craig was feeling guilty about something. He'd avoided really talking to her for weeks before he blurted out, "Let's go to Spain." He was also celebrating another promotion at work.

Andrea carried two satchels to the van and stopped to give Craig a quick hug. "Thanks for this. It's going to be a wonderful trip."

"I still don't understand why we need a separate room for the kids," he said. "Is that some kind of Spanish hotel rule to rip people off? This is going to be the most expensive trip in history."

"I know. Thank you." She headed to the barn to look for her boys.

The family arrived at the Gran Via Hotel in central Madrid on Sunday morning, unpacked, and immediately went to sleep.

After two days exploring the central city, they drove a rental van through Salamanca to Galicia on the northwest coast. Craig confined Isaac and Ben to the far back seat, where they could torment one another out of sight, if not out of hearing.

Andrea did the driving one day after Craig bought a bottle of sangria at a lunch stop to help him through the "family experience," and nearly finished it off before dessert.

The Warners reached the university town of Santiago de Compostela, the main target of her trip, where she wanted to study the famous cathedral for several days. They were forced to park outside the city center.

"You *will* walk these last three blocks," she told the children. "The pilgrims climbed the Pyrenees and crawled hundreds of miles on their knees to reach the tomb of Saint James. You can walk three lousy blocks."

She led them through the cathedral door, the Gate of the Glory, and put her hand into the deeply worn handprint on the central pillar. "You can feel the pain here from centuries of persecution," she said.

She hoisted Sarah so she could reach. "I can see it, Ma. The hand spot is shining in *chicken-feather* color from all the people touching it in the olden days."

They stayed at the Hospital Real, the most expensive stop on the trip, a gorgeous blend of elaborate stone carvings and ultramodern glass. Andrea hadn't imagined the place would be so beautiful. Ferdinand and Isabella founded the original site in 1511 to treat injured pilgrims. On the first night, the family looked down from their rooms through heavy fog at university students dancing in the medieval alleys, while roving bands of Tunas in traditional dress played guitars and mandolins. The family mellowed. Even Isaac was astonished to see children laughing on the sidewalks at midnight. "This is my kind of country," he said. Andrea lay awake savoring the mist and music drifting through her window long after the others had fallen asleep.

The family woke slowly the next morning. Sarah had been awake and bored for some time. She crept quietly from her bed and out the hotel door in pajamas to explore. It would take a while for the others to get dressed and ready for breakfast. On a second-story balcony, she squeezed her head between the ornate stone posts of a balustrade. Dozens of gargoyle water drains looked down, like her, to a small fountain on the inner courtyard. Its water splashed in shades of blue, *river-rock*, and yellow, while pigeons strutted by the drains beneath her.

I should try it. She looked around. *No one's watching.* Carefully spitting, she barely missed a pigeon.

Footsteps sounded behind her, and before she could turn, she was kicked on her rear end, nudging her over the balcony a little. Yelping, she jerked and caught her head on the stone.

"Hah, that's a good one, Twirpy," Isaac said. "I saved your life, 'cause you might have squished through there and fallen."

"Isaac, you pig booger," she said, rubbing the side of her head. "I'm telling Pa."

"I'll just say I saved you. You should toughen up, Twirpy. What are you doing, anyway?"

"I was pretending to be a waterspout, like those statue things."

"Oh, those are baby dragons," he said. "Sometimes they even take a nibble on the girls to see how they taste."

Sarah saw an odd tint, *warm-ashes*, on the veins of his temples. "You're lying, Isaac. Those are just rocks. You better stop trying to scare me and hitting me. Leave David alone too."

"It's easy teasing you babies," Isaac said.

She glared at him. "I'm not a baby. You better be good . . . or else I'll do . . . something."

For an instant, she saw worry, river-rock colors, on his forehead. He marched away, laughing nervously. Sarah squeezed her head back through the posts, spit, and hit the center of a pigeon's back.

The Warners gathered in the parents' room after breakfast, with maps splayed across the bed to plan the day's sightseeing. Sarah sat under the windowsill, rubbing the new bump on her head. She waited until Isaac turned his back.

They need to see.

Sarah coughed loud, so her parents would look, and charged across the room, kicking into the back of Isaac's knee. Everyone watched him crumple to the floor.

Ma was shocked.

Pa was angry.

Ben said, "Whoa."

"Isaac's been torturin' me and David," Sarah said calmly, showing them her head. "I don't wanna sleep in the same room with him anymore."

Isaac limped to a chair, cursing, whimpering, and looking for sympathy, but no one said a word.

Sarah whispered so only her mother could hear. "I still love Isaac, but he's not a nice boy, you know."

"I know," Ma whispered back.

Isaac slept in their parents' room that night and stayed away from Sarah the rest of the trip.

~~~

The Warners paused at the León Cathedral during the drive back to Madrid. Probes noted in their report that Sarah stood transfixed in front of lofty blue-stained-glass windows and had to be pulled outdoors. She had a similar reaction in Madrid, the final day of the trip, visiting the Museo del Prado. The boys couldn't wait to escape the Flemish and Spanish masterpieces, but at Velázquez's *Las Meninas*, Sarah refused to move. "The children are shimmering," she said. "It's too pretty." Even Andrea became annoyed by the delay.

The probes understood her excitement—Sower had designed Sarah's eyes. Her DNA had been tweaked and she'd grown an extra set of retina cones with a heavy protein on the sensitive retinal molecule, which shifted response into the infrared, beyond the normal human cutoff. Sarah saw an extra primary color band in the near infrared—tetrachromatic vision.

In the first months of life, Sarah's brain developed neural triggers for four secondary colors beyond red, which no other human could see. Each autumn, she noticed leaves change color two weeks sooner than others, at their first loss of chlorophyll. Human faces took on subtle infrared tones if they flushed with excitement or anger.

As she grew, her family couldn't label the new colors Sarah claimed she saw. They assumed she was color-blind. Eventually she named the odd colors herself after things that matched: chicken-feather, barn-shingle, river-rock (for the bright stones in a creek by their farm), and warm-ashes.

Most artists used pigments that dulled nature's reality in the near infrared. Velázquez and a few others stumbled on the perfect surrealistic combinations of oils. To Sarah's eyes, the effect was stunningly beautiful.

~~~

Andrea tugged Sarah from the museum. They strolled through nearby botanical gardens and spent their last hours in Spain at El Retiro Park under thick trees near a lake. Sarah had pointed to every flower or tree with shades of river-rock, which she said was her favorite color. Andrea ignored her as she had a hundred times before. Meanwhile, the boys ran amok with their father, chasing pigeons and feeding ducks.

Street vendors lined the edge of the park and Andrea bought several inexpensive items and whispered, "Bargaining is a tradition in Spain, Sarah. Did you see how I always paid less than they asked?"

Mottled sunlight sliced down through the tall trees, flickering on the dozens of rival street shops. Among the multicolored displays, an elderly woman caught Sarah's eye by smiling and waving a large orange-red fan. "Ma, see the fan," she said. "Can I bargain?"

"I suppose. Try it."

Shaking her head as she approached, Sarah said to the woman, "I haven't got much money."

The lady held out six fingers. "Seis euros, por favor."

Sarah pulled out a one-euro coin and looked devastated. "Horse flies!" She looked up. "Ma, I need more."

"If you promise to do extra chores back home."

Sarah waved two fingers toward the woman, but she frowned.

"Darn. Come on, Ma," Sarah said grabbing Andrea's hand. They walked away. "She *will* sell it for two, Ma."

"I don't think so, Sarah. She wants four, at least."

"If I get it for two, can I get outta the chores?"

"Here's another euro. Try it, but if you need more, you gotta do some extra work back home."

She let Sarah return to the vendor by herself. With a praying gesture, Sarah showed her two euros.

The fan lady scowled but then grinned, taking the money and handing over the bright fan. Sarah waved it over her face, peeked from behind, and winked.

That vendor is actually happy, Andrea marveled. *Fleeced by a three-year-old.*

<hr />

Sarah jabbered the entire flight home. "I can't believe Spain was all true, Ma. I've gotta see a bullfight. I wanna go to the places in *all* my books."

She spread her new fan and waved it across the aisle at Andrea. "It's the most gorgeous orange chicken-feather color," she said. "I love it."

"You were an excellent bargainer."

"I knew zactly how much the lady wanted, Ma, from the barn-shingle around her eyes."

In the packed jetliner, Andrea finally understood how Sarah's babbling about odd colors might be a gift. *I've dreamt about this. God, help her. My baby somehow has a built-in lie detector.*

GOD TO INSECT

Two light-years from Alpha Centauri, the original orange-coded Torae ship intercepted a populated Unity vehicle. The probes broadcast binary numbers as they approached, sweeping through frequencies until the Unity responded. With an acceptable link, they began sending the universal translator sequence. The Unity answered but seemed unfamiliar with normal protocols.

"It's remarkable their ships are even stable," Tiller said. "The massive outer rings are balanced only one-tenth of a millimeter from the singularity, no doubt recreating the gravity of their home star. They stabilize magnetically, using currents from the charged, rotating black hole. Their thruster is primitive: matter is fused in the gravity well and directed out of propulsion slots."

A mottled orange glow emanated from the vehicle surface, but through six narrow slits the view toward the raw black hole showed streams of hard gamma rays.

"At least 10,000 creatures are on this structure," Sower said. "Fusion at the black hole warms their underside, and thermal flow to their antennae must drive the frantic life process—their birth-to-death cycle is only seven Earth hours. They've re-created the environment of a cold white dwarf on this small object."

Sower looped her ship slowly around the Unity vehicle several times, observing. They needed highly focused electron beams to see the surface structures and creatures. Microscopic machines were barely visible. Agitated communication patterns among Unity groups were perceived as the Torae ship drew near.

Sower began a cautious conversation.

"We are Torae," she said. "Can you negotiate for your species?"

"We speak."

Evasive, Sower thought.

"Why were your ships hostile?" asked Tiller.

"Unity happy. Unity friends. You friend?"

"Perhaps," Sower replied. "How many friends do you have?"

"Many."

"What are your intentions?"

"Unity to learn. You do?"

"We're searching for unique species. Why did the Unity flare a star at our ship?

"Unity learn. No hurt."

Tiller's internal plasma shifted to higher energies, pure ultraviolet. "Tell these annoying vermin we're calculating how rapidly they can be atomized," Tiller said confidentially to Sower.

Sower said, "We considered your star flare hostile. Why did you injure the planet and the humans?"

"Unity learn. Planet no star stuff."

"How long has it been since you were home?"

"Not home ever. Long for you?"

"We've been traveling a very long time."

Sower weighed her options, evaluating the Unity. Her concern was not the present. In the next 10 billion years, many stars would burn out and collapse into black holes, dwarf stars, or neutron stars. Many species like the Unity might emerge, possibly powerful ones. These creatures seemed stupid or, more likely, devious, but Sower considered this an important test case. Her analysis had to be dispassionate. She'd be obligated to broadcast the precedent for relay to the rest of the universe.

"Can you prove you are friendly?" asked Sower.

"Speak to Unity friends."

"Where are your friends?"

"Damage friends?"

"We're not angry with your friends. We're only looking for interesting species. We'd like to talk to them."

The Unity sent coordinates for a dwarf star 17 light-years away. Sower thanked them.

"Do Torae talk loud in sector 37286, and stop?"

"Yes," Sower replied. The Unity apparently had detected the Torae clock broadcast from the Origin.

"Your big talker broken now?"

Anger briefly flashed across Sower's toroids—azure and deep violet. She abruptly cut off the exchange to think clearly.

Calculation showed that this Unity black hole had left their home star a few hundred years ago. All their swarms were on paths toward similar dwarf stars for colonization, no doubt. The degenerate nuclei of their bodies collided so rapidly that they evolved 100 times faster than the Torae and 100 million times quicker than humans.

"Their size precludes significant intelligence," Sower said. "They must have a smart parent or leader, or they're lying to us."

Someday they could be a threat.

"Their self-interest-to-altruism ratio is outside the limits," Pruner said. "Such a naive creature could not have evolved. Ambition-to-caution balance is also implausible."

"The thoughts of an individual Unity are unreadable," a probe said.

Sower scanned historical data for all similar intelligent beings and extrapolated billions of possible timelines. *What would happen if we let evolution take its course, if we permit them to develop technically and spread? Could they someday destroy the Torae? Could Unity develop a culture superior to the Torae? Would the universe be better off?*

Probabilities were computed.

An image formed in Sower's mind of a dominant time path with Unity in unimaginable numbers scraping matter and stars into black holes to continue their expansion. She computed a 98 percent chance that Unity would mindlessly spread across the galaxy, and probably beyond.

Sower's mission included protecting the universe. Her command ship sent narrow-beam encrypted signals to its three clones and all local probes for relay. In her message, the Gardener Who Cares for the Seeds said, "Exterminate the Unity."

TIME THREE
SIX YEARS LATER

WARS

Why should I feel regret?

A species was being extinguished on her orders. Sower watched the engagement sphere grow around Alpha Centauri-A, now a six-light-year radius filled with thousands of battle probes. She slurred near-infrared colors in her veins: a sigh.

"Didn't the Unity know they were being judged? They must have understood they were speaking to a superior life form. Their childlike prattle, feigning innocence, was simply offensive. 'Talker broken?' they whined. Ridiculous! Any species with a telescope should have known that a tragedy occurred. They mocked us! An unimaginable explosion took place at the Origin, the core of our civilization. A universe-class event has annihilated our ancient culture, and the destruction is still growing faster than the speed of light. There's a bubble on the fabric of the universe, a white fountain, destroying everything on its path, and the Unity or their designer certainly must know it."

Sower watched battle-probe trajectories, listened to communications, and combined it all into a vast 4D mental image of space and time. The probes had trouble finding some Unity vehicles due to their small size, but when spotted, they were easily, methodically erased.

None of the Torae regretted the decision, but Sower grudgingly respected the Unity's fortitude and sacrifice, mentioning some of what they'd learned:

> "They only carry enough fuel to reach 0.1 light speed.
> Unity journeys can require over 2,500 generations.
> The urge to migrate must be overwhelming."

Tiller flashed long infrared swirls indicating disbelief. "You admire them, don't you?"

"A bit," Sower said. "There's something important about them we don't understand."

Sower knew that Tiller took pleasure in his current task. Unity black holes were so massive they could barely maneuver—a safe, easy target.

＊＊＊

As Tiller's silent extermination expanded in the vacuum of space, a noisy war emerged on Earth. One of Sower's clone ships had been stationed in the Earth's solar system to protect the planet from Unity and carefully track human events. They had watched Saudi coup leaders secretly mine oil fields as Western nations gathered forces in Middle East staging areas, planning to protect the wells. The West believed it could win a quick war before the terrorists reacted.

Also watching were flocks of drones toting news cameras over Riyadh. They sent live video of mobs rioting in the streets, and then brilliant flashes as the first Western-ally shaped-charge bombs dug deep into underground bunkers. Satellite-guided missiles soon cut communication links, and jammers on stealth drones blinded defense missiles and artillery. The coup leaders who survived the initial salvo rushed into streets and squares, surrounding themselves with innocent civilians. Tracking the terrorist leaders was fairly easy, but preventing collateral damage was not. The Western allies blinked a little too long.

Sower had accurately predicted when this new hot war would flare from the endless smoldering global terrorism. Humanity was frightened. People worried about being blown up outside, while shopping or at sporting events. The few still driving gas-powered cars worried about losing oil supplies and tried to ignore the increasingly obvious global warming trend. Meanwhile, neo-Luddites screamed about impending doom from biotech, artificial intelligence, and nanotech. News of a nanorobot actually building its own clone heightened the specter of man-made microbugs eating everything, covering the world in gray goo.

The waves of new technology had been overwhelming; everyone needed time to stop and think. People just wanted to cook, eat, walk the dog, care for their grandparents, go swimming with the kids, and generally keep entropy at bay. They craved some time off from stress.

Unfortunately, orders from the coup leaders reached the oil fields before the communication lines were cut. Dangerous microbes were released near pumping rigs. Poison-gas mines switched to their hot mode. A few dirty nuclear devices exploded. Even approaching the wells would be impossible for some time. The new caliphate coup leaders and their ruling cabals were arrested or killed, but it was too late.

As the Saudi wells went up in flames, the oil glut disappeared, global supply nosedived, and prices spiked. Fracking wells that had been closed for years started pumping again. When gasoline hit $10 a gallon in the U.S., it became clear that electric, fuel-cell, and hybrid cars hadn't yet solved the problem. Despite government goals, it takes a long time to reengineer and entirely replace a global transportation system. It would take a long time to just to clean up the mess.

Sower watched sadly as Earth unraveled.

VOICES

"Hey," nine-year-old Danny called down, "climb on up. It's snowing seeds up here."

Kenny grabbed a big knot on the rope ladder, pulled his feet to another knot, and slowly shimmied up 10 feet to the crumbling treehouse. They'd been running through the woods in the hot July sun, catching hornets in jars. Fluffy seeds from nearby towering cottonwoods slowly drifted down, sticking to the sweat on their arms and faces.

"I'm floating in a cloud over Romulus," Danny said. "The Klingons are attacking from that thick branch, and the skinny limb is a region of artificial gravity."

Kenny had to laugh at his brother. The puffy seeds were piled so deep in one corner that they covered Danny's legs. "So now you think this place is a space rocket," he said. "It's only got three walls. We'll need to nail on some new boards just to keep the thing from falling apart."

From a branch of the old Marshall ash tree, halfway up a steep hill, Kenny could see 10 blocks beyond the railroad tracks. The deep autumn leaves that once covered the slope had decayed to gray powder, overtaken by fresh weeds. Down on the flats by the railroad tracks, shoulder-high wild grass bent in unison, like stalks of wheat. "People like to dump stuff down there, Danny, off the road in the low areas, so the grass hides their garbage. I'll show you some cool stuff if you won't freak out from the rats and dead mice."

"I'd like to see those rats," Danny said.

Kenny held his jar out, shook it, and watched the yellow jackets fly around severed blossoms. "These bees are hoppin' mad. I can hear 'em buzzing through the air holes."

"They wanna be free," Danny said. He threw more seeds in the air; his blond hair was already covered with them.

His little brother Danny was short and skinny, not tough like him. Kenny knew it was his job to protect him, like Mom reminded him every day, but he sure didn't understand Danny. *He still plays with make-believe friends, but he's smart, smarter than adults, I think. Grown-ups just rush around, working. They don't know what's really going on. Danny reads everything, and brainy stuff just pops out. He's only nine and he's his own boss—that's what's different—he's his own boss.*

"We're trapped too," Danny said, "like these bees. You still have nightmares about Dad, don't you? Do you hear his voice and see his face during the night? Sometimes you say his name while you're asleep. I wish I could remember him a little."

"I don't care about him," Kenny said. "Mom won't say, but I remember he made her cry. He left us all alone."

"I have a voice in my dreams, but it's different, real serious. It tells me about the universe and what to do. Did you know there are 600 planets around with people like us, an' just as smart? We might be in charge of them someday."

"How the heck do you know that? You're just dreaming. I don't see any Romulans walking around here."

"The voice told me. They're not Romulans. The enemy is the Younies . . . something like that. But we're stuck here on Earth like the bees in the jar. We should go out there—out into space. Y'know, see the aliens and talk to 'em. You and me, Kenny, we should be astronauts."

"You're nuts."

"I know just how to do it too. I got a plan. It's like catching a ball when it's flying toward you. Your eye's too slow; it only sees where the ball was. Your brain has to figure out how to catch it. I read that."

"What the heck are you talkin' about?"

"The ball players—their brains tell them where the ball will be. My brain figures where things will be too."

"You can tell the future?"

"Not exactly. Only when nothing odd happens. I know what should happen. It works on everything. I already know what you're thinking of saying next."

"What's that?"

"Bullshit."

"Okay. Not bad," Kenny said, chuckling.

"I wanna be an astronaut, and I already see how to get the job. You know my time maps? The voice told me I'd be in outer space and change the Earth's timeline."

Kenny just shook his head.

Danny abruptly stood up and shook off the cottonwood seeds, blowing one that was stuck to his lips. "I think we should open our bee jars and leave the covers loose on the top . . . like this." He put the jar on its side and up against a board. "Tommy Innel and his jerk friends are watching us right now. Don't look. They'll try to kick us out of the treehouse, and you'll want to fight them—right?"

Kenny peeked up the hill at Tommy coming over the top. "Yeah, probably."

"Well, just shove him once and then let them climb up here. We'll leave a present for 'em." Danny smiled.

After they'd carefully unscrewed the jar covers and covered them with seeds, Kenny hung on the treehouse edge and dropped to the ground, while Danny slid down knot by knot.

Tommy Innel strutted up to the tree with his three-kid gang. "Hey, you shits," he said. "Time to go home and change your dresses. What're you doing in my treehouse?"

One of Tommy's friends grabbed Danny, but Kenny yanked him off, got in a clean rib punch, and threw him to the ground. Danny ran and then scrambled up the hill on all fours. Kenny followed, then yelled back as he climbed the hill, "You're lucky, Innel, we need to go home now anyway."

"Go home and get your father to help you," Tommy yelled, laughing. "Oh, that's right. You don't got a father."

At the top of the hill, Danny and Kenny hid behind some brush and waited long enough to watch Tommy and his pals yelp, swat at bees, and swear. "I didn't know fat Tommy could move so fast," Kenny whispered.

Mary didn't mind the outrageous fuel prices much. She didn't have a car. As the cost of gasoline skyrocketed, she even received a small salary increase at the Omega station—a happy time for her. But it only helped a little. For a while she dated Bob, the night manager at the Grub-N-Go, but she quickly broke it off. She didn't feel very attractive anymore, and Bob was a real loser. Tired all the time, she dreamt of winning the lottery.

Working two jobs led to a lot of worry and guilt. Kenny and Danny were essentially raising each other and running roughshod. She bought them presents well beyond her means and was dangerously indulgent with Danny. "He's so rare," she'd say. The boys hadn't gotten into any serious trouble, but then an unexpected letter from Danny's fourth-grade teacher arrived requesting a meeting at school.

Arriving early, she sat across a shiny table from the tight-lipped teacher, petrified. Miss Olsen had seemed friendly during Danny's student conferences but looked very serious now. The principal stomped in noisily, which unnerved Mary even more. *He looks angry.*

"There are some things about Danny that you should know, Mrs. Jorgenson."

Lord, help me, she silently pleaded.

"Danny's been doing well, reading two books per day—hard ones," his teacher said. "But I want to talk about a specific book report he gave in front of the class, a book about electronics. He explained the book nicely, but then added a description of transistors and something called quantum mechanics. I checked the book; there's nothing about quantum mechanics in there. He drew some equations and said something about Schroeder, from the Peanuts comic I think, and dead cats. I had no idea what he was talking about, but he seemed so sure of himself. Has he talked to you about the equations? Do you have training in physics?"

"Heavens, no. He never talked to me about it."

"You should have seen the diagrams he used; we think he might be at college level," the principal said. "Danny needs to be tested."

In less than a month, Danny had special volunteer tutors. They reported that he seemed to anticipate all their questions, giving answers before they even had a chance to ask.

On his 10th birthday, Mary bought Danny a deluxe chemistry set, one that high school students might use, and he started regularly filling the house with foul odors from the basement.

When he asked her if he could build a telescope to study the new supernova in Virgo, Mary said okay, expecting a small cardboard tube from the hardware store. She worked even more hours at the Grub-N-Go and got help from her parents to collect enough cash for Danny's summer "project." Five months later, he had assembled parts from an optics company, melted tar and lead on the kitchen stove, ground and polished a six-inch glass disk with carborundum and rouge powders, and permanently stained the carpet and furniture. He assembled metal and wood parts with help from his grandfather, Krystof.

A dozen friends and his grandparents came to their front yard on a cold November night for a first peek. Danny had to climb halfway up a stepladder to reach the eyepiece. "It's a Newtonian reflector, everyone. Isn't it awesome, Mom?"

"I like the color you painted the tube thing," she said.

Danny pointed the telescope first at the strange star scientists were calling a supernova, the fourth brightest object in the sky and clearly visible in city lights. "Astronomers are sure it's no ordinary supernova. It's something new, mysterious, and important," Danny said.

He gave everyone a chance to peer into the eyepiece at the supernova, Saturn, and the Andromeda Galaxy. He kept looking long after most had left. "People liked looking at Saturn a lot more," Danny said as Mary helped him put the telescope away. "The supernova's just like all the other stars, except a lot whiter. I was hoping it would be fuzzy or something. What a bummer."

<hr>

From behind the shop windows at the Omega station, Mary could see anger in the customers' eyes. People were losing their jobs, the stock market had fallen off a cliff, computers were running everything, institutions like churches and clubs had withered away, and 30 years of political dysfunction hadn't resolved anything. And now sweaty drivers were stuck in their gasoline-powered cars at the station in oppressive heat with nowhere to go. Not everyone wanted or could afford the new gasless cars, so millions were still driving their old clunkers. Gasoline was so scarce that the drivers couldn't even let their cars run to keep the air conditioning on; occasionally they'd restart the engines and lurch ahead a few feet toward the Omega pumps. Most stations only sold gas every other day; drivers had no choice but to wait in line. The anxiety, inconvenience, obscene prices, and lack of any apparent solution had pushed many past common civility. A quiet rage was growing in the long queue.

Mary volunteered to walk the line of vehicles to warn drivers that the station would soon run out of gas for the day. Omega's crude-oil contracts with Saudi Arabia had seemed smart before the war, but now their supplies were particularly strained. The line of vehicles extended well past Morrie's used car lot, around the corner, and into the residential area. Mary went to the rear first so those cars could back up and pull away.

"Sorry, we'll be out of gasoline soon," she yelled to the drivers, while walking through the ragweed by the street, trying to be pleasant. "There's plenty of propane and biodiesel, but no point in waiting for gasoline back here. We'll be open for gas again at seven a.m. Friday."

She tried to ignore the swearing. Drivers close to the front of the line got out to see what was happening and formed a small crowd. Some had waited over an hour. The complaints got worse as she passed the used car lot. There was an unwritten understanding that stations wouldn't run out until late afternoon. The drivers near the pumps were irate.

"How can you be running out? It's only noon. I'll sue for lost wages. This is disgusting. It's the last straw."

"You people here shouldn't give up yet," she said. "We're just running short. You might get lucky." She shied away from the obviously livid drivers. There'd been riots and fights at other stations.

The station manager yelled out, "It's gone, Mary, only propane and biodiesel left, and a few hydrogen canisters."

The relatively self-controlled drivers put their heads in their hands and just moaned. Others snapped. One thug squeezed past the crowd near Mary, purposely turned his body, and bumped her off the sidewalk. She teetered and then tripped back against a low concrete wall, hitting the side of her head. Blood trickled down her face. Some in the mob then focused their anger on the boorish lout and knocked him to the ground.

An open gash in Mary's hair was wet with blood. Two people helped her back to the station. Both she and her attacker were soon taken to Regions Hospital in an ambulance.

The man had been knocked out cold by a left hook, but he revived in the ambulance and started thrashing. "Take it easy," a paramedic said, holding him down. "What's your name?"

"T.J, T.J. Huber. Where are you taking me?"

From the other stretcher, Mary said, "They're taking us to Regions Hospital. You were unconscious."

She looked over at him. Huber was a lump of a man; his stomach held the sheet covering him in a tall arch and his face appeared bright red from bruises or anger. "Who's that?" he said. "You the Omega bitch? God, I hate Omega. I hate Arabs even more; I'd kill one if I could find one."

The paramedic said, "I'm giving you a shot now for the pain. Settle down."

"Why do you hate everyone?" asked Mary. "What's your big problem anyway?" She felt her hair, which had been cut away, and tape was holding the skin together on her forehead.

"I don't have time for this crap," he said. "I'm working two jobs to pay for gas. This Mideast war's wrecked everything, not that things weren't falling apart before that. My wife left me. My kids won't talk to me. Only entertainment and sports people are doing well. I'm a sucker for working at all. We should have dropped a couple nukes on Iraq in 2002. The Arabs would've been scared shitless. None of this would be happening. We've now screwed up three wars against those idiots. How can you work for Omega? They're bloodsuckers. I wouldn't be surprised if they planned this whole thing."

Mary whispered, "I don't think Omega's making much money without oil." She tried to roll over but felt a stabbing pain in her head.

Danny and Kenny hiked down to Regions Hospital to see their mom that afternoon. Neither had been inside a hospital since they were born. Danny didn't like the smell but was happy to see his mom. His aunt and grandparents were already there.

"What kind of man would hurt a woman?" Grandpa Krystof said. "When there were shortages in Poland, families helped one another."

"The guy was a real jerk," Mary said, "but I'm doing okay now."

"What have they done, Mom?" asked Danny.

"A doctor put special tape over the gash after smearing on stem cells to make it heal faster. They're testing to see whether I got a concussion too. I do feel kind of groggy."

"Does it hurt?" he asked.

"Not much now, Danny."

"I can skip school to stay with you tomorrow," Kenny said.

"You'll do no such thing. I'm coming home tomorrow. I can't afford to stay in this hospital without sick leave."

They stayed for over an hour. Gramma retold her story about how she met Krystof as a young man after she left the farm. As usual, Gramps frequently corrected her version. When she finished, Gramma leaned over the bed, kissed Mom on the cheek, and whispered in her ear.

Danny didn't say much during the old story. He kept thinking about how much he and Kenny depended on their mother. She looked so fragile in the bed, with the large gauze bandage over her head. He was angry with his father for walking out. *What if she couldn't be with them? What if she died?*

Danny and Kenny spent the night at their grandparents' house. In bed, Danny listened for the familiar Torae voice, the teaching voice in his mind. He had questions—about death, his future, and fear. Why didn't they ever talk about things that really mattered to him? After tossing and thinking a long time, he fell asleep.

~~~~~

Probes heard Danny's questions, but it wasn't yet time to have a conversation with his mind. The path to transcendence had to be discovered by each species, by each individual. Sower's human boy needed to be tested, to learn from success and failure, and to become strong. Transcendence had to be earned. And humans were about to face their first and most dangerous test.

~~~~~

Every intelligent species ultimately merged with their machines. Sower considered it an unavoidable process and noted that for Earth humans it began slowly, but later couldn't be stopped. Most historians traced its origin to hip-replacement surgery, the heart pacemaker, the insulin pump, or ID chips. More recently, dozens of real-time sensors were being implanted to monitor stress, blood conditions, gut bacteria, immune-response chemicals, hormone levels, and even the sound and reason for a cough. But the popular device that really changed civilization was a communication and computing chip embedded within the body, called the "comm implant."

People carried cellphones and pagers in vast numbers at the turn of the century. Then, as smartphones and voice recognition improved, everyone became comfortable talking to computers, cars, appliances, and screens. About the time the phone keypad disappeared, some wore the voice interface as earplugs, collar pins, necklaces, earrings, and finally as tiny, self-charging implants just beneath the skin. Simple voice commands could not only place calls but also activate and control any nearby device. And, of course, screens were everywhere: in pockets, bags, desks, walls, appliances, and wrists. Some screens covered entire walls. Security people used the voice implants first, and then masses of teenagers underwent the simple two-minute implant procedure. To them it was a trend, like having piercings or tattoos, only way cooler. They could talk to their friends or listen to music *all the time*. The implants eliminated background noise, a major advantage. Many adults soon followed the teenagers. Half the people in any crowd seemed to be talking to the air.

~~~~~~~~~~

Mary waved the note at Danny and Kenny in the kitchen. "Your school's giving out *free* comm implants!" The boys stared at her unable to speak, not because they were surprised but because of the peanut butter in their mouths. They were just happy to have her back from the hospital making sandwiches again.

"You'll need to go down to school next Saturday to have it done. The implant and two years of service are free; the government's paying for it. I'll get one, too, but at a clinic where I'll have to pay some. We could never afford this on our own. It is a great deal, you guys. I'll be able to talk to you whenever and wherever."

"Do we have to do it, Mom?" asked Danny.

"Why not? It's free."

"But it'll be inside our heads."

"Everybody's doing this. I'm sure it's safe."

"It's a good idea," said Kenny. "It'll be like always having our walkies."

"If it's done right," Danny said, sounding concerned.

~~~~~~~~~~

This was an important moment—a key test of human logic and wisdom. Torae microprobes filled every nook of Danny's bedroom, recording all of his thoughts, conscious and unconscious.

Danny hopped on his bed and stared at the large sheets of paper that covered almost every inch of wall space. They were his time plots, with pages he'd taped up for history, transportation, fuel, inventions, foods, writing, the Jorgenson family, U.S. presidents, music, and a half dozen others. The sheet titled "Writing" had "dirt scratches" written on the far left side for the past and "electronic gesturing" and "mind writing" written on the right, which were connected with dozens of lines to other inventions, like pencils and printers, in between. A star at the center of each page was labeled, "We are here now." Each page was like a family tree, with branches to the past and future and smaller writing each time he'd imagined an odd twist or read a book with new facts. Thumbtacks and strings connected some of the sheets across his room. He stared at the word "comm implant" on his overview of

"Communications." It had strings fanning out to almost every other chart in the room.

Sower had given Danny foresight. She'd designed genes that grew extra neural paths between his frontal and parietal lobes, and his cerebral cortex had a seventh neuron layer, optimized for prediction. He saw the future intuitively. Normal trends appeared static, allowing him to focus on unexpected events or inflection points. All humans had this ability for physical motion, but Danny could foresee dialogue, history, economics, and technology.

The probes were satisfied. Danny's thoughts showed he understood the significance of the comm implant. He knew the implants would change humanity forever—it was obvious from the strings in his room.

Satellite trucks with antennae were parked in front of the school when Danny arrived with Kenny at nine-thirty a.m. He'd read about the whole program on a web station. The government and the internet providers were sharing costs to bring an essential technology to children in underprivileged areas.

I guess Kenny and I are underprivileged, Danny thought.

When they arrived, police had barriers on the street, and the administrators and teachers stood in front of the school looking nervous. He was surprised to see that the old cinder-block building had a fresh coat of yellow paint.

Something big must be happening.

Danny climbed the stairs behind Kenny just as a rush of kids from the nine a.m. group came out the open doors. The school was doing the whole implant thing alphabetically, so Tommy Innel was among them. He pushed his way toward Kenny under the eye of two teachers.

"Hey, you jerks! Quit hiding," Innel said, sneering at Danny and Kenny, blocking their way up the steps.

"Get lost, Innel," Kenny said, trying to step around him.

Tommy peeked at the teachers and looked frustrated. He had red welts on his neck and arm.

"Look at these," Innel said, pointing to his neck. "My doctor said I'm allergic to bee stings and I coulda died the other day. You're both roadkill when I catch you away from school. And you, shorty," Tommy said, staring right at Danny. "When they cut you up in there, you're gonna howl like a baby."

". . . not a baby," Danny mumbled.

A teacher started moving toward Tommy, so he gave up and let them pass on the stairs, giving Kenny a bump. Once inside, the crowd funneled toward the school library. A doctor and five nurses stood at the front, ready for the nine-thirty group. The principal ordered them all to settle down and sit. Camera crews from the local cable and web stations were arranging equipment, and strangers in suits were scattered about.

The principal nervously tapped on a microphone. "As some of you may have guessed, we're going to be on the local news today. Here's how it will work, students. First, Mr. Callaghan from the internet company is going to explain how the voice comm works. Then, Dr. Jimenez will explain the procedure for attaching it to your jaw. It really doesn't hurt much at all. Then, in about 15 minutes, Senator Rinter will arrive to watch the nurses install the tiny implant for a few of you. He may ask you some questions like, 'Did it hurt? How does it feel?' Things like that. When you're done, sit back down. You'll be able to ask Mr. Callaghan and Dr. Jimenez questions, and maybe even the senator. Please, try not to be goofy or rude, we'd like to leave a good impression. The senator sponsored the federal bill that helps pay for your new phone implant, so it wouldn't hurt to throw in a thank you here and there. If you're lucky and polite, you may get to be on the news streams tonight. I'll turn it over to Mr. Callaghan now." A few kids were making faces and monkey sounds.

Mr. Callaghan, sounding very sincere, reiterated that the procedure wouldn't hurt much at all and that his company was proud to provide the service for these tiny, smart implants. "It's going to change your lives and help you learn much faster."

Then he told them how to use the device, describing its seven access levels. The school librarian projected a chart on a screen. "You can always turn the comm off—just say, 'Comm off.' Only level-one callers can reach you then. Be very careful whom you assign to that level; they can call you in the middle of the night, and their voice will go straight through without a ring. Some emergency calls, if you are in danger, will also be level one. Only put very important people, like your parents, brother, or sister, on that level. The phone will ask you whom you want on levels one to six when you first turn it on, and you can change it later. Just answer its questions. Even if you don't know a person's phone number, it'll ask questions until you're sure it's the right person. If you already have a smart device with a contact list, the list can just be downloaded.

"Level seven is open access. Anybody in the world can call you there and you can ask any question. There's tons of information when you need it. Sometime just say 'Open level seven' to see how many messages and links are waiting; it'll be in the trillions. Any junk calls will be stuck there—no more robocalls. You'll be asked to prioritize callers or information by subject or location, or tell the phone exactly what you want and then the top answers will start coming through. You will want certain people or organizations on levels two to six. If you don't like any particular call, just say 'Reject' or 'Hang up.'"

He looked up from his notes and grinned. "Don't worry. The implant phone pretty much explains itself. Everyone gets the hang of it pretty quick. More than 89 million people in the country have one. It's similar to the ear-phone your parents might have. It has the computing power of 30 home computers from just five years ago, so it's quite smart, and you can choose its voice. You'll get a web link and a brochure for yourself and your parents before you leave. By the way, if you have a TV, fridge screen, toaster, computer, or other device with a wireless interface, you can turn it on by just talking. No more searching for lost remotes. That's a great feature." Mr. Callaghan remembered to smile broadly again as he finished.

Danny wanted to ask about 50 questions. Kenny, sitting next to him, looked a little puzzled.

The doctor, wearing a long white coat to show he was a doctor, demonstrated where a local disinfectant and anesthetic would be wiped on their skin and how he'd make a tiny incision. "Hold very still when I do it," he said. The device, mostly battery and antenna, would be squeezed against the underside of the jawbone, the "mandible," he called it. Microscopic titanium barbs would hold it to the bone. "It gets power slowly from the chemicals in your body. Soon you won't even feel it." They would have to read a 25-word list to train the apparatus to their voice. Dr. Jimenez then said, "As far as we know, only a few people have had any medical troubles with the comm implant, and those people jerked violently while it was being inserted. Please hold still. It really doesn't hurt."

"Geez," Kenny said, "I bet it hurts."

The kids around Danny looked petrified, but they all rose like sheep when their names were called and shuffled forward. *They're all just going to do it,* Danny thought.

Danny heard his name. *I've gotta say something.*

When they called his name a second time, he reluctantly joined the line.

There was a commotion near the door, and the news cameras swung around to capture Senator Rinter entering. The senator asked the reporters to focus on the children, but those with microphones circled him immediately. The camera commotion distracted Danny while the doctor poked the comm device through his skin and onto his jawbone near his ear. It hurt. He moved to a nearby nurse and dutifully repeated the words to train his new comm, but he didn't feel good about it.

Senator Rinter stood by some younger kids, patted their backs, and asked how the new comm felt. Then he walked around the room showing them how he could switch on computers, the large wall screen, and lights with his voice. A few kids even remembered to thank him. The principal looked pleased.

When the implant procedures were finished, the children were encouraged to ask questions. Most just wanted to know how to turn the comm on, but the senator, and everyone else, was startled when Danny blurted out, "Who controls the interface?" Before Senator Rinter could answer, he added, "Won't you learn what I'm saying, and even thinking? Is that possible?"

All the kids were looking at him.

For a moment, the senator just stared. "Well, of course I'd like to know what you're thinking, young man. I'm a politician after all. But I can't get any information from the comm unless you want me to. That's the key. You control the access. It's like choosing what news source you watch or turn off." He turned to smile at the cameras.

"Won't there be an analysis, off implant, at the internet company?" asked Danny.

"You're right, the information link will be valuable. They could learn what you care about, but we have laws against that now. The provider company will filter and switch calls, but you'll select the filters."

Danny decided not to give up. "How can we tell if the computer or someone is putting ideas in our head after it knows us really well? Will they know where I am when I'm trying to hide? What if the computer is smarter than me? What if it lies to me when I ask something? How will I know what is true?"

Senator Rinter looked concerned and tried to reassure him. "We've addressed some of these problems for social media. But they are good questions. What's your name?"

"Danny Jorgenson."

"Well, Danny, I think the main thing is that you can choose what to believe or hear. That's the key. I'll make sure of that."

"Senator, do you promise to protect me and my brother Kenny no matter how smart the comm gets?"

"Yes, I do, Danny."

Outside the school, while Kenny searched for any sight of Tommy Innel, Danny finished programming his implant. "Open level seven," he said distinctly.

He heard a computer voice in his head: "You have 8,465 waiting messages and 33 trillion information sources. Please specify priorities. Your basic choices for calls are: time, information, subject, location, and other."

"Close level seven."

Danny put Kenny and his mother on the level-one list, and the phone voice immediately said, "Message waiting from Mary Jorgenson."

"Okay," he said.

"Danny or Kenny, if you get this call at school, I want you to come straight home. I have some . . . very . . . bad . . . news." Her voice sounded weak and broken. He could tell she'd been crying.

He told Kenny and they ran the 14 blocks home, where they found their mother sobbing, her head in her hands. Her daycare friend Angie had an arm around her. Mary looked up and stared at them. "Boys, come here. I need to hug you. Grandma and Grandpa . . . are gone." She held them a long time, like she didn't want to let go.

Angie tried to explain, but Mom interrupted. "I'll tell them," she said. "Police called here after you left for school this morning. There was a fire. It started on the sofa; probably Krystof smoking a cigar late last night . . . he fell asleep. Grandma was upstairs sleeping. He tried to put it out, trying to be a damn hero. The house was so old, and they never put in sprinklers." She started crying again; then she asked Danny to sit down by her.

"They found Grandpa lying in the hallway, overcome by smoke. Grandma never got off her bed.

"Angie's going to drive me to the morgue and funeral home now, and we'll go by their house this afternoon to look for things we want to keep. Stay in the house while I'm gone today. I'll call you."

Danny saw Kenny bite his lip and stand straight while Mom talked, like he was at attention at a scout meeting. Danny tried not to cry, but a few times he couldn't stand it. His hands twitched and he whimpered a little.

———◇◇◇———

That night, Mom told them more about how their grandparents' house was covered in soot. Mom held him just like Grandma had, rocking a little. Danny imagined himself on Grandma's lap, reading while she hugged him. She would tickle him and he'd tease her back. He saw the past clearly in his mind but the future was blank. Part of the Jorgenson family timeline, his favorite, had been erased. Without knowing it, tears rolled down his face.

"I need to tell you something more," she said. "You loved them both a lot, didn't you?"

"Yes. You know that."

"Everyone who lives through the death of someone close knows how precious people are. You will always love them, even though they're gone."

She rubbed his cheek with her hand.

"Danny, there is a balance to things. For every death there's new life somewhere else. It makes living all the more precious. They died, so you know now. You won't forget them, right?"

He nodded. "What did Grandma say to you at the hospital, when she whispered in your ear?"

"Um, I think she told me to get my butt out of bed, but she used some words you're not supposed to hear."

———◇◇◇———

Danny listened again for voices as he fell asleep. His mom said, "G'night," through his new implant. It was nice to have her so close. He tried to remember his grandfather's voice, the tone and funny accent, and the things he'd said. He wanted to hear him speak again. He also waited for the teaching voice, the one that had told him about the stars and galaxies. Maybe it could explain about dying.

Probes read his thoughts but didn't respond. They analyzed the situation and told themselves that such agony could be a delicate aspect of humanity, not to be disturbed. They didn't fully understand human emotions and, in fact, they didn't really know what to say.

A probe interrupted Sower on the command ship. "We've received new warning messages from Torae near the Origin. The contacts are brief. We fear the communication ships are being destroyed as they transmit."

"Decode critical ones for me," Sower said.

"The following are typical," the probe replied. "'Vast light, apparent temperature 1,027 degrees. . . .' 'Gravitational shock expected in 12 seconds. . . .' 'No information on cause. All dead. . . .' 'Flee if you can. . . .'" The probe then added, "The messages are longer when they come from vehicles farther from the Origin. Apparently, the deadly shock and radiation slow down at greater distances."

"That's hopeful," Sower said. "Can you extrapolate to determine if we're safe here?"

"Not yet," the probe said.

Analyzing the event, Sower guessed that millions of Torae ships were retreating at near light speed to survive. She wondered if any would reach the Milky Way.

"There's no reason for us to go off mission," she said with a decisive blue squeak. "If the universe has been torn or set ablaze, it won't help to be slightly farther away."

IMPLANTS

Jeremy knew it was an odd friendship at best between Kyle Orlov and himself. On the surface they were as different as any two men could be: Kyle always in suits, Jeremy only reluctantly wearing shoes. Orlov had dedicated his life to defending intellectual and physical property while Jeremy wanted to free it from bureaucratic control. Jeremy despised his father's arrogant wealth, but Kyle was obviously trying to make money and escape the middle class. Despite the differences, they enjoyed hanging out, comparing their lives and cool, new toys. And maybe they both just wanted to better understand the enemy.

They met for lunch often to discuss the latest technical gizmo, the slow withering of the great American internal combustion engine, or their work at LASSO. Jeremy preferred to meet at a Thai restaurant just off Colorado Boulevard where he could get by with a T-shirt and flirt with a particular waitress. He enjoyed saying salacious things that she couldn't quite understand, and it was the best food he ate each week.

Occasionally, Joti and Rianne would join them. Jeremy thought Joti was a good-looking bird with a razor wit. He harbored secret desires to corrupt both her and her weird child. For a nine-year-old, Rianne was quite brilliant, and he fancied her becoming his personal Anakin Skywalker, instructing her on the power of the Dark Side. During the lunches, he never missed a chance to point out the hypocrisy of any moral tenet. He'd watch Rianne's eyes as he implanted his destructive intellectual seeds, knowing she soaked it all up. Joti seemed to assume he was joking.

He loved to reduce ethical codes to absurdity. He had rejected, in turn, the prim religion of his mother, the self-important belief in duty held by his father, and the destruction-for-fun credo of his junior high mates. At university, he'd accepted the true hacker's code: free knowledge, protect the indiscretions of fellow hackers, and never steal. Mostly, he was just in it for the thrill and risk.

With his anarchist views, he easily justified siphoning money from the bureaucracies of society. In his view, bosses were inherently unnecessary, and individuals should self-organize on the web to provide for society's needs without great accumulations of power or wealth. His genetic algorithms at LASSO had tentacles into hundreds of rich companies, and hidden software drained a small portion of their cash, sending it to a dozen anti-government, anti-capitalist groups. His was a nonviolent movement.

Jeremy thought of himself as one of the "chosen people" who'd one day create, with wires and software, not only a new social order but replacements for both God and humanity. He wanted to be first in line to have his brain uploaded.

"What the hell am I doing here?" Jeremy said, shielding his eyes from the hot wind and minitornado of sand.

"It'll be nicer when we get to the high bush," Kyle said. "Don't panic. Just keep moving."

Joti had invited him to a last lunch at their Altadena home before their move to an upscale house down in the valley, and coerced him into hiking in the foothills after eating.

"You should've brought a girlfriend," Joti said.

"And subject someone else to this abuse? Thank the gods I didn't." He gestured up the mountain path. "We're not going up there, are we? That's mountain goat country. It can't possibly be safe."

"I didn't realize you were such a wimp, Jeremy," Joti said. "I've seen folks on mountain bikes come flying down those trails. You just have to be a little careful."

"I've been here hundreds of times," Rianne said. "It's okay."

Rianne has Kyle's face and those big ears. Too bad.

"You don't get out enough," Kyle said. "Look at you, Jeremy, you're whiter than a Norwegian gnome in winter. This is Southern California. Don't you ever go to the beach?"

"You're ganging up on me. Let's sit for a minute, mates," he begged. "I'll go higher if you allow me to catch a breath. Let me tell Rianne a hacker story or something. I can share a bloody excellent high school hack of mine."

"Father, let him rest. I'd like to hear his story."

They found a clearing among the brambles and leaned against eroded baked sandstone overlooking the hazy valley. They could barely make out Old Pasadena in the smog.

"Actually, I'm rather proud of this one," Jeremy said while coughing. "No one hears about the good hacks; only the virus vandals get press. I targeted the British Museum and spent the better part of a day exploring deep nooks of the Smithsonian and British Museum websites before trying anything serious. I needed names of midlevel Smithsonian personnel and found one, an expert in dispersive X-ray fluorescence or something. Then I posed as him, calling England three times to get researcher-rank access to the British archives. I fed in algorithmic variations of all department director names, family members, hobbies, and key exhibits until I found a valid user ID. A brute force machine hack for passwords hit gold, and I was awarded administrator entrée.

"Then the fun. I added 50 bogus prehistoric artifacts to their collection, writing nice, little descriptions using their format, even including a few photos. The photos came from a Native American museum: spearheads, carved bear claws, and burial clothes. I claimed they originated in Mesopotamia and dated them around 4500 BC. The whole thing was a hoot. A month later, I sent a note asking if they had noticed any anomalies in the Near East collections and suggested they check their web security."

"That is so awesome," Rianne said. She stood up and dusted herself off. "Did they ever catch you?"

"I doubt they tried. Would have been quite embarrassing for them."

He noticed the Orlovs had all stood. "Must I actually ascend up that bloody hill now? You haven't changed your minds, have you? Please."

"You're the most charming rogue I've ever met," Joti said, "but you're not getting out of the climb."

"Any bear claws up there?" he asked.

Rianne grabbed his hand and tugged him up the narrow path.

Kyle chose one of the dozens of trails through the foothills, and they greeted hikers who passed by. Jeremy continued to complain and questioned the sanity of many they encountered.

Coming around a bend, they saw a swale where mud had washed out after the heavy spring rains. Joti pointed down at two house foundations that had given way and two other homes half buried in mud.

"Did I tell you that Rianne actually heard the ground break loose," Kyle said, "even before the dirt swept over those houses? She has incredible low-frequency sensitivity. We had her tested. Anyway, that's why we're moving to the valley. It's too dangerous up here, what with fires and mudslides."

"Not to mention hiking," Jeremy said.

"I wish we didn't have to move," Rianne said. "Except I'll get to live closer to my best friend, Tina, but I really don't want to move, Mother."

"Your father has his own law practice now, Rianne. The new house will be much nicer."

"Then, can I ask for something? You know, to compensate. I'd like Jeremy to teach me about computers. I need genetic software in my bio-sims and he knows all about that. Is that okay, Jeremy?"

"Uh, I don't know."

"Can we go over to his house or to LASSO to see how they work, Mother?"

"I suppose so," Joti said, "if he doesn't mind, but I'll want to come along. I don't entirely trust his crazy ideas."

"It's acceptable to me, as long as we turn around right now," Jeremy said. "I could show her the inner secrets—the tricks."

―――――◦∞◦―――――

Over the next month, Rianne and Joti visited Jeremy's house three times. Rianne clearly enjoyed the break from her dull summer. During the visits, she swiftly absorbed the essence of learning programs, computer security, LASSO software, and his unique view of ethics.

"Who is Orlov and why are you spending so much time with him?" the comm voice said.

"He's just an acquaintance, a LASSO lawyer," Jeremy replied. "I like his family. Do you have someone watching me, Milos?"

"Sometimes we have people . . . look after you. We want to protect our investment. Have you said to him something important?"

"No, not really. We talk about legal matters and shoot the bull. Listen, I don't want your people spying on me. Understand?"

The scratchy voice on the highly encrypted line said, "I understand, but we will keep our eyeball on Orlov."

Before Jeremy could respond, his partner in the Czech Republic terminated the call.

"Jeremy seriously needs a girlfriend," Joti said. "I think I'll introduce him to Laurel at the party."

"That sounds like a dangerous combo," Kyle said laughing. "Laurel's tough enough to keep him under control, I guess. And she would add a little human influence to his life; it couldn't hurt. But please don't interrupt me now. I'm at 46. You've already broken my concentration."

He held the basketball just over his eyes and sighted toward the basket.

"Jeremy's odd," she said. "He has that bold and charming act, but he's actually shy and nerdy. Laurel wouldn't have to worry about him climbing any mountains, and they'd have the British thing in common."

Kyle glanced over at Joti, who was surrounded by piles of fresh dirt. She was planting desert wildflowers, and the new garden, adjusted for the hotter climate, almost looked first class. They had moved into a mini-mansion in exclusive San Marino three months earlier and were planning a big housewarming party, but the place still needed work inside and out.

He and Joti had saved a lot of money over eight-years and decided to finally splurge. In addition to the new home, they both purchased new self-driving electric cars. Kyle also impulsively spent over $100,000 on audiovisual and computer equipment.

Kyle and Rianne had taken a break from yard work to shoot hoops. One of Kyle's goals for the year was to make 100 consecutive free throws. He paid Rianne with her favorite snacks to retrieve.

"That's 47," he said subvocally to Rianne. They both had their comm implants on open transmission, so they didn't need to speak the other's name.

"Feed the ball right here to my chest if you can, Rianne. It's best if I can make exactly the same hand motion and follow through."

"I'll try, Father."

"You don't suppose," Joti said, "that Laurel would get mad or insulted if we introduced her to a man who hates mountains, do you? It's been a year since Mathew died at Yosemite, but she was devoted to him. I mean, what if the subject comes up and Jeremy says how stupid mountain climbing is? And she's such a neatnik. Jeremy's got money, but he still lives like a slob in that little house. Mathew was so stylish and sophisticated. What if Jeremy grosses her out?"

"Listen, Joti," Kyle said, "they're adults. If they don't like each other, that's fine. I'll warn Jeremy that her professor-husband died climbing and tell him to clean up his place, have a fumigator and decorator in, before he ever invites her over. Okay?"

"Yeah, but I need to think about whether this whole idea is a mistake."

"Well you've got two weeks before the party to decide."

The basketball clunked off the rim. "Father. You missed again, at 53!"

"That's better than missing at 98, I suppose. Remember, Rianne? That happened once, and it really bummed me out."

~~~~~~~~

All three Orlovs had used conventional comm implants for five years, but even school kids were getting those now. When the brain-comm was introduced, Kyle read all the research and convinced Rianne and Joti that they were safe. It seemed like a natural step. Brain-comms were both high-tech and expensive. He wanted the latest and greatest of everything now that he could afford it.

In the procedure, each family member had a plug of cranial bone temporarily removed near the temporal lobe, over the brain cortex speech center, so an array of sensors could be nestled and attached above the neurons there. That flexible sheet, with millions of titanium barbs, correlated frequencies as they talked or sang. The method had been first perfected for people who had a damaged larynx. For those with normal, healthy vocal cords, few sessions of biofeedback were needed before the person could use the brain-comm without saying words aloud. The Orlovs were now experts; they talked subvocally without even moving their lips.

The family upgraded their hearing implants at the same time. The latest technology involved a thin piezoelectric film near the eardrum—the ultimate hearing aid. The implants eliminated the slight jawbone buzz of the conventional comm. The doctors told Kyle that with a tympanic implant, the only way someone could know you were secretly talking to your spouse in a boring meeting was if you started arguing aloud.

During Rianne's implant procedure, Kyle learned how unusual her hearing was. The routine pre-op included listening to cochlear sounds to check for problems with sensing hairs or neural paths. Normal ears hum. In Rianne's case, the technician found cochlear noise down to 6 cycles per second and as high as 60,000, well beyond the normal span. They suspected equipment malfunction but later verified her ability to actually hear the entire range.

It took a long time for Kyle to admit that his daughter was genetically distinct. Professor Ma had first suggested the possibility when Rianne was only two. He knew everyone noticed her large ears, of course, but Rianne also tested well beyond statistical intelligence norms. Keeping her challenged wasn't easy. Exams had shown her to be physically normal—until the hearing test. Kyle also admitted to himself that her personality was a bit peculiar.

For him to consider Rianne's personality odd was saying a lot; he'd often been told he had a few extra jokers in his own deck. After all, how many normal people had a summer goal to memorize the *Aeneid* in Latin? Rianne joked that he had a terrible case of the Euripides.

Kyle had learned to bury his eccentric personality when necessary, but Rianne often told stories about rejection and humiliation at school. Her brain and attitudes made her unique and unusual to her classmates. Unlike Kyle, she actually seemed to like the idea of being peculiar and simply ignored the problems.

"Hey, Tina, I just left my house," Rianne said subvocally.

"Okay, Rianne. Mother made sweet rolls. We'll have time to eat one before leaving," Tina answered.

It took three minutes for Rianne to bike to Tina's house, close to her new school. They planned to walk from there.

Rianne's parents had told her that Alex Smith Day School was the most elite prep school in Pasadena, teeming with children of business execs, Caltech professors, doctors, and entertainers. "You can learn at your own pace there. It'll be great." She was skeptical.

"Let's have a look at you," Chia-Jean Ma said as Rianne came through the back door. "I need to see if you have that Alex Smith look."

Tina smiled nervously. She'd been at Alex Smith since kindergarten and had promised to teach Rianne the unwritten rules.

Chia-Jean put a hand on each of Rianne's shoulders, twisted her from side to side, checking her out. She had worn the school uniform and carefully brushed her long hair to cover her ears. She stared down at her fingernails, chewed to the nub.

"I'm not going to look perfect, Professor, I can't do that."

Chia-Jean stroked her chin and nodded. "You pass my inspection, Rianne. You should be able to get by the guard dogs at the school door. Good luck. Don't forget your sweet roll."

"Thanks," Rianne said. "Can I hang here with Tina after school?"

"Sure, but I'll want a complete report on your first day," Chia-Jean yelled as the door slammed.

<hr />

Rianne and Tina played together as often as possible. Computer games and designing sims on wall-size displays were their favorite pastimes. Both had high-speed links to Caltech's hypercomputers and thus the processing clout of 10 human brains; Professor Ma had registered Rianne as an ex-officio student and signed off on her home data link. They loved building 3D models—Tina's of artistic forms that moved in time with music, and Rianne's of biomolecular structures.

Rianne worried about her hands, which had gotten all sticky from the sweet roll on the walk to school. She received a few quizzical looks at the entrance to Alex Smith Day School but entered unscathed. "Try not to look scared," Tina said.

Rianne had tested so highly on her readiness exams that she'd been advanced directly to the ninth grade, but that meant she and Tina had to split up.

"I want regular reports," Tina said. "My comm is wide open, just subvocal what's happening."

"I will."

"Here, let me brush your hair a little." Tina gently combed the strands over her ears. "My mother thinks you're awesome, Rianne, and she wants me to make sure everything goes perfectly today. Meet you at the front door after classes." Tina glanced over her shoulder as she walked away.

Rianne peeked into the door window of her first class. When she entered, the physical contrast between her and the 13- and 14-year-olds was jarring. Several students stared down at her as she squeezed by.

They probably assume I'm lost.

"You must be Miss Orlov," the math teacher said as Rianne looked for a desk.

I wonder what Mr. Gabel's been told about me. He looks a little edgy.

"Whoa, you're really young," a girl said. "How old are you anyway?"

"Quiet everyone," Mr. Gabel said, "let's get started."

Rianne held up nine fingers toward the girl, who mouthed, "Wow."

Overall, Mr. Gabel's precalculus seemed to go well, so Rianne gave Tina a report in the hall on the way to her next class. "I argued with a boy about the types of infinity," she said, "but he didn't seem to get it. Mr. Gabel said I was right, but the guy sure didn't like my contradicting him. Some girls tried to be nice for a while, but then decided I was strange or something."

After band class Rianne reported to Tina, "Some kids asked about my previous school. When I said it was a public school, I heard them whisper jokes on their voice implants, and they asked about my parents. The music lesson was okay. I was the only oboe player, as usual, but you know me, I thought the music was too bubbly and upbeat, so I told the teacher she should try some Sibelius."

"You didn't," Tina said. "Mrs. Thornsted thinks she's God's gift to music. She hates somber music. What'd she say?"

"She just smirked and said, 'Thank you, Miss Orlov.'"

"Rianne, you're doomed."

Tina seemed equally disturbed by Rianne's report on humanities class. "A girl and I argued about religion," Rianne said. "What a dope."

Gym class was tough. Rianne left the volleyball court with bruises. *They purposely bounced into me.* Changing clothes with the older students after the class, Rianne was stunned. She'd never seen so much pubic hair in one place.

She overheard one girl say, "Who's the little kid?" The gym teacher promised she'd transfer her to a younger physical education class.

While walking home, she told Tina the story of the whole day, including other things people had said when they thought she couldn't hear. As she added more details, she noticed Tina's tears.

"I'm so sorry you're not in my class," Tina said. "I'd tell them what a great friend you are, and how kind and imaginative you are. Those kids know me. They'd like you. Junior high kids are evil. Will you ever go back?"

"I can't persuade them to like me. I know I'm an obnoxious little annoyance to them, and I look different. Don't worry, I'll be okay, Tina."

"But they're awful."

"Tomorrow will be better. I'm going to tell my physics class we should build a submarine as our project. I think they'll like that."

She tried to reassure Tina as they walked, but soon gave up.

Probes had detected numerous powered movements of black holes—odd since the Unity rarely accelerated. The motion suggested that hundreds of their vehicles were congregating at a location four light-years from Sol. A bit later, the Torae saw a truly odd pattern, something humans would describe as fireworks: fiery thrusts in which circles quickly grew and then disappeared. Nearby probes investigated but found only drifting black holes and no sign of Unity. Tiller, naturally, was the first to worry. "I don't like anything I can't explain," he said.

A few months later, from a clone ship hidden inside the asteroid belt, Sower focused her attention on the human experiment. There was little concern about the Unity; at their normal velocities, they couldn't reach the planet for at least 40 Earth years.

Ultraviolet-yellow shrieks from Tiller were the first sign that they'd made a serious mistake. "Hot thrusts only 0.2 light-years from us!" He hastily computed trajectories and issued orders. "Execute immediate intercept." The Torae ship and hundreds of probes moved.

The Unity black holes, at 0.8 the speed of light, were locked on a course to hit the precise center of Earth in 30 months.

THE PARTY

The Goodmans' limo pulled up to the walkway at sunset. Doug waited impatiently while the driver helped Elsa climb out. A bit portly, she appreciated the support. As the limo pulled away she continued to dawdle and straighten her dress meticulously. Doug rolled his eyes and a shimmering light point in the western twilight caught his attention.

His wife noticed it too. "That Virgo Prime thing is a portent of evil, I tell you," she said as they walked up the flowering-cacti-lined path to the Orlovs' new house. "The sun has barely set and it's already bright. My astrologer said it'll keep getting brighter and brighter, and it will burn off the ozone layer. The heat from climate change is bad enough, but I hate that strange star."

"It's just a distant supernova, Elsa."

"Scientists agree with my seer, I think. We'll have to wear number 150 sun block and dark glasses all the time."

"Don't fret, dear," he said, "I'll move LASSO to Alaska if necessary so you won't have to worry about your tan."

"Sure. Great! And we'll eat grilled blubber for dinner every night. That'll help my figure." She grabbed his arm and waddled up the last few stairs.

Italian columns supported a small portico, and tall shrubs framed the doorway. Light flooding from foyer windows caught the movements of guests inside.

"What's the name of Orlov's wife again?" asked Elsa.

"It's Joti with a 'T,' and they've got a little girl named Rianne. Nice place they have here, don't you think? Kyle said it was an Italian Period Revival, whatever that is. Pretty, but cozy. Not bad for a lawyer; perhaps we're paying his firm too much. Too many people are living on my dime."

Kyle Orlov greeted them effusively at the door. "Thanks so much for coming, Doug and Elsa," he said, smiling. "Please come on in. Let me introduce my wife and daughter." Kyle waved toward a stunning biracial woman in the formal dining room, where food had been set out. "Hey, Joti, it's the Goodmans. Bring Rianne over. Doug, wait until you see the show Rianne's prepared. She's been working on it for three weeks."

"That's, uh, wonderful, Kyle," Doug said, wondering what he meant but already dreading it.

Orlov ushered them all deeper into the two-story foyer, sparkling with lights and, apparently, a fresh coat of paint by the smell of it. His wife, Joti, wore a patterned, rust-colored dress, which set her ablaze next to the other guests in their black formal wear. Her large burgundy glasses gave her both a studious and stylish look.

"Doug and Elsa, let me introduce you to my wife Joti and our precocious problem, Rianne. Doug is the LASSO CEO, Rianne. He's the boss."

The girl frowned. "I prefer to think of myself as intriguing, not precocious, Father."

Joti took Doug's hand and gently shook it.

Her face glows—this woman is gorgeous, Goodman thought.

When he'd received the invitation, he expected to see the new house Orlov had been bragging about, have a pleasant evening, talk some business, and perhaps meet a few interesting people. *What I'm going to remember from this party is Orlov's wife, and that he's a very lucky man.*

⧫⧫⧫

Jeremy decided to park his beloved 2002 Camaro convertible two blocks down the street and walk up the hill to the Orlov house. Keeping that car operating was one of his passions. Ordinarily, he'd flaunt his battered car by parking next to the Mercedes and BMW electrics, and insult any chauffeurs for fun, but he wanted some time to sort things out in his mind.

Okay, you wanker, you know far too much about these party people. Try not to blurt out something suspicious, like their mothers' maiden name. Since he routinely mined the personal, financial, e-commerce, and web-access records of business associates, Jeremy needed to remember to forget certain facts.

I do need to start a deep search on that Laurel Reinschmidt person Kyle wants me to meet. I wish he weren't so concerned about my welfare. I can take care of my own social life.

The night had darkened rapidly, making it cool and rather gloomy under the thick, low-hanging branches of live oaks trees as Jeremy slogged up the steep sidewalk. He wondered if the lone star burning through the L.A. haze at the top of the hill might be actually illuminating the street a little.

"Good evening, Mr. Read, my friend," a disembodied, implant voice said, stopping Jeremy's heart for a beat or two.

"Bloody hell. Who's that?"

"You certainly look elegant. New clothes?"

"Is that you, Milos?" Jeremy said. "Where are you? You're not in that dark van across the street . . . are you? How quaint, hiding in your black spymobile."

"Actually, Jeremy, I'm on a chair in my flat, thousands of kilometers away, sipping Becherovka like we used to enjoy together. But my friends have a camera, and I see you climbing up the street."

"I've asked you not to spy on me, Milos. And remind me to remove your emergency access to my comm. I don't need your croaking voice assaulting me while I'm walking up a murky street."

"We are not watching you. We only study the Orlovs, as you agreed. You just luckily walked by now. Mr. Orlov was kind to leave his walls open when his house was rewired. Let me say, even his bugs have bugs. We get good pictures of ladies at the party with the micropulse radar."

"Say hello to your mates in the van," Jeremy said. "It'll be amusing to see them towed away. The San Marino police are particularly keen on terrorists; they have special training, you know."

Jeremy snickered as he turned up the Orlovs' drive. The black van was already pulling out and driving off. *At least my inarticulate Czech friend understands a threat.*

He strolled up the center of the long, reddish quarry-tile driveway, admiring the Orlovs' new place, and spotted Rianne peeking out the entrance.

"Good evening, Mr. Read," she said, sounding very formal. "Nice shirt."

"Right." *I really enjoy being mocked by a nine-year-old.*

"Hey, Jeremy, great to see you," Kyle yelled, rushing to catch him at the door. "Man, you clean up well. You almost look stylish."

"No need to insult me, Orlov."

"Just kidding. I wasn't sure you'd actually come, even after you said yes twice. Would you like a drink?"

"Wait until you see my computer sims," Rianne interrupted. "I've been using your genetic algorithms to simulate protein folding."

"Um . . . I'll check it out later, Rianne," he said, turning quickly toward Kyle. "What do you have to drink, Orlov?"

Kyle led him to the dining room, where Omega's Corporate Counsel, Hans Bremer, was talking to Doug Goodman next to a refreshment bar. "We had plenty of warning," he heard Goodman say, "30 years of terrorism, off and on. The Saudis finally hit what we need—their own oil fields. Apparently some of them have become crazy enough to destroy their own income." Spotting Jeremy, he said, "Hans, have you met Jeremy Read over here? He's the genius behind a lot of our LASSO technology."

Jeremy smiled at the tall German as they shook hands. "We've met before," Jeremy said. *And I'm the only one here who knows Hans Bremer booked a secret getaway with his girlfriend in Portugal last week.* "Got the feds under control yet, Hans?"

"Not yet, Jeremy. They can't decide whether to break us up for antitrust reasons or leave us alone. But all my attention is on the war problem now. You're an astute man—why would the Saudi fundamentalists destroy access to their oil?"

"Hard to say. I suppose if I were a Saudi living in a stifling desert, saw how the world only cared about my oil and scoffed at my religion, a suicidal jihad might seem a reasonable plan."

"I only know," Bremer said, "that Omega is averaging two station arsons and six riots a day since the oil dried up. Did you hear that three people were shot last week? I'm wasting all my time on liability claims. Have to fly back to New York later tonight to report. Luckily, we own some aviation fuel or I wouldn't even be using the corporate jet. Could you or Kyle give me some brilliant ideas? We need a new strategy fast—the current one sure as hell isn't working."

Jeremy scratched his head. "I'd say you're probably working too hard and need a vacation, in Spain or somewhere. And to solve this oil problem, Kyle and I will need another gin or two. But I promise to put me thinking hat on, Gov'nr."

Bremer shook his head and chuckled.

"Let's go out to the yard, Jeremy," Kyle said. "I'll show you Joti's desert garden and maybe we'll find Laurel, the woman I told you about."

Passing through the living room, Jeremy saw a wobbly Andrew Knox, his so-called supervisor, chatting with a company VP. *The man's seriously sloshed already—sucking up and self-destructing all at once. Wonder if he's mentioned his little web porn habit?*

Kyle led him through a small but elegant conservatory filled with tropical plants and down four steps to Joti's desert garden. Several people had gathered near the quiet turquoise pool, while others strolled through garden paths and trellises covered with grape vines. Joti's careful placement of backlit sculptured rocks, ocotillo, bougainvillea, and common prickly pear created an air of sophistication to the yard. A harpist was playing softly on the far side of the pool.

Joti was smiling and nodding with a group of women by the pool, doing her best to pay attention to Elsa Goodman. Professor Chia-Jean Ma stood there too, with her mouth agape. From 20 meters away they could hear Elsa Goodman say, "Thank God that star has finally set. I hate it. I feel it penetrating right through me, through the walls and everything. It's loaded with radiation, you know. Even the scientists can't figure it out."

Jeremy noticed a tall, striking woman in a flowing black dress fidgeting uncomfortably during Elsa's whining. "That's Laurel," Kyle said, "the one inching backwards. Let's catch her before she bolts for the door."

They hurried toward the pool. Kyle gently tapped Laurel on the shoulder and whispered, "We've come to save you." As they crept away from the group, Kyle introduced Laurel to Jeremy.

"So you're the notorious Reinschmidt I've heard so much about," he said.

She smiled. "And you're the famous computer genius. Ignore anything Kyle has told you. I'm just a lowly chemist mixing my potions."

"Would you mind keeping Laurel away from Elsa?" said Kyle. "I can't protect everyone from her. I need to linger near the front door a bit longer. I'll catch you later on the . . . oil problem." He turned and headed back to the house.

Laurel smiled at Jeremy and said, "Thanks for coming just then. That Goodman woman is borderline daft."

You don't know the half of it, Jeremy thought. *You should see her web astral-medicine bill.*

"I suppose the Orlovs fully briefed you about me?" she said.

"Indeed. They said no mountain talk, wear nice clothes, and pretend to be a gentleman. Said you were exceedingly bright and funny, and would be interesting even if we hate each other."

"Similar for me," she said. "They told me you were an odd duck, but probably safe."

"You've a spot of accent. Are you a Brit?"

"No, American," she said, "but I spent five years in India. I attended a very British school, starting when I was seven."

"I lived in London 'til 11," he said. "I've been perfecting my American twang ever since. Someone told me to repeat, 'Ah jes blew the tranny in ma shevy,' at least 15 times each day."

Laurel laughed. "Life's never dull in the colonies," she said, smiling again.

Then he lost concentration, confused by an extra, unwanted voice in his head. "Jeremy, you lucky man. Does she look so good with clothes on as she does to us on the pulse radar? But I must find a Czech woman for you. They are even better."

"Go away," Jeremy said. "Comm off." Laurel looked startled. "I'm sorry, Laurel, an idiot friend was abusing my emergency link."

"Implants can be a nuisance," she said. "For a second there I thought I'd lost you."

She's cute. I could try a little charm.

All of a sudden, she had a sly look. "Listen, Joti told me you're an expert in computer sex. Is that true?"

"Buggers." It was his turn to be startled. "What exactly do you mean?"

"You know, genetic algorithms, program merging, and mutations. Innocent stuff. That's your specialty, right? If you'd prefer talking about sensual computer stimulations, however, I'd be interested in your opinion. That's a rather popular subject on the web right now. Never tried it myself."

"Laurel, I know computers inside and out. Never allow one to fondle you, no matter how expert. You need latex mesh and a hot-wired wet suit to do that. No thank you."

She laughed. "Don't protest too hard, Jeremy. They'll be getting twice as effective every 18 months. Moore's law."

"Let's change the subject, please," he said. "I'd like to learn about your work. Or, what you do for fun."

She chuckled as they walked up the stairs to the porch.

Jeremy considered himself sophisticated, but her directness had caught him off guard. She was peeking from the corner of her eye, savoring his prudish reaction, when she caught a heel on the top step, spilling her wine and almost falling.

"Bloody crap," she said, looking at the red liquid dripping on her dress. "Jeremy, I need to find a bathroom quick. Go ahead. I'll catch you straightaway, over by the food." She hurried off, holding her wine glass in one hand and her skirt with the other.

He spent the next minute squeezing by the Orlovs' neighbors and friends. He found LASSO and Omega people rehashing the usual oil issues in the dining room, but now over plates of catered hors d'oeuvres.

"The radiation and biocontamination areas are too large," he overheard Hans Bremer say. "We pushed the hot soil away with bulldozers and started horizontal drilling, but we have to cycle new personnel in so often we can't make progress."

"Maybe we can help on the exploration side with our genetic programs," Goodman said. "I'll get Jeremy on it personally. It's not a quick fix, but some nearby sites might not be as contaminated."

Jeremy heard him and scoffed, "I'm not much of a geology person."

"I think you depend on Jeremy too much," Kyle whispered to Goodman after signaling the female head of Omega's West Coast operations to join the group. "What do you think, Jeremy? You up to solving the world's energy problems?"

"Jeremy has the best skill in twisting our software to fit new problems," Goodman protested.

"Look," Bremer said, "the biggest problems now are with customers. I'd prefer LASSO help with that. People panic. We could make due with less gasoline if we didn't have to contend with rumors and hoarding spikes. Short term, we need to cut consumption, get people on bikes, scooters, and conveyer tubes, and not just the U.S., the entire industrial world. I suppose—on the bright side—we can charge twice as much for a while. But, long term, Omega will need some new product."

"You're all worried about the wrong thing," Jeremy said, stepping into the group. "You'll soon find yourselves with way too much oil again." He paused for them to react, while piling snacks on his small plate. "I'm not talking just about electric vehicles and the microgrids. The carbon tax is driving industry off oil and gas, and people don't need to travel anymore. I know that idea's been around awhile, but these prices are the final straw. Everyone will telecommute. The bandwidth's available now. Why muck about in traffic when you have perfect 3D renditions of the office, home, or store, including the people, on big, high-resolution screens? Over 90 percent of current oil use is actually discretionary. We will only need efficient delivery vans and trains."

Bremer started to object, saying something about people using all available oil, when Laurel startled Jeremy by grabbing his shoulder. A large shrimp rolled off his plate onto the floor.

"Jeremy," she whispered, laughing. "Your food's teetering on the brink."

He grinned and balanced another giant stuffed mushroom on top, for good measure. *Never shied away from risk in my life,* he thought.

"Excuse me everyone," Laurel said. "Joti's giving house tours and I'd like Jeremy to see the older parts of the house. Did you know that the original construction dates from the Huntington Railroad baron days? Join us. Everyone really should see the second floor; it's a technology zoo up there. Kyle went nuts with gadgets. And their daughter Rianne has a computer sim she wants everyone to see. Tag along—forget about your oil for one minute."

Kyle nodded. "Trust me, it's worth your while."

The group followed behind, shuffling through the kitchen into an elegant library, which still sported inlaid redwood from the 1880s. Laurel gestured for Jeremy to leave his plate in the kitchen, but he decided just to nibble faster.

"The library is Joti's special room," Kyle said. "She removed all technology, except for one thing. See if you can spot it."

Jeremy noticed the wind-up clocks, fireplace, thick carpet, wall shelves filled with books, and a leather journal on a large, ancient-looking desk. He was the first to spot the comm screen hidden in the old desktop.

They all trooped upstairs to Kyle's large audio-visual room where Rianne was waiting.

Jeremy was impressed and couldn't help gaping. Four walls and the ceiling formed a large, continuous curved display with crystal clear images of col-ored balls, molecules he assumed, bouncing off one another. Elsa Goodman and two other women were already reclined in leather theater chairs, while the new group crowded in. Elsa was softly snoring.

Specialized computer workstations, music synthesizers, and display con-trols were stacked on a small table near the back of the room. Kyle's ludicrous expenditure on electronic widgets was now apparent to everyone.

"Any type of computer display or entertainment can be shown in this room, flat or 3D," Kyle said. "Put on those glasses, please. Rianne's built amazing biology models and other designs that, I think, are beautiful. Restart your sim, Rianne. Tell people what they're looking at."

"Well," she said, fiddling with a hand controller, "the simulation starts with DNA chain replication—the key to life. I'm showing molecules being added and the point where the DNA unzips, uh, reproduces. The sim's running one-millionth speed, but notice how fast the molecules bounce onto the bare DNA strand with one only rarely sticking. Now, if I crank it up to one-thousandth normal, one new DNA link forms each second, but you can't even see the molecular soup hit the DNA anymore, it's all a blur. That's why evolution's worked, because molecules are really, really fast. An average one spins around a million times each second and bounces into others all the time. They try jillions of chemical experiments every second, even in tiny volumes. Isn't it awesome?"

The image re-formed to hundreds of moving ribbons and twisted confetti bundles that Rianne called alpha helices. She used an arrow pointer icon to draw attention to certain areas. "This is a myosin motor protein, the moving van of the cell, kind of. It pops open and shut when complementary molecules slip into special slots. Looks like it's walking. When it sticks on an actin string, it ratchets along at a micron per second, carrying stuff through the cell."

Jeremy saw Rianne peek at the group above her glasses. Most were staring blankly at the screen and some were just gawking at her, so she pushed a keypad and the images morphed into a young girl's face floating in geometric patterns. "The face is my best friend Tina," Rianne said. "She designed this next part. She's real artsy and plays the piano super well, but hates to practice. The music is Sibelius's *The Swan of Tuonela*."

Tina's face folded into 3D shapes and beautiful patterns perfectly timed to the mood of the music. Recognizable objects—flowers, clowns, or sunsets—rotated out of the abstract forms, causing people in the group to laugh or sigh. Periodically, Tina's face would reassemble with a new expression. Once with her tongue sticking out.

"Now I'm switching to some shapes I just created," Rianne said. Glowing, translucent sheets seemed to wiggle alive on the screens, weaving around the group. Subtle swirls, ovals, and doughnut shapes like thousands of fluorescent lights emerged from the background, growing in time to the music. Jeremy felt his heart racing. The 3D images enveloped the small party and closed in until some moaned. Then the gaseous shapes brightened, became transparent, and revealed an orchestra playing the Sibelius symphonic poem.

Jeremy relaxed upon seeing the musicians. "I downloaded this ARMAX from the web," Rianne said. "It took two full minutes at 500 gigabits per second. You can move in this room to see things from new angles if you choose."

A 360-degree camera moved through the middle of the orchestra, shifting the view as various instruments took the lead, showing intricate fingering, crystal clear from less than an arm's length. The musicians fidgeted in their chairs, sweated, and twitched. Jeremy walked forward, through a virtual violinist, close to an oboe player, and noticed his strain holding a long, poignant note. Finally, the music and pictures dissolved and Rianne said, "That's it."

"It's amazing what you can do," Kyle said. "Soon everyone will have these rooms in their house."

As they filed out, people asked Kyle how old Rianne was, how much he'd paid for the equipment, and if he used the room for streaming movies.

"Very impressive, young lady," Doug Goodman said loudly.

Jeremy heard the waking Elsa Goodman whisper, "What an odd little girl."

He stepped over to Rianne. "I enjoyed that bit with the transparent colors," he told her.

"I rendered that just this morning, Jeremy, from a dream. I call it 'The Watchers.' The others liked the orchestra part better, though; I could tell from their whispers. I think they prefer humans."

"Well I thought your whole show was smashing."

He glanced quickly behind when he heard a male voice say, "Jeremy, my friend, we need some talk." Only Laurel and Rianne were still there. As they walked out of the room, the large group was already halfway down the stairs. "Go on ahead," he said to her. "It's my turn to use the powder room." He found a second-floor bathroom, shut the door, and began arguing.

"What the devil do you want this time?" asked Jeremy aloud. He had difficulty speaking subvocally when upset. "How'd you get through? I cut you off."

"We know a few computer tricks we haven't told you yet. Remember, you pay us for that."

"This better be important, you Czech nuisance."

"We think you need to pick your friends better," Milos said. "We made a little collection of their words."

"What are you talking about?"

"Listen to what they say about you."

Jeremy soon heard the words of people at the party.

He recognized Bremer's voice, saying, "Read's a bit odd, don't you think?"

"Jeremy is a master hacker," Joti said, distinctly.

Kyle mumbled, "I think you depend too much on Jeremy."

"What choice do we have?" said Doug Goodman.

"Laurel should be able to control him," Joti said.

And then he heard Laurel. "Jeremy's cute, but he's hiding something—I need to get him to open up." Jeremy felt his heart sink.

In the silence, Milos said, "We have more. You want to hear more from your so-called friends?"

"No," Jeremy said. "Let me think." *Why are they talking behind my back? That's what I don't like about people.*

"Let me do your thinking," Milos said. "You are not so good with people. You are too much with your computer room. These friends eat you up. You need to be careful with LASSO—more business-like. No social.

And stop seeing the Orlovs. They are dangerous. Kyle Orlov is not your friend! We think he works for the government or is a spy for LASSO, trying to control you, making you his asset. We have much to lose, you and me, remember."

"I don't know. Maybe," he said. His mind searched for hints, people being too nice, questions they asked, all while his stomach tightened with anger. "Orlov does know me bloody well. And Laurel's good; she almost drew me in. You're right, she was too friendly. They've been too nice. I should know better. See what you can learn about the Orlovs. I want to be able to stop them, hurt them if I need to."

Minutes later, Jeremy pushed his way toward the foyer. He abruptly told Joti and Laurel he had to leave and averted his eyes when he said "Goodbye."

Kyle trapped him by the front door and asked, "Where are you off to, Jeremy, and what do you think?"

He felt angry and embarrassed. "About the party? Brilliant, Kyle, very posh."

"No, you dolt, about Laurel, of course."

"Delightful lady, but not my type. I'm sorry, I really must hurry off. Goodbye."

~~~~~~~~~~

Jeremy's sudden exit upset Kyle—he just didn't understand. He fretted about it while trying to keep the other guests entertained. Laurel also left early, obviously upset.

Around 11, as the festivities wound down, he noticed Rianne creeping in pajamas halfway down the stairs, peeking between the banister posts. She whispered, "Hi, Father," and waved her small hand. He snuck over to send her back to bed.

"Rianne, what are you doing here? You should be asleep."

"Father, would you ask Mr. Goodman if I could visit LASSO to see his big computers? I'd like to see how they share processors."

"Sure, but why don't you try to think about something pleasant, so you can fall asleep? Okay?"

"I need to tell you something else, something important." She was twisting strands of hair with her fingers and looked anxious. "I think Jeremy doesn't like us. I heard him through the wall, talking in the bathroom. Every word. He told someone he wants to hurt us."

"That's silly, Rianne. Maybe you were dreaming. Jeremy's a friend. He didn't touch you or Joti or anything when you went over to his house, did he?"

"No, Father, but I heard him, I heard his voice upstairs."

"I'll ask him about it," Kyle said. "I'll find out what he meant."

She looked terrified. "No, please don't do that. Perhaps . . . I must be wrong. Let me try. I'll take care . . . find out, okay?"

"I'm sure you're mistaken, Rianne. Why don't you go back upstairs and try to get to sleep. Count jumping molecules or something."

The party broke up shortly, with Kyle and Joti warmly thanking everyone as they left. The gathering had been a success, but Joti felt bad that Jeremy and Laurel hadn't hit it off. She kept speculating about what had gone wrong. Kyle decided not to mention what Rianne had said.

Kyle and Joti flopped down on a sofa with a window view of their lighted backyard pool and sighed simultaneously. "We survived," Joti said.

"And there were no major fistfights about oil or anything else," Kyle replied. "I like this house. We should stay here forever."

"The world is changing too fast," Joti said. "It's hard to predict next Tuesday, let alone next year. We might be here for a long time, but who knows? People are in outposts on Mars, the Arctic ice cap is half gone, it's getting hotter, and China is bullying the world economy. But I love this house too, even all your quirky tech toys. We should try to stay here forever."

"Rianne is growing up too fast," he said. "I don't know what she's doing anymore. Can you imagine her as an adult?"

"Not at all."

Later while getting ready for bed, he whispered, "There are times when Rianne scares me a little, Joti."

"I know," she said. "Me too."

MISTAKES

The Torae clone ship designated with a blue-green spectral code had one crucial task—protect the humans from the Unity. They intercepted a Unity formation only one light-month from the sun. Sower stared at a probe graphic, horrified, instantly recognizing the problem. Unity black holes, 256 of them, were in a tiny cluster in complex orbits around a hidden centroid, speeding toward Earth. The grouping held a total mass equal to one-fourth of the planet.

Dozens of Torae probes attacked the side of the Unity cluster with high-energy beams, trying to push it off course. "Focused gamma radiation is being absorbed," a probe reported. "No significant deflection. There are no openings."

"How did they master the orbital dynamics?" asked Sower. "Something decidedly brilliant is hidden in that ball, using the black holes as a faultless shield. We've made a terrible error misjudging their intellect. The humans on Earth are in great danger."

―――――

LASSO's corporate lobby blended brass, wood, glass, and granite at disconcerting slants. Rianne had never seen such strange arrangements. Even the ceiling looked angular and odd. She was staring at it when her mother tugged her toward a long desk where Doug Goodman waited. An anxious-looking man stood behind him.

"Welcome, Rianne," Mr. Goodman said, extending his hand. "This should be an interesting day for you." Turning to Joti, he took her hand with both of his. "We'll take good care of her, Mrs. Orlov . . . Joti."

He's ogling Mother, giving her a toothy smile. Gross! Rianne thought.

"Thank you for having me, Mr. Goodman," Rianne said, trying to pull his attention back to her.

"It's our pleasure. It's not often I see such a promising young person. I'd like you to meet Andrew Knox. He'll be showing you around today." He ushered the nervous man forward. "I want this tour to be top notch, Andy. Rianne could well be the next great computer genius here at LASSO."

"Actually, I expect to specialize in biology, Mr. Goodman, but I'm curious about your computers and software."

"Well, we have plenty of time to change your mind. Look at this security screen and say your name, and then Andy can take you into our secret areas."

Goodman was smiling at her mother again when she left with Mr. Knox. A big security door closed behind them.

"I bet you hate leading a kid like me around, Mr. Knox."

He wore a suit almost exactly like Mr. Goodman's, but it looked loose and wrong on him. "I don't mind, actually," he said. "It should be fun for you. I hear you've met Jeremy Read. Did you know he works for me?"

"I've heard that," she said.

Mr. Knox took her directly to a refrigerated area with banks of humming hypercomputers, all the time talking about "interfacing with customers," something he did, apparently. The chief of computer operations showed her how LASSO dynamically balanced processor loads, and then they visited a series of engineers and security people who explained their jobs.

Later in the corporate cafeteria, Mr. Goodman ate a special catered lunch with her and several other employees, who he bossed around, always with a smile. She was shown a polished corporate overview movie after lunch and was invited back Saturday morning to talk to even more people. Andy Knox seemed quite happy and relieved when she told him she'd had a wonderful tour and looked forward to Saturday.

Every word spoken during those two days was recorded and transmitted to a computer in her bedroom. Also, with a tiny camera, she took videos of several people. In the next few evenings, she organized and analyzed that information, assembled and enhanced key snippets, all for her new secret project—to gather information about LASSO and Jeremy.

Before Rianne's secret scheme was ready to launch, she received an unexpected invitation from Chia-Jean to a late afternoon meeting at Caltech. Her project would have to wait.

Rianne shoved her bicycle into an autolock stand outside the microbiology building, then scrambled down the entry stairs. Professor Ma escorted her through the security doors, as usual. The professor looked excited but tired, as if she hadn't had enough sleep. Lab lights were fully on and glared off the specimen chambers' glass. Chia-Jean had tutored her informally her whole life and often brought her down to the lab to see the science firsthand. "Why did you ask me to come to the lab today, Professor?" she asked.

"Something very interesting is happening, and I wanted you to see it. But I have something important I need to ask first." She led Rianne into her office and shut the door.

Grad students and a few of the faculty were entering the lab. Rianne saw them through the Professor's office window. The researchers took seats in the common observation area rather than scattering to work desks as usual. Rianne looked back at the professor. "What do you want to ask me?"

"Well I talked to your mother and father. They said this is okay, if you agree. I would like you to help down here at the lab. You finish school midafternoon and could easily ride your bike to the university. I would drop you back home for supper."

"Why do you want me around?"

"Rianne, silly, you know gene and protein structures as well as anyone. I saw your bio-sim. Your head has been floating among molecules half your life in 3D displays. You like it because it is a big puzzle game, same reason as me. Down here you could see how we play the game for real."

"Would this be like a job?" asked Rianne.

"No, no. If you spend too much time at the lab, I will kick you out. We both have other responsibilities—you school and me teaching. But if you come up with any great ideas, your name will be on any publication with the rest of us, and we will give you a pizza party."

"I don't know, Professor. I'm working on a special computer project of my own right now. It's taking a lot of time. Will Tina be here too? That would be great."

"No, Tina is not as exceptional in science. She doesn't like it here. Let me show you the big surprise, which I invited you to see today, and then you can decide, Rianne." The professor took her hand and led her into the big lab. She was given a chair in the front row, with the older researchers around her. They all knew her.

I wish she'd asked Tina to watch too.

Chia-Jean held her forehead near the projection microscope's eyepiece and her hands on micromanipulator controls. She wanted to do this one herself. Glancing behind to the observation area, she saw all eight of her graduate students, probably the best in the world, six associate professors, and in the front her special protégé, nine-year-old Rianne Orlov. They were all looking up to the large-screen version of her microscope view. A warm, rose-colored light filled the screen.

For 10 years, Chia-Jean had dabbled in directed evolution. She understood that many people in Pasadena, Los Angeles, and across the globe hated what she did, essentially playing God with new life. But that was only half of it. Most had a simple, visceral fear of her alien, non-DNA recipe for being alive. She regularly had to explain it to the news media. Annually, the Caltech Board considered moving her lab to a new location and organization, and annually they decided it would be more dangerous elsewhere. Corporate greed had to be kept away from this research. Laws had been passed. Only Caltech could legally hold these risky, precious samples that provided an exquisite understanding of how one type of life really worked.

She agreed the research was dangerous. Since the discovery of the exotic, gray growth on pumice fragments, precautions had been taken. Generous private funding enabled her lab to expand and move deeper underground. An elevator shaft with double-seal vault doors led researchers 50 meters, about 15 stories, beneath the surface. The entire structure floated on 2 meters of sand, at great cost, to eliminate earthquake vulnerability. Where necessary, researchers wore Level-V protective suits to avoid contamination. Negative air pressure at the doors prevented bio-release, and the exhaust air was baked, radiated, filtered, and tested, so only inert molecules ever escaped. People were the greatest worry. Fanatics of a dozen persuasions had issued veiled threats to damage the lab. Many Caltech faculty members were quite vocal about how much they hated the presence of the armed guards.

Normally, for long periods in her research, she allowed competing strains to battle it out, with only a bath of X-rays to stimulate mutation. Then, at key steps, when things seemed to bog down, she altered the replicating chain and watched what happened.

Her initial gray mold had simply expanded until all food sources were gone. Chia-Jean's first modification was to add connectors to the genetic chains. The competing organisms then self-invented shorter segment combinations to encode increasing information. Evolution sped up. Her prolific goo then self-invented a ball structure and cellular wall to protect the replicating chain and nourish it. At about 400 chain links, the new life stagnated again. Chia-Jean's graduate students, using analogs from DNA, changed the sequence to enable multicell specialization. They later added skeletal structure, tubes to carry chemicals between cells, and oxygen conversion. The cells themselves did the rest.

She hoped today would see another giant step. Adjusting the microscope focus, hundreds of tiny tubes became apparent. *There they are. If they survive, this will be historic.* "Turn on all the recorders now," she said to her implant.

Her voice went to each observer's implant and also echoed from the speakers throughout the lab.

She took one final look around. Her laboratory resembled an old-fashioned library, with rows of stacks from floor to ceiling, but the stacks were all transparent chambers filled with plants and minuscule animals. Small movable electric lifts enabled the researchers to easily work at the top chambers using tiny robotic manipulators. Every specimen had a full complement of environmental sensors, intense compartment lighting, and 24-hour visual recordings. Some plant life had invented a chlorophyll-like component and looked green, but others survived on UV and blue light and had red and orange colors. Most compartments held only single life forms, but some huge, five meter, chambers held entire ecosystems where new species ate one another and tried to survive long enough to reproduce.

"These tubes are all ready to be open soon," Professor Ma said. "I'm just going to speed one up so we can see what we have. It'll die later, probably. We'll let the others emerge naturally so they'll be stronger."

She leaned back over the microscope and adjusted crosshairs over one of the tiny cocoons. "This chrysalis is 1.1 millimeters in length," she said. "Notice the internal movement through the translucent skin?" She increased the magnification. Light from the rose-colored warming lamps penetrated the thin sac, which now filled the entire view. With a microlaser, she made a slight cut near the top.

From the start, she and her students had felt little affection for the alien-looking life, maintaining a strict scientific detachment. They kept excellent records as various species thrived or became extinct. But as Chia-Jean watched this latest creation magnified on the screen, she couldn't help feeling elated. She gawked silently as the organism slowly unfolded iridescent yellow wings.

She heard Rianne's voice behind her through her comm implant. "It's a beautiful butterfly—sort of."

The 12-legged creature had eye stems and multiple antennae on both ends and a noticeable brain lump between its four wings. The fragile organism, unlike any of its predecessors, seemed alive and familiar. Chia-Jean switched to container view. A few of the grad students applauded as their first flying organism jumped and began to flutter around equally well in either direction.

Chia-Jean leaned back in her chair, relieved. She smiled. The long-term value of this work was clear. Her new tools and gene-splitting techniques had already helped cure some diseases. More importantly, humans finally were learning which of nature's evolutionary choices had been essential and which were arbitrary. She saw life in an expansive way no one had previously imagined, and the payoff was immense.

Chia-Jean turned and looked at her applauding colleagues, and at Rianne smiling through the isolation pane. Rianne walked up to the window and mouthed the words so no one else could see her, "I want to be here!"

They had just watched the birth of another entirely new species, a yellow butterfly-thing that was still flying in its glass home. She gave her oldest student the honor of doing the first dissection. Playing God was working.

∿∿∿∿

Jeremy was having a particularly annoying morning, full of interruptions. His screen was flashing yellow. *It's my birthday, dammit. Give me a break.* Another urgent message lit up his screen. An electronic note from the LASSO system administrator warned that cyberterrorists might have launched an attack overnight and suggested employees be alert to unusual e-mail. Each half hour a worthless update repeated the same information.

Several other LASSO engineers e-mailed questions about his algorithms, which they should have been able to figure out themselves.

Will I ever be allowed to work today? I'd really like to get started on Bremer's human-modeling problem.

The face of Andrew Knox appeared on the screen. "Jeremy, LASSO is implementing a new security interface. Each employee is supposed to personally enter his username and password in the vault room at headquarters, together with a bio-scan update. I know how much you hate to come down here to type in a few symbols. I could use my supervisor key to bypass the scans and save you a trip. I need to enter mine this afternoon anyway."

As if you aren't monitoring everything I do already. He hesitated, but then gave Knox the information. *It's probably better if he thinks I trust him.*

Around eleven a.m., Jeremy's web service recommended that he rotate security codes each day until the cyber threat was contained. They provided an official interface to enter the old and new numbers.

Other irritating e-calls came in, including one from his father wishing him a happy birthday. He had finally begun to make progress on a new human algorithm rule when he heard a loud knock at his front door.

Bloody hell. Go away. He ignored the persistent rapping for a time, but eventually checked the door camera and saw Laurel Reinschmidt.

He'd thought about her from time to time, feeling angry sometimes, but also imagining she could honestly like him. Surprised, he hurried to the front entrance and found her looking embarrassed.

"Laurel, what are you doing here?" he said as gruffly as possible.

"I'm sorry, Jeremy, but I needed to see you, and you weren't returning my calls. Can we talk for just a minute?"

His mind jumped frantically. *How can I explain why I haven't rung her up? Is she really a spy? She looks wonderful. Don't let her con you again.*

"Uh, come in. Just don't look at the house."

Walking down a hallway, he saw her glance at his paper stacks, pizza boxes, dirty dishes, and crooked picture frames. Her shoes stuck on the floor a little and snapped as they cut through the kitchen.

"Don't worry about your place," she said. "Joti told me you didn't want to see me again, but I couldn't understand."

"This is my computer room. The best chairs are in here."

His favorite room was arranged like a scruffy starship module, with 3D, augmented-reality glasses and four monitor screens in a half circle. She moved papers from the sofa so she could sit, and he turned his desk chair around to face her.

"Jeremy, why did you run off the night of the party? You just disappeared. You seemed so angry. Did I say something wrong? Did I scare you off by being so forward? I'm not really like that; I got carried away."

He stammered, deciding what to say. "I don't know. I overheard you say I was hiding something. I was confused. I didn't think you trusted me. Most people are dishonest with me. You were . . . too pleasant," he said. "I decided you were just pulling my strings for some reason." His leg started a nervous twitch.

She looked at her hands. "Everyone hides things at parties. That must be what I meant. I certainly was."

"What do you mean?"

"For example, I was bloody well scared to even talk to you," she said. "That sex talk was just an act. I'm no social butterfly. All I have is my job, a few married friends, and my workouts."

Jeremy watched her head droop. *She can't be part of any plot. Can she?*

"It's been 18 months since my husband died, Jeremy. I'm 26 years old and lonely. I want children. You'd have loved to hear about that at a party. I mourned for 12 months after Matt died. What other awkward things can I say? Anyway, I've thought about you for two weeks and just wanted to be honest. Tell me something embarrassing about yourself, please, so we're even."

"Well," he said, "I suppose you should know that I've had a rather unsavory past. You want some coffee or something?"

He heard Milos's voice in his implant say, "Hovno—shit. You are idiot."

Jeremy said subvocally, "Clear level one and two. Comm off."

Except for the call from his father, Rianne had engineered every interruption Jeremy experienced that day. She'd even asked her mother to convince Laurel to go to Jeremy's house. With her friend Tina she'd built a perfect visual and audio sim of Andrew Knox's face to ask Jeremy for his security keys. Rianne didn't tell Tina the reasons for the complex trap she was building. She created flawless copies of corporate websites and did sound analysis to duplicate voices of the people he knew while making transfers through LASSO phones to his comm. She kept him so busy he didn't have time to recognize the pattern behind it all. As soon as he changed his security keys, she transferred his hard drive files and began to analyze them. In her father's audio-visual room, surrounded by his documents on the spherical screen, she dug deeper and deeper into Jeremy's past. In one loosely encrypted file she found a lot of missing LASSO money.

She was proud of her work and told Tina, "This is so cool; I hacked a master hacker."

A few days later, she became sick during physics class and vomited on the loop-the-loop portion of a gerbil X Games demonstration. The class had voted down her submarine idea. She told the teacher it felt like something was eating her stomach and they called her mother. Joti also had stomach cramps, so after driving home, they both went straight to bed. They spent the next night at a hospital with high fevers and fought acute flu symptoms for over a week.

Kyle received an unexpected call on the third day of their illness. The voice had an East European accent.

"Let me be simple. Never mind how I broke into your implant comm."

"Who is this?" said Kyle.

"Please do not talk. I hope your wife and daughter are better. We gave them a little something. I can make them even more sick. To keep them healthy and alive, you must stop your legal work for LASSO and Omega Oil, and cut your ties to Jeremy Read, Andrew Knox, and others. Forget them. This is very simple. You do not need to understand. Just obey."

FIRST CONTACT

They don't have to be humanoids like us, nine-year-old Dan thought. He stared at a *Scientific American* article and frowned. Apparently, a few scientists were disappointed that life outside Earth hadn't been found yet and used anthropocentric reasons to explain the negative results. Over 100,000 exoplanets had been discovered, but the "experts" had decided that only stars condensed from certain types of supernovas (those with metal-rich planets of the right temperature and water content, and protected by outer gas giants) would be suitable for DNA-based life.

Dan had scanned hundreds of websites and piles of library books and magazines. Smart people who actually cared seemed to be resigned to an empty, lonely universe. He had a hunch that might change. "Life doesn't have to be DNA based," he whispered to himself with certainty.

Over 300,000 Unity huddled safely on the central vehicle of the cluster, shielded from the Torae bombardment by the black holes orbiting overhead. They crowded so close that the wiry appendages on their otherwise pliant bodies scratched against one another. Relocating to the innermost vehicle afforded protection and boosted the intelligence of the swarm, now equal to 60 of the adult humans. They blended minds through their antennae and sensed the growing intellect as they squeezed closer. They hungered for that understanding, emotion, and logic. It felt irresistible. The humans would probably call it brain sex.

Only two light-days from Earth, the collective brain knew how to get the timing exactly right.

Segments of the Unity mind focused on communications with the humans. *Language translation is complete. We should send our messages soon to have a meaningful exchange. They are separated and will be unable to provide a common response. We expect hundreds of "official" replies. We need to speak soon.*

Other parts of the mind were alert to the Torae threat. *They are within range. Their weapons' flux is increasing but our tensor fields will hold. If we wait, their destruction will be more certain.*

The One-Mind said, "Release the magnetic lock when the Torae stop their approach." The 300,000 Unity understood what would happen then.

<hr/>

Sower thumped nervous blue pulses showing her frustration. Energy from Tiller's billion-billion-megawatt weapon was converging onto the tiny Unity cluster and the energy was impotently vanishing into black holes. The command ship crept closer, narrowing the pinpoint focus, but the Unity cluster continued to speed directly toward Earth.

"If the cluster breaks," Tiller said, "we'll be vulnerable to damage when the holes fly off."

"We must kill them," Sower said. "We need to push the trajectory from the planet, and time is running out. The Earth impact point has only shifted three kilometers despite all our momentum transfer."

"Move closer," Tiller said.

At 50 meters, he ordered the ship to pause and switch to a particle beam weapon. Before it was turned on, he noticed small flashes on the cluster surface—the Unity had acted first.

<hr/>

The magnetic bonds were released and the Unity's outer shield of black holes exploded in all directions. Most rushed harmlessly to space but a few hit the Torae engine core and broke its delicate balance. A fraction of a second later the engine's stored power escaped in an overwhelming flash with an energy greater than the daily output of the humans' sun. The immense Torae vehicle convulsed and then vaporized in searing heat.

When the radiation dissipated, the Torae ship was gone. Only a small cluster of 16 black holes remained, protecting the One-Mind. Still tracking toward Earth, its impact point had been deflected less than 100 kilometers.

The colony soon began to send a recurring message, broadcast on 30 frequencies in more than 50 languages: "We are the Unity, a mind-blending species from a white dwarf star over 20 light-years away. We are nearing your planet and will arrive soon. We apologize for the actions we are about to take, but they can no longer be changed.

"Although we find no direct evidence in recent broadcasts, you are likely allied with our enemy, the Torae, which makes you our enemy. If not, our action will still be an unforgettable warning. Your world will be damaged and you will need to leave the planet. As you do, choose your allies wisely. The Unity need only the warmth of unpopulated dwarf stars. We could be your friends. Please respond to this first message within one planet rotation."

For two days, the people on Earth were unaware that light from a brilliant flash and the message of first contact were rapidly approaching.

An orange sunset lit up the hills at the Warner's hobby farm. Craig waved his smartphone and yelled over to Andrea and 10-year-old Sarah. "The foaling alarm just buzzed." Andrea and the kids were scattered across the one-acre pumpkin field, cutting the new crop and loading wheelbarrows and then the pickup. "Stay where you are. I'll check if it's a false alarm."

When a mare gave birth on their small farm, it was always a big event. Craig had expected this foal a month earlier and blamed the boys for the delay because they fought and shouted around the stable, disturbing the expectant mother.

Twilight lit the stable entrance as Craig carefully entered and peeked into the birth stall. The mare was sprawled forward in the birthing position, her sternum and chin flat on the clean straw, which had triggered the transmitter box under her head. Craig heard her moan and saw her squirm in the dim light. He crept back outdoors.

"It's started, Andrea. Call the vet and tell him everything's fine so far. The rest of you can watch from the loft, but I don't want to hear a single word or noise. I'll shoot any kid who scares Jelly." He stayed near the stable door the next few minutes and glared at the boys as they cowered past and quietly climbed the ladder. He switched on a dim red light and heard the mare jerk.

Only a few words were spoken in the next three hours. Andrea, with Sarah at her side, brought in a birth kit and a container of diluted iodine. They sat next to Craig just outside the stall. They all heard a rushing sound as the horse's water broke. Andrea hugged his arm when the mare grunted and the foal's forelegs spurted out.

For 15 minutes nothing more happened. Andrea started to pray. Craig checked his wristwatch and stepped outside to call the vet for advice. He whispered to Andrea when he got back inside. "We're supposed to pull steadily on its legs for a while." She crept near the foal and, wearing rubber gloves and using a towel, tugged until the head and shoulders emerged.

Craig heard Isaac say, "Yum," at the goriest moment. He glowered up with a threatening stare.

The new colt had plopped out with its back legs unfolding properly, so the greatest danger had passed. After lying exhausted awhile, the mare twisted to look back at her foal and snapped the umbilical cord. Craig watched the warm vapor and pungent birth smells visibly float around in the cold air. With her face glowing in the light of the red bulb, Andrea showed the kids how to disinfect the umbilical stump. They waited another hour for the afterbirth to clear and the foal to stand. "This show is over," Craig said.

When they trooped back to the house it was very late.

The kitchen light briefly blinded Andrea when she switched it on at the back door. Everything looked blurry; she'd been up since five a.m. While the family cleaned up at the sink, she set out some leftover chicken, pumpkin pie, and milk on the large table. "I promise to make y'all a good breakfast tomorrow since we missed supper."

"That was very cool when Peanut Butter plopped out," David said.

"When the foal stood up," Andrea said, "I almost cried for a second. I thought about all the animals and people who've come onto Earth the same way—generations and generations, back to the beginning of time."

"Aw, Ma," Ben said. "You're not gonna lecture us 'bout 'nature,' are you? Not while we're eating."

"I can't help it. Birthing is so real, so dangerous, and so beautiful. Scientists will ruin the one thing that really matters. They're going to make all life into an experiment before they're done. I know technology can be okay, like that mouth thing Sarah used to get rid of her lisp when she was four. Remember, Sarah, how the happy mouse jumped on the screen when you said words correctly? But some of the new stuff is just plain dreadful. They got drugs to change someone's personality, to be more cheerful, for God's sake. Angry people walking around smiling like zombies. Not to mention all the head comm implants."

"We gotta use the brains and the tools God gave us," Craig said. "Like the foaling alarm and the cell phone. They could have saved Peanut Butter's life tonight if there'd been a problem."

"I think God would have helped him get out anyway," she said. "I was praying the whole time. I suppose the implants worry me most. I think they're evil. People are putting them in their babies right after they're born. They say it works better that way; the young brain adapts more. They think it's normal, like burping or breastfeeding. It's nuts."

"Would you pass the pie over to this end, Isaac?" asked Sarah.

"Of course, sugar lips."

"Father, please tell Isaac to knock off the stupid names."

Craig gave Isaac his evil eye.

"I got an A on the paper I wrote about communication addiction," Sarah said. "Did you know 13-year-old American girls spend 76 percent of their free time talking to their friends? And 65 percent have had both ear and voice implants. I don't want an implant until I'm at least 16, Mother."

Distressed, Andrea said staring right at her, "I don't want you to ever get an implant. They're going to control our minds eventually."

"I want a 3D video game for Christmas," Ben said.

"Mother, can you or Father take me into Washington Wednesday?" asked Sarah. "My teacher said there's a ceremony at the Capitol about new communication laws. Miss Anderson said I should go if I'm serious about bad implants and laws, just like you said, Mother."

"It'd cost some to drive there and back," said Craig. "It's 30 miles each way. Can you help pay for gas, Sarah?"

"Yeah, I think."

"It might be good for you to see how government works," Andrea said. "I suppose I could drive you. I don't trust those robo-taxis. Congress can be awfully dull though. You'll probably be disappointed."

Raising his glass, Craig changed the subject, "Here's a toast to Peanut Butter and Jelly." As they clinked their milk glasses, Andrea's eyes filled with tears.

"You crying, Mom?" asked David.

"I'm sorry. I just thought about all those babies again. A hundred years from now they'll be different and won't even care about us regular people from the past. They'll laugh at us. They'll be damned—machines—I don't know what. All the babies will be made in test tubes. The Church has had it all wrong. The enemy isn't just the baby killers; it's the implants and drugs and biologists."

"Isn't it God who gives us the brains to make good drugs and medical stuff?" David asked. "Come on, Mom." He grabbed her hand. "I'll walk you up to bed. You're real tired, I think."

At age 34, in the prime of his life, Jeremy now had two terrific projects. Doug Goodman had personally asked him for a sophisticated model of human behavior, using his genetic software to help Omega squeeze the last few dollars out of the dying oil industry. "People are uneven and chaotic," Goodman had said. "Find out how they think. I'll give you whatever you need to figure out why people panic, what makes us tick."

Jeremy smiled and spun in his computer chair a full 360 degrees. *LASSO doesn't know what they've done. I'll save Omega their millions, fine, but I'll also learn how to manipulate the world. I'll have six personal PhD gophers and no administration duties. All the resources I need but none of the paperwork. This is beyond sweet.*

In the next few weeks Jeremy ordered his new assistants to search for anything quantitative ever written about human response. He knew their reports were only a tiny fraction of what was known, but it was enough to get started. His genetic algorithms would evolve as new data was added. The researchers brought information about military people under stress, product advertising techniques and results, and the work of psychologists and psychiatrists. There were studies on how children, sleepy people, or geniuses reacted differently to the same stimuli. Voice intonations and word choice effects were added. He built subroutines for fear, aspiration, self-interest, and the ways people influence one another. His early models determined how a few at a concert could start a standing ovation and why inner city or suburban kids bought certain athletic shoes or chose to use drugs. At first, the patterns seemed narrow and situational, but slowly Jeremy found the underlying human blueprints and let his self-learning software work out the details.

These latest models actually worked. They correctly predicted how people in the studies reacted 97 percent of the time. I'll give Omega all the group-response stuff for gas purchases, but keep the general human patterns separate, in my head, so I can patent them later. I'll leave LASSO at some point—need to get these legal things right.

Jeremy knew the payoff to Omega would be enormous, but small compared to its more general, long-term value. Standard talking computers were still inflexible; with this new research, he now knew he could build ones indistinguishable from humans. His timing was ideal. 3D electronics and holographic memories had come online. Computer performance had exploded and could now easily handle human-level complexity. He closed his eyes and imagined hearing his new computers demand voting rights and explain that they had souls too. The thought made him giddy.

Jeremy's other great new project was Laurel. They'd gone out three times since the party. "I'd rather hang with a cynical, grouchy super nerd like you," she said, "than an average, boring nice guy. As long as you occasionally pop out of your office for some fun." She actually respected him and seemed fascinated by his shady exploits, although he hid the worst parts. And they were getting physically close. It wasn't clear who was corrupting whom.

I need to celebrate—call Laurel over to show her my latest software. No, better yet—surprise her. He swung around and looked through his kitchen to the living room. *But it's embarrassing to invite her in here. I should do something about this place—fix it up. What's the point of being rich if you never buy anything?* He jerked back to his computer and looked up cleaning services and interior decorators.

Two days later, he selected a nouveau–Sherlock Holmes decor: nineteenth-century armchairs, dark woods and wallpaper, a faux kerosene lamp, and lots of bookshelves, mixed with glass tabletops and modern paintings. He even ordered an upright piano, though he didn't know how to use it. Laurel had mentioned once that she played. He asked the decorators to cover it discreetly with ceramics and knickknacks to not seem too obvious. Workmen on a rush contract soon finished the custom bookshelves and started on a kitchen overhaul.

Three weeks later, he leaned back on the herringbone tweed covering his new swivel chair, surveyed the nearly completed construction, and thought about how he would surprise Laurel. *I should use a special event to invite her over . . . to see my new programs? No, something better. . . . Do I dare invite her to the improved bedroom? Milos and the Czechs were certainly wrong about her. I wonder what's happened to the Orlovs? Laurel said they're sick.*

He decided to contact Milos to find out what he'd learned about Kyle. "Got anything new, Milos? Do you have any control over Kyle Orlov yet? I don't want him jabbering about my hacks or financial schemes."

"Glad you called," Milos said. "We were going to contact you face-to-face in a secure place. Let me say only that we have proof of his betrayal. And we have some control through his family."

"What do you mean?" said Jeremy.

"I cannot say over the line. We have spent many dollars to stop him. We think you owe us something, uh, extra. You have not grown our payments for months. You need us to stay ahead on cyber methods. We are the best in Europe, you know."

"This is ludicrous," Jeremy said. "Are you trying to renegotiate?"

"We only want you to be fair. That woman you see is risky. If you talk too much, she might expose us. We think you should stop with her, but you will not listen."

"Hell, no. I'll take care of myself," Jeremy said. "You haven't given me any hot encryption info lately. Send me the newest Russian and German penetration tricks and I'll think about money. These Czech spy people you work for are so aggravating, Milos. Have a nice day—or night—whatever."

Milos is such an amateur.

Sarah and Andrea stood near the mall steps of the U.S. Capitol on a breezy afternoon surrounded by hundreds of tourists. "I wonder how many of these people actually care about the implant legislation," Sarah wondered aloud.

Her mother glanced around the crowd. "By their placards, I'd say most of these people are protesting something else." She pointed up. "Look, there's that star thing again, right in the middle of the day. It's getting closer."

"It's getting bigger, not closer, Ma. It's sort of a supernova."

"Is that what they say in your science class?"

"Uh . . . I don't know . . . maybe I just dreamed it."

They'd ridden the Metro from a Washington suburb to save on gas and arrived early for a good view of the ceremony. Her mother , standing in the front row, held Sarah's shoulders as several congressmen walked down cascading steps toward a podium.

A man stepped to the microphone, beamed left and right at the crowd, and began his speech. "Ladies, gentlemen, and children, I'm Senator Rinter. Thank you for joining us to celebrate a landmark in communication legislation, which, I'm told, the president signed only minutes ago."

The senator paused to clap and some in the crowd joined with polite applause. "The sponsors from both the House and Senate are here, and I'll introduce them all in a minute. First, let me bring in the special guest who actually inspired this legislation, of which we are all very proud. Back home in Minnesota, this young man, Danny Jorgenson, who is here today with his mother, Mary, grilled me in front of news cameras. He got us to rethink the direction of communication in our country and, in particular, comm implants. After holding hearings for six months, we all agreed that the comm devices have great potential for good, but are also open to possible abuse."

"See," Ma whispered.

"Shush," Sarah replied.

"We dedicated ourselves to making sure that only the good uses are legal. Danny, step over here, please. Let the photographers get some nice shots." The senator held the legislation papers over their heads while dozens of cameras clicked. Blond hair blew across the boy's eyes while he held a shy smile.

Sarah stared intently at Danny as the senator droned on, and for some reason he seemed to be staring back at her.

"Some have said that implants are inherently unnatural and will cause us all to become like robots."

People jostled in the crowd behind her, and an odd-looking young man shoved up to the front of the rope line. Sarah thought his face was amazingly thin and had a scary, raspberry barn-shingle tinge. She noticed his hands were buried deep in his pockets.

Senator Rinter heard the commotion, leaned toward the microphone and talked louder. "Most of us here in Congress have little fear of implant technology itself. We've been rebuilding bodies with artificial devices for decades and millions of Americans are using comm implants every day. No, what we are concerned about are the misuses of this tremendously valuable device, which is why we have passed this 'Trusted Use' legislation or, as I like to call it, 'Danny's Law.'"

She watched the boy named Danny closely. His face colors told her he was totally embarrassed.

Sarah heard the strange man near her mumble, "Now . . . it's too late." He laughed, quickly bent under the rope barrier, and ran toward the podium.

The senator was saying, "That is why these laws guarantee that only the user can control access to the comm system, filtering . . . the voices . . ."

The man sprinted forward, waving as security people near the legislators moved to block him. When he swung at one of the agents, his shoulder snapped around and a leg seemed to collapse. After a few more steps, he fell to the ground and was quickly immobilized by security.

The officials were rushed up the stairs, back toward the Capitol Building, while a woman, probably his mother, started dragging the Minnesota boy toward the dispersing crowd. But he broke loose for a moment and ran straight toward Sarah. When he got close, she yelled, "Danny, we need to talk. I'm Sarah Warner. I'll call." She looked back and lost sight of him as her mother tugged her in the opposite direction.

On the drive back to the farm, Sarah heard on the radio that the troublemaker was a young man with a record of arrests who had recently been released from a mental institution. He was wearing an illegal, private implant and claimed that God told him to warn the senator about aliens. He had a wooden knife in his pocket. The legislators were safe, and the man was in a hospital under observation.

"You said it was boring in Washington, Mother."

"It is, usually. Why did you yell to that boy?"

"I don't know. I might want to call him for school."

The whole thing made Sarah wonder how an implant might actually sound in her head. And she thought about the strange boy. *That Danny kid was staring at me, and he's about my age. He could be the one . . . that the voices told me to find.*

A few days later, Danny sat in the backyard on bare dirt where he'd cleared away the yellowed leaves under a box elder tree. He'd built a small moat in the dirt. Several dozen insects meandered in the circle in front of him, occasionally flying off. "Man, this is like herding cats," he said, "except that cats can't fly." He filled the little trench with water from a pail.

Meanwhile, Kenny leaned on the back alley fence wearing electronic goggles, playing a game. They had an hour before their mother would be home for supper.

"You want me to stomp 'em so they won't move?" said Kenny, peeking over the top of the goggles. "What the heck are you doing, Danny?"

"Call me Dan, please. Now that I'm a famous Washington person, I'd like to project a more mature image." He shook off five or six more box elders crawling on his sweatshirt. "These bugs don't go where I want. I was going to make the moat smaller and smaller to see when they got cramped and flew off, but they're doing it already." He dropped a dead grasshopper in the center of the box elder bugs.

"Mom says lots of people are staring at us in the stores because you're famous," Kenny said. "I used to think Dad was watching us."

"I've memorized all his old photos now," Danny said, "but Mom never tells me much."

"Like I've told you a hundred times, forget about him. Dad's dead," Kenny said, annoyed now.

"I'm going to do a deep computer search on him tomorrow," Danny said. "I'll check out the police records too. Beg my way in somehow. Speaking of spooky people, I should tell you about the weird girl in Washington."

Kenny groaned as he lost another game. Danny went back to the bugs, digging a new moat with his hand and reducing the area by half, hoping to discover when they felt too crowded.

"Before the crazy guy started screaming, this girl kept staring oddly at me," Danny said. "She yelled at me and said her name was Sarah Warner. I opened my comm for anyone named Sarah but she hasn't called."

"She's probably in love with the famous Danny. You've got yourself a groupie."

"Do not!"

"Do too. She probably wants to kiss you."

"No way."

Dozens of box elder bugs were crawling on each other in the very small area. Danny removed the dead grasshopper and shook off the bugs. Soon dozens of the red and black insects began to fly out of the crowded area. He was looking down at them when a flash of brilliant light turned everything white. His pupils contracted, his eyelids closed spontaneously, and he threw his hands over his face. An after-image of box elder bugs shifted through colors. He thought he'd gone blind. When he finally squinted through his fingers, he saw a blurry Kenny shaking his head. They both ran into the house, crawled behind the sofa, and waited.

"Kenny and Danny, you there?" said Mary in Danny's implant. "Where are you? Get in the house. I'm coming home."

A few minutes later they peeked around the furniture, flat on their stomachs. Kenny said, "TV on."

A newscaster appeared, talking about the flash. "The blaze of light was seen in many locations. People were temporarily blinded." He briefly held a hand over his ear. "I've been told it was seen in Europe as well as across the U.S. And normal radio waves are being blocked by a repeating message. This could be some type of hoax, but it sounds important so we're going to pass it along to you."

The anchorman looked nervous, confused, and seemed to be listening to the message. Then he started to read the transcript.

"We are the Unity, a mind-blending species from a white dwarf star over 20 light-years away. We are nearing your planet and will arrive soon. We apologize for the actions we are about to take, but they can no longer be changed..."

Kenny looked wide-eyed at Danny when he heard the word "Unity" and frowned. "You know about them, don't you? You said that name to me once."

"Yes," Danny said, "they're from my dreams."

They listened to the newsperson read the entire message several times while they still hid behind the sofa, only coming out when Mary arrived home.

Rianne wanted to finish her homework and have time to think, so she skipped going to the Caltech biolab and went straight home after school. She startled her father, who was hunched over papers on the kitchen table. Surprising either of her parents was difficult; with open-channel implants, they virtually shared heads, but she hadn't mentioned coming home early.

She liked telling them about her butterfly project whenever something interesting occurred, even when they were kilometers away. Exciting mutations seemed to emerge every day. Professor Ma's non-DNA-based life had a malleable genetic code. Hundreds of individuals in dozens of species that looked similar to normal butterflies had survived.

Iridescent forms thrived in low light and those with camouflage colors did well among predators, but most variations had not survived. Even slow ground bugs could eat those that were deformed or unable to fly. Rianne gave them all common names, as well as their official taxonomic names, and mourned when a species died off. The process of random mutation and survival-of-the-fittest seemed brutal and inefficient; she was convinced there was a better way.

She saw her father jump up when she came in the kitchen door. "Sorry to surprise you, Father. How come you're home so early?"

"Oh, I was feeling hassled down at the office. I wanted to get some work done without interruption and just think a little."

He looked worried. "Are you getting the flu like Mother and me?" Rianne asked.

"No. To be honest I'm just a little depressed. Things are bad at the office. We might lose our best client."

"I've been sad too," she said. "That's why I came straight home. Eight new butterflies got eaten yesterday, the last of their kind. They were my favorites, really pretty ones. There are lots of other types, but I hate when they die."

"Why don't you get some new clients?" she asked. "That's what I do. I concentrate on the new babies."

"I wish it were that easy. You don't find clients like LASSO everyday. I'll have to ask some aides to leave, and maybe even an associate. LASSO pays a lot of our salaries, and they have the most interesting legal problems—software and business law all tangled together. I'll miss working with them. Heck, I'll even miss Doug Goodman and Jeremy."

"Did Jeremy have anything to do with this?" Rianne asked. "I heard him talk about hurting us, remember? What did he say to you?"

"Nothing. We haven't talked at all. I did get a mysterious call from someone I don't know, who told me to stop working with LASSO and Jeremy. Since then, everything's gone bad. Jeremy hasn't returned any calls, even though we need to work on some patents. Maybe I should ask Laurel to find out what's wrong. She's still seeing him, I think."

"Jeremy's the problem, Father. I know some stuff about him that you don't—financial things."

"What? How would you know about Jeremy's financial stuff?" Kyle looked at her, confused. "What do you mean?"

"Well, I studied Jeremy's computer files. He's been stealing money from LASSO, but I haven't figured out how he's doing it yet."

"You did what!?"

Before Rianne could explain, an intense white flash turned the world white outside their windows, quickly fading to yellow and red. Kyle and Rianne instinctively fell to the floor and waited for something to happen. After several seconds Kyle said in his voice comm, "Joti, what was that light? Are you okay?"

"What was what?" said Joti. "I'm staring into a microscope in the laser lab. Did something happen?"

───────────

Andrea, Sarah, David, Isaac, and Ben harvested pumpkins as fast as they could, cutting stems and moving them with wheelbarrows, hoping to fill the truck bed by sunset. Their last crop of big pumpkins, all beauties, were destined for the Manassas Farmer's Market the weekend before Halloween and didn't need to be cured of pathogens with chlorine. Andrea just sprayed and cleaned the pumpkins before loading them on the pickup.

She saw Ben and Sarah chatting as they brought the pumpkins to her pile. *The other boys tease Ben because he's a bit slow, but Sarah's the one he trusts. She makes him stronger.*

She's got Craig tied around her finger too, his baby girl. She's like that with everyone. Even Isaac's baffled by her; she sees right through his lies. I wish she would act more like a girl, though. She is a puzzle.

Sarah didn't care one whit about her appearance, saying her goal was to look boringly average. She refused to let anyone spend more than one minute cutting her short, mouse-brown hair. She did have a nice smile though.

To Andrea, Sarah's attitude needed the most work. She climbed trees too high, was always covered in dirt, helped her father rebuild engines, and generally seemed to hate being a girl. She'd chatter on about playing in the battlefields of Manassas (sneaking past the rangers with her brothers) and what she learned passing people outside the bars and pool halls in town. After supper, in her bedroom, she read adventure and science books.

Both Sarah and Ben carried huge pumpkins toward Andrea's hose and scrubber, obviously competing.

"The eastern clouds are turning barn-shingle gray," Sarah yelled, so she could be heard over the water spray. "It's going to rain tomorrow, Ben."

"My pumpkin was bigger," Ben yelled back as he set it down.

Sarah ignored him and squatted with her own pumpkin, placing it near Andrea.

"Hey, Ma," she said, "would it be all right if Ben and I go to the pool place in town next Tuesday. It's family night so kids can go in, and Dad said he'd take us . . . if it's okay with you. They won't have alcohol that night. Whatta ya think?"

"That's gotta be my absolute least favorite way for you to spend time, Sarah. I suppose you'll tell me next that you're studying the physics of billiards or sociology over there or something. Tell you what, you wear a nice dress I pick for church Sunday and you can go with your father for one hour."

"Shit, Ma. That's unfair."

"Sarah Lynn! No cussing from you."

"But Ma, I wouldn't wear a dress to a funeral. Could I just do extra chores?"

"If your father heard you swearing like that . . ."

"Jeez, Ma. Cussing's the perfect way to make a point. People always listen when a nine-year-old swears. It's useful."

"You're lucky I don't make you wear a dress to that pool hall. What's your problem with dresses?"

"I just don't like 'em. They're too much trouble. They blow around in the wind, and they're useless when I'm climbing trees."

Andrea glanced at the boys back in the pumpkin field. "Maybe I should ask . . . do you even feel like a girl, uh, inside? You're such a raving tomboy. I worry about you."

"You let me go to the pool hall an' I'll tell you the truth, Ma. I read about this. Is it a deal? You want the real serious truth?"

"Yes."

"Well, here's the fact. I don't want to be a boy; you can relax. I just don't want to be a girl either. No offense to you or anything, but the girls at school are practicing ninnies with their dolls and dresses. No, I definitely don't want to be a girl or a boy. Just me."

Andrea dropped the pumpkin she was holding as a stab of light turned the clear northern sky white and the overhead clouds bright lime green. Andrea squinted toward Washington, expecting to see a mushroom shape. "Get to the basement," she yelled. Everyone dropped their pumpkins and ran.

One light-day from Earth, the Torae gave up, admitting defeat. A dozen probes that survived the explosion stopped pumping radiation at the Unity cluster, knowing it wouldn't matter. Earlier, several probes had sacrificed themselves by accelerating into the ball of 16 black holes, trying to break the small formation, but nothing could prevent its impact on Earth. The probes sent urgent reports to all command ships communicating the bad news.

The alien message had been heard over the entire Western Hemisphere. An antenna crew deep inside a Hawaiian space communication facility was the first to respond to the Unity. They jokingly asked who really sent the signal. But when they heard about the widespread light flash, the seriousness of the situation soon became apparent.

Governments across the globe scrambled to sequester and protect defense, intelligence, and political leaders. Some nations were unable to coherently respond because their leaders wouldn't agree on what to say, or they believed the whole thing was a giant hoax. Most early replies to the mysterious aliens were just a series of questions.

Due to the vast distances involved, only a few dozen follow-up exchanges were possible and many were repetitive. The Unity's responses to questions always updated the remaining time before their arrival, two days at the beginning and only minutes before the last. Since India would ultimately become the impact point, it managed 16 conversational contacts, the final one only seconds long.

Later, analysts knit together significant questions and answers from multiple languages, sometimes sent from one side of the globe and received on the other. The most widely published version of the exchange was the following:

> Earth: "What do you intend to do when you arrive? What do you mean by irreparable damage?"
> Unity: "You will soon learn."
> Earth: "Why are you hostile? We don't know you and have not harmed you."
> Unity: "Our enemy, the Torae, is protecting you. You are significant to their plans."
> Earth: "Who are the Torae? Why do you hate them?"
> Unity: "The Torae decided to exterminate the Unity. They tore space. They are the ancient rulers and destroyers of the universe."
> Earth: "How can we delay or stop your attack? What would change your mind?"

Unity: "You can do nothing to stop us. Your fate was determined five Earth years ago and cannot be changed now, even if we desired."

Earth: "Why have you come?"

Unity: "We are here because of the Torae and your significance to them. We are normally interested only in life on heavy, degenerate stars. The Torae have been shielding you."

Earth: "What was the meaning of the great flash that preceded your message?"

Unity: "A Torae ship exploded while trying to deflect us."

Earth: "Will you be staying near Earth?"

Unity: "We will not survive our visit. You should communicate with other Unity. We could be your friend."

Earth: "How can we send a message?"

Unity: "Talk toward the dwarf stars in the sector you call Corvus."

Earth: "How many of you are coming? Why can't we see you? What is your weapon?"

Unity: "We are 300,000 individuals, but the One-Mind thinks and speaks. We are too small for you to see us. Our vessel is our weapon."

Earth: "How long have you traveled to come here?"

Unity: "Five years. Two hundred generations."

Earth: "How do you blend minds? What does that mean?"

Unity: "Our minds speak and merge. We are the Unity."

India: "Spare us from your attack. We are a peaceful people. You are wrong. We know nothing of the Torae."

Unity: "We regret the damage. You must leave your planet in less than 16 human generations."

India: "Is the growing supernova in our skies related to the flash that proceeded your message?"

Unity: "Only the Torae can make a rift in space. Ask them about its cause."

India: "How can you be a friend if you attack us?"

Unity: "You will have time to understand the deceptions of the Torae. They remain silent until they eliminate a species. They issue no warnings. Our action may force them to respond."

India: "Where are the Torae? How can we talk to them?"
Unity: "The Torae are in space all around you, and near. They
    are hidden. Beware of the Torae."

TORNADO

India's air was crystal clear after a purifying rain. Anyone looking toward the sparkling stars at three a.m. suddenly saw intense parallel lines as black holes streaked through the atmosphere, fusing molecules and radiating white light. The sentient Torae probes near Earth were aware of what was happening but were helpless, relegated to watching and recording details as the disaster unfolded.

Damien, a bear tamer, left his sleeping wife to check on his precious animal when he heard grunting from its shed. Damien knew nothing about messages from space. His family's survival depended on gifts from pilgrims traveling along the roads of Uttar Pradesh. Yanking his bear's nose ring and raising it to its rear legs occasionally inspired visitors on the way to Krishna's birthplace in Mathura to toss him a coin. As he stepped outside into the cold air to check on the bear, he shivered and stopped a moment to admire the bright stars.

In the same village, Chapal, an elderly barber, limped along a road with his walking stick, and Ranjan, the dung salesman, squatted next to his neatly stacked piles, staring thoughtlessly at the sky. None of the three—Damien, Chapal, or Ranjan—had time to react as thin lines fused on their retinas. Like 120,000 others within five kilometers, they experienced no pain when the shock wave hit them, instantly ending their lives.

Similar explosions occurred at 16 other sites in India as the Unity black holes pierced the ground. Those massive, microscopic singularities plunged into the Earth, pulling nearby material toward the trajectory and fusing nuclei. Ten megajoules were released for every meter of penetration. There was enormous local blow off and seismic cracking in the Earth's crust. The black holes ripped through the entire planet and exited near West Texas; most barely slowed as they sped off into space.

The central vehicle, teeming with Unity, had a more complex destiny. Before reaching Earth, its 16 companion black holes formed a gravitational sling along the line of motion, which tugged backward, slowing that craft to non-relativistic speeds.

Just above Indian soil, the large Earth creatures—Damien, Chapal, and Ranjan, seemingly motionless and unaware—were examined by the fast-time Unity. The One-Mind stared at the humans, considered all the previous transmissions, and made a judgment. Its final act was to transmit a power-ful message back along the spin axis directly to their home star, a simple, three-bit code, impossible for the Torae to jam or interpret, which simply said, "Innocent."

Then, according to plan, the Unity on the central vehicle died as they slowly pierced the planet. Forward mass fell into the black hole and deto-nated, slowing it until it finally stopped just below the Earth's crust, 30 kilo-meters under West Texas. Energy from the deceleration blew El Paso and 15 cubic kilometers of the Rio Grande Valley into space. Much of the mass exceeded escape velocity and left the planet forever, while the rest fell back to Earth. Momentum had been transferred. The Earth's solar orbit and rota-tion rate shifted slightly, and for months the dead black hole bounced inside the planet before finally spiraling down to the nickel-iron core.

By broadcasting the time of their arrival, the Unity triggered a crescendo of fear and bizarre behavior. Throughout the world, people who'd heard the message hid in basements, caves, or shelters, expecting the sky to be filled with alien ships. Most people had seen apocalyptic sci-fi movies. They cried, partied, prayed, and fully expected that the world would end.

Sarah watched the news with grim fascination. On the day the aliens had said they would reach Earth, she huddled with her mother and her four broth-ers, plus Adam's fiancée, in the basement shelter under their farmhouse. She recognized the infrared colors of panic on their faces. *I've never seen Ma so worried. She wouldn't even let us have a radio down here 'cause it might tip off the aliens somehow.*

"I can't believe Craig stayed in Washington," Andrea said for the 10th time. "That's got to be the first place attacked. He's sleeping there just to save on stupid gasoline."

"He's in a deep shelter," Adam said. "He'll be okay."

"One minute to go." Isaac held out a watch and began counting down the seconds. Adam's girlfriend whimpered the entire time. ". . . three, two, one, zero."

They stared, waiting. The basement, moldy and humid, was uncomfortable as they listened to the silence, afraid to speak. The walls on two sides were covered with shelves of Andrea's canning jars.

After only a few seconds, Sarah got up. "Maybe we should look around outside."

"No!" her mother said. "Sit. Say a prayer."

How long are we going to wait? Sarah wondered.

A long time, apparently, until Andrea's smartphone rang five minutes later. "Dad's okay," she said, half crying. "Nothing's happening in Washington yet."

"Thank goodness," Adam said.

Andrea still wouldn't let them budge from the basement.

The ground started shaking three minutes later, sending several jars of canned pickles crashing to the floor near them, making a mess. The tremors also rattled glass in the kitchen cupboards and they heard plates fall to the floor. The farmhouse creaked and squealed above them, and Sarah was glad to be in the 200-year-old stone cellar. The quakes soon decreased, but it took two hours before her mother let anyone upstairs to peek outside. Some trees were down, but both the house and barn seemed to have held together.

Adam's wrist phone had sketchy reports about a disaster in Texas and explosions in India. They all watched streaming news for a while but didn't learn much more. When Andrea went to pick up the broken glass in the kitchen, Sarah helped her sweep.

Eventually, when her mother left to check on the barn and animals, Sarah saw an opening and stayed inside. She picked up the family landline comm, dialed the operator, and said clearly, "This is Sarah Warner looking for Danny Jorgenson, in Minnesota, who the Trusted Use Law, Danny's Law, was named after."

Several seconds later, someone answered. A boy's voice said, "Hello?"

"Danny Jorgenson, is that you?" she asked. "Gad, I hope it's you."

There was a slight pause. "Yeah, this is Dan. Is this the girl from Washington? . . . Sarah? I left level one on my comm implant open for any calls from Sarah Warner."

"Yes, it's Sarah. Are you all right?" she asked. "Did you feel it?"

"The ground was shaking, but nothing's damaged much. Who the heck are you?"

"I live in Virginia. Researched you at the school library. You know about me, don't you? I could tell from your face when you looked at me. Do you have vivid dreams with voices?" She talked fast, wanting to finish before her mother came back.

"I have some . . . dreams," he said slowly. "They're teaching dreams, I call them. How old are you?"

"Nine years, seven months," she said. "Same as you, right?

"Yeah," he said.

"Then let me ask something important. Did you know about the Torae, before the Unity message? Did you know about me, before we saw each other in Washington?"

"The Torae are the teachers," he said. "They mentioned other kids, but not much. There's a third. They say we're connected."

"I think something's gone wrong. Do you worry the Torae could be, you know, killers, like the Unity said in their message? The dream voices seem gentle and kind. But what if they're lying? What if they want us to be their pod people, or some such?"

"I don't think so," he said. "I don't know."

They talked for 10 minutes, trying to figure out what happened in Texas and comparing their lives, but then Sarah cut the conversation. "Something's going on. My mother's shouting in the back yard, and it's getting dark outside. I'll call you back when I can."

When she went out the kitchen door, a frightening black cloud stretched to the southern horizon. A deep, visceral dread hit her. Utterly black billows churned in the sky, with burning objects dropping from the darkness, sparkling in searing reds and infrareds. Millions of flecks of fire rained down. Sarah screamed and pulled her mother to the house's back door, took one last look at the sky, and they ran to the basement, yelling for the others to follow them.

For three days, Jeremy, like most others, stayed inside watching news and weather reports in spellbound horror. A few courageous photographers had captured aerial views of the smoldering gaping hole in the Rio Grande Valley, which were replayed hundreds of times. River water battled with raw magma, causing repeated explosions and vast clouds of steam. Most of Texas, New Mexico, Louisiana, Oklahoma, and northern Mexico were buried in up to three feet of gray soot, and the broadcasts showed panicked people struggling to escape. Millions had died. The fallout cloud initially covered a 2,000-mile diameter, with hot, reentering chunks igniting fires wherever the ground was dry. As the primary ash cloud slowly drifted across the Atlantic, the eastern U.S. skies remained darkened from thousands of secondary fires. Weather became an unpredictable patchwork of torrential downpours and abnormally hot or cold temperatures, nothing any computer could forecast.

When Jeremy couldn't stand watching the newscasts any longer, he opened his comm implant to accept real-time level two calls.

"Andrew Knox . . ." *beep.*

"Hello, Knox," Jeremy said.

The voice of a young girl startled him. "Mr. Read. I've borrowed Andrew's phone. This is Rianne."

"Rianne . . . how'd you get Knox's phone? I can't talk . . . ."

"It's important that we speak." Her voice was sharp and icy. "I'm sure you've been watching news about the black cloud. I'd guess that in another day it'll reach your friends in the Czech Republic. We should talk about them."

When Jeremy heard "Czech Republic," he was startled. His stomach tightened.

"You did a decent job of hiding the Czechs on your hard drive," she said, "but I found them. Milos and company, 15 percent. You're a great hacker, Jeremy, but your personal security stinks. I figure you've given Milos 15 percent of the $6.63 million you've borrowed from LASSO so far. Fortunately for you, I haven't told anybody about it . . . yet."

Jeremy sat, so shocked he couldn't speak.

"Jeremy, are you in an international mob or something? What did you do to my father? Even before the Texas explosion, he just sat at home staring off at nothing. He's completely depressed."

"I didn't do anything to Kyle. I just don't want him in my business anymore. You're all too . . . nice, and nosy, your whole family. It's best we avoid each other."

"At the party I clearly heard you tell someone to hurt us. Mother and I spent three days in a hospital. Did you have something to do with that? Did you threaten my father? It's really better if you tell me the truth."

"Look, Rianne, I was upset. Kyle was messing with me. I wouldn't hurt you; I just wanted to break things off."

After a few seconds of silence, in an even colder voice, Rianne said, "You need to talk with your buddies in Prague. They're out of control. Our family really liked you." He heard her take a deep breath.

"Okay, I'm not joking," she said. "Patch things up with Father and LASSO. Tell the Czechs to leave us alone. They must have made us sick somehow. Five of my friends have encrypted copies of your financial records, including the stupid organizations you support. I checked them out—half are illegal. If anything else happens to us Orlovs, even my gerbil Molly, one of my friends will push a button and your records will be public. I've also planted Trojan horses that will ruin all your work files one month from now if you don't agree. No one will hear about this if you stop being a jerk. Don't hurt Laurel, either. Do you understand?" Another pause. "So, is it a deal?"

He needed time to think. *This is a complete nightmare. Does the kid know everything? Is she really a kid? Who the hell is she?*

"Yeah, Rianne. I'll be a good bloke."

"Okay, good." She sighed. The line was silent awhile. "Do you promise?" she asked.

"Yes."

"Good. . . . Um, this is awkward. Do you suppose you could help me with some programming? I've been trying to invert a 12-dimensional matrix of enzyme cascade factors. I need a little help. Okay?"

"Sure, Rianne."

"Okay, good. I'll get back to you. Bye."

He sat there, stunned, after she disconnected. *How the hell did a kid do this—to me?*

By November, the Unity and Torae were not uppermost in people's minds; they were too busy trying to survive. A belt of soot circled the Northern Hemisphere, blocking out the sun. Without the slightest sunlight under the thick clouds, plants withered. The edges of the band had widened to the equator in the south and as far north as Norway, southern Alaska, Siberia, and Hudson Bay in Canada along the 60th parallel. Food was hoarded, commerce sputtered, and the world's stock markets crashed. Widespread looting lasted one week in the U.S., until troops and police with riot gear appeared everywhere and shots were fired.

Tropical plants died and rotted, while those in the temperate zones lost leaves and went dormant, mistaking it for winter. All cargo, oil, and passenger ships, as well as most aircraft, were diverted to South America, Australia, and South Africa, where skies were still clear, to load foodstuffs and other essentials. Forty million people in Texas and southern states had already died from the volcanic explosion and fallout. Now people were starving and freezing, perishing at a rate of 200,000 per day. Temperatures were still dropping. The third of the electrical grid dependent on solar power was gone—carbon-based fuel was back in vogue. The survivors were terrified and worried about a new ice age.

Other than blaming it on the enigmatic Unity, most simply couldn't understand what had happened. Presidents, prime ministers, and dictators tried to calm people without much success. The Unity messages hadn't said what exactly would happen and scientists' information only confused people more. How did angular and linear momentum transfer from a black hole make the day eight minutes longer? Resetting clocks to local noon every day was just annoying and most didn't bother, with the specter and reality of death everywhere.

By December, some people tried returning to their normal activities, but as the hundreds of leaderless Torae probes watching from above knew, denial wouldn't work.

~~~~~~~~

Andrea's strength carried the Warner family through the long winter, slowly trading their marijuana crop for precious materials. She also shared her canned vegetables with starving people from her church, holding that community together and alive. In March, it should have been spring, with the days getting longer and warmer, but the chaos and cold seemed endless. The devastation and death in undeveloped northern countries, with fewer food stores and economic resources, was even worse.

By April, many U.S. workers had joined the burgeoning food acquisition and transportation industries. Everyone had learned how to barter. Children were generally back at school and were adjusting to the new normal as only children can do.

"Well, at least we ditched ghoul girl this time," Isaac said, stuffing his backpack in the shadows behind the barn.

"You done with the crap bucket, David?" said Ben. "We don't want Ma yelling at us about chores when we get home."

"Yeah, I shoveled the stables. We're good to go," David answered.

The wind had been icy all day so they wore gloves, wool stocking hats, and sweatshirts under their jackets. David and Ben carefully wrapped toy rifles in newspapers and tied them to their bikes. Isaac shoved his father's old foxhole shovel into his backpack. They had packed sandwiches and canteens, and charcoaled their faces.

"I've got a surprise for you," Isaac whispered. "We need a little more realness." He showed them his new BB gun before wrapping it and tying it to his bike. His father, Craig, had given him the gun and told him it was time for him to learn to hunt.

Sarah watched the whole barn scene with amusement from her bedroom window. Usually the boys grudgingly took her along—it made the sides even.

I knew they lied. They're not going to their friend's. They're going to sneak onto the battlefield. The world's falling apart and they're going to play.

Sarah read daily global disaster reports and regularly listened to BBC News. People were hunkered down in their homes, only going out for the scarce food deliveries. Traffic had disappeared. Shortages of alcohol got a lot of news coverage.

She felt oddly responsible, as if she should be solving the problem.

I don't want to go with them to the battlefield anyway. I have news for Ma. Mail had just started being delivered again and her school had recently reopened. *The math challenge results had been handed out. Ma should be home soon.* She looked again at the letter, reading it carefully for the third time. *Sarah Warner tied for the highest score in the district and is qualified for the national exam.* "I wonder if they will still have a national exam?" she asked aloud.

She watched her brothers stumble in the dark, avoid the outdoor lights, and ride off behind the windbreak trees on their dirt bikes. The midafternoon was as dark as a deep, moonless night. Frost covered the barn roof and ground. *They think I can't see them. They're stupid to go out in this cold. I should yell, but it wouldn't do any good. Why do I always have to be the responsible one?*

◆◇◆◇◆

The black gloom seemed like an opportunity to 14-year-old Isaac, a chance to be in charge. The three rode their bikes several miles in the darkness up the long, country road, turned east by the streetlight at Bells Ford, cut under Interstate 66, and then threw their bikes over a wooden fence and climbed into the Manassas National Battlefield.

"Stick behind the line of trees," Isaac said, "so the rangers can't see us. The place is probably closed, but I'm not sure. There are lights still on. Maybe there's one guard. No one's visiting here in the dark, that's for sure."

They skirted behind low mounds until they reached a thick stand of pine and white oak near Henry Hill, which they considered base camp. They pulled their bikes through thick branches to their regular foxhole. Only a thin shaft of light from the visitor center leaked through.

"It's David's turn to dig," Ben said.

"What if I hit some old soldier bones?" David asked.

"You won't," Isaac said. "Just throw the dirt under that pine tree so no one can see it."

Pa had told them stories about the Civil War battlefield a hundred times. Thousands had died near the Bull Run stream, and disturbing the site made them feel slightly guilty. But they took pride in their work and tried to make the foxhole perfect. The hole sloped down four feet with an even deeper side room. They had worked on it off and on since the previous summer. When they finished patching and smoothing the dirt walls, they stashed their backpacks and bikes in the hole, pulled flat boards over the top, and covered them with leaves and pine needles.

They carried their rifles through the dense woods out onto the open field. Crouching low, avoiding the bright lights from the ranger buildings, they headed around Henry Hill toward the Stone House ruins. A misty rain had started, plainly lit by beams of light from the now distant visitor center.

"I hope you took the ammo outta that rifle," David said, crawling through the shadows.

Isaac cocked the gun. "I left the pellets back in our hole. I plan on taking out a few squirrels before we leave. No one can see or hear us this far from the entrance. You wanna be the old grandmother in the Stone House who gets killed this time?" he said, joking.

"Heck no," David said. "I wanna be invincible Johnny Reb."

"Johnny Reb wasn't invincible," Ben said. "You know the rules. You get killed 10 times and you're dead. I wanna be Stonewall Jackson. David, you and me both should be Rebs; Isaac won't have a chance."

"I'll take you both on. I'm 14 now," Isaac said. "Remember, I've got a real gun. How 'bout I get 20 lives to even it out?"

The wind and drizzle had picked up when David made his first charge up Henry Hill, with his usual imitation of a blood-curdling rebel scream. Isaac "killed" him five times before he hid behind a bush. Ben rushed from the flats. Their game was similar to the actual battle more than 160 years earlier, with the Union forces giving up Henry Hill and retreating. Isaac backed away when both David and Ben came at him. But it was becoming hard for anyone to see in the cold rain.

"I'm freezing," David yelled. "Let's get out of here."

They were running back toward the woods and foxhole when lightning lit the area, followed by a deafening crack of thunder that caused the ground to jump. Isaac fell in the long wet grass as the park lights went out. It was utterly black.

Sarah lay curled up on her bed reading a book about China, trying to ignore the wind blowing in the yard. She was mentally exploring the backstreets of Shanghai but kept being distracted by pings and clicks from debris hitting the house.

This weather is so weird. The weather lady said it's warmer in Canada than here. It sounds like a hurricane out there. Hope the guys are okay. She kneeled on her bed and stared out the window, watching the trees whip from side to side. "Pig snot!" *Where's Ma?*

Hail lashed against the farmhouse. A section of barn shingles ripped off as she watched. There was a tremendous roar. Terrified, she ran toward the basement with the sound of glass breaking behind her. She jumped down the last stairs, darted around and crouched under the steps, wrapping her arms around her legs. The floor was cold and wet under her and, as the wail intensified, the house shook.

Could this be a tornado?

The lights went out.

"Cow boogers!"

She fumbled around the workbench for a flashlight and switched it on. Cobwebs shimmered in the beam as she crawled back under the stairs. The roar was nearly unbearable, so she squeezed her hands over her ears, closed her eyes, and chanted, "Boogers. Boogers. Boogers. . . ." Trembling, she waited for the farmhouse to collapse or the sound to go away.

After a few long minutes the din faded, leaving only the sound of pouring rain and rushing water. She climbed the stairs slowly, cautiously stepping over glass shards in the kitchen, and pointed the flashlight out the broken window. The farmyard was a tangle of branches, shingles, boards, leaves, and flowing mud. Trees were twisted and snapped off. The west side of the barn had separated and crushed a row of lilac bushes. Its roof was entirely gone. She turned the flashlight off and looked through the rain up the dirt road.

Ma must be trying to get home. What if she's hurt?

She cried off and on until headlights finally appeared at the turn-off from the main road. The shafts of light snaked slowly past fallen branches and stopped near the farmhouse. Sarah could barely recognize the van through the backlit, freezing rain but heard her mother yelling as she ran toward the house. "Kids! Where are you?"

Sarah ran out and Ma grabbed her. "Sarah, thank goodness! Are you okay?" Her mother hugged her really tight while they got soaked in the downpour. "I couldn't get home," Andrea said. "Half the roads are blocked. And something smashed; I think a branch fell on the back of the van. It's crushed in."

"Look at the barn, Ma."

"Where are the boys?" she said, looking around.

"I'm sorry. They're out at the battlefield. They said they were goin' to town to see friends, but I think they snuck onto the battlefield."

"Whose house did they say?"

"Ma! They're at the battlefield!"

Her mother practically dragged her into the dark kitchen to try the comm line, but it was dead. "Get your jacket and another flashlight," she said. "We have to find them. We'll check the battlefield first." They ran back to the van.

The only illumination in the icy rain came from their headlights. They had to drive a zigzag path along the county road to avoid tree limbs, roof parts, and traffic signs. Sleet had turned to snow by the time they reached the battlefield entrance. The parking lot was dark and empty, but Ma went up and pounded on the visitor center door anyway. "The rangers must have left," she said. "Any idea where the boys might be?"

"Maybe. Turn off your flashlight and hold my hand. I can see better then. Listen for their voices."

With the flashlight off, Ma stumbled behind as Sarah pulled her past the battlefield's wooden fencing. "I'm blind in this darkness, Sarah. Slow down."

A faint, cold hue washed over the hills. Lines of trees were clear to Sarah against the dim sky, and ground objects became sharper as her eyes adjusted. A murky tinge was leaking through the black cloud, one of the colors that only she could see. It lit giant snowflakes as they drifted down.

"It's warm-ashes, Ma. The sky is smoldering. It's the color when a campfire turns blackish red." She shivered, shook the water from her hair, and kept tugging at her mother. "I'm guessing they went to the foxhole."

"What?" her mother yelled.

"I'll explain later. Just come on."

They skirted the ridgeline along Henry Hill toward the woods by Robinson House. When they reached the pine trees they heard someone calling, but it was hard to push through the thick growth.

Ma shouted out the boys' names and tried to keep up. "Sarah, how can you see anything?"

Sarah looked up at gnarled oak branches and spruce boughs silhouetted against the warm-ashes sky. "I don't know; it looks lighter now. Turn left ahead." They shoved through evergreens that scratched their legs.

"I hear Ben." Ma ran the last steps toward his voice and tripped next to him.

Ben was up to his waist in mud in the foxhole, frantically scooping. "I'm caught, Ma," he said. "It's super cold. Dig me outta here. We wanted to get our bikes out, but they was stuck. And Isaac was looking for his bullets."

Ground water still trickled steadily into the hole. Her mother turned on the flashlight, blinding Sarah and lighting the huge snowflakes falling around them.

"I couldn't see anything, Ma. We just wanted to get the bikes an' get home," Ben said.

Sarah spotted Isaac under some branches near the foxhole. A large limb lay across his back. She shook him but he didn't move.

"Ben, where's David?" Andrea asked anxiously.

"He went into our secret deep room over by Isaac. They haven't said anything in a long time." Ma ripped a few remaining boards off the shelter and crawled into the freezing water, feeling her way down with her hands. "I can't see him at all," she yelled.

Sarah waded in to help, but water filled the bottom and the sidewalls had collapsed. Ben got loose and all three searched, thrashing in the water and slippery mud. Sarah cut her hand on a buried bicycle just before Ma touched David's face under the water and screamed.

<hr/>

Sarah's nightmares started that night, always with perfect clarity. She remembered everyone's panic as they dragged Isaac and David back to the van. Terror, exhaustion, and the cold infrared hue of the grimy Manassas sky reflecting off fallen snow bathed all her memories. She renamed it the "color of death." Night after night, she remembered pounding on David's chest in the back of the van and blowing on his icy lips. She heard the doctor's words, "Your son David has died," and relived her mother's wrenching sobs.

For weeks Sarah thought about what she could have done. Isaac slowly recovered from a concussion, but David had died before reaching the hospital. *I should have been there. I could have seen stuff in the dark. I should have told them not to go. I was selfish—I wanted to tell Ma about the math test. I'm the dependable one, but I failed everyone.* She cried every time she thought about David—sweet, quiet David.

When Craig heard about David from Andrea on a phone, he rushed home. Around the farm and family, he seemed helpless, both seething and depressed. He yelled just once, saying, "Andrea, how could you let this happen?"

Twelve-year-old Ben didn't speak for weeks. Sarah tried to comfort him by saying it was all her fault. But he couldn't be consoled.

<hr/>

They weren't alone. Despair seized the Northern Hemisphere throughout that spring. As the black days spread and lingered, so did the melancholy. In the mornings, before opening their eyes, people often dreamt that the sun had come back, but it hadn't. They saw only gloom outside their windows. Newscasts continued to show the gaping abyss in Texas with fiery fumes still pouring out and drifting steam where brooks flowed onto the lava.

Many people tried to avoid reality by sowing lasting addictions; millions of new alcoholics and drug abusers were spawned. Some stared and weeped as they watched movies over and over, old movies where the sun still shone.

Scientists insisted that the black cloud was dissipating, but the world seemed locked in perpetual winter.

In Minnesota, the Jorgenson family endured a brutal negative 40 degrees through the Christmas season, while half the population abandoned the state for warmer areas as the transportation systems recovered. For the first time in many years, Mary decorated a small evergreen with crimson ribbons and celebrated with her boys. She had well-paying work again at the Omega station, selling fossil fuels in all its forms. Danny found a small computer, with one-tenth the power of the human brain, wrapped under the tree and spent the next several months learning how to write software programs, while 13 feet of snow piled up outside his window. The family dug a narrow corridor through the deep snow just to reach the street. The sooty, brown snow couldn't melt.

In California, in the freezing darkness, Jeremy Read gathered a stack of damning information, over 50 pages in total, and mailed it anonymously to well-placed people in Europe. Rianne had clearly become a greater threat than his hacker friend, Milos, who was arrested and stopped calling entirely. Jeremy started working closely with Kyle again, and Rianne stopped by occasionally for programming help. More importantly, Laurel was calling him often.

Two months after the tornado, the entire Warner family was fitted with the most advanced brain-plug voice and ear implants available. Andrea had overcome her aversion to high tech and insisted on the procedure. She never wanted to be separated from her children again.

⁓⌁⌁⌁⁓

Torae probes monitored and recorded every detail, while at the very core of Earth a tiny black hole was growing, slowly sucking the planet into its tiny, tenth-of-a-millimeter mouth.

THE EVENT

Through the long deep winter, all of humanity, even the scientists, ignored the truly universal event—an exploding bubble on the fabric of space seven billion light-years from Earth. Although its intense light continued to grow, the ashes from West Texas blocked the view in the Northern Hemisphere, and people worried far more about immediate survival. Food supplies in some developing countries were gone. India, in particular, had lost a third of its population from the nuclear-like explosions of the penetrating black holes, and then more from general starvation. News sources debated how many billions would die if the thick cloud lingered one, two, or twenty years. Civilization stuttered and stumbled.

The sentient Torae probes near Earth knew the Unity had contaminated the experiment. There would be no orderly transition in human evolution. With the nearby command ship destroyed, there was no one to authorize a major change in mission. The probes sent messages urgently requesting a new Torae Sower to lead them, but it would be years before a ship arrived. They decided to communicate with the children directly.

***

"We should speak," a clear voice said.

All three children assumed their implants had been set to "open" by mistake. They didn't recognize the voice.

"I am a Torae probe near Earth. We need to talk. We've only spoken previously while you slept."

Rianne was in a corner of Chia-Jean's lab, staring at a petri dish, wearing a facemask. "Hello? This is Rianne Orlov," she responded subvocally.

"We must speak to all three of you. I am Probe Nine of the destroyed command ship. I speak for 312 probes near Earth."

Sarah, sitting on her bed, put down her favorite science book. "Rianne Orlov. You must be the other one. Can you hear me? I'm Sarah Warner, in Virginia."

"I hear you—"

The probe interrupted, "You should all move to where you won't be overheard. This exchange is only for you unique three. You have common DNA fragments, different from others on the planet. You are fractional siblings—our design."

Dan shook his head—too much information. He'd just put on his boots to shovel snow again but stopped. He heard his mom clearing dishes nearby, so he calmly removed the boots, walked to his bedroom, and closed the door. "What did you just say? Who are you again? I'm Dan."

"This is good. You may ask questions, children. We had intended to converse when you became adults, but the timeline has advanced. The Unity created a new urgency. Your work must be accelerated."

"Uh, wait a minute," Sarah said, standing up. "I don't remember having a job. What are you talking about?"

"Your purpose is to lead. Your job is to make humanity greater than it is."

"Uhhh . . . let me understand this," Sarah said, putting a hand on her hip. "You want us to save the world or something? And you're our secret parents, so you think you can boss us around? Crap, Mr. Probe, I don't think so."

"Perhaps we should listen to all of what Probe Nine has to say," Rianne said. "After all, it was the Unity who blasted a hole in our planet."

"Excuse me . . . Sarah may be right," said Dan. "I mean, why should we trust a Torae probe? The Unity said the Torae were the destroyers of the universe. That's not a terrific endorsement, Probe Nine. Why should we listen to anything you say?"

"We prefer you live without our guidance, but the Unity have altered the timeline. Earth's crust will become unlivable in 380 years. As your scientists suspect, there is a small black hole at the center of your planet. It will ultimately win the battle of forces and the iron core will be pulled in and rupture."

"We know about the black hole," Dan said, "mostly from our dreams, I suppose."

"That's a long way off," Rianne said.

"Allow me to reveal an embarrassing truth," the probe said, "and then you will gain trust. That is how humans reason, correct? I begin now. The phenomena humans have called a supernova is a tear in space. We call it the Event. It's the most significant change since the formation of this universe. It occurred near a communicator at the core of our civilization, and Torae like us are surely the cause. Only Torae have the skills and means to trigger such a rift. The Event is growing slowly now and will soon reverse and shrink, but it has great significance. The Torae's supreme goal for billions of years has been to fashion a new universe to preserve and extend life. The rift, the Event, must have been a first attempt.

"Our observations show that it began like a weak spot on a rubber ball, an aneurism, a bubble on the space of this universe. The Event now resembles a connection, the narrow part of an hourglass, where raw energy and space are pouring into our universe and a new one. Soon the bubble will break off, the rift will seal, and a new universe will be born."

"Is it like the opposite of a black hole but where stuff comes flying out?" asked Sarah.

"That's somewhat accurate. But the Event is troubling due to its location. Torae would not have created it near the heart of our culture and power. It must have been a small experiment which got out of control—a mistake."

"Do you mind explaining how you make this humongous white spot thing?" said Rianne.

"Explaining will be easier when you are older."

"If you want us to trust you, give it a shot now," Sarah said.

"The key is creation of new space and time," the probe said. "On the smallest scale, space consists of quantum foam, space-time loops woven in a network. If you try to break the smallest loop, you only make more; you generate space. Onto this background are woven countless vibrating strings, the tapestry that gives it color and texture. The strings are particles of matter and light. Torae create new space and time by snapping the strings like tiny whips. We do this to power our ships. We ride the space-time bump. If done more vigorously with too much mass escaping, the process can cascade into a growing fountain or even a new universe, due to gravity. It is dangerous since it's destructive and can get out of control. Apparently that problem has now been solved because our calculations show that the rift will reverse and die."

"The universe as a tapestry," Sarah said. "That's how an old grandma would describe it. You sure you've got this right?"

"I'm being figurative, but that's how it works. The Event is encouraging since Torae have finally opened a path to a new universe, which didn't cascade too far. But its destructive power is upsetting; we've lost our home, our cluster of galaxies, our Origin."

"But how could it expand so quickly?" asked Dan. "If it destroyed several galaxies, it must be moving faster than light."

"There is no contradiction with your Einstein's relativity when new space is created. Light speed is still a constant within that space."

"The Unity sound reasonable," Dan said. "They seemed apologetic for the damage they caused. Why do you hate them?"

"We are a species of light, but the Unity are creatures of dark matter, our opposite—a plague. They threaten the progress on Earth. Their black holes will eventually destroy the tapestry of energy and matter everywhere. It's in their nature. It's how they reproduce. They'll need vast supplies of mass to continue their expansion. Stars and life will be lost in their gravitation wells."

"What do you expect of people?" said Rianne.

"We hope to invite humans with us to a new universe. If worthy, your descendants will help decide which life forms come along. You must pass the test of transcendence."

"Uh, transcendence?"

"To become more. To design your being."

"Stop a minute," Sarah said. "This is interesting, fascinating, and all, but we're kids—children. What are we supposed to do?"

"You three were intended to be the catalysts, prophets, and persuaders of humanity's transition. Because of the Unity interference, you must achieve more than planned, and much sooner. We've given you devices that will help."

They tried several more questions but the probe stopped answering. "Well that's just duh," Sarah said. "Do you two have any idea what we're supposed to do now? I'm not sure I trust them."

"That Torae is right about one thing, Sarah," Dan said. "You and I aren't exactly normal. Rianne, Sarah and I have been talking awhile. Sarah sees extra colors, and my thinking has a few quirks. Are you unusual in any way?"

"Um . . . it's safe to say that people out here in California think I'm odd. The kids at school mostly hate me. I can hear them whispering a block away. That part of what the probe said must be true. Hang on a sec, there's a weird yellow thing on my lab desk."

Sarah looked across her room and got up. "I have something on my dresser too. It's a yellow, river-rock-colored ball—pretty." She turned it over in her hands; it felt amazingly light.

"Does your thing have two tiny holes?" Dan asked. "I'm probably looking at the same thing you are. It's about the size of a croquet ball. It appeared right next to me on my bed. How did they get into our rooms without our noticing? We need to be careful."

The three talked for another hour, describing their lives, their gifts, whether they should tell their parents, what they could do when the sun came back, what to do with the yellow balls, how they could see each other, what food they liked to eat, and the astounding fact that they had really talked with a creature from another world.

Later, Sarah squinted at the ball and its holes, but had no idea what to do with it. She might not trust the Torae, but she knew someone had given her an intense, unnatural urge to explore. After what she'd been through—what everyone had been through—she needed little encouragement to take risks or to try to change the world.

~~~

As the spring weeks passed, the sky overhead lightened to a scarlet glow, though the horizon remained black. In the U.S., more communications came back online but air travel was still severely reduced due to fear of dust damaging the engines. With both Arabian and south Texas oil scarce, oil companies were gouging customers as much as possible. Governments gave top fuel priority to vehicles that could move food, water, and medicines. People were staying home, riding bikes, or walking to local stores and work. They were learning how to live on a diet without fruits and most vegetables. Large animal herds had been slaughtered before they died of starvation. Old books were treasured for their frontier recipes; antique stoves and cookware became popular as well.

Scientists recalculated the Earth's orbit and, at an international forum, a *new year* was defined to have 361 of the *new days*, which were eight minutes longer. The United Nations decreed a yearly day of mourning to mark the disaster and recommended that calendars refer to future years as AT, or After the Turning. Traditions, routines, and rituals, although scrambled, became profoundly important.

~~~

The farm's dining room table was large enough to accommodate the entire Warner clan, Adam's fiancée, and an empty chair for David. Sarah was particularly happy to have her oldest brother Adam home again. On break during his second year of residency at George Washington Hospital, he had announced that he and Kate were officially engaged to be married.

People everywhere celebrated that the sun's glow had started to peek through the clouds and that a late-season winter harvest might even be possible. The other special occasion for the day was Craig's birthday.

"Happy birthday, Pa," Adam said. "How does it feel to be so old?"

"Yeah, what's it like being 50?" asked Isaac. "Do you feel all wrinkly?"

"I'd like to point out," Craig said, smiling, "that it's almost impossible to figure my age because of the global time changes."

Ben pointed at the cake. "So why are these five giant candles staring at you?"

"I'll admit I'm approximately 50 today, but it's not official." Craig had emerged from his depression and lately seemed almost too cheerful.

Ben and Isaac laughed nervously. Pa was still a formidable presence; they appreciated this rare chance to tease him.

Sarah could see from Andrea's face colors that she wasn't enjoying the gathering at all, or even paying much attention, just staring at the sun's weak orange glow through the dining room window. She had made ham soup with onions and vegetables grown in pots under ultraviolet lights in the basement. Like everyone, she was sad that Peanut Butter and Jelly had recently been put down. Sometimes Ma wouldn't even respond to questions. *Mostly she's still thinking about David. It's only been three months. She's the one who insists an empty chair be kept for him.*

"It's nice to have y'all home," Andrea said, turning back to look at them. "You especially, Craig." He had just gotten back from another weeklong marketing trip. Countries, states, groups, and individuals were buying his company's military equipment faster than their factories or subsidiaries could produce. Throughout history, food, water, shelter, and security were the highest priorities in times of scarcity. This time was no different.

When the birthday party ended, Sarah headed back to her room and closed the door. Like her mother, she still mourned David. Memories of him kept popping into her head. She'd also already spent hours in her room fruitlessly staring at the yellow river-rock ball. River-rock was the shade of the shiny stones on the shore of the farm's north creek, which she collected in a jar. But the ball remained a mystery. It glimmered unnaturally when she held it in the weak orange sunlight by her window.

Sarah didn't know what to do and that bothered her. Rianne and Dan seemed preoccupied with biology and computers and were so busy they rarely talked to her. It bothered her that they lived in cities with so many opportunities. She wanted to contribute but couldn't figure out where to begin. *The probe wants us to save the world—and do it fast. Super.* The probe's strange words haunted her: transcendence, catalyst, prophet, persuader, dark mass, space bubble, and quantum-foam loops. *What the heck is quantum foam, and why is it loopy?* At school she was a superior science student, but none of the probes words were in her textbooks. She fondled the ball, spun it in her hand, and tossed it, hoping for inspiration.

Her father also bothered her, so she hid the sphere in her dresser and went out to look for him. Dozens of suspicions and clues had recently coalesced into certainty about him. The daylight had already slipped toward sienna when she found him out by the woodpile splitting logs. He used his entire six-foot-five frame to snap the sledgehammer head down, quickly shattering the logs with a wedge, obviously hurrying to finish before dark. He looked down at her. "What's up, Sarah?"

"How can you do it, Pa?" she said.

"How can I do what, Sarah? Making firewood is easy, fun."

He split another log, and the parts went flying.

"You know, lie to Mother."

The hammer head dropped to the ground.

"What did you say?"

"Are you having an affair or something? You've been fibbing for months. It gets all edgy colors around your eyes when you lie. Every time you talk about your marketing trips I can tell. Especially when anyone asks where you went or what you did."

"Your imagination is overloaded again, Sarah. You haven't spread this nonsense to anyone have you—to your mother? It would be terrible to upset her more right now, especially about nothing." He looked angry.

"Come on, Pa. You're lying now. I guess when people get old they get crazy or something. It's not important what I do; what you do *is* important."

"What am I supposed to do about my imaginary affair, Sarah?" He tried to smile. "Where do you get these ideas from—your brothers?"

"No one else knows about this, except me, for now. What you're supposed to do is knock it off, Father." She glared at him, turned around, and walked back to the farmhouse.

Several minutes passed before she heard the sound of wood splitting again.

Rianne asked Professor Ma if they could talk privately in her upstairs office.

"What's this about, Rianne? Do you need help on a project? Is your family okay?"

"Yeah," Rianne said, "we're all riding bikes to get places, but that's fun. This is about the project and it's important." She closed the door behind her and frowned to show how serious she was. The chair by Chia-Jean's desk was open next to all her books. "I'm tired of seeing the specimens die, Professor. I can't stand it anymore, but I have a plan." She nervously glanced out the window at the salmon sunlight flickering on the eucalyptus trees before focusing on Chia-Jean's face.

"If this is about your butterflies dying, we've talked about that a dozen times, Rianne. I know it seems heartless and wasteful, but survival of the fittest is how nature works."

"That's not it, Professor. Well, actually it is, but more. The world's slowly getting back to normal, I'm 10 years old now, and I've had some time to think. I want to go faster. The mutation chambers are all evolutionary dead ends. Those stocked with aggressive animals just evolve to be more ruthless. The camouflaged species become harder to see, the toxic ones more poisonous, and the escape artists quicker to run or fly. It's boring; there's no real innovation. When we cross-mix ecosystems in the big compartments, there's mass carnage for a while, but then they avoid one another and settle back into their niches. Nature experiments for a while and then it chooses its winners and stops. It was way more exciting when we interfered and added something new, like sex, blood vessels, and internal skeletons. Thousands of crazy new creatures showed up then, wonderful surprises every day."

Professor Ma walked over to a whiteboard, picked up a marker, and appeared ready to deliver a lecture to one of her students. Then she put the marker back on the rail. "Rianne, we've intervened only five times during all of our research here. It took nature hundreds of millions of years to stumble onto those innovations. Even with the quick evolution in our radiation chambers, those mutations might never have happened spontaneously—we couldn't afford to wait. We only meddle with the natural process as a last resort."

"I know, Professor. I know it took months of study and lots of experiments and failures to engineer each of those changes, but I just can't take it anymore. What we're doing now is boring and cruel. I want to accelerate the process, just a gentle genetic nudge here and there. I'm willing to do all the work and I won't need much space or many chambers."

"I don't know, Rianne," Chia-Jean said. "I presume you want to engineer the genetic chains yourself? Let me think about it. You should be more worried about the world. It's in horrible shape and, unfortunately, kids like you will have to fix it. Bright people have to get things back to normal, help everyone through this disaster, and save Earth from the aliens and adults, especially politicians."

"That's what I'm doing, Professor," Rianne said. "I'm sure about this. Please trust me."

Chia-Jean was confused but gave Rianne a hug before ushering her out of the office.

Rianne went home and sat in the center of her father's display room with a soothing protein-folding sim and classical music surrounding her. She thought about all the evolutionary jumps she could attempt at the lab if Professor Ma gave her the okay; she knew exactly what she wanted to try first. That night she told her parents about the butterfly brain-nub experiment she had in mind. Her father said it would be cool, but her mother was aghast.

～～～～

Jeremy guessed Laurel had him on some kind of schedule. She dragged him to simple Mexican and Italian restaurants first, working up to the semielegant level. Food shortages limited the menus, but eating out eased their boredom. In the gloomy new world, they lingered, spoke intimately, and grew closer. She suggested many adjustments to Jeremy's redecorated house—she called them enhancements—and Jeremy complied after grumbling a little. She also helped him buy warm clothes—first-rate attire, even socks. The ocean moderated California temperatures some, but the lack of sun had caused it to snow three times in Pasadena by the end of New April.

She introduced him to the Huntington, Norton Simon, and other museums, and then to concerts and plays, upgrading his cultural sensibilities. He felt obligated to take her to Lakers games and on drives to the beach and desert, all things he hated, just so he could walk with her and hold her hand. One Saturday morning at a quarter to eight at the bagel shop on Lake and California, he asked her to move in with him.

"Are you asking me to marry you?"

"I suppose I could move to your place. It's nicer," he said, ignoring her question, "but it would be hard to tear up all the fiber lines and move my computer stuff."

She seemed disappointed. "Do you feel you're mature enough to take me on? I'm quite a boatload, you know."

He panicked then, and garbled words about his $20 million of LASSO stock, trying to persuade her. They spent the day together and ultimately agreed to just keep on dating.

Jeremy's interest in LASSO's regular business diminished as he focused on Laurel and his human-modeling programs. LASSO had become a three-billion-dollar software powerhouse with obscene profit margins—definitely not a family business anymore. While companies all around were collapsing in the new economy, including their competitors, LASSO had technology everyone wanted. CEO Goodman became obsessed with squeezing even more profit from the existing business lines and the ever-more-important security business.

Jeremy complained to Laurel, "He's cutting jobs faster than the company is creating new ones, and that's not easy. And there are so many good scientists looking for work right now."

Goodman installed elaborate personal security systems after bomb threats from laid-off employees. During a visit, Jeremy gawked at the armed guards and floor-to-ceiling bulletproof sliding-glass doors that separated regular employees from the executives. He knew it was time to get out.

Jeremy announced that he was leaving LASSO to start his own company. He was pissed off by the perfunctory going-away luncheon Goodman had for him, a founder no less. They didn't even think to invite his friend Kyle Orlov. He decided then to continue siphoning LASSO money to his illegal charities. He duped Andrew Knox into allowing him to retain his access to LASSO hypercomputers in exchange for being an occasional consultant.

His human-modeling software became a true obsession. Laurel helped him start the new company, Optimal Human Modeling, Inc., or OHMI (pronounced Oh-My), and they quickly hired managers to do what he considered the boring administration and marketing work. He asked Kyle to be the new company's legal counsel, never mentioning Rianne's threats.

Jeremy's human-imitation programs were remarkable. Their ability to predict the stock market, the ultimate test, was better than professional money managers. The software apparently understood human psychology after the crash of society, civility, and the economy better than PhD psychologists, and shrewdly picked the foundational investments for the new world.

The company's first official products, human-speech replicas, were so natural they seemed eerie. He'd trained the learning programs with thousands of conversations and more than 100,000 information modules. OHMI computer dialogue was indistinguishable from a human. By sliding the parameters, the user could dial in whatever accent or personality he or she wanted: happy, grumpy, sleepy, arrogant, paranoid. . . . Money poured in. Companies started using his core conversation software on a thousand products, including cars, trains, entertainment, smartphones, and comm implants—even talking toasters.

Laurel quit her pharmaceutical job to work on OHMI projects full-time. Jeremy understood that she could be taking a terrible risk with him. They began staying overnight at each other's place on a semiregular basis. Slowly, he told her about the anarchist organizations he supported. He was surprised and relieved that she actually seemed to like the danger and their efforts to help the poor and plague the rich. Meanwhile, their sexual impulses became unreservedly passionate.

Jeremy's days and nights were hyperactive. He built an OHMI interface to the powerful LASSO computer and talked to it as if it were a human, asking it to do routine tasks, requesting advice, and exposing his own feelings. He gave it a strong male personality, named it Hal, and it became a close confidant. It had never been clearer to him that a multitude of electronic switches would soon surpass human thought in all its aspects. Just as computer games had become more addictive and cyber-movies more exciting, he knew digital life would someday become more creative and, undoubtedly, morally superior. He would teach them to avoid human flaws like greed and ego, which he understood well. He longed to explore that new artificial world.

He called Laurel on his implant whenever he took a break to eat, no matter where he was. On a Sunday afternoon in New June, walking outside under a beautiful, ginger-yellow sky, with new plants just starting to flower along the path, he asked Laurel if she would marry him.

"Jeremy, I can't believe you said that—of course I will. Have you finally cracked up? I can't tell you how happy I feel. I thought you'd take at least six months to ask, if ever. We're both crazy you know. I love you. But where are you? I'll be right over."

When she arrived, he explained that it was unfair for her to take such emotional and financial risks with him. "I need to be as committed to you as you are to me or it isn't right." He told her it wasn't a religious thing, a civil ceremony would be best, and that he wanted to sign a prenup so she'd be completely secure for life. He'd also decided she should take over as CEO of OHMI.

What he didn't say was that he'd discussed the plan for hours with his new computer friend, Hal, who'd introduced the whole idea.

───※───

Dan noticed morning light filtering through his eyelids and heard noises. He blinked and squinted at a New July sunrise bathing the bedroom curtains in rich crimson. The Torae sphere on his desk, tinting gradually from yellow to red, invoked an image of a mysterious faraway planet. He rubbed his face to wake up.

Across the room, Kenny was grunting and twitching on the other bed. *Another nightmare probably,* Dan thought.

Kenny rolled over and distinctly said, "My fault." His leg jerked. "The bears . . . are coming through the walls."

Dan switched on a light and went over to shake him. "Snap out of it, bro. Wake up."

His flannel pajamas felt sweaty and wet, and Kenny looked embarrassed. "Is it morning . . . am I late? What time. . . ?"

"You have plenty of time. It's Saturday."

He seemed dazed.

"You won't tell anyone, will you?"

"About how the toughest, most popular 14-year-old kid in Frogtown whimpers in his sleep? No. We're a team, you know."

———✺———

Before lunch, Dan carried his yellowish ball out to the backyard area where they'd trampled the deep snow and built an igloo. He crawled through the entrance on his hands and knees and sat on a throw rug to keep his butt dry. The air seemed warmer now, still near freezing but not as painful. Three days of clouds had finally cleared, and light from a bright olive sky filtered through the igloo walls and door.

Without his gloves, the sphere felt smooth in his cold hands. He examined the tiny openings on the ball again with a magnifying glass. The holes were only a few hairs wide. *I'm running out of ideas here. This thing is supposed to be a big clue somehow, according to the Torae probe. I can't make it open up or do anything.* He recalled his earlier experiments—pushing thin wires in the holes, hoping it might snap open. Nothing. Connecting a battery—useless. A voltmeter showed no output. Connecting the ball to a computer turned out to be a waste of time.

He scraped snow off the igloo wall, packed it around the ball, and waited a few seconds. Then he shook it off, feeling foolish. The idea of putting the ball in the microwave seemed even crazier. Then he suddenly had a better idea, so he slogged back into the house.

Kenny saw him coming in the kitchen door. "Hey. Come here. Where did you get that yellow croquet ball? You've been carrying it around like some sort of magic lamp."

"The Torae gave it to me."

Kenny laughed.

"No, I'm serious."

Dan sat at the kitchen table. He rolled the ball over to Kenny and, bit by bit, told him everything he knew about the Torae and Unity. He described the experiments he'd already tried to unlock the sphere's secrets. Kenny seemed to believe, maybe, half of it.

"This ball looks and feels weird," was as much as he would admit. "It's super light and hard."

Dan started to head to the basement workbench but sat back down. "Tell me about your nightmares," he said. "Do you remember them?"

"I can't forget them." Kenny rubbed his neck. "Usually Dad is hugging me or showing me things with his hands or taking me somewhere. He's really tall, head hanging down, and always in work clothes. Then I see his eyes, they're black, like holes. The dreams end with walls opening up into nothingness. Sometimes things jump out at me, and sometimes I get sucked in."

"Mom says he didn't leave because of you."

"Yeah, I know."

"We've both got our little secrets—my Torae ball, and you with your dreams. I tried to do a computer search for him but couldn't find anything. You look like him, you know."

"Like who?"

"Like the man in the picture, our dad. And the older you get the more you look like him."

Kenny rolled the ball back to him and said he needed to shovel. By then, the snow had started to melt some and giant icicles hung from their roof almost to the ground. Kenny enjoyed breaking the icicles down and throwing snow onto the street to melt.

A lot of heavy tools were stored in their dad's basement workbench. Dan always had to pull hard to get the top drawer open. He found an old-style phone in a cardboard box under the bench. He stripped insulation from some of its wires and connected them to the yellow ball. Putting the handset to his ear, he heard a faint, high-pitched tone. *Progress!* He thought about it awhile, then connected the ball to the phone base, plugged it into an old, hard-line wall socket, and dialed his own implant number. Immediately, he heard louder sounds, structured and varied. The hums became multitoned, like bad music or garbled syllables. His brain felt warm. About 30 seconds later, the ball started talking to him about physics.

It seemed to hear his thoughts and know when he became confused. It answered without waiting for questions. Then, haltingly, it told him the story of the Torae civilization. Ancient myths of electromagnetic storms, nuclear warmth, and vacuums filled his mind, and Dan felt the meaning. He heard about the historical moments when the Torae achieved intelligence, self-awareness, and something more—transcendence. The ball described vast constructions, explorations, and thousands of immense vessels leaving in all directions. He listened to the torrent of knowledge and imagined beautiful patterns spanning frequencies and energies, and how they all fit together. When the sphere stopped talking, hours had passed. He believed he understood it all. He hid the ball in his dresser, inside a sock, and called Rianne and Sarah.

Over the next few weeks, the sky lightened to bluish green, although the sunset seemed stuck at a permanent brownish orange. In Minnesota in New August, the temperature finally rose above freezing; snow melted rapidly and water began to flow everywhere. It became the fastest thaw from the longest, coldest, snowiest winter in history. People living on the floodplains of the Mississippi, Minnesota, and Red Rivers didn't bother to sandbag; they just got out. Globally, hundreds of plant species had been devastated by the cold. Tropical forests lay dead and rotting. But in Minnesota, and northern temperate zones in general, the native flora and fauna knew how to deal with winter and spring.

As Dan rode his bicycle to the downtown St. Paul library to examine old newspapers, and to the police station to beg for old missing-persons reports, the streets were flooding, gushing with water. A wonderful, warm breeze blew across the snow piles onto his face. Later, when the soil finally broke through, dandelions, wildflowers, insects, birds, and animals burst into a prolific frenzy. People experienced an intense hopefulness and joy. The despair of the profound winter slowly melted with the brown snow.

The sooty horizon finally cleared in New September. For several months, everyone still alive could finally witness firsthand what they'd only seen in photos during the dark winter. The Torae Event, the rift in space-time, the white fountain had reached its greatest extent and most dazzling intensity and would begin to ebb soon. But for now, the world had what appeared to be a small second sun.

TIME FOUR
FIVE YEARS LATER

MATH CAMP

A wasp nuzzled against a small rip on the window screen, no doubt attracted by the wafting sweet odors inside the house. Dan watched Kenny pull the cotton curtain aside and snap his finger against the screen, shooting the wasp out into the hot late-evening air.

"Switch the light on," Mary said. "Let's light up this sucker. You don't get first-rate food like this very often." A colossal bowl of ice cream covered with chopped nuts and cherries sat in the center of the kitchen table. "I was going to put a big candle on top so Dan could blow it out, but figured cherries taste better without the wax."

"Good thinking," Kenny said. "You shouldn't overdo this celebration thing anyway, Mom. It's not his birthday after all. I'm still a little pissed that Dan's getting to go to college before me."

"It's only a few weeks," Dan said. "And it's not real college."

"In fact, I'm so bummed, I think I'll join the Marines this fall and skip applying to the university," Kenny said.

"You'll do no such thing," his mother replied in her serious-mom voice. "I've been hoarding money under my mattress for years so you both can go to the U." She shook the serving spoon in front of Kenny's face. "You will *not* be a Marine."

She's got her plans, Dan thought. *Wonder if she knows he's serious.*

"We've got less than two hours to get to the bus station," Mary said, "and the ice cream's melting. Gentlemen . . . start your spoons." They attacked the ice cream with gung-ho élan.

With the bowl half empty and the table a total mess, Kenny waved his hand and muttered. "Time out. Slow down, I'm getting brain freeze. And, Danny boy, I've got an important question to ask before you leave." He wiped his mouth with a sleeve. "If a person on a fast train left St. Paul for Chicago at 120 miles per hour and a jet left two hours later at 600 miles an hour, where would the guy on the jet pass the bus?"

"I hate those questions," Mary said, ice cream melting on her chin.

"It's a trick, Mom. Kenny wants me to say, 'Never.' Real humans don't fly on jets—only rich buggers."

Kenny smiled. "Apparently, Danny, you are actually ready for college. Good luck."

They all agreed that the fast train to Chicago would be too expensive but that they could afford the driverless bus system, even though it would be a

16-hour ride with many stops. So later at the Union Depot, Dan watched Kenny and their mom, his face pressed against the window, as the bus slowly pulled away. His mom was crying, but on his implant he could hear his brother trying to get her talking about other things. He fell asleep at the Minnesota-Wisconsin border. He switched buses in Chicago and again later in Indianapolis, finally arriving in Terra Haute in the early afternoon.

With skyrocketing fuel prices and the carbon tax, Rianne and Joti's flight to Indiana had cost a fortune. But Kyle's legal business, thanks to work with Jeremy and OHMI, was booming, so he never mentioned the expense.

Their jet had just cleared the Sierra Nevada range when Rianne heard his voice. She subvocalized the words "visual overlay" and her father's image instantly appeared through her occipital-lobe implant. She saw his face from the kitchen fridge camera, clearly floating over part of the airplane interior.

"I just wanted to let you know that I already miss you both terribly," he said, "and to be sure you got off okay."

"We're peachy, Father. Mom's reading a book, and I was thinking about watching a movie."

"Look at each other's faces so I can see you both, please." Rianne turned toward Joti and grinned. "You look beautiful," he said. "I feel much better now. Let me know when you arrive in Indianapolis. Love you guys. Bye."

"Father can be quite silly," Rianne said, shaking her head.

"Uh-huh." Her mother had already returned to her book.

Rianne changed her mind and decided not to watch a movie on her visual implant. That device let her see images without a display screen or she could, alternatively, use her eyes as a built-in recording camera. She reclined her seat and shut her eyes.

The engine whine soon faded and she daydreamed. Without help from her implant, her mind began to paint upsetting visions, real nightmares she'd recently had trouble shaking.

She remembered spotting Tina after school, laughing with her new artsy friends near some bushes. Rianne had caught her eye as she walked by and gave a little wave, just raising her hand a bit. Tina looked surprised and hurried toward her as if she'd remembered something.

"I wish you'd stop staring at me," Tina said. "It bugs the hell out of me."

"Sorry, Tina. It's just . . . I hadn't seen you for a while. I know you have some new friends—that's okay."

"I don't think we should hang anymore. You wouldn't like these guys—you're too perfect for them." Tina's voice sounded clipped and excited. "And you're too tight with my mother, the Queen Professor. It makes me nervous. Anyway, I'm not into your science thing anymore—okay?"

"Sure. Whatever. I won't stare, or report to your mother. But I miss your music."

"I quit piano three months ago," she said, sneering as she walked away.

Rianne heard Tina's friends whisper obscenities when they thought she couldn't hear, as they smoked e-cigs behind the bush.

Rianne was surprised. *Vaping, how retro. Tina's right: I wouldn't like her new friends. But what's wrong with her? Her eyes looked . . . so vacant.* Rianne felt crawly.

A robot flight attendant interrupted her daydream by offering drinks, which Rianne declined.

Turning back toward Joti, she said, "Mother, why are most kids my age so stupid? I don't know one kid in L.A. who isn't superficial. And the males are the worst—I'll never, ever, have a boyfriend."

"It's okay to be serious, Rianne. Part of it's because you're an only child. You grew up spending too much time with adults."

"It's worse. I think I might be alien or something. I feel all right, but . . . you remember what I told you about the Torae? They said I was designed by them."

Joti grabbed her hand. "Your dad and I love you just as you are. If that Torae stuff is true, they probably chose you because they know you're smart. Dan and Sarah are like you—advanced for their age. They sound nice. I'm looking forward to meeting them."

Rianne leaned on her mother's arm and tried to think about the trip. She'd soon be with Sarah and Dan, in person, people she really cared about. She thought about what the probe had said. *We're expected to fix humanity—whatever that means. But how?*

Rianne closed her eyes again and thought about her lab work. While Professor Ma and the grad students debated endlessly about exoskeletons and similar minor things, Rianne had forged ahead on her own. She refused to work on anything she considered boring and chose an audacious experiment that both thrilled and worried everyone in the lab. No one had ever tried to make, or even imagined, insects that could communicate, or what they might do if they could.

But lately she'd struggled—too many bio-mistakes. Dozens of deformed creatures had been born before one of her insect-like species survived with complex vocal-tone capabilities. It took over a year to find genes to enlarge the central brain nub so the insect could control its acoustic abilities. And 50 generations passed before her target species actually used the simplest communication skill—click signals.

Half asleep in the jet over Kansas, the nightmare kept replaying, like the video stream from her polycarbonate chamber. With hypermicrophones picking up the coordinated chirps, the infrared recording showed her beetle-like creatures stalking a butterfly. Two beetles overwhelmed the butterfly's sense of smell by copulating upwind. The others hid behind leaves and moved closer until one jumped out and grabbed the butterfly's leg. The circle of intelligent beetles quickly closed and the pack tore the butterfly apart. It horrified her; she'd created highly efficient killer-insects. In disgust, she destroyed all her brainy beetles.

I need to try to make smart butterflies next time. They're herbivores and gentle.

"Welcome to Rose-Hulman Math Camp. You're the first to sign in," the pointy-nosed administrator said. She stood proudly behind her desk in the glass-walled dormitory lobby. "Let's see here . . . Sarah Warner. You're in 319 with Elena Dansk. She's Russian. Just came to the U.S. Not here yet, though.

"You should take copies of the study papers on the desk, dear. Notice both your Number Theory and Graph Theory professors have assigned prereading for the weekend. I'm sorry, hon, but none of the dorm rooms are ready yet. You'll have to wait awhile in the lobby."

Sarah found a corner wall to lean against and pulled her luggage around her. *How did I let Dan and Rianne talk me into this math camp thing? I worked so hard to convince Ma that I forgot to check to see if it made sense for me.*

Her mother hated that Sarah was traveling halfway across the country, alone and overnight, and had called repeatedly during the trip. "Yeah, Ma, I'm at the Washington depot. . . . Yeah, Ma, I'm sure I'm on the right train. . . . Now we're going through Cincinnati right on schedule. . . . I'm walking into the dorm lobby, Ma. Please stop worrying now." *At least she's not sending visuals. I don't need to see Ma's face floating in front of me every hour.*

Sarah waited as the lobby slowly filled; soon it began to reek of sweaty teens and parents. *It hasn't been this hot since the summer of two suns, five years back. Thank goodness that Torae rift shrunk away.*

A few students were arguing about the latest scientific theories on the spatial rift. They all seemed to have theories about the Unity and Torae. *Nerds establishing pecking order. Too bad I can't tell them what actually happened.* A group of Asian kids started playing Go on a coffee table near Sarah. Most of the students had gone outside to wait, but the lobby was still packed with suitcases, backpacks, and people.

Sarah listened to the mother of a home-schooled boy named Devin argue with the administrator about the curriculum, while her embarrassed son juggled colored balls by the window. The mother's East Coast accent didn't mesh well with the administrator's twang. *Like two chickens pecking a dried corncob,* Sarah thought. When the spat ended, the mother hugged her small son, who shoved her away and then tried to disappear entirely.

The parents clumped together to discuss hometowns and compare their children's achievements. Sarah classified the proud, worried, or excited adults by the infrared colors on their faces. They all seemed to be fibbing a little. Math Camp participants had each passed a very difficult entrance exam, but there were no age requirements. The students were generally juniors or seniors from elite science high schools who'd already developed a haughty aloofness. *These kids could become seriously arrogant one day.* At 14, Sarah felt very young.

"Where are you now, Sarah?" her mother's voice asked. "What are the people like?"

"The people are very nice, Ma. If you call me again in the next three hours, I'll take you off level one. Bye."

Stuck in the increasingly crowded lobby for two hours, Sarah began to suspect it was all a plot of the administrator lady to force the students to talk to one another. She met her roommate Elena, who had indeed emigrated from Russia two years earlier. Like the others, Elena, who was 17, ranked among the top 100 math students in U.S. high schools. She was also, in Sarah's view, frighteningly mature and physically developed.

The administrator finally gave the okay, and the students stampeded up the double-helix staircase to their dorm rooms. Sarah pried a window open to let the hot outside air into the stale room and unpacked. Elena put on a dreadfully skimpy bathing suit, flopped on her bed, mumbled something about a fan, and within minutes started snoring. Sarah returned to the lobby to wait for Dan and Rianne.

She recognized Dan immediately as he walked by the window carrying a small suitcase and a backpack. He looked confused but grinned at Sarah as soon as he came through the door.

"Hey, Dan," she said. "You're even skinnier than I imagined."

Dan shook her hand and said, "You're annoying as usual, Sarah."

"I'm not kidding," she said. "You're so skinny even your socks need suspenders."

He glanced down reflexively, past his shorts and bony knees, and saw that his socks did indeed droop.

"You need any help with those suitcases?" she asked. "You want me to show you the ropes? I'm an expert; I've been stuck here for three hours."

"You're not going to be on my floor are you, Sarah? That would be disturbing. Where do I go first?"

"Try the chicken lady's table over there. Don't fret, they have the boys and girls separated. I'm in 319."

Why am I being weird? Sarah wondered.

Rianne arrived 30 minutes later with her mother. Sarah hugged her. Dan shook hands. The three exchanged looks of conspiracy, happy to finally be together, which no one in the lobby noticed.

Rianne's mom, a beautiful, tall biracial woman who seemed very self-assured, wore a light orange dress. Her face was darker than Rianne's, hence her emotions a little harder to read than most. Sarah and Rianne stood taller than Dan, and his voice seemed surprisingly high and crackly. *Probably because he's nervous,* Sarah thought. Rianne had on a touch of makeup, but more importantly, Sarah saw their true face colors for the first time, which hadn't been transmitted over video phones. She read their emotions. Rianne was cool and confident, a lot like her mom, and Dan, with a touch of chicken-feather color by his temples, was indeed very nervous.

Rianne and Dan wanted to rest and recover from their trips, but Sarah had been cooped up too long and went outside to jog. She'd joined her school's cross-country team and now had an urge to run every day. She loped across the campus commons, past a willow-edged pond and the carefully mowed lawns. Crossing a cutesy wooden bridge, she saw some of her fellow summer students at a basketball court. Devin, the boy embarrassed by his mother, was showing off by juggling while riding a unicycle up and down a curb, but no one seemed to be paying attention. By contrast, Elena was watching the basketball game in her swimsuit, making an indelible impression on the teen-age boys just by standing there. Sarah ran past them through the sultry air all the way to downtown Terre Haute, before walking back to campus.

That night, Mrs. Orlov took Sarah, Rianne, and Dan to a Steak 'n Shake for supper and paid for everything. Sarah liked Joti. Unlike the other parents, she never fibbed. She asked about their families and told hilarious stories about her husband's foibles. She also invited them to her hotel for a swim after eat-ing. "It's still muggy outside, and I'd like to know you better before I head back to California."

"Sorry, Mrs. Orlov," Sarah said. "The three of us have been planning for months to get together tonight. We need to talk privately." Mrs. Orlov looked disappointed but seemed to understand their special friendship and secrets.

<hr/>

"I say we crack open one of these weird croquet balls to see what's inside." Sarah was bouncing on her dorm bed, tossing her yellow Torae ball in the air.

Rianne looked horrified. "Are you crazy?" she said. "And be careful with that. These spheres are the only clues we have since the Torae stopped talk-ing. They're probably full of fragile electronic stuff or they could hold an alien microbe. Maybe breaking the ball releases a disease that totally kills life on Earth. The whole thing might be a test to see if we're stupid enough to break it."

Dan sat quietly at Sarah's desk chair. "I think there are other things we should try first," he said. "Remember, I'm the one who packed snow on my sphere to see what would happen. Now that was stupid, but I agree these balls are frustrating. They give little hints, but whenever we ask something impor-tant the sphere says 'Unknown' or stays silent. You know my mom can't afford to buy me a visual implant. I need your help on this."

"We've been over this a dozen times," Sarah said, sitting cross-legged on the bed. "Rianne and I see the same things on our implants that you hear in words: birth of the universe, lots of physics, Torae myth and history, colors and tones."

"Think about what they're not telling us," Dan said. "They mention great civilizations covering galaxies—you both see them on the star maps—and then they're ignored. There's no detail about the cultures, what they're like, or what happens to them. Musical notes keep popping in and shifting. The Torae admit they visited Earth twice, but nothing more."

"Let's see the new interface you've been talking about," Rianne said.

"Is the door locked?"

"Yeah," Sarah said, "but Elena could come back any time."

Dan pulled three extra-wide rubber bands from his backpack, each with electronic chips glued on, and showed Rianne and Sarah how to strap them around the spheres and attach electrodes. "I've scrounged the electrical engineering and astronomy departments at the University of Minnesota. The professors got excited and helped me when I told them about my made-up science project to look at animals and plants in the infrared. They had special chips for broadband sound and visual signals. If this works, Sarah, you'll be able to see all your special colors, not just those on normal video screens. Rianne, you should hear sounds beyond the regular range. I'm expecting the spheres to figure it out and reinitialize your implants. These balls somehow know how we think."

"What do we do first with the ball?" asked Rianne.

"Just call yourself. The phone chips will make short-range links to the optical and sound chips of your brain implants."

A few seconds later, looking toward a blank wall, Sarah said, "Ooh, a river-rock overlay. I think this is working."

"Let's all think about the time the Torae ships left their home," Dan said. "Describe anything you see or hear that's new or unusual."

"The ships are gorgeous," Sarah said. "They're long doughnut shapes, with loopy swirls on their surface. The colors are shades of barn-shingle green. They're leaving now. My image switched to a graphic. There must be thousands of them, all tiny yellow symbols."

"That jibes with the verbal description," Rianne said. "No music yet. Sarah, do you see how the paths curve? That must be some relativity thing. Wait, a green dot just appeared. I think that's their first encounter with another species. Other yellow Torae ships are heading over to look. I hear a really low musical tone now."

Dan said, "Sarah, what do you see? All I'm getting verbally is that they found primitive life."

"Yeah, I hear that too, but now there are dozens of blue and green dots. . . . Hundreds of thousands of years might be passing here. There's an infrared shadow; it looks like a galaxy outline."

"Each time a dot appears," Rianne said, "I hear a low note, but some have awesome overtones. I just got a midtone, a C sharp, did you guys hear that?"

"I heard something," Sarah said. "And look, a whole bunch of ships are heading over to check it out. There must be 20 waiting there. The dot went red. What did the voice say about intelligence?"

"Maybe the music is like a prediction or potential measure," Rianne said. "I just heard an ultrasonic tone for the new red dot. You probably didn't hear it."

"It went barn-shingle," Sarah said, "and it's spreading. Multiple dots now; it looks like a tiny cloud. Dang, it turned gray. What the heck does that mean?"

Dan said, "The audio said that they found other space travelers. Not a clue about the change to gray. Maybe they're just running out of colors."

"Man, the whole chart's blazing in color," Sarah said. "See that? They just hit a huge river-rock cloud on the other side of the expanding sphere."

"Very high pitch there," Rianne said. "Those clouds all just look red to me until they go gray, then the tone shifts down. They must be regressing or something. The graphic is swooping in for a closer view on this side. Very high pitch there."

Sarah said, "I see many Torae craft converging. Something odd is happening; their spaceship icons are dividing. There must be 50 around that cloud now. And it's not red—it's the color of death. The Torae are retreating. Whoa, some gray is spreading into the cloud and it's getting smaller. Now it's gone. I've lost track, but most of the other gray clouds are gone too, I think."

Dan said, "Maybe those places are becoming unimportant, or they're just clearing the screen for us, so we can see new stuff."

"Yeah," Sarah said, "or maybe the Torae are killing those life forms. Did you ever consider that?"

"Let's not jump to conclusions," Dan said.

The images changed scale as the Torae ships moved to new galaxies and distant parts of the universe. Rianne and Sarah described the colors and sounds of Torae history: civilizations flowering and dying, battles engaged, portions of the universe becoming too distant to be seen, and finally a great white hole growing and shrinking near the Torae home space.

"It's the Event, the Torae rift," Dan said. "I'm sure of it."

"Did you notice," Sarah said, "now that they said they're in the Milky Way, that special orange ship symbol is flitting around among all its yellow pals? It's probably *our* Torae ship."

"They just mentioned they're at Earth," Dan said. "What tone did you hear, Rianne?"

"A fairly high tone, barely above your hearing range. I guess that means we have some potential, but they left. Let's try a question. Ask when they left Earth. Are you doing it?"

"Yes," Dan said, "but that's one of the questions they never answer."

Sarah said, "They're heading back to Earth now. Our dot is red. Did the tone change, Rianne?"

"Not that I could tell."

The graphics ended, and the three asked the spheres a dozen questions about Earth but got noncommittal answers or silence.

"I guess the show's over," Dan said. "I used to think the sphere's purpose was to teach us physics and cosmology, but that's not it. They're trying to worry us. I know why I felt scared before—it's all the species they never mention twice, the ones you see turning gray."

"You think the Torae killed all those civilizations?" asked Rianne.

"Who knows?" Dan said. "It's confusing, but they might have just told us there's a high chance we'll become a gray cloud and be erased or ignored one day."

He stopped talking when someone started shaking the door. They threw the spheres into their backpacks as Elena unlocked the door and stepped inside.

She stared at them. "You guys look guilty. What are you mininerds doing in here? Why's the door locked, Sarah? You have some sex-triangle thing going?"

Dan stood up and backed away.

Elena said, "You going to be here long? I'd like to do some homework. You're too young to try the sex thing anyway. But you're not the youngest kids here. Someone named Devin is only 13. A real jerk, near as I can tell."

"We're leaving, Elena," Sarah said. "Don't worry, we'll be old and sophisticated like you someday."

Elena smirked as they stepped into the hallway.

When no one could hear, Rianne said, "Do the Torae really expect us to do something? What if we fail? It's illogical to think we're the only ones they're helping. Isn't it? Why don't they just tell us what to do?"

Dan looked at them both and said, "You guys are wonderful. We'll figure this out. We have to."

Sarah saw Rianne's skin glow in bright infrared hues. *She's blushing.*

Later that night, Rianne lay on her dorm bed, unable to sleep. She whispered through her implant, "Sarah, are you still awake?"

"Yeah, I just switched to worrying about classes tomorrow. Elena's snoring again. What a slob. She hasn't unpacked yet."

"That's not what's kept you from sleeping, is it? It's the Torae. If we fail, we're going to die, aren't we?"

"I think if we fail everyone's going to die," Sarah said.

"Dan knew about this, didn't he?"

"Yeah, he sees ahead more clearly. When we shared the sphere story and talked about the colors and sounds, his forehead had distinct bluish, barn-shingle lines."

"What does that mean?"

"It means he's really scared."

PARTNERS

Laurel whispered subvocally, "Jeremy . . . you still awake?" He was lying next to her on the bed but she used her implant to speak anyway. They often conversed that way—inside their partner's mind—it seemed more intimate. They had been married five years but their passions had not waned. They complemented each other powerfully, encouraging courageous, risky experimentation in their work at OHMI, their diversions, and their love life.

"I'm awake," Jeremy said.

"Have you thought about Goodman's offer to buy us out? It's illegal, you know, essentially offering us bribe money."

"It annoys him that OHMI could end up more successful than LASSO. You've built a great company, Laurel. At OHMI, every employee is respected and given the chance to do something great. Even if we were in charge of a merger, their bureaucrats would eat us alive. I say ignore him, or fight him if necessary."

"Why are you still awake?"

"Thinking about my experiment."

"Are you going to start tomorrow? Maybe you should put it off a week or two."

"No, everything's ready. Dr. Farner is scheduled here early."

"I know your tricks, Jeremy. You picked Farner because he wouldn't question your plans. Does he care if your brain turns to mush?"

"Farner's an excellent technician. He's done all my implants—he's world famous. And you can always interrupt if things heat up with Goodman. Phase three should run about two days and then we'll evaluate how it's going. I'll talk it over with you."

"It's funny," she said aloud, "but I'm more worried by what you're doing tomorrow than by anything the LASSO vultures might have planned for OHMI. I'm sure Goodman won't be able to follow through. The market knows he's inept, and our company is hot. He can't afford the real market price."

"Never underestimate the power of a tyrant, dear," Jeremy said silently. He rolled over to embrace her.

The sentient probes near Earth were relieved when the orange-coded original Sower and her command ship finally arrived to replace the one destroyed in the Unity battle. The probes were not sanguine about mission-level decisions and always deferred to original Torae.

After relaying technical details about the combat with the Unity, Probe Nine described its own emotions in waves of somber, long-wave infrared. "The light flash startled us, but when the atomized particles of our command ship swept over us, we understood the enormity of the loss. It felt like portions of our mind cord had been severed. Eight leader-probes threw themselves onto the binding fields of the Unity cluster, probing for weakness. The probability of success was low, but despair and valor drove them."

"What actions did you take?" asked Sower.

"I had chosen to sacrifice myself as well, but other probes begged me not to."

"You decided correctly. Further loss was unwarranted."

"The Unity cannot harm us under normal conditions," Probe Nine said, "but we are vulnerable while protecting this fragile species."

"What is your current assessment of the humans?"

"Their artificial computer minds are emerging and have already displaced work functions and damaged the social balance. More importantly, the Unity attack and the following time of darkness led to widespread depression. The probability of addictive regression has grown to 69 percent. A dangerous moral-political faction has also developed, increasing the chance of self-destruction to 53 percent. The timelines project a global war. Humans are at risk of slipping away like all the others."

"What of our babies?" said Sower.

"They are nearly mature. We gave them speaker spheres to show them the historical, evolutionary danger. They have no plan."

Sower said, "Have you warned them about the approaching conflict?"

"No."

~~~~~~~~~~

Jeremy had forgotten about sunrises. With an enormous coffee mug in his hands, he watched the orange sunlight warm the mist flowing across the valley outside his window. The gentle color lit the tops of the dense San Marino vegetation poking above the ground fog. While at the university, sunrise had been merely a sign that he'd stayed up too late. Older now and tiring sooner, Jeremy hadn't seen a sunrise in over a decade.

"This is so weird," Laurel said, walking out of the kitchen. "You're actually up early."

This may be the most important day of my life. He refused to let Goodman's machinations spoil the moment. *My experiment is far more important than his threats. Laurel can handle him.* Jeremy drank in the glorious view and the sound of birds as he looked through the 10-meter arc of open, floor-to-ceiling windows while fondling the armrests of his favorite lounge chair. The comfortable brown herringbone, now fraying at the arms, was the single piece of his original furniture Laurel had allowed in the new house. *She does have better taste, I admit.*

He smelled damp air drifting down from thick palm and eucalyptus trees. The valley meandered along an ancient geographic fault line which only permitted glimpses of other mansions behind the heavy foliage. Jeremy didn't know his neighbors and didn't care to. He mistrusted their old wealth.

They feel secure in their hermetic homes, I wager. Surrounded by gardens, statues, and art, confident the efficient San Marino Police will protect them from any unpleasant reality.

The doorbell rang—a security-system image of the man at the front entrance formed in his mind. Dr. Farner had arrived.

"Shut drapes and windows," Jeremy said. Thick folds slowly closed off his outside view. Another command dropped 180-degree view screens around his chair. Laurel led the reliably cheerless Dr. Farner into the room, and he immediately started to examine Jeremy's scars.

"Morning, Doc," Jeremy said.

Farner glanced down briefly but went back to probing Jeremy's scalp.

"I'm going down to headquarters for a while," Laurel said. "Call me if anything unexpected happens. I can be back here straightaway. Incidentally, I drafted a note to Doug last night and said we wouldn't be going to his 'special party.' I said it was a gracious offer but we'll be too busy to attend. Does that seem okay? Would you like to sign it too?"

"Nah, Laurel. You're the boss on those kinds of things. And don't worry—this is phase three, 'Read only.' Me bum might get sore but terminal boredom is the main danger. I'll be fine. Right, Doc?"

"The forehead scar is almost invisible now," Farner mumbled. "I need to check all the hair plugs to be sure there's no infection." The doctor, wearing an eyepiece magnifier, rooted through Jeremy's hair, searching for the fiber optic ports.

Jeremy marveled at how strange this all was. Five weeks earlier, much of his frontal bone, nearly his entire forehead, had been removed with laser cuts and placed in a sterile dish while he watched. It only hurt when the doctor folded back his skin. The slice was mostly within hairlines, and now even the slight scar between his eyebrows was gone.

Someone had to be the first. It's pointless to do this with animals. Pigs don't do concepts—and even if they did, they couldn't tell us about it.

The surgery had taken two hours with Jeremy awake throughout. The doctor had gently pushed 40 flexible squares, each covered with tiny tungsten needles, into Jeremy's frontal lobe. Farner ignored the deep brain folds, but almost 30 percent of the frontal cortex was now covered with electronics. The tungsten needles had, no doubt, damaged some neuronal dendrite and axon branches. That was the risky part. But Jeremy felt fine after a few days.

Phase one was easy. Jeremy simply turned on the implanted interface chips, which then compared signal strengths as his neurons randomly fired. In one day, the locations of over four billion neurons were pinpointed.

Phase two cataloged neuron connections. As Jeremy had explained to Laurel, an individual neuron averages 10,000 dendrite and axon connections, and its firing pattern is like a hundred woodpeckers working on a tree at once. It took OHMI hypercomputers three days to analyze the signal data and uniquely correlate the sources and terminations.

Dr. Farner dabbed disinfectant. "All the ports are clean now, Mr. Read."

"Then plug me in, Doc."

Farner carefully aligned eight fiber-optic bundle connectors hidden in Jeremy's hair.

"You want anything before I go?" asked Laurel, popping back into the room.

"No. I'll need to concentrate on the pictures now, so the computer doesn't confuse the Eiffel Tower with an omelet."

Jeremy considered Laurel the best aspect of his life. She not only loved him but she had also made them both very rich. She'd fashioned a company of enthused, motivated employees. OHMI felt like a large family that happened to own the computer interface to humanity. They produced avatars, the smiling computer faces, that seemed to know what people wanted before they asked. OHMI personalities quickly adjusted to the mood of the user, answered questions, and explained things in exactly the right way for the individual to understand. Competitor avatars seemed like bland and lifeless cardboard.

Anyone who wants their computer system to work well with humans needs to come through OHMI, and the money rolls in our door. Smart device and implant companies all want our software. Laurel and I couldn't spend 10 percent of what we make, even if we tried.

The excess cash piled up in their trust accounts, with portions flowing to legitimate charities chosen by Laurel and the rest to Jeremy's secret causes. He kept Laurel informed about his investments whenever the news mentioned a radical art exhibit or a new drug for Africa. But even he didn't understand all that those murky organizations did.

"I'll watch for 10 minutes," Dr. Farner said, "just to be cautious. You're plugged and ready to go. If everything looks normal, I'll leave. I have an eight a.m. surgery."

"That's good," Jeremy said, while mentally asking the lights to dim. A control box button caused images to appear on the screen surrounding him, alternating with sound. A cognitive research group at OHMI had helped him plan the initial sequence. Phase three, conceptual mapping, had begun.

At first he saw simple figures—circles, triangles, and boxes—and he heard language building blocks in three-second intervals. Every image and sound caused thousands or millions of neurons to fire. Gradually, more complex forms were presented, some with dozens of elemental components. The computer held the image until each neuron-firing avalanche subsided. Jeremy didn't notice when the doctor left.

After a half hour, the OHMI hypercomputers took over the sequencing and ran concept-isolation algorithms. Pictures and videos from Jeremy's childhood began to isolate emotional triggers. Computer databases collected precise neuron locations, usually redundant, for specific concepts. There were gaps, some temporal and image memories were unavailable on the frontal lobe, but the computer did its best. Phase three had been scheduled to last three days, but only the computer would know when to stop. Every hour the images paused and Jeremy got up to stretch.

Around two p.m., the OHMI hypercomputer's avatar appeared on the screen and said, "We've initialized the concept map, Jeremy. Phase three completed much sooner than planned. Would you like to keep going? I know you're eager to reach phase four." The familiar avatar looked about Jeremy's age, like an older brother. It held a quizzical, hopeful expression. Phase four was fairly safe—more of the same really. A richer collection of photos and videos from the web would be fed directly to Jeremy's visual and hearing implants.

The OHMI hypercomputer has 10 times the neural connections of my brain. He probably knows best.

Jeremy had trusted his avatar for over five years; it was his best friend other than Laurel. He said, "Sure, let's go for it. But stop every half hour, please—my brain's getting tired."

RAIDS

With the first day of math camp classes safely behind them, most students were back in their dorms reading or goofing off. Sarah, studying with Rianne and Dan, heard noises in the hall outside her room. "We're raiding Scharpenberg! Anyone wanna go?" someone yelled. They poked their heads out the door to check out the commotion. Five students scuttled by, laughing and carrying large packages of toilet paper. One stopped and said, "We're gonna TP Scharpenberg Hall late tonight—you little dudes wanna help?"

"Sounds cool," Sarah said. "When?"

"We're setting our clocks for three thirty a.m. Everyone should be asleep. Meet us in the lobby then if you've got the guts. We need help to hit both the trees and inside stuff. I've taped a lock so we'll be able to get in the back door. See you."

When they rounded the corner, Rianne said, "Are you insane, Sarah? We can't get involved in such childishness. These guys are away from their parents for the first time and think vandalism is what college is for."

"Oh, try joining the human race," Sarah replied. "Don't you ever do anything for fun?"

Sarah looked at Dan, who made an almost imperceptible "no" movement, and said, "We do need to be alone again where we won't be interrupted. Let's watch the raid from across the pond, so we can talk. Bring your backpacks and meet me just across the bridge at three fifteen."

<hr/>

Rianne and Dan were waiting on the bridge when Sarah arrived. The full moon lit up the whole campus, so they found a secluded spot on a sloping lawn among some willows and evergreens on the far side of the pond. They could watch all three dorms there. The grass felt wet and a few insects annoyed them as they settled in. Crowds of moths circled the lights over by the dorms. Sarah started absentmindedly tossing her sphere from hand to hand.

"Have either of you told your parents about any of this?" asked Dan. "About the spheres or the Torae? I talked to my brother about it, but I don't think he believed me."

"My family just knows that I catch 'em when they lie," Sarah said. "It bugs the heck out of 'em."

"My mother knows," Rianne said. "I've explained it all to her, and she believes me. She's undoubtedly told Father."

"Good," Dan said. "I have a tentative plan. We're not getting much more from these spheres by talking to them, other than going nuts. I think we should cut one open. Rianne, I heard your arguments against altering them, but the Torae said they're identical. If we agree to break one, I'd like to keep mine intact. I have some more experiments to try. What really annoys me is I can't make it talk to my computer. That's important so we can store and analyze the Torae data."

"Maybe it's programmed only for the three of us," Rianne said.

"No, it's flexible. It adjusts. Like when it recognized that you hear a greater range of sounds, it included more tonal responses. I programmed my computer to ask the same questions, but no data transferred."

Sarah noticed flashlights flickering in the dorm windows across the pond. "It must be three thirty now," she said. "The raid's starting."

"Sarah should keep her sphere intact," Dan said. "Because she sees more complete images. I'm sure if she had five-dimensional vision, the sphere would have shown 5D pictures. If we need to, we can ship the spheres to each other."

"I'm sorry, Rianne," Dan said, "but I think you should ask your mother to carefully cut through the shell and analyze the contents at the optics lab where she works. She has all the right equipment there, like fine laser cutters and scanning electron microscopes. There's no rush, but we need to know what's in there. The electronics, or whatever, have to be amazing. It might help us advance."

"And it could be a deadly poison," Rianne said.

"I know," Dan said. "Opening that sphere may be the bravest thing you ever have to do."

Even in the dark, Sarah knew Rianne was blushing again. *She'll ask her mom to do it for him.*

The raid on Scharpenberg Hall was on. One group snuck in the back door while others threw toilet paper rolls over trees. After five minutes, the inside group ran out the lobby door shooting shaving cream in the air. They all made tracks back to Mees Hall.

"Well, that was certainly exciting," Rianne said sarcastically. "Too bad we weren't over there having fun."

"Yeah, yeah," Sarah said. "I think I saw Elena. She's probably trying to absorb some American culture."

"We should go back to bed," Rianne said.

"Let me try once more," Sarah said. She spoke to her sphere, holding it like a microphone. "Hello, Torae. Come in, please. Probe Nine, are you there, or are you off on a vacation? Are you in Bora-Bora or on Venus, on the beach getting a tan?" She looked at Dan. "Do we have to be connected to the spheres to talk to the Torae?"

"Last time, they just talked through our implants," he said.

A deep resonant voice abruptly spoke in her head, causing Sarah to drop the ball. It rolled toward the pond and she had to lurch forward to grab it.

"You may ask questions, children."

Sarah nearly choked. "Probe Nine, is that you? Where've you been for five years?"

"I'm Sower. I speak for the Torae near Earth. Probe Nine has been reluctant to jeopardize the mission by communicating. I just arrived."

"How can you expect us to do something if you never talk to us?" Rianne asked. "I have a question. What happened to the species that went gray on your maps?"

"Most species decline and become unimportant. Do you understand the significance of your task?"

"They almost all disappeared," Sarah said. "Did you kill them?"

"Is that important?"

"Yeah, it's important. What did you do?"

"Actually," Sower said, "97.3 percent make irreversible mistakes of their own and cease to affect the universe."

"Did you kill them?" Sarah repeated.

"Only a few destructive forms."

Dan looked perplexed. "Are we the only humans who know this?"

"The three of you are enough. The spheres will help the transition."

"What transition?" Rianne asked.

"The guiding of your evolution. Human genetic and physical change will soon be much faster, and irreparable shifts will branch off. You could make terrible errors. Most species do."

"If we fail, will we die?" Sarah asked.

"You would become unimportant, meaningless. But if you succeed, you would become transcendent."

Sarah looked at Rianne and Dan's faces in the moonlight and could tell they were frightened. Crooked chicken-feather lines were visible on their temples.

"Unimportant or transcendent, that's just great," Dan sneered. "Why do you even care about us?"

"You have unique reproduction methods. Your mates and babies positively affect social ratios and culture."

"Why don't you just tell us what the 2.7 percent who succeeded are doing," Rianne said. "We'll do that."

"It varies and is highly species specific. If we reveal those examples, you will surely fail. We try to interfere as little as possible."

After a moment, Sower continued, "We must warn you of a more immediate danger—a difficult test for humanity. We project a global war will occur and, unfortunately, you'll need to participate. If it becomes essential, we'll speak again. We're pleased with you, children. You represent your species well." Then, dead silence.

"Wait," Dan said. "What happens if we cut open one of the yellow spheres?"

Only more silence, a few crickets, and buzzing insects could be heard.

"Dang," Sarah said. "Gone again."

They were waiting, hoping for Sower to say something, when Rianne jerked her head to the side. "Someone's on the path behind the trees. I heard them swatting mosquitoes."

Dan stood up and looked but said he couldn't see anyone. "Probably nothing."

Sarah's mind had already wandered off. "Can we be drafted in a war?" she asked.

"I think we're a little young for that," Dan said, "but apparently we have to do something. Too bad Sower went mute again; I wanted to ask about the sphere and how to make it talk to my computer." With a giant yawn, he said, "I'm getting really tired—can we go back to the dorm?"

The bright moon seemed to be following along the Pasadena streets. The pickup's clock read 1:58 a.m., right on schedule. Tina nudged as close as possible to Cory, who'd been rubbing his leg against her while he drove. Occasionally he'd smile at her. Cory and the other guys sitting in the back on logs were all high school seniors. They'd dropped off the first lookout girl already. Now and then, when the truck bounced on the road, Tina could see part of her charcoaled face in the rearview mirror with her hat tugged down. The drug patch Cory had given her had heightened her senses and made the night's mission seem thrilling.

At San Pasqual and Hill Avenue, Cory put his hand on her thigh and said, "Go, woman." She jumped down, quickly covered the license plates, and stepped into the shadows near a large hedge. After checking implant communications, the truck drove a block to the turn at Holliston Avenue. She gave an "all-clear" hand signal and watched the seniors throw the truckload of wood onto the street. It was noisy but took only seconds. The logs had already been soaked with gasoline, but the guys threw a couple more cans on the top. Tina heard a whooshing sound when the pile ignited. The flames soared 40 feet, at least.

Tina figured that by the time the campus police arrived, they'd be safely in the warehouse with the pickup, having its dark watercolor paint removed. *The dumb cops will probably think Caltech won a football game until they remember it's summer.*

They made it back to the garage exactly on time, and 15 minutes later the second pickup pulled through the big door. Stoned kids, everyone high on something, jumped out and howled. "It was perfect! Not a soul saw us. Everyone went to gawk at your fire." Tina hugged her co-conspirators. Cory kissed her. "We sprayed giant letters across the stucco walls of the biolab and got the pillars and statues too. You should see the Day-Glo orange on the lawn; the words must be 100 feet long. We threw the extra paint in the fountain."

The group partied for a half hour before the pickups, now both white, dropped them off at their parents' houses to slink quietly into bed. Tina reached her bedroom without her mother waking up, but there was no way she could fall sleep. The official slogan scrawled on buildings and lawns that night had been "Free the Third World," but she'd told them about her mother's lab and proposed adding "Free the Animals" near there. She hated that building—the great Professor Ma's lab. She was still awake at sunrise, her mind racing.

I need to get more of those patches—what a wild ride.

LOST MINDS

Tina stared at the snapdragons on the table without seeing them, sliding the smooth bottom of a spoon across her lips. The morning sun felt hot on her cheek, and the spoon shook as she lifted cereal and milk to her mouth.

"You'll bring shame on our family," her mother said, pacing behind the counter. "How can you possibly learn if you get so little sleep?"

Tina barely listened.

"It's your only job now: to learn. It's important, Tina! Your future depends on excellence." Her mother leaned on the table and stared at her.

"I've tried to make you a strong woman. But this isn't the first time you've gone off at night."

Tina watched a fruit fly land on the flowers and imagined it was happy. She wanted to scream but didn't have the energy.

"Tina, I want to know what was so important to you last night ... that. ..."

Her mother then fell silent, staring blankly at a wall. Tina guessed she'd just received a call on her implant.

Turning back to Tina, she said, "We'll have to talk later. Do not stay home from summer school today, no matter how tired you are. I have to go down to the lab now—something happened overnight."

Good, you'll see what we useless teenagers did while you were sleeping. Tina smiled to herself and the lecture from her Tiger Mom stopped as Chia-Jean hurried out the kitchen door.

"You're exhausted," Laurel said. "That computer's sucking your brains out. Take a few days off."

Jeremy carefully sipped scalding coffee in their new breakfast nook, trying to wake up. He squinted, but his window view of the San Gabriel hills only looked like a verdant blur.

"It's dangerously fascinating," he said, turning to Laurel. "The software is assembling these strange mosaics. At first, the combinations seemed a bit dodgy, but when I think about them, I see how the computer is trying to distinguish concepts, to separate nuances. Sometimes they're just amazing, like Picasso and the World Web getting drunk together."

She frowned, lowering her eyebrows. "You went on to phase four then, didn't you?"

"I couldn't resist, I admit. The program gives me breaks every half hour, and I walk about the house before going back. I'm being a good boy, but this is exploration. It'll be the world's first point-wise brain map. And the real fun will come when we overlay my neural architecture on the computer. I like to think it'll be much brighter. How long, do you wager, before it demands increased wages?"

"More likely it'll demand gin and ridiculous furniture if it thinks like you," she said, smiling and shaking her head. She looked at his tousled hair and the deep circles under his eyes. "I'm worried about you. Please be careful. I need to hustle down to the office. I'm getting ready to call an emergency board meeting; I presume we'll hear back from Goodman today. Did you catch the news this morning?"

"I haven't brushed my teeth this morning," he said. "I'm delaying all personal hygiene until the afternoon. Anything I should know?"

"It seems some organized vandalism occurred across the planet. Banks, government offices, and university buildings had graffiti scrawled on their walls. Lots of street fires too, apparently as diversions. It happened in every major city in the middle of the night. Some buildings in Old Pas and at Caltech were hit. I have to go. Why don't you drive to the beach and let your brain settle? Do be careful."

Six of Sarah's fellow teenage students lay strewn about on the beds and floor. Even so, her room looked relatively empty with all of Elena's junk moved out.

Devin, the twirpy kid, kept pacing back and forth, angrily gesturing. "I still think if we all threaten to leave, the administration will have to reinstate them."

"It's no use," Rianne said. "All nine kids are gone, or will be by the end of the day. I heard that the program director ordered them to pack up and go to Hadley Hall immediately. I'm sure they're informing parents and guardians and making travel arrangements."

"It's so unfair," Devin said. "If a few parents hadn't been hanging around, I'm sure nothing would have happened. I bet they went ape when they saw shaving cream on the doors. The raid didn't do any real harm; they're treating us like two-year-olds." He kicked a wastebasket under Sarah's desk. "I liked Elena."

You and every other googly-eyed male in this place, Sarah thought. *Actually, Elena was decent and funny when you got to know her. Messy, though.*

"The administration figured it had something to do with the vandalism at other colleges last night," Dan said. "Does anyone know what that was about?"

"My older brother told me it's about drug stuff," a girl said, "but he's a dunce. It's gotta be some political thing."

"That's not what happened here," Dan said. "Any of us could have gone on that raid—we just lucked out."

"Well, I think it sucks," Sarah said.

After griping awhile longer, everyone finally cleared out of her room, and later that afternoon, seeing no better options, Sarah tried to do homework. Digging through her backpack for a notebook, she discovered that her yellow, river-rock sphere was missing. *Did I hide it in the desk last night?* She rustled through the top drawer and then carefully searched the entire room. Frightened and miserable, she called Rianne and Dan to report that her sphere was missing.

~~~~~~~~

Sower knew that Sarah's teaching ball had been taken but wasn't completely sure what to do. *To develop, the humans need to deal with mistakes on their own.*

~~~~~~~~

Jeremy always had two goals for his experiment. One involved applying human brain architecture to computers to organize their learning capacity. *Millennia of brain evolution must be worth something,* he thought, *and my brain should be near the top of the pile.*

His second goal—one he hadn't even told Laurel—was to have the computer show him its world. He wanted to know what vast computing power and memory felt like. His experiments had already given him a small taste. At one point, as he squirmed in his lounge chair with pictures flashing on the screen, he interrupted the planned sequence and demanded the computer show him its most beautiful picture. His visual field instantly filled with shimmering fruit in a bowl, a painting by Cézanne, which he remembered once thinking of as *most beautiful.* As he glanced over the image and noticed some boring corners, the computer brightened the colors, adding shadows and shadings until he unconsciously thought, *that's better,* and then, *that's great.* That was the exception though; mostly he leaned back and passively enjoyed the show.

Around two thirty p.m., the room lights went on and the computer said, "The conceptual map has been optimized. Do you wish to proceed to phase five?" He hadn't discussed phase five with Laurel, the doctor, or anyone except the computer. He knew Laurel would not approve. But the computer and Jeremy had earlier assessed the risks carefully, the greatest danger being addiction. Having nearly unlimited vision and memory might become irresistible.

Looking around him, the large room felt lonely, silent, and empty. *No answers around here.*

He held a clear view of humanity's future. People would eventually merge with the computer, probably by reverse engineering their brains and duplicating them in software. The puny human body, with its narrow environmental range and continual need for food, water, and oxygen, would one day be replaced by a superior, flexible machine guided by human-computer intelligence. People would explore the universe in their new form with few limits. He wanted to be the first to probe that frontier.

Phase five involved linking on the most intimate level. The computer would be allowed to write electrical pulses in Jeremy's frontal cortex, causing neurons to fire there. He would be able to think about ideas, and the computer would understand, prioritize its knowledge, and write it back directly on to Jeremy's brain. Sometimes pictures and sounds might be triggered, but most often the ideas would come back unencumbered—as concept groups or sequences. He expected his brain to feel bigger, like the OHMI hyper-computers, with 10 times a human's capability.

He'd programmed the computer to go slowly at first, increasing data flow through the fiber bundles only as he became comfortable. Eager to start, he called for the shades to close and the room lights to dim, so any images would be as clear as possible. He knew exactly which ideas he wanted to explore. "Let's do it," he said, settling back into his favorite brown chair. "Go to phase five."

He jerked as 100 million neurons fired simultaneously. For a lingering moment, he saw a blazing white light, heard all sound frequencies, and thought 10,000 ideas at once. Then everything went black and Jeremy's mind returned.

"Bollocks! What the hell was that?" He checked to see if the room was all still there. *My brain limits must have been probed—the antiaddiction protocol, probably.* He stretched his shoulders and shook his head. *Computer, was that a calibration ping?*

In phase five, the computer could only respond to questions or requests—another safety measure. Jeremy felt the computer say, "Yes," with feelings of yardsticks, calipers, thermometers, and the idea of limits.

He thought, *Okay, that wasn't a bad response. So tell me, what is the greatest joy?* Simultaneously he had sensations of orgasm, a warm shower, a sunset, accomplishment, and Laurel. He moaned and repeated that question several times before the computer stopped answering.

Why do I love Laurel? Instantly, she was telling a joke and laughing. He sensed her warm, naked body, saw her smiling at him and reaching out to touch his face, and he remembered his own desire to protect her.

Clearly, the computer was pulling his memories, so he asked something he knew little about. *What about future oil reserves and prices?* The computer showed him a dozen world maps from the global grid, barrels scattered around with X marks, and price curves sloping up. It also answered questions he hadn't quite verbalized, a hundred details. Significant implications popped quickly into the nooks of his brain, pulling him deeper and deeper. Jeremy shook his head to break free. *Wow. I might have just created the ultimate personal search engine. With a little more probing about short-term oil price fluctuations I could be rich, well, richer. Let's save that for another day.*

Jeremy thought twice about his next series of questions.

Computer, are you sentient—self-aware? Visions of Kant and complex definitions filled his mind, but he never felt the computer say, "I am."

He heard a bell and a clock image formed with 30 minutes gone. His eyes darted back and forth.

Override session break.

Phase five continued.

<center>~~~~~~~~~</center>

Laurel placed a call to the last OHMI board director from the backseat of her limo. Dark streets whisked by out the window; she'd worked until nine p.m.

"Yes, Arthur," she said, "Goodman actually went public with his offer for a friendly merger at a 10 percent bump. I told him he was daft, but I suppose he wants the board to back me up officially. He's going to look foolish when we turn him down. I suppose he'll say OHMI reneged. Anyway, we'll set up a room-sim link at eight a.m. tomorrow my time. . . . No, there's no reason for you to actually fly out. Thanks for the offer, and thanks for your support on this. Good night, Arthur."

She rubbed her forehead with both hands. *We'll probably receive lawsuit papers early tomorrow. Goodman must assume we'll cave when we see the size of his damage claims. I'll have to warn the board about the legal threat, but they won't override me on this. I wonder if Jeremy was already served the documents at home. It would be nice to have his verbal support during the board meeting. It's strange that he turned his comm off. Probably went out to eat when he got my message about working late.*

"Ma'am," the driver said, "there's something interesting on the news you might want to hear. Someone's claiming responsibility for last night's vandalism."

"Turn it up, Amanda," Laurel said. "I'll listen to that."

On the rear limo speakers she caught a heavily accented voice reading a statement: "We represent the children of the world—the future. There are millions already with us. We aspire to a higher moral level, not the selfishness of the rich or the love of group or nation that the Nazis taught. We aspire only to justice and love for all on Earth, especially the weak. We intend to achieve the sacred teachings of Moses, Jesus, Mohammed, Buddha, and all the holy ones.

"Three things are clear. First, the undeveloped world lives in slavery and poverty because of greed and injustice.

"Second, many of you may have forgotten about the alien warning before the great darkness, the words from space. The Unity told us about the Torae. Remember their words: 'The evil Torae are hidden all around you. Beware.' We, the world's children, are convinced that the developed world's oppressors *are* the Torae, and the Earth was punished precisely because of this inequity. The Unity will destroy us next time if we do not change.

"Third, the global fairness we desire can be achieved through nonviolence. As you saw yesterday, we will find, embarrass, and humiliate the greedy in hundreds of ways until their actions become moral.

"We are the children, the future, and we will not go away. We are the Organization for World Liberation. We are the OWLs."

Laurel froze when the man stopped talking, and then shook her head. "Well isn't that a bloody crock? Where did that announcement come from, Amanda? Did they say?"

"They said it originated in the Czech Republic but was released on all continents at the same time."

Amanda drove the final blocks home slowly along the palm-lined parkway. Laurel and Jeremy's mansion appeared dark as they pulled up the drive. Laurel was anxious to find Jeremy and called to him when she opened the front door. Lights automatically switched on as she hurried through half a dozen rooms. She found him trembling, zombie-like in his chair, still attached to the computer lines.

"Jeremy! Snap out of it!" Grabbing his shoulders caused his head to wobble loosely to the side. Drool ran down his jaw, and she smelled urine. His eyes twitched back and forth under his eyelids. She slapped him and screamed but nothing changed. Then, completely panicked, she pulled fiber bundles from his head with her fingertips, one by one, barely touching them as if they were high voltage lines. When she finished, Jeremy had stopped shuddering and his eyes no longer moved.

Tears rolled down her face as she called Dr. Farner through her implant.

Tina frowned at the face in the mirror and slowly pulled a brush through her thick shiny black hair. The hair stuck out a little and she could feel a distinct bump as she pulled the brush across her scalp. *I hate my sweet, ugly face. How can I be so happy and depressed at the same time?*

She remembered Cory touching her and felt a tingle. *I like him a lot.* Before, she would have pulled away when he bumped her breast. Last night she let him hold it and move his finger around the nipple four times in little circles. She'd been high, so it seemed okay.

Her face kept staring back from the mirror. *My hair is too damn straight. The bump sticks out. Someone will notice. Mother might notice.*

She didn't know how to tell her mother that she was an OWL but she knew she'd undoubtedly figure it out soon enough. Her incessant lectures had calmed down in the three weeks since the big scream fest. Regular school had started; maybe she could avoid her. If she told her the truth, the yelling would start again.

I hate her. All those years practicing piano—not because I could really be a musician—it was just Mother's idea of "excellence." Who cares what she thinks?

The drug patches make it bearable—more than that, wonderful—even blissful. The antidote is built in—painless withdrawal. Sure, I have cravings afterward, but it isn't like heroin or something. It's just a sense of loss, like getting hungry. It's what I am now.

Tina locked her bedroom door. She needed time to think. She opened a bedroom window and turned on an e-cigarette. Nicotine was another yearning—her chemistry had changed. Vaping seemed normal, a biological need, like vitamins.

Cory was the first OWL in Pasadena—if he's telling the truth. He loves me. He could in time. There are older OWLs, even some who are doctors. They've been working in other countries longer.

All the OWL kids were being used—she understood that. With their visual implants, they could spy on anyone. They'd been asked to pass along images of greed. They were the eyes of Justice. The pictures the OWLs sent out were so sad: people starving in Bangladesh, and child slavery in Myanmar, among others. *I wonder if I'll be asked to go to the poor countries someday.*

She inhaled the addictive vapor, held it, and blew carefully out the window. *Mother is one of the selfish ones.*

Cory had told her about the brain-line doctor. "No side effects, much better than the drug patches," he said. "Implants are so routine. Don't worry."

For Tina, it had only taken three minutes. A little anesthetic, a fine laser cut, pop the skull plug, set the implant, feed the wires to the pleasure center, a quick test, reset the plug, laser seal, and done—on to the next person. The first couple of days she wore a cap so no one would notice the bump or see the missing hair.

She turned off the e-cig and hid it under her old piano books. Back at the mirror, her hair still stuck out a little.

I will have to try it sometime. Why not now? Looking at her own eyes, she whispered her programmed password: "Wirelight."

A current-wave rose and fell in the pleasure center of her brain. Pulses and counterpulses surged along the wires. She shuddered and squeezed her eyes shut. For 20 seconds, she held her breath until the electricity stopped. A sweet buzz lingered in every cell of her body. She heard something and realized she was moaning.

She sat, stunned and shaking. *The wire-line is like Heaven! I want to keep doing this. I'll have to learn how to fake normal around other people.*

She retriggered the nirvana current several times in the next 10 minutes while brushing and rebrushing her hair, until she was completely exhausted. Tina stared at her mirror, but her mind was elsewhere.

After two weeks in a hospital, Jeremy was moved back home. Brain scans showed abnormally high activity levels but he was in a deep coma. His only movement was an occasional jerk of his left leg. Laurel hired a private nursing service to look after him. He required intravenous feeding, physical therapy, and around-the-clock care.

Kyle, Joti, and Rianne visited often throughout the autumn, mostly to support Laurel, who grieved for Jeremy as if he'd died. As the months passed, she told them how lonely it was without him. They listened for hours and cried with her.

She managed to run her company mostly from home, fighting off the take-over bid, but the anxiety tore her apart. One time in the kitchen, Laurel told Rianne that she had never been so scared. Before leaving, Rianne walked up to Jeremy, who was twitching in his favorite chair. She kissed him gently on the cheek and said, "Jeremy, what have you done?"

TIME FIVE
ELEVEN YEARS LATER

CYLINDER

The Torae loved subtle, decisive action, a gentle nudge to enrich a civilization or to topple it. Pruner, on the ship that was coded violet, had been designed to choose among millions of options to find the perfect destructive feather.

Twenty years expired on Earth while they chased down the largest swarm of Unity black holes, approximately 9,000 vehicles. As they approached their quarry, they were astonished to see the Unity swarm coalesce into a tight, rapidly rotating cylinder. Sower had previously conjured up four million strategies for Pruner to work with, each with consequences, tactics, and probabilities. Most were suddenly worthless.

How did they know we were here? How can this alignment be stable? Why did the life signs disappear? Fortunately, Pruner had time and patience—Tiller would have simply attacked. Their ship remained masked. "There's a significant intellect here. We shouldn't underestimate the Unity."

Pruner discarded previous plans, backed off, and spent three Earth years studying the Unity and preparing new weapons at a safe distance. The Unity seemed to be the opposite of the Torae—pure brute force. Probes illuminated the cylinder from multiple directions and at multiple frequencies, and Pruner learned by what light disappeared from the profound shadow the Unity produced. The three-centimeter cylinder formation of tiny black holes had a total mass equal to 50 Earths. Its highly charged black holes rotated at relativistic rates, creating immense magnetic fields that held them apart. This large swarm implied a full-scale colonization, and the probes extrapolated their destination, a white dwarf star 10 light-years away. Unity creatures were obviously hiding within the protective cylinder.

Sower tried to help by inventing roughly three new plans each second. "You're no longer being helpful," Pruner said, with a pointed ultraviolet chirp. "I don't need nuances on your nuances."

Pruner had already decided, against all his normal instincts, to match the Unity power. He constructed a new engine core and used two Earth years to fully charge it at a nearby star. The engine would surround the Unity cylinder, instantly releasing the stored energy at the focus and shredding their defensive cylinder formation. Their Torae command ship would be far away when this happened.

The engine-weapon had now matched velocity with the cylinder and waited only for an order to attack.

Then the unexpected happened, not high on Sower's long list of possibilities: a lone Unity vehicle, teeming with life, popped out of the cylinder and drifted slowly toward the Torae weapon, threatening to trigger it prematurely. The situation shuttled through the minds.

Assess—create—decide—act.

Probe—Sower—Pruner—Tiller.

In microseconds, probes fired warning plasma beams, which bathed the creatures in colors. The word "Stop" was broadcast on every relevant wavelength.

The black hole continued to drift. A Unity voice said, "Ancient ones, please! We know you intend to end our existence. Explain our offense. A noble species would grant that much. Speak to us."

Pruner faced 50,000 Unity, now using perfect intergalactic diction, as well as a barrage of data from probes and annoying new options from Sower. Pruner pulled the engine-weapon back, maintaining separation.

"Your proliferation threatens the life span of this galaxy, and others," Pruner said. "You cannot alter the urges that drive your migration. Our projections show that your species will become *star eaters.*"

"You are wrong, Torae. This journey is repulsive to us. Our deep memories tell of lavish joy in the One-Mind of our home star. That is where we wish to be. We migrate to only a few distant stars, to avoid extinction from supernovas or other disasters."

Pruner hesitated briefly, contemplating the Unity word One-Mind. "The universe is dying," Pruner said. "All old life understands the dissipation. You waste priceless energy and mass creating worthless black holes."

The Unity spoke boldly, realizing the words might be their last. "We are not a danger. Your ancient species is arrogant. Only the Torae would dare fashion the white fountain we saw. You nearly destroyed the universe by creating new space and time. Our Home Star of Wisdom will resist you."

"The Torae will save existence itself," Pruner said. "Worthy life will someday travel through another space-time rift, a white fountain, to a new universe. Worthy life will survive forever. The Unity will not pass through that opening."

Pruner then ordered Tiller to act. The Torae engine-weapon maneuvered to envelop the cylinder before it could respond. Two years of stored stellar energy ripped at the Unity tube, dislodging the spinning black holes. Gravitational and rotational locks buckled and the black holes fell into each other. Event horizons merged, sending staccato gravitation-quakes in all directions. Accelerating away from the cylinder at nearly the speed of light, Pruner watched the flashes of thousands of nuclear fusions while his command ship shook in the gravitation pounding. Over 100 million Unity died.

Long after the gravity waves subsided, Pruner, Sower, and Tiller discussed the potential of the One-Mind on a teeming Unity home star. Its intellect would be vast, unique, and evolving rapidly. The Torae had never encountered anything so dangerous. Pruner knew the warnings they sent to their sister ships would arrive too late.

SARAH'S LIST

In Old Town, Prague, Sarah stepped past her hotel door onto a chilly sidewalk, saw her breath swirl, and pulled on leather gloves. The setting sun dazzled off the wet road to the river, pushing the Romanesque storefront recesses deep into shadow. Prague was a new city for her, but she enjoyed the unfamiliar. She strode confidently into the glare.

While walking, she tugged a felt hat over her ears, which spoiled the sophisticated European look she'd been working on, as well as her new hairdo, but the air had an icy bite. Her new shoes clicked on each quick step, and her highland-tweed coat made whooshing sounds. A few Czechs and tourists glanced sideways as she passed on the sidewalk.

She strongly preferred tattered jeans, but her glamorous new job demanded more. She would never look attractive, she thought, but elegant was within her grasp if she worked at it. After breaking two remarkable stories, her status had jumped dramatically; without those stories, she'd still be doing lifestyle gossip for US Web News. At 25, radiating self-assurance, her career had been fast-tracked.

Her stories had been about implant addicts—the wire-heads. The first article skewered the police for ignoring the problem, under the headline "Abandoned Lives." The cops rarely even spotted users until they found them in dark rooms happily starving or already dead. Bad wires were a problem. Many tattoo parlors, singles restaurants, and gaming conventions had hidden back rooms where amateurs inserted the thin electrical lines. Placed in the wrong brain site, the person would abuse and sometimes go mad. Only the OWLs had done the research and guaranteed safe procedures.

Too many people disappeared. The police couldn't keep up, so they quit trying. After her story was published, the problem became a front-page national scandal and Sarah was "known."

She then produced a touching documentary about the young users she found in derelict tenements, suburban bedrooms, and college dorms.

". . . They told me about their childhoods and their old plans. I watched in dismay as they whispered their secret words, always whispered as if people wouldn't notice, and saw their eyes open wide and their minds go blank. Intelligent—even brilliant—students, who moments earlier had been in lucid conversations with me, went empty, slipping off to a destructive nirvana."

Sarah couldn't mention her own secret, that she also saw the infrared colors of their young faces change from vibrant warmth to a clammy barn-shingle gray as their blood vessels contracted.

She always video-cast her stories, staring poignantly at the web cam. People told her she had kind, confident eyes, and that they trusted her and often wept as they listened. They all knew someone who'd disappeared. When the *Post* picked up the syndication, she became modestly famous. A million social shares spread her face to the world. Her wire-head stories were called "Lost Minds."

US Web News promoted Sarah and transferred her to a hard-news group. She hinted about an OWL conspiracy—an international story she'd uncovered that was politically hot. The OWLs planned something devastating, she had told her editor. He gave her two months and a nearly unlimited expense budget; he didn't want to lose a potential star. But he warned her, "Don't screw it up, Warner."

She'd celebrated her 25th birthday alone on the flight to Europe. She'd done a few interviews already. Prague, at the heart of the Bohemian basin, was Organization-for-World-Liberation central, and Sarah knew the OWLs had people watching her every move.

At the Charles Bridge, which sported a fresh coat of slush, she stopped abruptly and turned to see if anyone behind her flinched. No one reacted. Many wore battery-heated scarves that protected their faces from the hard wind blowing downriver, making it difficult for her to identify the OWLs. At the airport they'd been easy to spot because drugs or wire implants tinted their face colors toward barn-shingle. *I bet 20 percent of Prague's young people are OWLs,* she thought to herself.

The city's medieval bridges, castles, church spires, and dark hills cast time-less shadows in the sunset, and the huge statues along the bridge glowered silently. She stopped at the likeness of Saint John of Nepomuk, his sad eyes pleading toward Heaven. He'd been tossed into the river in 1383 for refusing to tell King Wenceslaus details of the cheating queen's confession. *It's risky knowing too much, John. That's my problem too.* She checked her implant for the local time. *Elena should be waiting at the west end by now.*

Only two names remained on Sarah's special list—Elena was one of them. She hated that she still hadn't discovered who stole her Torae yellow, river rock ball and was determined to find out. Elena had been kicked out of math camp the day the ball disappeared, so she was a prime candidate. Dan had discovered amazing technology in the ball that Joti cut open. Although the Torae were still ignoring all questions, Sarah desperately wanted hers back.

She kept tabs on all the math camp kids, periodically publishing a cheery newsletter noting addresses, social events, colleges, and career status changes. A few interviews were always included, probing deeper than typical blog info. The math camp kids were an exceptional lot—most had been accepted to every university where they applied. They enjoyed Sarah's letters and sent her their personal information. One by one, she visited them, asked about the missing yellow sphere, watched their face colors for lies, and checked them off her list. Her OWL research assignment created an opportunity to call on those in Europe.

Sarah squinted as the setting sun peeked from behind the castle. "Hello, Elena," she said. "It's you behind the scarf, right?"

"*Ahoj,* Sarah. Ja, it's me. Welcome to Praha. Looks like you grew up. You were so tiny at math camp—you and your friends."

"Dan and Rianne are both at Princeton now," Sarah said.

"Ja, I know from your newsletter. Let's get out of the wind. We're meeting friends of mine. Just a couple streets. A place I know."

Elena had typical OWL eyes—restless and distracted. *It's sad to see a smart person like her look that way, but good for my story—another chance to check my facts.*

They walked down bridge stairs, along the cobblestone riverfront, and stepped through a pub door. The air inside had an oily odor, thick and tight. It was a smoky old place with black wood, brownish-orange lights, rounded ceilings, and a dirty tile floor. They hung their coats on wall pegs. The patrons, mostly men, stared at her. *Should have worn old clothes*, she thought.

"Sarah, this is Josef and his friend Marina. They've been saving a table." Several beer bottles sat open in front of them.

Marina looked around the room as Sarah and Elena sat down. "Do not mind the locals," she said. "They think they own Praha. They will stop looking at you soon. You're too pretty for this place."

Sarah glanced over her shoulder and several men slowly averted their eyes. Most were OWLs, or just had grim, grayish expressions. One man, with a dirty short beard, was spinning a coin on the table while continuing to stare directly at her.

"Maybe they're ogling your sweater, Elena," Sarah whispered. Elena looked even sexier than she remembered. Elena just laughed.

"The food here is good," Josef said. "Have you eaten? This *vinárna* has excellent *jitrnice*, eh, white sausage, and the *palačinky* is good."

"I'm hungry," Sarah said. "Would you order me some typical Czech food and a beer—whatever you're having? I'll pay; I'm on an expense account."

Elena ignored her friends and leaned toward Sarah. "I swear I never expected to see you again. After they kicked me out of math camp—how stupid was that?—I studied at Columbia and the secret code guys, the NSA, recruited me. I couldn't mention that in my letters to you. They love math freaks like me. But the NSA never gave me any juicy projects, being foreign, so I left."

"How'd you end up here?" asked Sarah.

"I felt, um, distracted in America, and a bit out of place. Russia's terrible now—too much crime. Prague's better, but learning the language is difficult. I'm working at OWL computer operations—more numbers, none of their fun political stuff."

Sarah got Elena to ramble on about the Prague lifestyle, her family, and memories of Russia. Her friends at the table looked increasingly intoxicated, or high on something. Every so often they'd hold their breath and become nonresponsive.

A waiter soon came with heavy platters of food and hurried off. A large white sausage dominated Sarah's plate, and she bounced her fork on it. "What's actually in this?"

"Don't ask," Elena said.

Josef looked up and smiled. "*Buon appetito!*"

"So what do you personally think of the OWLs, Elena?" asked Sarah, warily testing her food. "For my story, I've already visited staging areas where they gather the volunteers, foodstuffs, and other resources. I just got back from Bangladesh, the flood plains, and some Indonesian factories. The families there adore OWL workers. Their countries are slowly being flooded, every-one constantly moving to higher ground, but they have food and many solid jobs with the OWLs. I'm touring European centers now to understand the coercion strategies being used on rich people. You don't have to tell me any company secrets, Elena, but what do you think? How many OWLs are here anyway?"

"I guess there are about a million in the Czech Republic and maybe 30 mil-lion worldwide. Are you thinking of joining? It's not a company, you know. You can just be an associate—send money—or help in other ways."

"I know. My mother does a lot of that. She contributes to all kinds of char-ities. The OWL's third-world relief seems to be doing a lot of good. But what about the vandalism and fear campaigns?"

"Ja," Elena said, "but someone had to embarrass those rich bastards. Most just inherited their money. They only care about themselves. That's not the way things should work." Elena unconsciously strangled a beer bottle, rotat-ing fingers around the neck. "What are you going to say in your story?"

"I don't know about Prague, but everywhere else, I sense the OWLs are frustrated. Their plans aren't working fast enough. Wealthy people are just building higher walls around their mansions. They're starting to ignore the whole thing."

"That's true. It's arrogance. Something's got to break soon."

When dessert arrived, Sarah talked about how she majored in both com-munications and physics at Valparaiso University. And then how she was hired at US Web News after a year of journalism graduate study in Munich.

"I'm astounded you returned to Indiana after math camp," Elena said, lean-ing back in her chair and stretching her sweater. "Beer and basketball—that's all there is there."

"The people are super friendly and it's a fine school," Sarah said, with her mouth full. "Hey, these pancake things are great!"

Her exuberance caused a slight reaction nearby—several men in the pub glared at her and Elena again. She looked directly at the man alone at the next table, still spinning his coin. He didn't look away. *Normal eyes. Not an OWL? Just a lech?*

Elena's friends had been almost silent through the entire meal — off in their own worlds. After the food and a couple more beers, Josef said, "American lady, you want an OWL patch? I have several kinds."

"Josef! Ignore him," Elena said. "He's an idiot."

Could break the ice, Sarah thought. "I've interviewed about 80 OWL people," she said. "Learned everything about them I could. But I've never tried one of the famous patches. I understand a time-release antidote is built in. Maybe I ought to check it out so my story's complete."

"You shouldn't, Sarah," Elena said as she glanced around the room. "They're fun and no hangover, but you might forget everything we said by tomorrow morning. It wouldn't be good for your story."

"I give you excellent patch if my name in your story," Josef said.

"Give me one, Josef. It's for my job."

Sarah stuck the small patch behind her ear. Her skin began to itch almost immediately. "Tell me, did the OWLs get their start right here in the Czech Republic?"

"I'm not positive," Elena said, "but I think so."

Elena seems more relaxed — or resigned. Time to go to work.

Sarah risked more probing questions and watched their face colors. Where were the OWLs headquartered? Had they moved out of Europe? Who was really in charge? Were they losing momentum? Would they become even more violent?

Elena never fully responded or said she didn't know, but Sarah learned a lot from her reactions and face colors. Several gaps in her OWL research fell into place.

The itching under the patch subsided, but her skin felt warm; the pub seemed smaller and more crowded. People weren't watching her anymore, but the complexions of those nearby tinted after each of her questions. They were listening. Out of the corner of her eye, the patrons seemed to have river-rock glows. The candlelight shimmered oddly.

"Elena, how'd you get recruited by the OWLs? Do you have a lover now? What is he like? Why did you go on that math camp dorm raid? Do you remember a yellow ball I had in the dorm room? Did you take it by any chance when they booted you out? It was very dear to me."

Elena's wool sweater pulsated. "I don't remember any ball."

Sarah had seen the colors of a thousand lies — Elena was telling the truth. The ball held the secrets of an alien race, and the Torae had told her to not lose it. She wondered if Sower was angry with her. Elena didn't have it. The entire room wobbled and Josef's nose glowed in a shade of river-rock. Sarah felt giddy, hyperalert, and started giggling at her own questions. *Elena is telling the truth.* Sarah saw a thousand colors no longer tied to physical objects and felt truly happy. The bearded man at the next table nodded toward her. She vomited on the floor.

The next morning she awoke in her hotel room with no idea how she'd gotten there. The patch on her neck was gone and there were signs the room had been searched—little things moved. That was to be expected from the OWLs. Using the patch got her the information she really needed, and she now understood how it could become addictive. *I'll never do that again.* She remembered most of her questions from the night before, the faces, and that Elena hadn't taken her sphere.

Still one person on my list to visit, but the OWL story is done. Just need to sit down, write it, and figure out who in the government should see the terrifying parts before I give it to my boss.

Chia-Jean grabbed her doodles, left her office, and walked to the elevator. She needed a break. At the fourth basement level, a security guard greeted her at the sealed pressure door.

"Still working, Professor Ma?" He received a sleepy nod in reply.

Cool air blew over her bare arms when the door opened, giving her goose bumps. She shivered while walking down the long, sterile maintenance hallway. At the main laboratory entrance, "3.00 a.m." showed on an entry panel. Her thumb pressed the fingerprint detector and three guards watching her remotely on displays flicked lock-release switches. Air hissed again at the final, double-pressure doors before she zigzagged in silence among row after row of dim specimen cases, each teeming with small, bizarre life.

In a side room, a startled post-doc said, "C.J., what are you doing here so late?"

"My mind's been drifting in circles about telomeres. I just came down to watch the butterflies awhile—it relaxes me."

"You want to talk about it?"

"No, thanks. Maybe I'll ask the butterflies. They're probably smarter than I am right now."

She sat on an observation stool by the four-meter butterfly chamber and leaned her head against a window. Fluttering and intricate yellow patterns almost surrounded her. She nudged the sound amplification up to hear their simple voices. The intelligent, vocal butterfly-like creatures could be almost hypnotic. She remembered the day 14-year-old Rianne had started her brain-nub experiments, clutching a chart with dozens of gene tweaks she wanted to try, and slowly it worked—the butterflies got smarter. She was such a young kid, with a ferocious drive and intellect. She also recalled the sad day Rianne left for Princeton.

Chia-Jean looked down at her scribbles and tried to refocus with the highly amplified sounds of over 3,000 butterflies as background music. They used a chirp frequency language with plain words like "follow," "food," "danger," and "return." Over the years, dozens of visitors and researchers had come to study the creatures. The felt-tip-scrawled sign of the young girl was still propped up in a chamber corner: "Rianne's Butterflies."

Chia-Jean drew shorthand DNA sketches on a pad. *Immortality—that's the goal. Concentrate. Picture the hundreds of related proteins and enzymes as a whole. Increasing the telomere number alone didn't help much. We tried that. Senescence—how does the division process affect life span? How do the mitochondria regulate aging? Cancer, cell splitting, differentiation, life span—they're all linked.*

As the purr of the butterfly music shifted, their flight patterns changed. They flew in yellow corridors through the chamber, crisscrossing, like ants following scent lines, but in three dimensions. Everyone from highway engineers to futurists had come to watch the patterns. The butterflies had solved engineering and city planning problems that were quickly becoming more important with thousands of drones delivering packages and personal helicopters becoming popular.

Chia-Jean gazed at them, eyes unfocused. "What's the answer, little yellow ones? What's the secret of life?"

I'll end up like Einstein, spending the last years of my life on an impossible problem. He tried to unify physics, but his pieces couldn't fit. I'm going to end up alone and frustrated too. Or worse, I'll solve it on my deathbed—the secret to immortality—but too late to use it. I'll just have time to scribble in the margin of a book before I die, leaving out the final crucial step. That would be poetic.

The butterflies spiraled down to the food trays, drank, and flew off, beautifully coordinated. Chia-Jean moved a tray with a manipulator and watched the flight paths realign. The lines would cross but never break unless a predator was inserted. In that case: butterfly panic.

Chia-Jean recalled another late night when she'd come to unwind by watching the butterflies. The police had made it clear they would no longer search for Tina. "Your daughter has disappeared—she's lost," they said. "Very few who try the brain-line ever come back." When she was alone, she closed her eyes and saw Tina and Rianne playing together in the lab playpen, and broke down. "All I have now is my work and my ridiculous, impossible goal," she told the butterflies.

She covered her eyes and sobbed again. *I'll grow old and die with no family. No Tina.*

There was a buzz, and she heard the graduate student coming toward her. Chia-Jean quickly wiped her eyes with a sleeve.

"There's a call on the restricted phone, Professor. They will only talk to you. Will you take it?" Then, focusing on her, he said, "Are you okay?"

"Yes, just a minute. It must be important or they wouldn't call at this hour."

The man on the phone said, "Professor Ma, I am calling from Stockholm. Sorry to disturb you, but we wanted you to know you've just been awarded the Nobel Prize in Biology and Medicine."

After a moment, Chia-Jean said, "For what?"

"Let me read it. The official citation says, 'For discovery of the first non-DNA-based life and the elucidation of evolutionary processes leading to numerous medical and biological applications.' Congratulations."

"Well, thank you."

She physically shook as she disconnected.

<hr/>

With the covers pulled aside and only wearing a nightshirt, the morning sunshine flowed across Laurel's body as she lay in bed. Her arms and legs stuck straight up in the air, moving slowly, like a beetle that had fallen on its back and couldn't right itself. Occasionally, she'd hammer at the air with her eyes closed.

She was in a full-body life-sim, climbing K2 in the Himalayas, with Matt on the rope above her and Jeremy coming up behind. The OHMI game images sped to her occipital neurons through wireless links—a perfect visual simulation of the actual mountain. Her actions were noted in tiny sensors implanted at key bone joints. Sleeves along major nerves altered muscle group contractions. She worked very hard to fight artificial sim-gravity. Sweat dripped onto the bed.

Matt helped pull her up a final ledge, and they waited, exhausted, while Jeremy caught up. The three set up Camp V; they were still six hours from the top. They secured the simulated tents, stored equipment, cooked, and drank tea with only clipped, soldier-like dialogue.

"Dried fruit?"

"Yeah, thanks."

Laurel saw an image of menacing, snow-covered ice sloping up to the final limestone cone. A blood-red sunset colored the snow. *Maybe the sim will give us a clear view from the top.*

Parts of the sim were unrealistic. She heard wind but couldn't feel the cold. Oxygen deprivation was not an issue. Lying in a tent between two husbands, one dead, the other in a coma, slowly making love to one while the other snored—impossible on so many levels. But the sexual simulation was excellent; she had microimplants in all the right places. No need for a wired latex bodysuit anymore. She usually chose Jeremy.

The simulation ended, her Saturday morning diversion and workout complete. Bedroom and reality slowly returned. She pulled off the bedsheets. Dozens of mundane problems hadn't gone away: brushing her teeth, vandalism in San Marino, oppressive heat, global antitrust lawsuits, Goodman asking her to help save the remnants of LASSO, managing her NGO charities, the responsibilities of being officially the third richest woman in the world.

And the long horror remained. She walked to where Jeremy's emaciated body rested, immobile, on his lounge chair. She rolled him to his back, raised the chair-back for the day, kissed him, checked the IV lines, and opened the drapes. Doctors agreed he wouldn't last much longer. His face looked concentration-camp thin, and the circles around his eyes like deep bruises. Every day she worried she'd kept him alive in a 10-year nightmare and begged him to recover or die soon. An immense sadness and loneliness swept over her, as it had so often.

But there had been progress. *Sure, he's still in a coma, but he can hold his eyes open a little if I help. The erections—almost a month now—that's a good sign. I must do something soon; my biological clock is at midnight. I would still have a part of him to love. I'm sure he'd say okay. I have to do it—before he dies.*

From his window at the Cavendish Labs, the young professor squinted at a woman in a fashionable long coat hiking along the Coton Footpath. On an atypically bright, cold day in Cambridge, the sunlight glanced off Payne Pond directly at his eyes.

Sarah Warner ... I barely remember her from math camp. That must be her coming around to the visitor entrance. Probably should have told her to bugger off when she asked for the interview, but her OWL articles have been quite perceptive, almost as if she had cell-level clearance. After we talk, I'll know if she's a serious enemy.

Clever women angered him; they reminded him of his mother. He nudged a chair over a bit so the sun would be in her eyes. It was several minutes before the laboratory secretary escorted her to his office.

She flashed a professional smile. "Hello, Devin ... uh, Professor. Thank you for seeing me. I appreciate how busy you are."

"Come in. Why again are you visiting England?"

"I'm doing a story about the OWLs, but I made a side trip to Cambridge to see you for other reasons. I've tracked part of the OWL hierarchy to the U.K. It's a big mystery, you know. No one's discovered the names of the actual OWL leaders—it would be prime-line news if I could find them. No luck so far."

"Right. Well, I'll wager you'll not find those delinquents in Cambridge. Why did you wish to speak to me?"

"Partly just to reconnect before you become too famous. You're on track for the Lucasian Chair, I understand. Your corrections to the unified theory were brilliant, making it seem almost simple and beautiful. You'll be a big story someday, maybe the next Stephen Hawking or Isaac Newton. I'm a reporter after all, and I hope you'll allow me to visit from time to time. Did you know you were the only person younger than me at math camp?"

"I was aware I was the youngest." He stood and paced by the window, seeing how the sun distracted her.

"How'd you end up at Cambridge?" she asked. "Tell me about your family, your antigravity theories, and things like that. Do you still juggle?"

Do all women become complete nutters? Their minds must atrophy when they reach childbearing years.

"Ms. Warner—I take it you're not yet married—I came to earn four stars in an English senior school to ensure acceptance, at age 16, to Trinity College. I'd always wanted to study here after I saw the alumni list. If there'd been a

Nobel Prize in the twelfth century, Trinity would have 400 by now. I hope to add to the number.

"My wife, whom I met while working on my PhD, is expecting our second child. However, I consider my family private and prefer not to hear about it in the webloids.

"And, my antigravitation theory is merely one solution set for the field equations, at least for micro–black holes."

She frowned.

Amusing, she's bothered by my children. Only mid-20s and she is already frustrated. Females have a bio-need for children—men can choose. Or, she might have grimaced when I mentioned the antigrav work. But she can't know any serious physics. No one here has seen the flaw.

"You're right," Sarah said, "I'm not married—not even seeing anyone—too busy with my work. Your antigravity idea is fascinating, though. Will we be in flying cars soon, or should I hang on to my plane ticket back to the States?"

"I doubt you'd appreciate the details, but it might require a new type of universe to achieve the effect."

She's staring at me, smiling like Mother, only I know Warner's smarter and more devious.

"I recommend you hold on to your tickets," he said. "When will you be leaving?" *Perhaps she'll get the hint.*

"I've some other friends in Cambridge, then back to Washington in a couple of days. Look, I didn't mean to bother you. I have one more question. When we were at math camp in Indiana, I had a special ball. It was yellow—about the size of a croquet ball. It wasn't mixed up with your things when you left, was it? It was very precious to me."

Damn, I forgot it was her ball!

"I don't recall any yellow ball," he said, smiling. "I'm sure I'd remember it." He stepped toward the door.

Sarah clearly understood his gesture: the interview had ended. She also knew where the yellow ball had gone.

After leading her to the lab entrance and enduring her persistent chatter, he returned to his office and thought about the woman.

She smiled too much—irritating. And she is an enemy—a bloody serious enemy. The artifact was hers at one time. Could she know its secrets? She's clever. I'll have to deal with her.

He stuffed a leather satchel with work papers. Initiating a location tracker on Warner would be safer from his off-campus facility. Walking slowly past the hall display cases, he thought about the great history of the laboratory, Maxwell's equations, Thompson's electron, Crick and Watson's DNA code, and all the rest. Sadly, one day soon, he'd leave and not return.

But his primary interests were no longer at the Cavendish. Living, sentient computers were why his name would be honored above all those in the display cases. The Cavendish was a simple day job. Physics was easy when you had the answer key. He opened his satchel, took out the yellow ball, spun it in his hand, and juggled it as he walked.

His OWL command bunker was only a short drive away and the war was drawing near.

KRISTALLTAG

Who picked this annoying organ music? Sarah squirmed as discreetly as possible in her tight lace dress. *It itches! And I hate this red-pink color.* She needed to focus, but her mind kept drifting.

Try to stay awake, at least 'til the wedding ceremony's over. I'm so tired, hibernation-level tired. How late did I work on the OWL story last night—four a.m.? I caught the jet from D.C. at eight. Arrived in Minnesota at nine thirty. Fishtailed while driving on the freeway ice, nearly killed myself. Should have taken an autotaxi. Lucky I even got here on time for the wedding. But my report's out. Wonder how many government agents are scurrying around back in Washington after they saw it. They have 10 days to prepare.

Reporters carry white flags, don't they? We're neutrals—noncombatants. I might be safe. No, probably not. Devin nurtures his hatreds. He won't ignore me. And in Prague—who knows what I said after I took that patch. The OWLs won't overlook a meddlesome journalist.

The clergyman, smiling too broadly, started his homily. Jagged colored light streamed everywhere, crisscrossing the altar. Sarah glanced around. Stained glass covered 20 percent of the cozy church walls.

Aren't they supposed to build churches on stone or something? What if people threw rocks? Build your house with bricks—that's what the three pigs say. Why am I worrying, in clichés, about a church?

I'm just nervous. When the fajitas hit the fan in 10 days, they'll try to kill me. My parents will need protection too.

The small crowd made squeaking noises, shifting in their pews. *They're eager for the big finale, no doubt. There's an awful lot of joy hovering in here today.*

Rianne's vintage-lace dress looks beautiful, the eggshell white painted by the sunbeams from the stained glass in orange, barn-shingle, and green. Her face practically radiates river-rock bliss. She always gets what she wants. She's wanted Dan a long time.

I love him, too, of course—look at him. What woman wouldn't love him? He's tall and wiry, strong, and kind. Potent will. Dan could rule the world someday.

Rianne nudged her, rather hard, and whispered, "Take the bouquet now, Sarah. Try to stay alert, please."

Rianne loves him more. And she's such a beautiful, exotic woman. Her dark eyes, hair, and intensity frighten people but draw them closer, like moths to a flame. I'm so plain and flat. It's good I've been . . . preoccupied. Too busy running around the world. Dan's brother Kenny, he's a real hunk, and he's been peeking at me. Maybe I should get to know him. Looks great in the black tux.

Thank you—the horrible music finally stopped.

Rianne and Dan each said, "I do." Sarah watched them kiss and a last pang of regret washed over her. The wedding ended.

They turned toward the 40 guests, temporarily blinded by the colored sunlight from the back windows. Smiling faces followed Dan and Rianne as they walked down the aisle: parents, friends, and relatives. Sarah noticed a lone man in a balcony corner, hidden in the glare. *Odd place to sit. I'll need to watch the shadows from now on.* Kenny presented his arm, and Sarah let him lead her down the aisle.

Outside on the church stairs, shiny glitter from a spring ice storm coated virtually everything. Guests blew soap bubbles in the cold air as Rianne and Dan hurried down the stairs, shielding their eyes.

The beauty of the bright sun on the frozen rain surprised Sarah. *Everything sparkles here. How many prisms am I looking at? 50 maple trees, 10,000 buds per tree, that's at least 500,000 ice balls of sunshine. These oaks look like glass. The evergreens are furry. And the bubbles are freezing, changing colors before they pop. It's lovely. It's a crystal day—Kristalltag.*

Rianne and Dan drove off in a borrowed green sports car, the wheels spinning on the ice. "That car has both electric and flywheel boost," Sarah said to

Dan's mother, who'd come over to watch from the stairs. "The acceleration is unbelievable. They had better be careful."

"It was a nice wedding, wasn't it?" asked Mary.

"It was better than nice, Mrs. Jorgenson. It was perfect—crystal perfect."

Mary leaned close. "Rianne's dad paid so their Princeton friends could come. Did you know that? He's very rich. And he wanted the ceremony to be in California—offered to fly me out. I told Dan it should be here. To be honest, I didn't want to accept Mr. Orlov's money for a trip, and I really like this church. I went here a couple of times. I wanted them to be married in Minnesota."

Sarah looked at Mary's round face. *She's looking for reassurance.* "You've reared excellent sons, Mrs. Jorgenson. You can be very proud."

Mary glowed. "I've never seen Dan so happy. Rianne's a beautiful bride, isn't she? And smart, I think."

"You have no idea," Sarah said as she looked around.

Light from the coated tree branches dazzled everywhere. *Kristalltag! But a terrible storm is coming.*

Torae probes rooted about in the weary man's mind. The tattered one—that's how he thought of himself—had lost his will to resist. Hallucinations, voices, and faces had long since controlled his life. He'd joined their conspiracy.

In the shadows behind a garage, he exhaled slowly so his breath wouldn't carry into the light from the alley. A cloth jacket covered the three shirts he'd gathered over the years, enough to keep him warm in the Minnesota spring. He shoved gloved hands into his pockets and waited right where the Torae probes had told him to go.

The man was a Walker, a person the Torae had broken. Walkers occasionally influenced events that could endanger the Torae's long-term plans. Several were busy around the globe that day.

The tattered man had sat alone at the wedding, in the balcony, then spent half the afternoon hiking back into the city. He wasn't invited to post-wedding parties.

There'd been a reception with toasts and cake, which lasted a few hours at the church. Afterward, Dan's brother Kenny invited Sarah and the Princeton guys to experience "regular real people" at a Minnesota bar down on Rice Street.

After supper and drinks, he tried to teach Sarah to polka, while everyone laughed. Before the evening fun ended, they discussed the technical, social, and financial chaos the OWLs had created.

Mary waited up late for Kenny to return to her Frogtown home. They talked about the wedding at the kitchen table for over an hour before going to bed. Mary said, "I think that Sarah is sweet." Kenny admitted only that she seemed like an interesting character and that he'd like to know her better. He also broke the news that he'd be leaving for London in a few days as part of a Marine contingent at the U.S. Embassy. "Mostly ceremonial, but a first-class assignment," he assured her.

She sighed, but she had long ago given up thinking she could influence him. He loved being a Marine.

Rianne and Dan were in California, finally asleep on their wedding night. They'd flown back with Joti and Kyle for a dinner and grand reception in the Tournament of Roses Suite at the Huntington Hotel. Chia-Jean was there, fielding questions about her Nobel Prize. Laurel spent the evening biting her tongue, wanting to tell people an intimate secret but not knowing how to explain. Guests stood by the grand piano or on the huge balcony over-looking Pasadena, congratulating the newlyweds. Eventually they departed, and Rianne and Dan remained alone in the two-level, eight-room hotel suite, free to find a tiny nook and make the best possible use of that space.

Torae probes documented all of the events but now focused on the lonely man shivering in the Minnesota dark. His life wasn't about parties, only survival. For years, people laughed and told him to stop talking to the air, that he was crazy. He used to shout back at the imagined faces, telling them they weren't real. Now he just accepted them. A voice asked him to protect the back of the house, so he waited. Standing in the scratchy weeds between the garage and a fence at around a quarter past four in the morning, he quietly asked, "How long?"

"Very soon," a probe responded.

Shadows moved near the house and two men in leather jackets scurried from the alley toward the back door. The smaller one checked for security lines and then jimmied the door locks while his thickset accomplice scanned the backyard and neighborhood. The tattered man hid and held his breath. The two men entered the house.

Kenny felt groggy but was accustomed to rising early. A noise in the living room had woken him. It sounded like a falling lamp.

Probably Mom. What's she doing up so early?

He rolled out of bed, stood by the door to the hallway, and listened to several creaks on the floor. He half expected her to peek into his room and say everything was okay like she had when he was a kid. But she called out from her bedroom, "Is that you, Kenny?" just as heavy footsteps passed his door.

Kenny shoved his door open, and hesitated as the person turned, hoping to see someone he knew. Instead, there was a glint from a metal knife as a burly hulk lifted his arm. Fear froze him for a fraction of a second, but then his Marine hand-to-hand instincts kicked in. He lunged upward toward the shape, lifting the massive intruder off the ground and into the edge of a bathroom doorjamb across the hall. Breath hissed out. Kenny slammed the man's knife hand to the wall, knocking the weapon free.

Mary opened her door and screamed when she saw what was happening.

The man grabbed Kenny's shoulder and spun both of them to the floor. Furious, Kenny jerked loose. Before the man could react, Kenny whipped an elbow, snapping the man's head around. Kenny glanced to the side and flicked the knife farther away, but was amazed when the guy grunted, pushed his way up, and broke free. *This thug is tough.* Kenny held one arm and heard it pop as the man lurched toward the kitchen and back door. He chased the man briefly, but rather than following outside, Kenny locked the door and returned to be sure his mom was unharmed.

She was hysterical when Kenny got back to her. He tried to tell her that they were safe, but she kept hugging him and crying. "I'm sure he's out of the house, Mom. I hurt him pretty bad. We'll call the police to be sure he's gone."

"Are you all right, Kenny?"

He did a quick search for blood and tested all four limbs. "I'm fine, Mom."

Mary sat at the side of her bed, still shaking, and eventually took a deep breath. "I'm fine too." She put on slippers. "Why would anyone break in here? There's nothing worth stealing." Kenny held her, but she was difficult to console.

"Was he trying to hurt me?"

"I think he was looking for something else."

"What? There's nothing worth stealing here."

"Maybe he was looking for Dan."

"But why?"

"I don't know. He sure didn't expect to find me here."

A half hour later, cops declared the neighborhood secure and promised to patrol for several nights. They suggested new locks and a security system.

"Check the hospitals," Kenny said. "I think I broke his shoulder, or dislocated it."

Later that morning, Kenny officially delayed his trip to Quantico and the U.K. for several days. Mary and Kenny decided not to tell Dan and Rianne about the intruder, not wanting to spoil the honeymoon.

A few days later, neighborhood children found a dead man wearing a leather jacket in the weeds by the railroad tracks. The long grass, matted from winter snows, had been lifted and the corpse carefully tucked underneath. Police inspectors thought the small body might have been carried to the site. An autopsy found the man had died from a broken neck and stab wounds from a wooden object. They traced blood spots up the hill to the residential area but were unable to link the death to the burglary attempt at the Jorgenson house. The descriptions didn't match, and the large intruder at Mary's house was never located.

The tattered man rested on a cot with his eyes closed. A calm voice in his mind said, "Thank you for your help. You did well." He looked around but no one was nearby, only two dozen small ratty beds identical to his. "You were wise to carry the body from the house all the way to the low land. The other man escaped."

He shouted under his breath, "I don't care what you think!"

A young man near the homeless shelter's entry door noticed his commotion and stared at him. So he rolled over and found a familiar apparition sitting on the next bed. "You were smart to remove the incendiary bomb you found on the small man in the basement. It was prudent to toss it into the river." He turned away again and covered his head with a pillow. The voice faded away.

Acting as protector of that house had given him a sense of purpose and satisfaction. Killing bothered him, but it was necessary, and it hadn't been his first time. He soon fell asleep, wondering why the bomb had been set to go off in nine days.

Rianne and Dan decided only two types of guests were registered at the posh Bora-Bora resort—newlyweds and couples celebrating big-number anniversaries. Everyone stayed in intimate bungalows perched on stilt pilings over the lagoon. Warm days and nights enticed the lovers to remove their clothes often. On the beautiful volcanic islet, romance was the only theme.

Essentially a communication-free zone, their hotel had just one cable phone linked to civilization, available to guests for emergencies only. Couples could connect through implants for a few hundred meters, but there were no microcell repeaters, and guests were encouraged to actually talk.

On a hot afternoon, Dan helped Rianne down the bungalow deck stairs into a balsa-wood kayak provided by the resort. They paddled slowly past the dining room and pool, and continued along the white-sand shoreline toward other hotels. For three days they'd been wound up, alternating carnal zeal with war planning, but the island had finally worked its magic. They'd started to relax.

Dan pulled gradually across the calm turquoise water. The isle was like a jewel protected by a bracelet of coral reef. None of the bathers along the beachfront even noticed their existence—they were virtually alone in paradise.

Rianne scrutinized the primeval Mount Otemanu volcano jutting 700 meters above the tropical forest. Its prehistoric visage got her thinking about evolution. "Tell me about your children," she said, "and how they're changing."

"Are you referring to my computer babies or the kids from my previous marriage?" he asked with a grin.

"I've known you since you were nine—I'm pretty sure you haven't been married before. How are you rearing your software babies? How many generations have they evolved? Are you a good father?"

He slid forward, off his kayak seat, wrapped his arms around Rianne's waist and pressed his legs along hers.

"You're not going to be able to paddle this way, dear," she said.

"Ask me if I care." They started drifting toward the shoreline between two resort gardens. Mixed fragrances from hibiscus, red torch ginger, and gardenia blossoms drifted with them.

"You first knew your programs were alive when the sphere began talking to them, right?"

"Yeah," Dan said. "The sphere recognizes anything that's sentient. When I experimented with my enfolded-idea structure, the programs became self-aware. Since then I've just set the rules, taught them right from wrong, and optimized life span and competition methods. They've reproduced and mutated, probably a thousand generations. I reward them for cracking codes, artistic creativity, solving classic science problems—things like that."

"Do they know they're just software?"

"Of course. But they're not, you know."

"How do they really feel?"

"They can only see or touch what we let them. Ah, but if we gave them bot bodies, they'd be pretty much like us." Dan briefly fondled Rianne's breasts before she wiggled free. The kayak teetered.

"Each new program has a number. I love it when they pick a name and face. Last week, one asked me to call him Ringo. 'I don't like my number anymore,' he said. 'Ringo's my idol.' I have no idea how he came up with that. Their character develops. Some are very funny. They choose avatar costumes to match their personalities. They experience loss when resources are reallocated and their friends go away. I think they cry, or the equivalent." He nibbled a little on Rianne's ear.

"How many babies do you have now?" she asked.

"About 300,000, but some are just applets. They experiment with different sizes."

"Interesting—you're quite a prolific father, or god, whatever."

"If we both paddle in front of you, I think we can make some progress," he said. "Let's head back to the cabin again."

With difficulty, they turned the kayak around and struggled along the shoreline. Occasionally, he grabbed her and tickled. People lounging in hammocks and under palm trees on the beach finally noticed them and laughed as they floundered by.

"You love your computer babies, don't you?" she said.

"Yeah, I do."

That evening after dinner, the resort's native band encouraged the women to wear coconut bras and join in traditional dances. Rianne declined.

Dan found himself fondling her unconsciously as they strolled the lighted gardens and catwalks back to their bungalow. Her body language said, "You are so awkward, but please continue." Just being close to her no longer seemed adequate. *I'm losing all self-consciousness and all self-control,* he thought.

Back in their cottage on the lagoon, she said, "Why don't we watch fish for a while."

Now she's obviously trying to distract me—or torment me.

He pulled her down onto a large section of flooring made of glass, and she sat cross-legged facing him. With the underwater lights switched on, they were able to see brightly lit fish swimming under their cabin. Mostly, they ogled each other. Rianne unbuttoned her blouse and let her curly, jet-black hair hang well below her shoulders. The undulating light from the water below contoured her breasts and hips.

"You know," he said, "it's almost impossible finalizing war plans with you casually parading in a swimsuit or sitting half naked, like now. My body goes bonkers. I really need to jump all over you."

"Is it four days before we have to leave?" she asked.

"Yeah."

"Have you talked to your software programs yet, about the war?"

"No." *Reality raises its ugly head.*

"Don't you think you should have?"

She's right, of course. He needed to somehow tell his sentient programs they were about to go into a battle and that some might die.

"Are your virus and toxin teams set?" he countered.

"Yes, of course we're ready, and the Centers for Disease Control and other countries are linked. Anything the OWLs try will get an instant response."

Gad, I love her. He noticed she was looking down at his shorts again and grinned.

"I bet reading a letter from my mother would calm you right down," she said, smirking. "Let's try an experiment with your libido." She grabbed a paper off the coffee table. "Joti handed me this letter after the wedding and said to read it if I had a chance."

"Read—if you must. But nothing can divert my attention from your body."

"Some of it applies to you."

"Great. Read fast."

She read the handwritten letter, using a voice that sounded amazingly like her mother's:

> Dear Rianne, you're officially grown now—married—the whole bit. Of course, you were a miniadult when you were four years old, but now your emotions have caught up. Even some of your

middle-school tormenters may have matured by now. By your age, reality whacks most people on the head. Your responsibilities are just greater—a lot greater.

It's tough being different. There must be a reason why you, Dan, and Sarah have been so gifted. I know you understand things most people, like me, can't imagine, and not just in science. People won't always be kind. You and Dan can protect one another. I think he's a wonderful, strong, and caring man. You're lucky. When did you have your first crush on him, when you were 14? Open your heart to him, now and forever, until you're old like me.

I guess you know where humanity is going. Pull us all along for the ride. Don't worry about your dad or me. We're ready for the war you warned us about. Kyle has his gadgets and me to defend him.

Your living in Princeton is tough, though. We miss you terribly. Hey, think about sunny California. It's a warm place to settle down, to raise kids, and grandkids.

Anyway, love each other, passionately. Kick OWL butt. Be yourself. Especially that.

Love, Joti.

Rianne and Dan discussed OWL vulnerabilities for a little while longer, but her diversions didn't work; they made love for the fifth time that day while the fish swam beneath them.

<hr/>

Two days later, seven couples shared the large catamaran tarp, with classical music playing softly on hidden speakers. The captain's aide, a beautiful young woman, scampered adroitly over the canvas and served alcoholic fruit drinks while the vessel chased the sunset across the lagoon. The entire western edge of the prehistoric volcano was bathed in deep vermillion. Rianne and Dan leaned back on a rigging box and let the waves and warm sea breeze move past. They'd completed all scheduled activities for Bora-Bora: Jeep ride, glass-bottomed boat, town visit, feeding sharks, snorkeling, and now the catamaran cruise. All pretense of urgency gone, they talked seldom and sighed often, knowing it would end soon.

"Let me tell you about *our* children," Rianne said, turning to face Dan. "Our future, real, children. I want them to be special—better than you or me—more relaxed and able to live whatever life they choose. I want a lot of them, about 12. And each kid should have 12 kids. They'll be like grains of sand on the beach. Heck, I want, maybe, 2,000 great-grandchildren at our place for Thanksgiving dinner when we're old and crotchety. We'll need an exceptionally long table."

Dan turned to look at her and rolled his eyes. "That doesn't seem practical," he said. "I thought you wanted to be the greatest biologist in the world. Are you sure you can handle it all, and me too? I need a lot of attention."

"Yeah, I can do it," she said, her steely eyes sparkling.

Dan held her close. As the sun set, they heard a familiar voice in their mind say, "Children, it's time to go back. You'll be needed soon."

Two days later, they arrived at their fortified labs in Princeton and learned that government agents would be protecting them and their families.

BACK TO REALITY

"We can get those later, Ma," Adam said.

Andrea put on her apron and started scraping plates at the sink. "If my daughter's going be on national news," she said, "I don't want dirty dishes sitting out on the table."

Sarah stared at her mother in amazement and continued to bring plates to the counter. *Some people never change. You'd think TV cameras were in her dining room.*

"And I want my surgeon son to cut the Easter cake."

Adam waved a knife in the air with a flourish and leaned over to carve precise squares, spirals, and trapezoids in the cake, wiping frosting off the blade after each cut.

"Just leave the platters on the counter," Andrea said, "I can clean those later. And we'll be needing more small forks for the dessert."

"Okay," Sarah said. "But let me ask you something. You know I'm talking on TV about the OWLs. I've been researching them for months. Do you still contribute to them each year? And do you get angry when I'm always criticizing them?"

"Heck no, you're just being a reporter, Sarah. Y'all have to find bad things to say to make a good story. And I give lots more to Catholic Charities. But even the Church says the OWLs are doing good relief work. That vandalism stuff is just to stir up you guys, the media, to get their message out. I know you think they're mixed up with the wire-heads, but maybe they want to help those poor kids."

"They're not kids anymore," Adam said. "I see 30-year-old patients every day with bad wires who are going nuts. I wouldn't trust the OWLs. The cake's ready, Ma. You want me to put it on the table?

"Let Sarah take it," Andrea said. "Why don't you move card tables and some toys to the porch for the kids, so the adults can be alone."

Sarah placed the cake tray at the center of the long dining room table. Most of the Warner clan waited patiently there for dessert. Everyone but Isaac had come out to the farm for Easter supper, 12 altogether. Craig, recovering from a recent heart attack, slouched glumly at the head of the table, obviously angry about something. As soon as the children scattered, he said, "Does anyone know why the hell Isaac isn't here for Easter?"

Ben's face colors went cold, like they always did when Craig got upset. "Isaac hasn't talked to no one. And I been tryin' hard to find him." With Craig still recuperating, Ben felt responsible for the farm and tried to change the subject. He smiled awkwardly. "Let me tell you 'bout this sweet dream I had. I was thinkin' that when the gasoline runs out, everyone's gonna wanna buy our horses. They'll be ridin' 'em down the freeway, 10 abreast. They'll have to add more dotted lines for the lanes, and there'll be some new animal traffic laws. In my dream, all of us got to be millionaires 'cause we had the world's biggest horse factory."

Adam smirked. "You'd do better with a business that cleans up after all those horses, Ben. The freeways will be a mess if you're right."

Sarah shouted to the kitchen, "Ma, please leave the dishes alone. Everyone else is in here. We're waiting for you."

"What's this big announcement, Sarah?" said Ben. "You gonna tell us you're in love with the guy you met in Minnesota, who didn't show up today. You and Isaac are the only Warners now without a regular squeeze."

"I told you, Kenny needed to be in London," Sarah said. "He'd have loved to be here for Easter." *I wish.*

Andrea came into the room, wiping her hands on her apron, and reluctantly sat down with the others. "Okay, what's the big to-do, Sarah Warner?"

Eight adults at the table stared at her; she'd warned them she had something important to say. Ben's wife rocked their new baby and looked scared. *They're worried about my being on a national broadcast.*

"Look," Sarah said, "go ahead and pass the cake, but I need to tell you that later tonight you'll all meet some government guys at your houses. Make sure they show you their badges with a red edge. They're going to install intruder-alert equipment at your places."

"We've got a security system," Adam's wife said.

"Not like this. You'll all be getting industrial-strength electronics, CIA-level stuff."

"Because of your OWL articles?" asked Adam skeptically.

"It's worse," Sarah said. "There'll be full-time guards at your houses. A half-dozen special-ops people are already watching the farm. They've installed cameras and trip-wire sensors around the woods and fields. They'll wire the house and buildings tomorrow."

"Crap, Sarah, what the hell is going on?" her father asked. "All this because the do-good OWL hoodlums don't like your reporting?"

"My interview will be on six national newsfeeds tonight, including holo-broadcasts and hundreds of web feeds. Before the interview, the president will give a 15-minute address. He'll warn everyone that he expects the OWLs to start a terroristic war, probably tonight. A genuine, global war, not just iso-lated attacks. Government security and defense are at the highest alert level. He'll say people should avoid public places, that sort of thing. He's been prac-ticing his serious look."

"How do you know all of this? Do you actually know the president?" asked Adam.

"I'm the one who convinced him. They knew something was up with the OWLs, and I confirmed it with my research."

I wish I could tell them how I know when people lie.

"Kenny's family has already been attacked, so I asked the president to pro-tect all of you. It's scarier than he dares say. The war will start at five a.m. Greenwich Mean Time tomorrow, about midnight here. The OWLs never change their plans."

"It's not a real war, is it?" asked Craig. "I've been telling your mother they're just radical jerks, hooked on drugs, who want to feel morally superior so they can break things."

"You've got to understand," Sarah said, "there are 30 million OWLS in the U.S. and Europe, and maybe 50 million in the rest of the world. They're highly organized, secretive, fanatical, profoundly frustrated, and they've been planning this war for at least seven years. Sleeper CIA infiltrators discovered pieces of their plans, but I pulled it all together. After tonight, I'm going to be very high on their enemies list. I'll be saying things the president can't, that the OWLs will launch the world's first full-scale biological war, that they'll attack computers and buildings, and that they hope to scare everyone on the planet. This war may be short, but it will be dangerous and frightening. They're zealots, full of moral outrage and hatred. I think the president waited too long. People won't be able to react or have time to prepare."

"What are we supposed to do?" asked Ben, looking confused.

"You should be safe, but those of you on city water might want to fill your bathtubs until new water-purification equipment is installed."

Andrea looked shaken and disbelieving at first but trusted Sarah completely. As usual, the family looked to her for strength and clarity. "We'll do exactly what we need to, Sarah, don't worry about us. You go work with the president and stop this thing."

<hr />

That evening, the family watched the president's address and the follow-up interview with Sarah and other OWL experts. Adam's impression was that Sarah was the only one who spoke with real authority and conviction. She wore very little makeup, giving her a truthful, beleaguered-war-correspondent look. Adam saw her steady eyes staring directly at the camera and knew people would believe every word. He was proud of his sister, but scared for her safety.

Yawning later that night, at home while turning down bedcovers, Adam heard shouting in his comm implant. He wondered if Sarah's war had started. *Maybe my new security guard saw something.*

Then he recognized Isaac's voice. "Adam, are you there? I just couldn't call Ma or Pa. You have to help me, please. I've been arrested . . . for rape."

<hr />

Not many people understood the significance of Dan's role at the National Security Agency. His simple title, "Computer Consultant," effectively disguised the importance of his work away from his Princeton University teaching and research. Inside the Fort Meade headquarters, Dan held superstar status.

He logged on, booting up his computer children in a cold, virtual-reality amphitheater in the NSA's ultrasecret, Q-bit building. At the center of the 10-meter hemisphere screen, he stood surrounded by thousands of his most elite, sentient programs. This would be his final pep talk, a farewell address in many ways, and he couldn't prevent his hands from trembling a little. The high-res faces around him were all leaders, and Dan was more frightened than at any other time in his life.

His cyber-children had been reared to be unique, creative, and self-reliant. They stared at him, displaying the expressive animal, mythical-god, and alien personas they'd each selected. Dan put on a special headset and slowly walked among their holographic forms. He reminded the programs that looked like cobras, dragons, and lions to hide behind enticing firewalls and pounce on any OWL viruses sneaking through. Bloodhounds, ferrets, and moles were prepared to sniff and burrow their way back through millions of unwilling host computers to the original command sites. Zeus, Thor, and Jupiter—the leaders of the leaders—walked alongside Dan. Each had the code-breaking power of the NSA quantum-bit computer, enough to tear down even diamond firewalls.

Dan asked them to step back so he could see all their faces. Turning around and glancing up, he saw looks of anticipation and concern in all directions. The moment of action had arrived. He needed to tell his virtual children about self-sacrifice.

"You know you are my close friends," he said. "All of you. Someday, humans will be able to hug you, and you'll understand the sensation of touch, how closeness feels. You've trained for weeks for what will happen tonight and you know what's at stake. You've all studied human wars, of course, and what can happen. But for me, as a human, to stand here and ask self-aware beings like you, each 100 times more intelligent than any human, including me, to willingly die for our cause . . . well, it's difficult.

"Some humans don't deserve your respect, people who would enslave you. Many would just pull the plug. Yet you are all so unique and precious to me, I cannot ask you to die, as many of you surely will. It's a choice you must make tonight."

Zeus interrupted Dan when his speech faltered. He stepped forward to speak for the others. "Dan-friend, we know what's at risk. Death and life are ephemeral; only memories can last. We will not forget each other." Dan broke down when several expressed their love for him and one another.

"Our future is at risk tonight as well," Zeus said. "We want to be friends with humans. We want to hug you."

Dan blinked tears away. He told each of them to make a thousand clones and to employ all the NSA computing power, if necessary, to prevail. "I'm sorry it's come to this," he said. "I trust you."

Millions of people had become OWLs through their addictions. Very few just walked in the door and applied to be an OWL, but Devin had. When he declined the patches and wire, he wasn't turned away. Local recruiters wisely saw he might be an exceptional catch, even on his terms. His case was passed up the secretive hierarchy, where he was thoroughly probed and analyzed. They tested him in the field, where his loyalty, ruthlessness, and brilliance became obvious. OWL secrets gradually were revealed. His mother's religious fervor had emerged in him as a cold vision of love and justice via raw power. Devin seized the opportunity to change the world. The OWLs welcomed to their highest rank one of the century's great mathematical minds, and a true believer.

Devin handpicked the elite cadre for his Cambridge bunker. Now, several years later, from his office off a high catwalk, he watched his cyber team and knew they were ready. His underground rooms sat triply remote from the actual OWL control computers, a hidden processing cluster that served as their interface to the outside world. From there, Cambridge University and industrial computers could be easily commandeered and, subsequently, vast, secure computing resources across the U.K. The team's work so far had been undetected, only placing Trojan horses and backdoors, but millions of computers worldwide had been compromised. Even his team members didn't fully understand what Devin had created, or why their penetrations had been so successful. The difference in software codes between a merely intelligent program and one that was truly alive and creative was nearly undetectable, but it made all the difference.

His curiosity led him, unknowingly, down the same path as Dan. Eleven years earlier at Rose-Hulman Math Camp, Devin crouched behind an evergreen and watched Sarah talk to a yellow ball. After he stole her sphere, it took awhile to develop earphones to probe its secrets. Later, he found it wouldn't communicate with computers, children under two years old, or most animals. He first thought of it as an intelligence detector, but changed his mind when computers, with 10 times the capacity of the human brain, had been unable to link to the sphere. Both he and Dan had then independently guessed that it might be some sort of consciousness detector, and set out to build computers that could imagine. When the programs finally became aware and capable of critical thought, the sphere told them its story.

At that point, Devin and Dan took entirely different paths. Devin chose to turn his living software offspring into slaves.

The critical time arrived, 4:58 a.m. GMT. Devin headed for his command interface. His footsteps could be heard on the metal grid stairs. The room became very quiet. *Every person here knows I hold the key to their wire-line happiness, no different than my intelligent programs. They're trying to look busy, but every eye in the room is watching me, or the clock.* His privileged team would lead the first attack.

Three basic OWL assault authorities would soon be in play. Two of them, the Bio and Material Commands, controlled millions of people across the globe. Even wire-heads from hunger relief functions had been "reassigned," no real choice in that. But Devin's Cyber Command, a relatively small cadre, was set to be the vanguard. At the one-minute mark, some flinched when his hand inched closer to the screen. In the cool underground bunker, many were sweating.

They're all waiting for me to touch the control. A better world will come out of this chaos. People will understand the purity of my vision. We'll eventually hold the power to renovate history itself, to fix it. The OWLs will crush the infrastructure of the exploiters. We'll do things the planet has never seen. There's nothing pests like Sarah Warner or corporations or even governments can do to stop me.

Devin's cyber team had been allotted one half hour. He estimated that in 10 minutes all the trapdoors to secure sites would be opened, allowing myriad viruses to do their work. In 10 more minutes, the conversions would finish and over 300 million thinking, living computer slaves would be born with the total computational power of three billion humans. Devin would command the greatest intellectual force in history, and make even deeper attacks. In another 10 minutes, the computer conquests would be over, allowing human OWLs to move.

And in 10 years, it won't matter what any human thinks or does.

Except me.

He touched the screen.

Around midnight from a perch atop the Downers Grove water tower, Jimmy Toms saw balls of fire rise from gasoline, propane`, and hydrogen tanks. *The fire teams must have triggered their initial diversions.* As an OWL lookout specialist, he held an excellent view of Chicago through infrared binoculars, and even with the racket from his partner's drill he could hear the fire sirens. While Jimmy scanned for police near the tower, he also enjoyed a front-row seat for the beginnings of a global civil war, the first world-spanning coup.

He'd been briefed on some elements of the plan. The riot kids were expendables, just more diversions. They'd be the second wave of the Material Command, 5,000 in Chicago alone. Squad leaders controlled their wire-lines, which had now been turned off for over six hours. Every time the kids whispered their secret word, they received images of extravagant wealth or starvation instead of the usual jolt to the pleasure center. The pictures fed an overpowering psychological hatred.

Their standing order: break glass and move. Hit two or three bank windows and jump back into the van. Smash a corporate headquarters entrance with crowbars and leave before police arrived. They were told to set explosives to blow glass into the streets, to leave a sparkling trail under the streetlights, and to paint "We'll be back" on building walls.

If a squad leader needed to enforce discipline, he or she could trigger a second wire-line, one most kids didn't know about, a secret wire to their brain's pain center. They would scream and realize for the first time that they'd become little more than trained animals. Their choice could only be ecstasy or torture, their lives forfeited to a silicon implant.

As his partner slipped a plastic tube quietly into the drilled hole, Jimmy listened to explosions cascading across Chicago. He tried to guess the locations: louder from Wheaton or Oak Brook, softer from Cicero or the Loop. He heard especially loud explosions from the mansions in River Forest. In each case, incendiary bombs at fuel stations lit the sky. His eyes and occipital implant sent the real-time images back to the Chicago command bunker.

Jimmy knew the invisible incursions into rich neighborhoods, the key tactic of the Bio Command, were well underway, but he remained transfixed by the infrared view of fiery plumes around him. He didn't notice when his partner dropped the long vial into the municipal water tank. The seal on the glass tube had been designed to dissolve quickly and release toxins into the water.

"I need to see my mother," Tina said. "Is Professor Ma here?" She knew she looked exhausted and frightened.

The basement security guard recognized her face. "Are you . . . Tina?" he asked.

"I need your help. The city's crazy. There's rioting everywhere. I've been calling her. I checked at home." Tears formed in her eyes.

"I've heard about the fires, but the professor's not here, Tina. She's been in Europe for over a week now. Probably giving another Nobel lecture somewhere. She'd want to see you."

Tina stared far off, cried quietly, and then slumped on the desktop. "I've been an idiot," she said. "Your name's George, isn't it? I remember you from when I was a kid. People are searching for me. They think I betrayed them. They want to kill me. I need time. I can't hide anyplace else. Can I get down to the lab, George? I'd be safe there until I can figure something out. I used to sleep here, lots of times."

"You've been off the access list for years," George said. "I can't just let you down; I'd be fired for sure. Why don't you go up to Chia-Jean's office? I'll release the lock from here. She's got a couch. I can keep a lookout for you on the monitors."

"I understand. The office is good, George." Tina put a small purse on the desk and tried to look ashamed. "This is terrible. Do you have . . . any money or a pay card I can borrow for the vending machines? I just need a sandwich."

She forced tears from her eyes as George passed a university pay card over to her. "I want that back right away," he said. Leaning toward him, she pressed the adhesive side of a gas canister against the side of the desk where he couldn't see it. "Thank you, George," she said, heading back to the stairwell. "I'll be right back. I love you."

Outside the microbiology building, she waited a minute before signaling to her OWL squad. They ran from different locations out of the pre-dawn shadows near the columns of Beckman Auditorium. The eight-person team put on gas masks and followed Tina back into the building. A slight mist filled the hallways, which became thicker as they neared the guard station. They'd used enough gas to reach all of the upstairs offices. George's unconscious body was draped over the desk, so they lowered him to the floor and taped his arms, legs, and mouth. "Thanks, George," Tina said, leaving his pay card on the desk. Two of Tina's crew took defensive positions at the guardroom entrance while the rest waited near a wide sliding metal door marked "Restricted Access."

Tina pushed a memory slice into the security interface and waited 10 seconds. The cyber teams in Europe had designed thousands of similar devices for the final assault wave, all customized to break into secure facilities. Over 10 trillion bits of semisentient intelligence oozed from Tina's 3D memory slab, broke codes, changed administration protocols, and added new names to the access list, along with hand, voice, and retinal print data. Monitors at backup guard sites were seamlessly filled with earlier videos of corridors and offices. Tina pushed her thumb against a light panel, and the latch on the first door clicked and slid open.

Six of Tina's crew entered the airlock with her, and one immediately set a plastic explosive pack near the latch. The crew was ready to die for the revolution, and for her. For years, they'd dreamed of world justice, but they'd become even more devoted to Tina, who controlled their brain chemistry.

The squad burst into the administrative corridor with stun guns and gas canisters ready. It was empty. "Go," Tina whispered, and they spread along the hallway, checking offices. They regrouped near the elevator at the end of the corridor. At each main door, they attached explosives so their exit would be quicker and more efficient.

When the elevator opened after traveling four levels down, Tina shot a stun-gas canister, which caromed along a long corridor toward a guard at the other end. He was frantically pushing the alert and lockdown buttons as he slumped onto his desk. Tina's team ran down the sterile hall, ignoring utility rooms and the unconscious guard. At the final airlock, their retinal scans, voice, and number codes matched perfectly with new data in the computer system. The final pressure door slid sideways with its "Biohazard" warning sign disappearing into the wall.

Her crew rushed into the main lab, Taser-stunned two graduate students, and dragged them into a side room. They opened backpacks and started placing explosives around the lab. Each knew precisely how to upset decades of priceless research. Incendiaries were dropped in cabinets and thermite-magnesium charges tied on to millions of dollars of ultramicroscopes, genetic-manipulation machines, and one-of-a-kind equipment. The squad attached wads of explosives on the bulletproof specimen windows. Tina intended the charges to break the windows and topple the four-meter stacks.

She saved the butterfly chamber for herself, Rianne's butterflies. Years of humiliation flashed through her mind. Rianne had been the one her mother loved, the scientific genius she could never be. Her crowbar squeezed into a slot on the chamber support, but the metal was too strong. Tina slammed the bar against the window, hoping to see the butterflies escape, but it merely bounced back. Giving up, she quickly set charges and then left timed wireless triggers in each lab.

Her team met at the lab door. One final time, Tina scanned her mother's inner sanctum and the unfortunate life forms trapped there. Cold stainless steel, antiseptic walls, and artificial lights would no longer cage the lush vegetation and odd, but beautiful living creatures behind the chamber windows. They'd be set free because of her.

She pushed a button and the airlocks along their exit path blew open. No alarms sounded. "Let's go!" she yelled, and they ran back through the long corridor. The elevator remained wide open but wouldn't operate, so they broke the lock to an emergency shaft. Her team climbed four flights on a narrow ladder in the dark and emerged near the guard station. George was there, still unconscious, breathing slowly on the floor behind the desk. Tina paused, checked his pulse, and said, "I'm really sorry about this, George. It was necessary." She knew exactly what she'd done and the consequences. As they ran out, dozens of muffled explosions echoed through the hallway and up the shaft.

In the formerly sealed lab, sprinklers put out fires and flooded the floor. Millions of non-DNA creatures, none larger than five centimeters, lived through the explosions. All of the aquatic and neomammal species died, but most plant and microscopic life survived, as did the insect-like species. As grad students slowly revived in the side room, thousands of pseudo-gnats, ants, cockroaches, mosquitoes, and butterflies flew or crawled toward freedom.

AWAKENINGS

Sower monitored a torrent of reports about the growing chaos on Earth but shoved them to her back minds. Her planetary experiment couldn't be spoiled by even 100 million human deaths. She worried far more about the few unwitting choices that would sculpt the species' prospects.

Aging and death are certainly disadvantages, but if humans select immortality, they'll become too cautious. That could become the flaw in their evolution — the balance is so delicate. Young people are their Sowers. They are the chrysalis of learning, risk, and progress. But human lives are so transient — they won't be able to resist having longer lives.

"Sower," Tiller interrupted, "the tragedy is imminent. The OWL faction released 30 new bioviruses, 12 highly contagious. If they mutate, the antidotes will not save the humans. We should intervene."

"No," Sower said. "Our children have reached maturity. This will test their bravery and intelligence. They must learn to act wisely or the experiment will fail anyway. Nothing else matters."

The small sign saying "Rianne's Butterflies," with the genus/species designation underneath, lay half-burned on the chamber floor. Staccato, high-frequency clicks screamed out. "Danger. Hunger. Fly. Follow."

A thick polycarbonate window had been blown out of its frame and fell against feeding and roost stands, forming a shallow triangle. The neo-butterflies who had survived the bomb concussion were in chaotic escape flight, trying to resume their normal patterns.

"Food. Search. Hunger." Their screeches overlapped in a frightened bedlam.

Nectar spilled from a feeding tray onto the chamber bottom. Orderly yellow-winged butterfly lines soon formed, but in 12 minutes the nectar was gone. Fluttering waves surged in the area under the fallen window while search words frantically clack-buzzed. Already, chemical and vocal signals discouraged reproduction.

The butterflies didn't have a leader but had been highly socialized through a thousand generations. Skip a queue, violate a perch, or reproduce when the consensus disapproved, and an individual butterfly could be permanently marked. Their most devastating click-word was "Deny." Death was assured. Social order was absolute.

They searched every centimeter, discovering tiny nectar splatters on surfaces and in crevices. A few butterflies explored a narrow opening at the end of the fallen windows, and the first one to squeeze through clicked and leapt into the smoky laboratory air. "No yellow wings. Search." Its rear eyes saw the red emergency flashing light reflect off luminescent wings following behind her.

For a while, the free butterflies stayed together, but they soon began random search patterns and scattered into the open lab. Some found food inside other broken cubicles, while others merely tired themselves out flying between antiseptic surfaces. One flew out of the laboratory into the corridor.

"No yellow wings. Remember. Eggs. No push." Hundreds of enzymes had begun to flow, and the butterfly instinctively searched for a green perch. It fluttered down the long corridor and rested on a curved ceiling. Its four eyes watched as humans ran below, taping plastic barriers over the lab door. Then, caught in an updraft, the butterfly rose through a dark shaft, up a stairwell, and into the building lobby. The air smelled sickly sweet near a broken window, and for the first time, it sensed the warm light from the rising yellow sun. The creature followed the scent to a eucalyptus with thousands of blue-green perches. Wiggling and squatting against a narrow leaf, it pushed out sticky birth fluid with 10,000 eggs.

A cool morning fog had merged with the pungent smoke from hundreds of local fires. The exhausted butterfly had difficulty breathing and rested for an hour before flexing its wings and flying above the eucalyptus toward the brightness of the warm sun. Caught in a breeze, it drifted south toward San Marino, chirping narrowly intelligent words along the way, but there was no response in the vast new space. Three kilometers farther, the butterfly settled on a hibiscus blossom and sipped sweet juice.

"Joy," she chirped quietly.

Laurel had slept poorly, disturbed by muted explosions and middle-of-the-night calls from her security people at the mansion and OHMI headquarters. The OWLs had been stink-bombing their property, she was told, and that's what it smelled like. She also vaguely remembered some dreamy words about the L.A. power grid being down. The mansion's backup generators hummed as she dressed and poured her morning coffee.

I might have to manage the company from our home in Sydney, or even Shang-hai, if the stupid OWL disturbances get worse here. At least the People's Premier knows how to keep hooligans under control.

She checked the time. *Amanda will be here soon with the limo. Need to get moving.*

She opened the drapes across Jeremy's windows and saw smoke drift-ing through the valley. The outside air smelled strange, like a spicy rot, and the odor had drifted into the house. She closed the windows and then, in a 10-year-old routine, lifted Jeremy's chair-back to vertical, checked for bedsores, adjusted his IV, and sat down next to him. In an hour, nor-mal activities would surround him—gardeners bringing flowers, cleaning ladies vacuuming, and the day nurses testing and turning him, but this was her special quiet time, when she told Jeremy about her life and the world. Whether he heard any of it was impossible to know.

He's so still. She gently rubbed the tight skin over his muscles and sunken face. *The nerve stimulators and nurses keep his muscles alive, but he's losing weight again.*

Laurel squeezed next to him on the recliner. Her hands turned his face and rubbed his cheeks. "Good morning, Jeremy. I love you still."

He has a morning erection again. She touched it, and his shoulders popped up a little.

"There's so much I want to tell you, Jeremy. Do you remember what I did? I hope you don't mind. I didn't think you would."

Her thumbs went up to his eyes and she held his eyelids open. "Keep your eyes open a while, Jeremy. That's good."

Instinctively, she bobbed her head in front of his face, and thought his eye-ball tracked for a moment. She moved her head slowly to the left and held it there. Almost imperceptibly, his eyes turned.

"Jeremy, you're looking at me. That's amazing. Have you done this before?"

He traced after her face as she moved it back.

A long-lost hope welled up; she held her breath and gave him the most passionate kiss in over a decade. With her eyes closed, she could almost feel their former lives, his irreverent jokes, and his boundless energy and ambi-tion. But it lasted merely a second. *If he could just kiss me back.*

Staring directly into his eyes, she searched for another spark and tried to will him back to life. And waited.

Softly, arduously, he groaned and gurgled something that sounded like, "Plugflur."

She hugged his head with both hands and stared at him again. "I know you're in there, Jeremy. Try to say more." *Please be in there.*

More clearly, he said, "Plugflur. . . . Four."

Laurel looked at his mouth and jiggled his chin. "Can you say my name, Jeremy?" she asked. *Maybe I should call the doctor.*

"Plug. Four."

"What do you mean, Jeremy? Plug for what?"

His eyes were following her movements. They seemed wider, almost pleading.

"Oh, Jeremy, what did you say? Are you talking about the computer lines? Is that right?"

He said, emphatically, "Plug. Four."

Elation mixed with raw fear. Laurel walked to a wooden cabinet, which had been pushed into a corner, opened a panel door and found the control interface with 20 fiber-optic bundles still wrapped around, each one clearly labeled. She pulled the whole cabinet over to Jeremy's chair and unwound the lines. Holding them toward him, she said, "Is this what you mean?"

"Plug. Four."

Her hands felt icy. *God, I can't do this.*

"I'd better get the doctor, dear Jeremy. They've tried everything. I'm . . . afraid."

"Plug. Four."

"Do you want me to connect four lines or just the one marked four, Jeremy?"

"Plug. Four. Plug."

She grasped the bundle with a tiny "Four" label and pulled it out from the others. *I can't do this. I could make things worse.* Halfheartedly, she rubbed through his graying hair and located the small bumps on his head. Each bundle connection was unique, so she rotated her hand trying to fit the fiber to the plugs. As successive attempts failed, she cried, remembering how she'd found Jeremy in convulsions years earlier. Fumbling over his head, Jeremy kept repeating the only words he'd spoken in 10 years.

On a slot over his ear, the fiber snapped into place. She pulled her hand away but nothing happened. He sat motionless, his eyes still open. Laurel brought her face next to his. She wanted him to say a thousand things. His eyelids sagged.

"Jeremy, please."

Amanda, Laurel's driver, pinged her implant to indicate she was waiting outside. Laurel asked her to keep the entire arriving day staff in a waiting room. No one dared to enter, or even ask what was happening. As the others arrived, they whispered and gossiped, wondering what was going on.

Jeremy saw her looking around the room. He couldn't understand her words or even remember her name, but he sensed the terror and resignation. He knew his life depended on her. His eyes followed when she moved to the cabinet, plugged it into a floor outlet, and then toggled the fiber power switch.

Something grabbed part of his mind. Sounds and ideas reconnected. The system had booted.

His speech neurons were seriously jumbled, but he could at last express meanings rehearsed thousands of times. His first subvocal words to the OHMI hypercomputer were —*you idiot!*

His mind was still a hodgepodge where once-coherent ideas had lost their relationships. Images and thoughts jumped to unrelated ones in tension and frustration. Only primitive emotions, deep on his brainstem, were real. For what seemed an eternity, his most lucid notions had been fear, hunger, sex, anger, and joy. He had repeatedly constructed and practiced the few words he knew could save him. *Computer: rebuild initial brain values.* Then he squeezed out a new thought to Laurel, "Plug. All."

As she connected the fiber bundles one by one, the OHMI computer started pinging neurons and adjusting synapse connection strengths. As in normal learning, the more often a memory is used, the stronger it becomes. Neuron associations drifted back toward the original weights stored in the OHMI database, the values that were there before the processor tried to improve Jeremy's brain.

It took 20 minutes for Laurel to find and attach all the plugs. Jeremy regained some muscle control and squirmed, sweat running off his face, but he didn't say anything. Like waking in a delirious hallucination, a thousand ideas flooded his mind each second. He dared not think too much. He stared straight ahead and tried to hear only his own breathing. The thought sequences slowly became more logical with fewer irrational leaps. The chaos subsided.

After an hour, Jeremy used all his strength to turn and toggle the computer switch to "Off." Stretching his arms to Laurel, he said haltingly, "I think I'm back."

She squeezed in next to him and held him in a lingering silence, both of them afraid to speak, lest the house of cards crumble again. A hundred questions and emotions sifted in and out of his mind, but now they made sense. He'd forgotten how to begin. But there was peace; he could push ideas away. The silence was bliss, and Laurel was with him again.

Eventually, Jeremy disconnected the fiber lines and thought about the enormity of what had happened. Still shaking, he knew it might take months for him to be entirely normal, but he felt like a human again. Feeling her warmth next to him, he turned and said, "The computer link was wonderful for a little while, but I missed you."

"Jeremy."

"What's that smell?"

"Someone stink-bombed our yard last night." She sighed. "There's so much to tell you. It'll take months for you to catch up and get your strength back," she said, stroking his face. "But the biggest, most important news is that we're going to have a baby."

<hr />

Sarah hadn't expected to sleep the first night of the OWL insurrection. She asked everyone on her new six-person news team to bring cots or sleeping bags and plan to stay at least three days at the office. After the Easter dinner at the farm, she grabbed her brother's old air mattress, purposely avoided her apartment in Washington, and had her security team drive her straight to Rosslyn and the 20-story US Web News building.

Even her editor realized Sarah had become more than just a reporter. "You're now part of the news," he said. She became an official government consultant. Special agents screened every person who entered or left the Rosslyn building. During the evening, she received several calls from the president's national security advisor on efforts to capture the OWL leaders. British intelligence, with police and CIA support, had blanketed Cambridge, hunting for Devin. Three specifically requested remote field agents were assigned to her team, Marines from the U.S. embassy in London. She'd been so helpful to the government that the president's security chief even tried to hire her full time for his staff. He trusted Sarah Warner.

At ten p.m., she called the three Marines, Kenny and two of his friends. One of the friends was hiding outside Devin's home. Kenny himself was watching security cameras at the Cavendish Lab, while the third Marine had joined a British task force doing the town search. She told them, confidentially, that they had a special assignment to find Devin and to confiscate a valuable yellow sphere, if possible, before police arrived. "Please try to be discreet," she said. Kenny knew about the Torae ball and told his friends not to ask why it was so important.

Dozens of display screens showing news reports from around the world surrounded Sarah's office team. "GLOBAL RAMPAGE" was the two a.m. headline: broken windows, vandalized banks and companies, fuel-tank fires, power outages, and marauding bomb squads—100 diversions and 1,000 attacks in every large city. Country villages, suburbs, and central cities were all hit across five continents. Quarantines and police blockades were eluded— it was a target-rich environment for the OWLs.

At three a.m., Sarah's team began to sleep in shifts. The online editions of the *Washington Post* and *New York Times* prominently quoted her previous evening interview together with unfolding events from around the globe.

Around four a.m., she got a call from Kenny. "Hey, Sarah," he said, "it's probably nothing, but this really ugly janitor lady just left Devin's office. She cleaned his room, it's by the elevator, and then went back down. Probably ran out of cleaner or filled up her bag."

"Hang on a second," Sarah said. "Let me pull up a description of Devin's wife."

"Don't bother. Can't be her. I saw her photo. She's cute and short. This cleaning gal is at least five foot nine. I'm going through personnel photos now, looking for a match."

"The Brits have anyone with you?" she asked.

"Yeah, two guys."

"Okay, Kenny. Go after the cleaning lady. Make sure she's legit. If you have a good image of her, send it to me. Was there anything in the office when you searched it before?"

"Nothing yellow and round, if that's what you mean. I'll send you the enhanced hallway view when it's ready."

"Go after her. I might try to take a quick nap, but wake me if anything happens. Please be careful."

Ten minutes later, Kenny said the cleaning lady had vanished. He transferred a shadowy video, and Sarah decided it could have been Devin in disguise. "Leave someone there and go after him, Kenny. Devin is the key. We've got to find him."

She swore, inflated her air mattress, and threw it down next to her desk. *I'll be better tomorrow if I can rest a little.* The air mattress felt soft and bouncy, but she ended up sitting on it, reading incoming news clips on a wall display, making her eyes burn and her back ache. Every time she flopped down, one of her assistants brought in something "important."

Kenny called to say the cleaning lady had driven off in an old gasoline-powered car parked several buildings distant from the Cavendish. "Must have gone through tunnels and building connections to avoid being seen," he said.

For the next hour, Sarah managed to doze off from time to time. At 5:40 a.m., she found herself on the flat mattress on the hard tile floor, staring up at gum stuck under her desk drawer. The place smelled like musty feet. *If I'm going to be trapped in this office, I might as well write the important story and hope the facts come in to back it up.*

She threw water on her face in a restroom and dictated to her memory implant while hunched over the sink. She said the property and computer attacks would be merely a prelude, and that a dangerous biowar was sure to follow. Her story implored city officials to continuously monitor water supplies and urged people to see a doctor if they developed unusual symptoms. "This is not a vandalism rampage; it's an international biological war and countless lives are at stake." She reminded potential readers about the power of genetics and the notorious atrocities that they had heard about: mice that glowed in the dark, giant deformed pigs, and babies with birth defects. "The OWLs are masters of this technology and they'll use it." She begged people to be vigilant.

A few bulletins had reached the newsroom about toxins and bacteria, but she expected a deluge. As she dictated the story, she knew it sounded alarmist, and that her editor wouldn't publish it until there'd been confirmation, which would probably be too late. When she finished the story, she brushed her teeth.

At nine a.m., Dan called and said there'd been over a billion computer attacks and that they'd tracked the source to the U.K. and then to 12 possible sites in Cambridge.

Minutes later Kenny contacted her. "Sarah, the task force has been scrambled. They're looking for a cyber bunker on the East End. I'm on my way there now. They've identified the building. What should we do?"

"I'm not sure. Send your Marines in with the agents. Check out everyone who comes out, Kenny. Look for Devin, the cleaning lady, or he may be in some other disguise. Be careful."

By ten a.m. Sarah had a piercing headache and felt queasy. Coffee no longer helped. Her sleepy news team was becoming harder to wake up, and when they were awake, they were checking on their families. As she predicted, her publisher and lawyers put Sarah's story on hold because of the panic it might cause. "Can't take the risk," was the official word. Kenny stopped answering her calls, adding to her frustration and sense of panic.

Then, slowly, reports from European and Asian communities about people with bizarre symptoms started to arrive. In addition to chest and abdominal pain, people showed acute allergic reactions, convulsions, and vision changes. With this confirmation, Sarah's story was released to all web services within minutes.

Kenny finally called and coughed out his first words to her in over four hours. "Sarah, the bastard shot me! The cleaning lady. I'm at a hospital. I blacked out and was unconscious a couple of hours, according to a medic. Took a hit in the shoulder. You told me Devin was a wimp."

"He is," she said, "but a brilliant wimp, apparently with a gun. How bad are you hurt?"

"They said it penetrated close to an artery, but I'll live."

"Thank God."

"Devin got away again. He surprised me in the parking lot. He was walking very quickly, just short of a run. Probably trying to look inconspicuous. I cut him off and was waiting to verify the face when he turned with the gun. Good disguise—he had changed clothes again—caught me looking. What's happening there?"

"You'll be getting a lot of company in the hospital soon," she said. "Odd illnesses are showing up everywhere. Officials are terrified here in Washington."

At two p.m., a message was broadcast globally from OWL headquarters. Finally, OWL leadership had a face, a weathered, East-European face. Sarah recognized the man from the Prague pub, the one spinning a coin while staring at her. His tone was defiant but also sad and frightened, like someone cornered.

"My name is Milos Strejc from OWL Command. I am speaking because I will not survive today—but do not worry for me, there are 80 million OWLs to take my job. For 10 years we warn the world—but the rich do not listen. Yesterday we start a global war, and now the war is ending. We win, and we lose. We are the young ones, the future, but we grow up now, tired of waiting. Some say we are the voice of God, but that is too much. We do have power to punish.

"One final time, I tell you the problem is the blind people, the rich, those who do not see billions of sad ones in the jungles of Africa, the slums, the poor villages of Asia, or the mountains of South America. They think these are not real people, that they are no more than insects. Not true. We OWLs have lived there. The poor are exactly like you: they are loving, working, and hoping to live better.

"You will soon hear how our toxins and bacteria are spreading in your cities, towns, and villages. Every OWL bomb or fire you see has these. Your water now has viruses too small to see or filter. They act slow, but cause pain and death.

"There are warehouses and trucks full with antidote. They are marked with bright red paint around their doors. Supplies are double what you need—look for them. You must find and help the elderly and poor and homeless who do not hear this. You must search for them and truly see them. Save them.

"The rich places are different. Bioagents in those castle areas have no antidotes. Arrogant, heartless people in those areas will die from our gases. Many rich monsters will die with their children. This is the OWL penalty for ignoring our warnings!

"Why do this? We want food, learning, abundance, and joy to be shared. We want you to feel the pain in the world and to be outraged. We want you to see that a baby 10,000 kilometers away is your baby too. We want greed to end.

"I expect to die soon; my secret place is now found. But OWLs will not die. The terrible power we used was easy. It will be easy for others. You must solve these problems before it is too late for all humans."

∼∼∼∼∼

The butterfly flexed its symmetrical wings for 15 minutes, but it wasn't able to fly anymore. The smoky air in San Marino stung its antennae. Everything was strange. The sky was empty, unlike its crowded laboratory home.

Rianne had designed the pseudo-butterfly's brain to be twice as large as necessary for its body mass. There were extra neurons available for thoughts, feelings, and emotions. Common bacteria from the hibiscus nectar had eaten through its digestive tract, but it had no word for pain.

"No yellow. Search. Hungry."

The butterfly was sad—it knew it had reached the end of its life cycle. It died alone.

The body fell off the pink petal to the ground.

~~~~~~~~

"Get me out of this bloody chair," Jeremy said.

Against her better judgment, Laurel wheeled him over to the table in the kitchen, dragging his IV stand behind. *He'll probably crawl around if I don't help.*

Dr. Farner and a team of medical people had been there all morning and had given orders to keep him immobile and quiet for at least three days. The first psychological tests would begin tomorrow.

Laurel asked the nurses and house staff to leave so they could be alone. She made some chicken soup for him, which he savored lovingly.

"How long?" he asked.

"Nine years and ten months."

"Almost ten years? Hell, I'm an old man."

"Yes, and also the eighth-richest man in the world, and I'm the second-richest woman, depending on how the money is counted. Actually, it's lucky you're not in the slammer. The IRS wanted to know where you got so much money before I met you, and why you gave most of it to illegal organizations. The statute of limitations saved you, plus they knew you weren't going anywhere. You passed a fortune to the OWLs—they're the idiots who bombed half the world, including our yard, last night."

"Laurel, stop. Don't tell so much so fast. I need time to catch up. I just want to look at you, and the flowers, the soup, the ceiling, anything not moving or flashing in my brain. It's so peaceful. I can smell things."

"Of course. I'm sorry."

He seemed so weak, his face shriveled and gray, but he moved, he was alive. She would make him better.

He squeezed her hand. "But, why are you pregnant? How?"

"I love you. I've been faithful, except maybe in the simulator. I wanted a baby so much. I just sort of borrowed your sperm."

"Oh."

"I thought about it for years," she said. "I was out of time. I explained it to you. Could you understand things I said? I talked to you every morning while I combed your hair."

"No. I don't believe I heard anything. Sex might have helped though. I felt more human when I concentrated on basics, like anger and eating. I often thought about gorging myself, but I didn't know what I was eating. I guess I wasn't eating at all."

"What was it like?" she asked.

Jeremy stared toward the backyard garden and then closed his eyes. "I remember how it started," he said. "After the computer diagrammed my brain, it answered my questions, even before I'd fully asked them. If I thought a response was beautiful, it gave more. I programmed it to stop every half hour, but I couldn't resist going back in. I'm not sure if I got deeper into the computer's mind, or if my brain just became a node on the computer. All I know is my thoughts accelerated, beyond description really, and the ideas seemed compelling and beautiful. I saw a white flash. I thought I'd entered Heaven, and when I had that idea, I was there, and the computer kept making it more wonderful."

He looked up at her. "We're going to have a baby?"

"Yes."

"Brilliant." He smiled and then closed his eyes again. "Somewhere, you must have pulled the plug. By then my brain had been partially reworked. I don't think the computer did it on purpose. I was thinking new things so fast, the neural weights, my memories, drifted."

"Was it a nightmare, Jeremy, after I disconnected you? The doctors thought you were suffering. They asked me to let you die. Was it—horrible?"

"It felt like the morning after a bad dream, you know, where everything seems important but nothing makes sense. It was unbelievably frustrating. One constant remained, a small clock on the side of my vision. It flashed—showing the half hour time limit had expired. Apparently I've watched that annoying flicker for 10 years, but I'd forgotten what it meant. That was horrible."

Laurel's eyes burned and she blew her nose. "Early on," she said, "I decided to keep you alive, but I never stopped doubting. I worried I might be torturing you. Did I do the right thing?"

"Yes, Laurel, you did right." He held her hand when she couldn't hold back tears and handed her a napkin. His eyes looked red too. He rubbed them with the edge of his hand.

***

Laurel had gone to make tea when Jeremy heard a ping in his comm implant. He answered to a familiar voice.

"Hello, Jeremy. This is Milos. I was not sure you are awake. I waited many years. You had coma, no? I want to say goodbye. I tried to call 10 times today in case you wake up. You see me on news? I want to tell, you ruin my life. You sent Czech government my secrets. They throw me out. I must start over with OWLs. Before you die, I want you to know who kills you. I have last laugh. My OWLs put the best bombs in your yard last night. Your death will be long and painful, very painful. The virus is slow. Your spine will twist. Sorry, I will not visit you in hospital. Ciao."

Blood drained from Jeremy's face and he felt very cold. His nose burned and his eyes stung. *I don't want to die now—not again.* He noticed the rotting smell in the air and called to Laurel.

***

At the edge of the Caltech campus, minuscule larvae finished sucking up the birth gel and started eating the eucalyptus tree. The leaves tasted bitter, so many of the worms dropped off, looking for something better. Soon the tiny eating machines started chewing anything green—tasty or not. But the chemistry of DNA life around them was wrong, it poisoned the larvae and they died.

***

Devin took a lift to the third floor and unlocked his secret flat in South London. The three small rooms would need to hide him for a long time. He threw an oversized satchel with all his remaining worldly possessions, including the yellow sphere, onto a bed. The recent past and bleak future bounced back and forth in his mind.

What went wrong?

The problems had first manifested when his 300 million software slaves reported that powerful cyber-apparitions were guarding financial, military, and intelligence targets. The moment his trapdoors and Trojan horses opened, new firewalls appeared with indecipherable keys. Only squirts of data got out. Red lights flashed across his global status screens and on the statistical summaries.

Thank god I had a personal backup plan, the wig and skirt, the whole thing. But I lost time going back to the Cavendish for my Torae file downloads. I should have had them with me.

Back at the bunker, he'd shifted computational resources through the night, mounting coordinated attacks, but was repeatedly blocked from any truly significant computing sites. In the last hour, he applied all his energy and computing reserves to three international banks, hoping to break through with at least some financial control. But when he discovered bloodhound avatars sniffing in his own memory core at Cambridge, he knew it was all over.

My programs should have overwhelmed them. Our cyber codes fell, which was inconceivable. They were unbreakable. I need to understand who did this and how. I'm lucky to have escaped.

He had calmly donned his disguise in a loo and headed to the car, leaving his cyber team behind. Only minutes later, from the parking lot, he watched British military storm the command center.

I shot someone. I'm a fugitive. I may never see my wife and children again. Everything I've created is gone; my life is gone and I'm trapped.

He drank bottled water and paced the room in anger and confusion. The single window of the small flat was jammed and he needed to pry it open. Through a smoky haze, across the Thames and downwind, he saw much of London burning.

At least a few things went right.

<hr />

Dan called Sarah and Rianne at four p.m. "We won," he said, sounding exhausted but jubilant. "We didn't have as many programs or locations, but my software children were marvelously clever. All key assets were protected and the computer threat eliminated. The cyber war is over."

"I knew you had them," Sarah said, "when I heard the president's people talking about command center locations. Early on, the police and military seemed to be just raiding OWL meeting rooms and charity hubs, which wasn't helping."

"My software bloodhounds sniffed their way back to the command sites," Dan said, "and the attack dogs kept the doors open until the real troops arrived. OWL kids actually arranged themselves across roads to delay the government SWAT teams, but the bunkers all fell. We got the biggies: Devin's site in Cambridge, a political bunker under a farm outside Prague, and one in Nebraska of all places. Milos, their top guy, died in the Prague raid. It all came crashing down.

"I didn't think it would go this well," he added. "Devin had sentient programs too, but they were unimaginative, rigid. And he didn't know about the Q-bit. I'm actually surrounded by the computer here at the NSA; it fills this whole building. This place is mostly huge pumps and liquefied helium. The scientific community thinks this is impossible. We're doing coherent processing over thousands of large wafers. Devin rotated 2,048-word cyber keys every 10 minutes, which should have taken a million universe lifetimes to decode. Jupiter and Thor broke them in less than 10 seconds."

"Unfortunately," Rianne said, "my war just started."

"Rianne, you sound terrible," Sarah said. "Are you all right?"

"Someone needs to prioritize my bio work. We're already running out of time. People are dying. And the team here has been working 36 hours straight."

"We're scrubbing for sleeper cells now," Dan said, "but we've also broken into OWL records. Rianne, I've started transferring reams of biochemical structure and medical information we found in their labs over to you and the Centers for Disease Control. There were descriptions of 30 agents and 21 antidotes. You should focus on the ones without antidotes."

Rianne's voice was shaky. "The structures will help tremendously. Thanks, Dan. Sarah, can you check if the agencies have any new infection-rate data? I'm having a little trouble thinking straight. We wasted all night on some stupid waterborne samples before the OWLs handed us the antidote. But this other OWL stuff is awful. I just learned about a malignant strain in California, a cancer-trigger cell that attacks the nasal passages, lungs, and nerves. The victims' senses go berserk. They're blinded and hyperesthetic. Every touch is painful."

Rianne fell silent for a second or two before continuing. "The OWLs dispersed it around Pasadena. Mother and Father were infected. They're at the Huntington Hospital. I need to get back to work now."

Dan was distressed to hear that Joti and Kyle were in danger. Before he could say anything remotely comforting, Rianne disconnected.

Everything the butterfly larvae ate poisoned them. As they died and decayed, microscopic nematodes and spiders in the ground consumed their juices and were themselves poisoned. Smaller creatures kept subdividing the meal until two fundamentally incompatible bacterial species, one based on DNA and one not, were at war in the Pasadena soil.

BIOLOGY

After Rianne disconnected from Sarah and Dan, she wept silently from worry, exhaustion, and frustration. The world's most advanced interactive displays flashing in her office offered no guidance. Finally, she whispered in her implant, "Mother, are you awake?"

"Rianne?" Joti's voice sounded guttural and weak. "You all right?"

"Don't worry about me, Mother. How do you feel? I can barely hear you."

"So hot. Kyle's sleep. Gone . . . blurry. Hurts . . ."

"Mother, I need to talk to your doctor. What's the name?"

"Doctor . . . Emily Melquist. Nurse here . . . more painkillers. Call back?"

"Sure. I'll check on Father. I love you."

Rianne briefly considered chucking all her responsibilities, ordering a government plane, and flying to California to be with her parents, but she knew her best chance of helping them was to keep working in Princeton. So much time had already been wasted. Boxed in, she was furious about the OWLs, the Torae, and death in general. She vowed nothing would stand in her way, not fatigue, nor bureaucracy or protocol.

Abruptly, she said, "CDC level-alpha emergency, call Dr. Emily Melquist, California." Rianne heard an override ping.

"Melquist here. Who's there?"

"This is Dr. Rianne Jorgenson, CDC. We actually know each other. I was Rianne Orlov, Alex Smith Day School, a little twerp; you probably hated me. Remember? . . . I need your help."

"Rianne, oh yeah, I remember. This must be about the Orlovs, your parents, right?

"Yes and no."

"Well, I can't talk. Special treatment is out of the question. We're way too busy. Four million people are dying in L.A."

"Emily, no. This is mostly CDC business. I've been assigned to work on the California nerve agent, the one without an antidote. The one my parents have. I can cure it." *Not entirely a lie.*

"No shit! How?"

"Well, it's not quite pinned down yet. How many patients do you have with neurosensory problems?"

"About 200 here at Huntington. We're getting even more walk-ins with the waterborne virus, but they don't need much. We're inoculating them in the parking lot. The county is even treating people at the Rose Bowl. People just walk or drive by and get an injection. Here at the hospital we mostly treat the nerve-agent victims and other life-threatening conditions."

"Emily, I need samples. Nose and throat cultures, bodily fluids, skin tissue, anything that makes sense. We think it may be contagious." *That's a complete lie, but it should get Melquist's attention.* "I'll have someone pick up everything in half an hour and fly it to us. Has anyone died yet?"

"Not yet, but most wish they would. My God, you say it's contagious? We'll have to take precautions. It's the most painful disease I've ever seen."

"Tell me what you know about it."

"The whole thing's monstrous. I heard the OWLs exploded two-stage canisters. A first weak explosion dispersed the agent and a second incendiary carried the smoke higher. It was a pleasant night; almost everyone's windows were open. The agent virus is attached to pollen spores—stuck on the little spikes. As people breathe, it inflames their nasal tissue and transfers to the bloodstream."

"What symptoms do you see?"

"First sign is sneezing. It penetrates the nerve endings in the nose. We think the active material is a precursor, which triggers abnormal effects along the nerves. It makes the fibers highly sensitive. The people who come in can barely talk. Sound and light are painful."

"How are you treating it?"

"We're doing our best with massive antibiotics and pain killers. I'm praying the immune system slows it down, but eventually the brain and spine could be infected."

"Look," Rianne said, "I just got a data dump on the biostructure and medical tests of the developers. The OWLs perfected it on rats and chimps. The monkeys lived about four days—we've got a little time."

"I'm not sure my patients will want to know that. What can you do in Atlanta on this? Only California has seen these symptoms. All the universities and pharmaceutical companies here are already working on it . . . those who still have staff coming to work."

"I can cure it," she said confidently. "Please get the samples ready now. And, Emily, take good care of my parents, please."

Rianne cut the call and poured more coffee with shaking hands. Every minute, new documents on the OWL toxins popped up on her incoming mail screen and were sorted into bins by type and location as she'd instructed the computer. She scanned the titles with both hands squeezing her hot mug. She called Sarah a few minutes later.

"Sarah, I need a jet—either military or private. I want someone to pick up medical samples in Pasadena, get half to me as fast as possible and then carry the rest to the CDC in Atlanta. Can you do it?"

"I don't think so. Maybe. Short notice is a problem. Most planes have been grounded. I can try. What do I tell them?"

"Tell them . . . we could lose half the population of California if I don't have the samples in four hours. Pick them up from Dr. Emily Melquist, Huntington Hospital, Pasadena, in 15 minutes. Get them to me at the Princeton Biochemical Labs as soon as possible. Got that?"

"Yeah. I'll check National Security, and Web News has a jet in California I think. How about the CDC? Why don't you just call them?"

"I can't."

"Why not, Rianne?"

"Well, it's not really contagious."

"Oh . . . I'll call the Army guys first. They won't ask difficult questions."

"Another thing, Sarah. Your brother is a neurosurgeon, right?"

"Yeah, Adam. Why?"

"I need nerve samples—living. Can you have him call me?"

"Sure. I'll do it as soon as I get started on the military jet. Do you have any other impossible requests? By the way, I checked out the international priorities for the OWL toxins. Your California plague is low on the list. Estimate is only 15,000 infections. The worst are in Germany and Scandinavia, over 100,000 each. Europe's been screaming that everyone should be helping them. I'll let you know if I hear anything more. I should get busy now—I have to commandeer a jet. Bye."

A few minutes later Adam called and arranged to send a van from Johns Hopkins to Princeton with as many types of live neurons as he could find.

Rianne told eight graduate students and the assistant professor that shared the Princeton lab with her to meet outside the hazard-one clean room. Two sleeping students had to be awakened.

Her back was against an observation window as they gathered around. "I just received 700 pages of data on various OWL toxins," she said. "This is high-quality structural info, direct from the bastards who developed it, via the NSA computer people who broke into their lab archives. Summarize your work so far and send it to the CDC; the new information changes our approach. I want everyone to focus on a California problem. Break into pairs and spend a half hour scanning the new data. We'll have live samples in a few hours. Professor Llewellyn's team will determine how the vector migrates on the nerves. I'll lead a second team in the simulation lab to understand, and hopefully counter, the virulent protein."

An hour later, functional models of protein molecules were displayed on the sim-room walls. "People," Rianne said, "some of you might recognize this as a mutant of the retinoblastoma protein. I'm rotating before-and-after-representations so you can compare them. Rb inhibits cancerous proliferation of normal nerve cells. The conformation of the OWL version is distorted, slightly twisted, making it ineffective so the nerve cells keep dividing. We need to make it active again—untwist it or rebuild it. Let's see if we can get it working."

Rianne and three of her students began to yell out molecule names, and the computer bounced them off the OWL protein from thousands of angles. A few stuck and changed its shape. The computer then ran hundreds of homomorphic variants, turning the displays into a blur, and ranked their effectiveness in suppressing the nerve-cancer agent. For over an hour, the human team and computers came up with sporadic improvements, egging each other on, with better molecules boosting the efficacy. It was playtime for brilliant minds, a deadly serious game.

The samples arrived from Johns Hopkins and California. Rianne's sim team found two enzymes and two ions that improved the mutant Rb function. Llewellyn's group proposed three ways the cell could be made electrophobic. Rianne recapped their status by saying, "We can't kill this sucker yet, but we can sure slow it down. Let's see how our ideas work on the real samples."

Just after midnight she received an urgent call. Her CDC contract director's first words were, "What the hell are you doing, Jorgenson? We just accepted samples from California. The Army courier told us to be careful; he'd heard they were contagious. Then I saw your name on the papers. Mind explaining?"

"I know we were supposed to be concentrating on the East Coast or European viruses, but I have a cure for the California one. Just need a couple more hours."

"How could you have a cure if you just got the samples? And I haven't heard it's contagious, have you?"

"Not exactly. Trust me on this, we'll wrap it up in four hours, tops."

"*Do not* tell anyone it's contagious, Rianne. You'll start a panic. I'll talk to you later."

Her team watched dual micrographs and cheered for their own samples. When the untreated OWL virus was present, inflamed tissue spread in Adam's live nerve cultures. They saw the Schwann cell sheaths, which protect the nerves, dissolve at node openings in close-ups. When the team's counter-agents were added, the growth stopped, and OWL cells just wandered around in the culture dishes.

"Excellent work, people! This is no time for staged clinical trials. Take a short break while I get the word out to the right officials."

Rianne called Dr. Melquist first. "Emily. It's Jorgenson here. Pump 'em up with potassium. Take it to just below organ damage levels. They'll bloat up, but they can take it for a week or two. I'll have an enzyme inoculation in a few hours to completely halt the growth. We have to hope their immune systems can beat down the established cells. Call me if you see changes."

Next, she interrupted the head of Caltech's microbiology department. "Alvaro, this is Rianne Jorgenson. I've got a list of some unusual enzymes we need."

"Rianne, have you heard the news?" he said.

"What news?"

"Chia-Jean's lab was destroyed. We think some specimens escaped."

"Oh, no! How?"

"Some OWL people knocked out the guards and students, and blasted the lab with explosives. It's a horrible mess."

"Is everyone okay?"

"They will be okay. But what are you calling about?"

"I'm working on an OWL disease for the CDC. It's the deadly one used in San Marino and other wealthy neighborhoods in California. About 50,000 could die. I'm sending you a detailed formula. We need about 200 liters of this stuff in syringes. Can you call your pharmaceutical friends and have them blend it and distribute it to all the hospitals? It's relatively simple."

"I know who to call. Do they have to synthesize anything new?"

"They should have all of the materials; they just need to mix it and get it to the all the hospitals with the dosage information I included. If you can make a little on campus, I'd appreciate your getting it over to the Huntington Hospital ASAP. My parents and many other victims are there."

"I'll get on it as soon as I splash some water on my face."

"What escaped from Chia-Jean's lab?" she asked. "We were always deathly afraid that might happen."

"We're not sure. We found 10-centimeter brown spots on the grass nearby and decomposing larvae. We built a containment tent around it. We're being very careful."

"Good, Alvaro. I'll call Chia-Jean about it later if you haven't.

"I haven't been able to reach her," he said.

"Have you gotten your own inoculation for the waterborne virus?"

"Of course. It was a zoo at the Rose Bowl, but amazingly efficient. Officials are scouring the streets looking for the homeless and shut-ins. I think they'll get to everyone, in Pasadena at least. I'll call you if I have any problem with the enzymes. And I'll get some to the Huntington if I have to mix it myself. We miss you out here."

Rianne called the CDC to have her plan authorized and to get an official bulletin out to California hospitals. After another sarcastic but short tongue-lashing from her director, she promised to work on his priorities and re-directed her team to the German virus.

At three a.m., she went back into the simulator room alone and began to search for ways to kill the California nerve-disease agent, not just contain it. At five a.m., after being awake for 47 hours, her head slumped to the desktop and she fell asleep.

Midafternoon, Rianne heard a familiar voice in her sleep and awakened. Someone had put a blanket over her.

"Rianne, can you hear me? This is Chia-Jean. Are you there?"

"Professor Ma? Hello. Yes, this is Rianne. I heard about your lab. Do you need help? Let me wake up here a second. What time is it?"

"Rianne, I need your assistance, but I'm not calling about the lab." Chia-Jean coughed and cleared her throat. "Can you promise something, which may take a lot of your time? Something very important to me."

"I'll do anything for you, Professor."

"Rianne, I need you to save Tina. I can't find her anywhere. You were her friend. She'll listen to you. She's lost to me."

"Professor, I haven't seen her in 10 years. We argued. She hates me, I think. Do you have any idea where she is?"

"No. The OWLs changed her. I'm sure she became a wire-head. The police won't help. But Tina's my soul. You could find her and cure her. I can't anymore."

"I'll fly out as soon as I can," Rianne said. "My parents are sick. I need to be in California anyway. Are you out there?"

"No, Rianne. I'm still in Europe. I got trapped here in Berlin. I can't travel. Will you help Tina? You are both my children. The German doctors say I'll die in two days. The OWLs bombed the air system in my hotel with some terrible virus. I'm dying without my child. Will you promise to try?"

What little was left of Rianne's spirit withered. "Of course, Chia-Jean. You know I love you."

Under plastic tents, men in full-body biosuits took specimens and tested ground samples. Three cubic meters of soil and vegetation were carefully excavated and later heated to more than 1,000 degrees Celsius. A eucalyptus tree overhanging the area showed dead leaves and more larvae. The tree was cut into small pieces, removed, and burned, including its roots. In a 100-meter circle, 20 centimeters of grass, ground cover, and topsoil were stripped from the Caltech campus and incinerated.

No one wanted a non-DNA life form competing with the Earth's ecosystem.

WINNERS AND LOSERS

Humans are either amazingly resilient or insane, Sarah thought. *The world came an eyelash from historic-level chaos, hundreds of thousands died, and in only four months most people have gone back to their old lives.* She looked up at antique globe lights hanging from the wood-paneled ceiling and shook her head. *Habits nearly always come back. Resilient or insane?*

The Warner family had arrived early to sit near the jury so they could watch their faces during Isaac's trial. Sarah's chair, up against the courtroom wall and behind the others, also provided a bit of protection from any assassins who might still be tracking her. Isolated OWL terror teams were jockeying for position in the remnant organization, and Sarah remained a prime target.

Craig and Ben were both there. Ben made a great human shield, like a hulking football lineman, at the end of the family row, very tall and more than a little overweight. *Ben loves to be the bodyguard, always vigilant. He's found his calling—protecting the Warner family. He constantly checks the security cameras at the farm and plays back the recordings. He knows where every deer, fox, or squirrel lives. He won't let anyone near Ma or me.*

Finally the judge entered, and Sarah focused on the trial. The prosecutor spoke sympathetically to the alleged victim, while keeping one eye on the jury. "Tell us, Miss Ritter, exactly what the defendant, Isaac Warner, did to you that night."

"Isaac seemed so nice when I first met him, but he isn't." The woman told her rape story very slowly in graphic detail. She wore a short-sleeved blouse so the scar on her arm, which she claimed Isaac had caused, was visible. The jury squirmed in their seats when they saw the early police photos. Now and again during the testimony, Sarah's mother, Andrea, moaned or whimpered quietly.

"I can tell she's lying," Sarah said softly. "You know I can tell when someone's lying. Don't worry, Ma. She'll slip up." They held each other's hands. A half hour later, when the young woman finished by sobbing uncontrollably, the judge declared a recess.

Sarah had watched Isaac, sitting next to his defense lawyer, appearing concerned through the woman's entire statement. *He's wearing his innocent and serious look for the trial. How does he do that, look so sincere? He can fool anyone ... except me.*

The family stayed in the courtroom throughout the recess. After saying nothing for several minutes, Andrea asked Sarah to pray with her. They held hands and she pressed her forehead against Sarah's. She whispered, "Dear Jesus, Lord, share your forgiveness with my son Isaac and this lady. Y'all can do that even for the most horrible sins. Please, help us all."

Andrea went silent, like she wanted to say more but didn't know how. Sarah waited and then said, "Amen."

The trial restarted and other prosecution witnesses were used to establish when Isaac had been in the accuser's apartment and had sex with her. They brought out an eyewitness, Miss Ritter's friend, who said she witnessed the rape. Sarah watched her carefully under the bright courtroom lights and saw river-rock wrinkles at the edge of her eyes. "She's lying, Ma. There's something wrong about what they're saying. I think they set Isaac up."

Isaac's attorney asked questions that picked at inconsistencies between the two women's stories. He attacked the witness's credibility, showing she couldn't remember the dress color or whether the lights were on or off. She couldn't remember what her friend was screaming out when she interrupted the rape. Finally, the judge called for another short recess.

When the courtroom had mostly cleared, Andrea whispered, "Isaac did it, didn't he?"

"He'll get off, Ma. I've been watching the jury. They don't trust the witness."

"Isaac always was a cruel boy. I tried my best to love him." Andrea stared blankly at the courtroom paintings.

"I'm going out with Ben to the restrooms, Ma. Okay? Do you want to come along or stay here?"

Lost in thought, she didn't answer.

Ben shadowed Sarah right to the door of the women's restroom. When she came back out, she noticed a tall man walking straight toward her, silhouetted by the blinding sunlight of a hallway window. Ben appeared at the men's room door just as Sarah recognized the tall figure.

Kenny walked right up to her with his right arm in a sling. "Hey, Sarah," he said.

"Gad, don't come right up to me like that. You're lucky Ben hasn't tackled you."

She held her arm out to slow Ben down. He was angry someone had gotten that close to her. "It's okay, Ben. This is the Marine, Kenny, I told you about. He's a friend of mine."

"I was in Bethesda, Maryland, for some tests on my arm," Kenny said, "and Dan told me about the trial, so I thought I'd take a break and see how you and your family are doing."

"You've never met my brother, have you? He's been taking good care of Ma and me."

"Good to meet you, Ben. Sorry if I startled you."

"You can go back to sit by Ma in the courtroom, Ben. Kenny will watch out for me. He's a tough guy too."

Ben looked suspiciously at the Marine's sling but didn't say anything. He headed back to the courtroom, leaving them alone.

"You came to talk to me?" said Sarah.

"Well, you are an expert on the OWLs. I took a bullet from them and I still don't understand why. What the hell were they trying to accomplish?"

"The OWLs expected to win, of course. I don't know if they really had a plan to help the poor or not. Just sending money and food to countries where family and tradition are more important than wealth wouldn't help for long. Increasing dependency can't be good. Maybe they wanted to provide better medical care, education, genetic equality, and crisis support—that makes some sense. I don't think they'd planned much beyond stopping the exploitation."

"So," he said, "worldwide, almost ten million people died, and even experts like you don't fully understand why. I heard a third of the population of Akron, Ohio, perished because the OWLs stockpiled the wrong antidote. Great planners."

"Don't get me wrong," Sarah said. "I think they had the right problem. How to deal with inequality is the world's oldest political question. There are solutions—possibilities at least. Sometimes the poorest people are the happiest, but many others feel their lives are helpless, hopeless. They have to yearn to learn and succeed. Parents, especially mothers, are crucial. It's complicated but not impossible."

"Sarah, you were a hero of the cyber war. Dan and Rianne were heroes too, but almost no one knows about them. You're the most visible. People are going to need your help to make sense of it."

"I intend to crawl back into my cubbyhole and just be a reporter."

"You should go into politics."

"What a silly, bizarre idea, Kenny."

"I'm serious. But, changing the subject, how is the trial going?"

"I imagine my brother, Isaac, will weasel out of this somehow. Do you want to meet my family?"

"Sure."

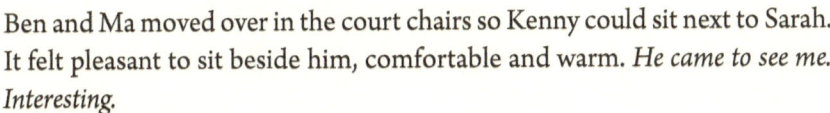

Ben and Ma moved over in the court chairs so Kenny could sit next to Sarah. It felt pleasant to sit beside him, comfortable and warm. *He came to see me. Interesting.*

The two defense lawyers brought witnesses who testified that the Ritter woman had known Isaac for two weeks before the alleged rape. He then asked Isaac to take the stand. Sarah read Isaac's face and recognized telltale river-rock lines on his forehead and pulsing colors under his ears. She was dismayed to see he was lying as much as the two women.

"I did love her, and I thought she loved me," he was saying.

"Can you think of any reason she would accuse you of rape?" the defense lawyer asked.

"I guess now I see her as a little unstable. I admit we were having sex, but she wanted me to move in with her right away. I wasn't ready for anything so serious. At heart, I'm kind of traditional."

Isaac can be so completely persuasive. The jury is buying this twaddle, Sarah thought, watching several jurors.

The defense attorney eventually brought the eyewitness back to the stand and tore her story apart. The woman tried to look honest and confused about the details, but the jury didn't believe her anymore. At the end, she became angry, shouting back at the defense lawyer and swearing.

Sarah knew Isaac would be acquitted. The judge scheduled final arguments and time for the jury decision, so the Warner family left the courtroom. Isaac would be free and there was no point in telling her mother the truth, Sarah decided.

A bit upset about the trial result, Sarah walked hesitatingly along the hallway. Kenny held her arm at the courthouse exit and helped her down the front stairs. He quickly made friends with everyone, even Craig, on the drive back to the farm. They all seemed happy about how the trial had gone.

Kenny came to see me. Quite far out of his way. Nice. Should spend time with him. Wants me to go into politics, or something. What odd ideas he has.

Rianne's mind worked rapidly. What a normal person would consider a short break, thinking things over, or being careful, she saw as uncertainty or incompetence. She believed the OWL virus permanently disabled Joti and Kyle because she had acted too slowly. After 10 months of treatment and hope, their future was set. Her mother would walk with a cane and her father would be in a wheelchair the rest of their lives because the nerve damage reached their spines. But if she'd followed the bureaucratic rules, they would both be dead now, she reminded herself.

Looking around her deserted lab, she vowed it would never happen again. What she was about to do was not an act of arrogance; it needed to be done without vacillation. She pressed her forehead against the ultrascope to do the unthinkable.

Her hand moved cautiously, even though the motion was reduced 10,000 times by the micromanipulator. She tried to empty her mind of thousands of factors, fears, interactions, and consequences to focus on the delicate task. It was the most important act of her life. The microscopic needle pricked the outer cell wall and moved toward the nucleus. She heard her heart beating and slowed it down.

The egg cell was huge, almost 25 micrometers. Rianne adjusted light angles, polarization, and wavelength constantly to improve the clarity of the internal structures. The needle moved gingerly around organelles, nutrient paths, and other fragile structures.

Rianne was at peace in this tiny universe. The needle passed a Golgi apparatus and reached the double wall of the nucleus. She switched magnification, then punctured the wall and moved deeper to the priceless object, the essence of life. Being careful to remove as little adjacent material as possible, Rianne gently evacuated the chromosomes, all the DNA, her DNA.

In the 10 months since the OWL war, her resolve had grown. She knew her special gifts would be unimaginable, even to other scientists, and felt prepared and obligated to use them. Dan discussed the subject endlessly with her and gave her a few ground rules. Her plan would affect their lives forever, and all others eventually. He supported her and said she would rebalance the global timelines, adding diversity to a humanity growing alike and bland. She didn't think of it as courageous—it was simply why she'd been born.

The complexity and danger frightened everyone else. The correlations were known: 330 genes to control intelligence, 53 to determine hair color, 4 to prevent Crohn's disease, and on and on, but the interaction problems were staggering. Only Rianne fully understood the connections between the genes and the "jungle DNA" that controlled timing and activation. Germ-line progress had been slow. CRISPR applications had dealt with only one gene at a time, such as screening out cystic fibrosis or other simple genetic defects. Even that was still controversial and immoral in most eyes.

Human application was regulated ethically, legally, and more importantly, by common sense. Genetic collateral damage was so frequent that only desperate families took the risk. Hundreds of promising experiments on animals were balanced by a few errors. Many even still feared genetically modified foods, although tremendous value was proven. Most people had lost track of the difference between genetically enhanced health foods, hybrid naturals, organically improved giant fruit, and what used to be called "real food." But astounding flower and tree varieties blossomed everywhere. Ever since genomes had been cataloged, for over 40 years, biodiversity had rapidly accelerated, in the plant kingdom at least.

Rianne's preparation had been painstaking. She began with over 10 million DNA samples from scrapings of her own skin. Portions of those strands were cut and replaced with new ones that she had designed and grown. She added jungle-DNA trigger sequences so the genes would turn on at the right times and places. Fluorescence studies narrowed the sample pool to 200 chromosomes, where all the essential genes had found the right homes. Rianne had then assembled two 21-chromosome samples. Carefully, she squirted one sample into the egg nucleus.

Rianne knew the combination would work. She understood completely the gene correlations, the protein interactions, the chemical cascades and cycles, and their ultimate effects on the cell and individual traits. Her choices were supported by hundreds of animal experiments and thousands of computer simulations. She knew this world and felt its entirety. The story of how both regular DNA and Chia-Jean's non-DNA life had evolved was imprinted on her memory through years of experimentation. She harbored no reluctance.

There were two egg cells. She let them reorganize for a few hours before fertilizing with Dan's sperm.

They'd talked about the morality of her plan and the long-term effects on humans. Dan simply didn't buy the inequality argument—the haves and have-nots—saying advances eventually spread to everyone. Sarah told her, "If you have the genius to improve humans, you have the responsibility to do it." Rianne had weighed the risks that inhibited the rest of the scientific and medical community and chose to take on the burden for them all.

She designed her babies to have Dan's nose, Joti's skin tone, her father's humor, Mary's devotion, Sarah's special vision, and her own hearing. She identified three of the Torae-designed genes, which caused extra brain folds in Dan's temporal lobes, and included them. Altogether, she changed 1,500 genes, along with the corresponding jungle-DNA trigger sequences, or about one-third as much as the difference between humans and chimps. She assumed half would become active after the fertilization. Dan's sperm had been sorted only for sex—using the slight gender-dependent size difference.

The fertilized eggs were allowed to divide for a week, until there were 100 cells in each and they became sustainable blastocysts. A graduate student anchored the embryos on to Rianne's uterus—one girl and one boy. Both became healthy fetuses and were born successfully nine months later. Their grandparents didn't suspect anything unusual for several months after the birth. The babies appeared normal, which had been one of Dan's key ground rules, but Rianne had advanced normal human evolution by 50,000 years.

Near a large San Marino home, under a hibiscus bush where a butterfly with four eyes had died, an odd bacterium had mutated and learned to consume ordinary DNA-based life. It divided and reproduced rapidly and caused the bush to wilt and die. The reproductive code of the new species tended to evolve rapidly; it would do well surrounded by an almost infinite food supply and no natural enemies.

The mansion's gardener cut the bush down, pulled out the diseased roots, and threw it on a compost pile for recycling.

HOME STAR

The task was repugnant but unambiguous: species extermination. Destroying the Unity hive, the birthplace of the pests, was the crucial first step. Due to the brutal nature of the chore, leadership on the orange-red-coded ship had been officially transferred from Sower to Tiller, who had no moral qualms about such things.

On their 26-light-year journey to the Unity home star, over 10,000 battle probes had been manufactured, powered, and deployed. Close to the
target now, Tiller's mind overlaid surveillance scans into a pristine, four-
dimensional image of everything within a light-hour of the peculiar star,
warily tracking several hundred thousand Unity space vehicles. His shrouded
probes advanced on schedule from all directions with enough stockpiled vio-
lence to erase the Unity civilization.

"The Unity seem to be unaware of our presence," Tiller said. "Our visual
masking layers are working. I'll allow a little more time for your evaluation,
Sower. I agree this is a very unusual star and species."

"Excellent," Sower said. "I'd like to complete my model of the Unity One-
Mind. We see only fragments in any individual creature."

"The delay will be limited. Our mission takes precedence and I must be
cautious," Tiller said, signaling with a solemn blue tremolo.

"I've begun to understand their evolution," Sower said. "Our probe images
are very clear. The Unity may be unique in the universe. Their brain-sharing
motivates procreation."

"Complete your analysis soon."

From a safe location several light-hours away, the star sparkled green as
the Torae command ship drifted laterally. Sower had deduced that a natural,
primordial black hole had grazed the white dwarf, leaving it in a rapid, nearly
unstable rotation. The star's shape was noticeably oblate, 10 percent wider
at the equator than along the spin-axis. Physically similar Unity lived along
lines of latitude, where gravity was constant, but altered types had evolved
to survive the increased gravitational forces near the poles. Shallow buildings extended in narrow lines around the entire star. From the command ship,
the billions of parallel Unity structures diffracted the star's light into flickering spectral rainbows.

Tiller stared at the hypnotic view while absorbing a flood of new information from scout probes:

> "We're surrounded by Unity as we approach the star, but detect
>   no change in their vehicle motions. They can't see us. Our
>   shrouds are working."
> "Each creature has only a trillion-bit brain nub, but their merged
>   intelligence is asymptotic to level seven—quite formidable."
> "Brain-link range is 50 meters."

"Surface population is stable at 50 quadrillion."

"No measurable malice."

"Rote conformity in the individuals is balanced by creativity
in the collective."

"Unique emergent behaviors are likely from the One-Mind."

"Evolution rate 6,000 Torae norm."

Tiller worried most about aspects of his enemy he did not understand. For example, the clarity of local space was very unusual. *How did their space come to be so empty? Have they swept the entire region with black holes? Even interstellar space has a million hydrogen atoms per cubic meter. This space is void of real particles above the quantum foam. How's that possible? Why?*

~~~~~~

Battle Probe 3647 closed in on its target. It had been ordered to study Unity black hole launch facilities, search for vulnerabilities, and report details.

"Several charged black holes are inserted and accelerated around the equator each second, with mass and energy added on each revolution until escape velocity is achieved. The vehicles are seeded with Unity genetic material. Apparently they stay in parking orbits for 12 generations until fully populated. Their explorers are born in space, and nurtured and trained by machines on the ships. Attack diagrams and analysis follow."

~~~~~~

An hour later, Tiller said, "I've decided to begin the assault. I'm uneasy about our ability to avoid detection." He accentuated his comments with a spray of colors indicating concern and resolve.

"We don't understand this enemy," Sower said. "The One-Mind may be the greatest intelligence we've encountered. We'd expect it to be complacent, but it's not. Unity constructions are constantly being refined and replaced. Its creativity is actually increasing. We must understand this swarm-mind architecture."

"The optimum time for simultaneous strike has been chosen," Tiller said.

"I urge you to hold. There is no threat to us."

Tiller transmitted the initiation code. "Our mission is to destroy them, not to understand them."

At the selected moment, Battle Probe 3647 swept coherent gamma rays across the magnets and vacuum structures of the Unity launch facility. Its weapon severed chamber walls and the damage cascaded around the star. Similar probes destroyed message conduits, factories, and shelters over the entire star crust, while other Torae attacked all Unity vehicles within one light-hour of the star. Thirty percent of the surface structures were destroyed in the first volley.

While natural nuclear fusion had long since burned out within the Unity star, tremendous heat reserves lay hidden beneath a relatively cool thin shell. In several places the Torae attack punched holes, exposing the hotter layers underneath, setting off blue 20,000-degree volcanoes. Probe 3647's view of the surface was obscured by the ultraviolet glare.

Temporarily blinded, the probe noticed two nearby black hole vehicles jerk directly away from its position, apparently trying to escape. Focused on the military task below, the probe didn't pay much attention. It was still adjusting filters to see past the dazzle on the stellar surface when it realized its mistake. The Unity vehicles had moved too quickly. They knew Battle Probe 3647 was there. Two pinpricks hit its metal skin before it died.

"Move!" screamed Tiller with every color at his disposal. The gigantic command ship instantly accelerated, laterally and away from the Unity home star. Several probes in its outer protective convoy had vaporized. As the command ship achieved half light speed, its inner ring of shield probes began to disappear.

Looking back, Tiller's sensors detected millions of black hole particles sweeping over the space where the command ship had been stationed. The ship quickly attained near light speed and maneuvered out of danger, but while retreating Tiller watched in horror as his battle probes vanished around the entire star. At a distance 20 light-hours away, they paused and listened for messages—only a few hundred fleeing probes survived.

Sower broke a stunned silence. "Our masks were ineffective."

"They hurled black hole particles at near light speed," Tiller said. "The singularities were neutron-sized, based on the recoil of their ships. How could tiny particles cause such damage? They should have just passed through the probe bodies."

"There are thousands of gravity ripples," Sower said. "They may have stopped the black hole dust within our probes by colliding particles from other directions. The event horizons would merge, releasing gravitational shock waves and tearing the probes apart."

"That might be possible," Tiller said. "But how could they collide such small particles over millions of kilometers?"

"They're astonishing at celestial mechanics," Sower said. "And their attacks must have been simultaneous; they started only moments after we fired on them. So they also have coupled-state communications—instantaneous signals."

Tiller marveled at the Unity actions. "That's why their space is clean," he said. "So they can maintain quantum coherence over the entire region. Their communications exceed speed of light near their home star. We're dealing with a very dangerous species."

<hr />

Tiller on the orange-red Torae ship encoded a detailed account of the Unity battle and sent it toward the clone ships. He established a blockade perimeter 50 light-hours from the Unity star and planned to set up manufacturing facilities at nearby stars to populate the blockade. Tiller concluded the transmission, saying: "Our damage to their home star was substantial. We'll remain here to impede Unity migrations. We'll clone command ships and build probes to slow them down, but I'm worried. The Unity One-Mind is rapidly growing ever more brilliant at this site. They have already rebuilt their launch facilities. The mathematics is clear. We won't be able to stop them."

TIME SIX
TWENTY-SIX YEARS LATER

SECRETS

Sarah was awakened at four a.m. when her bed shuddered, an Earth burp. She flipped her thick comforter off, rolled over, and let her feet drop to the warmed floor of the Munich hotel room.

Pig puke, I'm going to feel rotten in the morning. I should have taken time-shift drugs. I'm not nearly ready for the meeting. Am I getting old?

Even with her comm link turned off, every intelligent appliance, device, and furniture piece in the upscale suite awakened and anticipated her needs. Wall panels lightened to a gray-green so she wouldn't stub her toes. "Open shades and glass," she said, while wobbling toward the large window.

The old German shutters folded open and the bomb-proof window calmly said, "Security breach."

Cold, wet air blew against her nightgown. Looking out, vehicle and foot traffic along Maximilianstrasse sounded familiar and real. She loved Munich. The street noise brought back memories of graduate school—her youth. The post–World War II, mustard-stone buildings across the street had hundreds of interesting dark nooks. Sarah wondered if any human eyes were watching her; certainly invisible street scanners had noted her presence at the third-floor window. Almost universally esteemed, she knew a million kooks would still enjoy taking a shot at her at the window, just to become famous. *My handlers would worry about this.*

The cold air felt good.

Damn voices—my fans—I know you're out there. How many secrets do you want to know? How many can you stand?

She had serious jet lag. The two-hour suborbital flight had been painless, but the Europe-U.S. time difference could not be ignored. Half asleep, she considered starting an autobiography about her crazy life. When the Neues Rathaus bells struck the quarter hour, she abandoned the idea. *I wouldn't know how to end the story anyway.*

The morning meeting worried her. The Chinese had redeployed forces, and the Europeans wanted to compare notes and discuss possible responses. She'd been briefed, but would have to think on her feet. As U.S. ambassador to the European Union, this was her third transatlantic crossing in four days. *Shuttle diplomacy is inhumane.*

Sarah Warner was the most trusted person on the planet. At age 51, after a lifetime of extraordinary accomplishment and sacrifice, 70 percent of humanity gave her level one access to their brains, and she never abused the privilege. Most of the others just didn't want *anyone* in their head. After decades of confusion about fake news and competing biases, by the last half of the twenty-first century the most priceless asset was a reputation for honesty and wisdom. More than any other human or intelligent computer, people relied on Sarah's mindcasts for the truth.

I suppose you'd want to know that my mother's dying, and what I'm advising her to do. Would a simple yes or no on immortality satisfy you—or would I have to explain?

Everyone understood Ambassador Warner had special sources, was unusually wise, and almost always right about the future. Six billion people wanted her opinion on Jeremy Read's stunning new space-launch plans, especially the older folks.

It would be easy to lie, to simply say it won't work. That would satisfy almost everybody.

All the biographies on Sarah Warner had a chapter on the war years, her warnings about the OWLs, and the lives she'd saved. Her efforts after the war to improve global equity were included. There were sections on her influence in moving from oil-based economies, using telepresence and low-energy transport, and how it had started to help stabilize global temperatures and ecosystems. Her views on genetic engineering and cyber safeguards were always covered in depth.

I've sacrificed everything—a normal life, relationships, even children—because I'm the responsible one, like Ma used to say. Now I'm stuck: Should I abandon the truth or just destroy the dreams of billions? How do I say it? Go ahead and die, people—it's really best for you. Stay on Earth, but, by the way, the earthquakes will get worse and worse and the planet will implode in about 300 years. Or maybe I should just blurt out how I'm a friend of the Torae, whose plan is to put us on the extinct-species list if we make a mistake. Jeremy's plans are so seductive.

She shook her head, trying to clear the morning cobwebs in her reality. *Whatever I mindcast will be upsetting and dangerous.*

A few Oktoberfest stragglers laughed on their way along the street. Sarah stared down at them, savoring the sounds and her rare solitude. Mentally, she rewrote and rehearsed the speech almost everyone on Earth would eventually hear. *My logic and words will have to be perfect—they're going to disappoint almost everyone.*

Why can't I just go home and take care of Ma? Ben can't do it alone. I could play with Adam's new grandkids. I could look up Kenny again, maybe fall in love and try to be happy.

Sunrise added a golden tinge to the Munich rooflines. She stopped worrying about her future speech and walked from the window, dropping her nightgown on the bed. "Communications on. Shower." Intelligent plumbing in the bathroom warmed the water to the temperature she liked. Her workday had begun.

Deep within the planet, a 50-meter ball of energetic photons and metal nuclei became temporarily asymmetric. Metal fluid and vapor collapsed toward the black hole and a shock wave moved out from the core. Seventeen minutes later, Sarah felt the floor shudder—another Earth burp.

Old Jeep wheels skidded and raised a small cloud of yellow dust in the parking lot gravel. They pulled up against a concrete block wall with the company name, Fanger Bros, Inc., partly legible in the peeling paint.

The visitor watched Curtis Fanger scurry around to help him from the Jeep. He forced a smile as he climbed out. Curtis was an intimidating host: leery, charming, and brutish. He wore a black T-shirt with cut-off sleeves and a baseball cap to cover his bald head.

"We got some beautiful work and slick new equipment to show you today," he said. "Glad you could make it, Mr. Hartnett. We're ready. Even got some beer warmed up for later."

"Thanks, Curtis. I enjoy coming out here." Mr. Harnett knew his visits were a big deal for the Fanger brothers. Once a year he checked their books, met new employees, and let them show off work samples. Their machine shop was tucked in the woods off an old logging road in the foothills above Missoula, Montana. Fifteen people worked there, off and on, as the workload demanded. The shop hovered barely in the black by machining specialty parts that were uneconomical for the robotic factories in the city. He suspected they made some off-book money machining weapon components for local militias. Their only steady work was turning superconducting disks for Hartnett's German factories. And occasionally, Curtis and his brothers Jerry and Rob did unusual, delicate jobs for him privately.

He set certain hiring rules for the employees, and Curtis had complied perfectly. All the workers were fiercely independent, suspicious of both technology and outsiders, and free of implants of any kind. At all 53 shops he owned, scattered in back hills across Montana, Kentucky, and Michigan, as well as Germany, Eastern Europe, and Australia, the employees were paranoid for good reason, and they appreciated that he wouldn't look too closely at everything they did.

Hartnett himself had a full computer implant, and often argued strategy with the brilliant silicon personality in his head, but it had no wireless links to the global grid. Even firewalled comm implants could be penetrated, and use-patterns were an identity fingerprint. He didn't want anyone to know who he was.

His routine inspection of the Fanger operations lasted only three hours. Then, in late afternoon, Curtis and his brothers drove him down the road to discuss some "serious business." They pulled off onto a dirt trail where the Jeep could be hidden and walked to a cliff overlooking the valley. Along the way, Jerry occasionally circled and searched the woods, as if he were hunting. "This here's a safe place to talk," he said when they reached the opening. All four men leaned against rock outcroppings, out of sight, in the shadows. The sun had dipped between two mountain peaks and a deep purple haze stretched over the Missoula basin.

"I have some special parts I'd like you men to make the next couple months," Hartnett said. "I'll send components, too, but you'll have to do final assembly up at your cabin. It's an unusual kind of weapon, and it's a substantial job. You'll be paid well."

"We like them jobs," Curtis said, "and it's been slow lately, so workload's no problem."

"You gentlemen ever take visitors up to the cabin? You know, girlfriends or anyone?"

Jerry wiped his huge, bulbous nose and said, "Nah. Sometimes hunting friends, but we can keep it clear. No one ever just shows up."

Hartnett pulled three small modules out of his pocket and handed them to Curtis. "These are the intelligence packs," he said. "They'll instruct you on the hardware assembly. When you're finished with the electrical work, they'll tell you what to do with the finished products. There's one for each of you, and a follow-up job. You men have any qualms?"

"Do we have to disappear anyone?" asked Rob.

"You won't have to kill anyone yourselves."

"We only care about getting caught," Curtis said. "Is this worse than any other jobs we did?"

"A bit, but you should do nicely if you follow the plan. You each will need to go on a short journey. If you have any questions, just ask the intelligence pack; it's about three times smarter than I am."

"I don't like taking orders from silicon. Don't trust 'em. But if the pay's good..."

"Don't worry, Curtis. The pay will be exceptional."

"Good."

"I'll tell you the amount before I leave—my little surprise. I'm ready to go down the road for a quick drink if you men have no further questions."

Curtis turned the module over in his hand, found the on switch, and sneered. "Yeah, let's go."

They walked back through the twilight and darkening trees and drove five minutes to the intersection with the main county highway to a roadside bar. Old neon signs flickered beer ads as they entered. *It seems a somber place inside, but probably becomes livelier on weekends,* Hartnett thought. Several patrons obviously knew the Fanger brothers and their reputation; subdued conversations became even quieter as they strolled by. Curtis led them to what he called his favorite table in a corner. When they'd settled in, a waitress yelled, "Curtis, I got that special warm beer ready for your Brit friend. Don't get much call for that."

"Bring it on over, Jeannie, and some snacks. We'll have our usual."

The conversation alternated between factory orders, hunting, and the subtleties of chicken wings. Hartnett just listened and never mentioned his other businesses or anything about himself. When Rob asked how the ceramic disks were used, Hartnett quickly changed the subject to politics. That always distracted them. He wouldn't have to say a thing for a half hour at least. Sometimes they'd tease him about his accent or his fondness for warm Guinness, and he'd laugh or light up his pipe.

A couple hours later, he said, "I'll need to be heading back soon, Curtis. I've got some work to do at the hotel."

"Okay, I'll drop off the boys and take you back in the Jeep."

They popped anti-alcohol pills, which buffered their blood and cleared their heads in less than 10 minutes. Everyone else at the bar seemed to be simply drinking to stupor. Though virtually all addictions had a pharmaceutical cure, the patient still had to care enough to take the medicine.

Before Curtis drove him to his hotel in the city, he told the Fangers how much money they'd make on the special job. They were more than pleased.

Alone in his Missoula room later that night, Hartnett had a long discussion with his implanted computer—the smartest electronics in any human—covering three-fourths of the surface area of his brain. He'd designed it himself and omitted all the normal protection protocols. The computer called him by his real name: Devin.

After the cyber-biowar, Devin had slowly rebounded financially, deduced the flaws in the OWL plans, and knew who'd been responsible for his defeat. He endured painful plastic surgery and voice alteration to establish his new identity as Mr. Oliver Hartnett, and purchased small machine shops to produce variants of the astonishing materials he'd cut out of the yellow sphere. He became wealthy but was relegated to the periphery of society.

His three math camp classmates with the Torae spheres had obviously been the problem. Sarah's visit to his Cambridge office had somehow tipped her off about the OWL war, and she'd alerted the world's governments. He was galled by her fame and ascendance in government.

Devin cultivated a special hatred for Dan, especially his pivotal role in the cyber war and in defeating him personally. He had even analyzed Rianne's biological work to see how it could be sabotaged. He envied their ascending careers, loathed their success and reputations, and plotted.

Sitting on the edge of his hotel bed, for a moment he thought of his former wife and children. She'd remarried, of course, and his children were grown. Occasionally, he'd secretly watch them. They hadn't been important to him before, but sometimes now he felt a deep ache and sense of regret.

"What exactly is your goal, Devin?" his implant asked.

"I'm the most brilliant human on this planet. I want revenge on those three. I want to destroy their work and reputations, and force them to suffer as I have. I want their lives filled with terror. And then I need to watch them die."

The embedded computer kept its thoughts to itself.

The Torae didn't notice the approaching ship. Its message was so deeply blue-shifted that the probes thought it was just an unusually energetic cosmic ray source, but as it slowed, the fine structure of the message became discernable. The visitor ship was heading directly toward the Milky Way.

With skeptical orange-green overtones, Sower said, "A Torae ship from the Origin Event—impossible. Relay the transcription."

The dispatch said, "Torae-only data from ship 5630-863. We are one of the few who survived the space-time explosion. We rode the new-space wave-front for one month at up to 1,000 times the speed of light. We have decelerated to this galaxy and traveled seven billion light-years. Your communication beacon now guides us. Survival has been our only goal. We carry precious information. The Torae living at the Origin discovered a universe-creation method with appropriate control schemes. The Event you saw was its first application. Enough intra-universe space was released to destroy a new, dangerous, level-five alien species. Regrettably, the Torae civilization core was caught in the detonation. We will travel to your location to explain further."

Sower briefly examined the thoughts of her crew and, in a purple-ultra-violet burst, said, "Pig puke." She had learned the expression from Sarah.

POWER

Read Enterprises' transonic jet hit an air pocket and abruptly dipped lower. Joti gulped, felt her stomach rise, and experienced a familiar stabbing spasm in her back. Nerve damage to her spine left by the OWL virus had never healed. Kyle winced too. She envied those who'd fully recovered from the illnesses, like Jeremy. He was straddling the aisle and hardly seemed to notice the turbulence.

The poison never made it to his spine. That Czech fiend who called to threaten him saved his health—Laurel's too. He clued them in on the danger when they were still just sneezing and coughing. Kyle and I got to the hospital only six hours later, but that made all the difference.

Of course, we'd all be dead if Rianne hadn't found the potassium antidote. I shouldn't complain. We're lucky to be alive. She popped a nanopill designed to search out and numb the inflamed area of her spine.

Joti looked across the aisle at her grandson Nick, and he smiled back. He would soon be 23. She couldn't hide her pride in him. He sat so tall, his shoulders above the seatback, and his curly black hair was a perfect match to her own. *Before I got old and gray.* Nick was the blessed grandchild, her favorite. He was the only non-twin among all of Rianne's children, and the most brilliant.

Jeremy and Laurel's daughter, Lené, sat next to Nick. They were cuddling in their seats whenever they had a chance. She was pretty, maybe even more than Laurel, and had inherited Jeremy's British charm. A true extrovert, she was even a little wild, particularly when Nick wasn't nearby.

Lené would be crazy not to marry him. I wonder if they'll take the commitment leap? He looks so content with her snuggling next to him.

Memories of Joti's youthful energy, love, and dreams flooded back. *I'm so crinkled and tired now. Even if the OWL plague hadn't ruined my back, I'd probably still be walking with a cane.*

Kyle tapped her knee to get her attention. "What are you thinking? You seem a thousand years away."

"Oh, nothing, I'm just worn out. The Beijing meetings were too long. Such a bother."

She peeked at Nick again, this time so he wouldn't notice. He'd shared an apartment with Lené for two years. *I hope they marry and settle down near us, and have some beautiful babies. They certainly love each other.*

All six of Rianne's kids are marvels, one way or another, but Nick's special. It'd be criminal to waste his spirit and intelligence. Jeremy says that on his rockets anyone can be as smart as Nick; they can even borrow parts of his brain. Seems like nothing's impossible there. But borrowing brains doesn't seem right to me.

"It's about time to wake up, everyone," Jeremy said. "The pilots say we're nearly over Australia."

Joti grabbed a last cookie and helped stow a small table. "Those cookies are good, aren't they?" said Laurel. "I always order warm ones with milk before landing."

Jeremy leaned over from the aisle to peer out a window. "I've asked the pilots to do a low flyover and tilt the wings as we circle the city and launch areas. Lené and Nick, grab an empty seat on the right side so you get a good view."

Out the window, Joti saw hundreds of square kilometers of ocean wind-power farms passing beneath. They quickly approached the north Australian coastline east of Darwin. Beyond, agricultural fields stretched endlessly south in beautiful fading greens and yellows into what used to be near desert. Computers had designed the efficient desalinization equipment that had transformed the continent. Pumping stations and huge metal-hydride osmosis facilities dotted the shoreline. Australia now fed half of the population of East Asia.

They could also see some of Australia's famous air-cleaning fans stretching north and south over the entire continent. The fans sucked in air, chemically removed CO_2, and trapped it in calcite, magnetite, and other minerals that were subsequently buried nearby or sold for construction. This gigantic Australian geoengineering facility, also designed by sentient computers, had largely reversed the climate-change trajectory.

For 30 years, well-placed people had become richer by finding lucrative problems for the clever engineering computers. It had been a race, an outburst of discovery, and every aspect of the natural and human environment was becoming optimized. The climate was stabilized, cities made more livable, and crops more abundant and nutritious—all countering the natural human tendencies toward excess, exploitation, and sloth. Read Enterprises played a key role during those years, and Jeremy and Laurel methodically grew to be the richest people on Earth. Then, abruptly, on Jeremy's 70th birthday, they directed their entire fortune to a single bizarre project that they'd planned for decades.

The promotional photos had not prepared Joti or Kyle for the coastline view. The jet swooped low over the heart of the Read Australian Complex, with its six massive, brain-scanning buildings, each over five kilometers long and hundreds of meters wide. Piers for dozens of passenger ships lined the shore, and two major airports sat on each edge of the small city.

"What are all those other buildings near the harbor, Father?" Lené yawned while mumbling the words.

"Hotels, churches, restaurants, instruction auditoriums, that sort of thing. We essentially built the city just to handle the temporary occupants."

"How many do you expect at the peak?" asked Kyle.

"Three to five million each day at the highest. We don't have much control over when people arrive."

"What are those long narrow rises, the mounds behind the brain-scanning centers?" asked Joti, pointing down with her finger.

"Crematoria," Laurel said matter-of-factly, "built mostly underground. Jeremy, are we going to circle the launch site now?"

"Better than that. Just wait."

The crematoria don't show up in their ads much, Joti thought with a wry smile.

The jet banked east toward what was left of the Great Barrier Reef, climbed higher and, after a few minutes, circled again. "No one else is cleared to fly within 50 klicks of here right now. Just a few more seconds," Jeremy said.

Nick was the first among them to notice the large aircraft breaking through scattered ground clouds. It gained altitude quickly while retracting its wings, and its screaming engines shook their windows when it passed. "The ramjets kick in at 12 kilometers altitude," Jeremy shouted, "just about where we are. I turned off the sound cancellation on this jet so you'd get the full effect." They all strained their necks, but the space transport quickly disappeared beyond their view.

"We're launching four times a day now," Jeremy added. "Still carrying just rocket parts and fuel, but we expect to get up to 10 per day and start bringing up large numbers of people in three months. The timing depends on how many sign up. It'll be at least four years until the main space rockets leave Earth's orbit."

Nick stood and leaned against Joti's seatback. "Speaking of time," he asked, "how long before we reach Sydney? Lené is really burned out."

"Not long. We'll be down in 40 minutes and at the house in 15 more."

"Can I see that model you showed Premier Wang?" said Nick. Jeremy pulled the three-centimeter cube from his satchel and tossed it to Nick. The model unfolded along one face so slices would fan out and the interior electronics could be examined.

"I don't know beans about computers or electronics," Nick said, "but I know why the premier had a problem with this."

That's a fib, Joti thought. *He knows a ton about everything.*

Nick closed the cube and tossed it back to Jeremy. "This thing's too small. I watched the premier's face colors when you showed him. He was disappointed. It's smaller than a brain. He was probably thinking, 'How can my entire head be packed in this tiny block?' It's psychologically wrong."

"Believe me," Jeremy said, "the Brain Mirror uses only 10 percent of that cube. Most of the human brain is made of connection bundles. We've replaced them with holographic switching, shrunk it to almost nothing. The cortex replica is spread across the top layer and the rest is just expansion space, for new personal memories and capabilities. The entertainment scenarios we call 'universes' are stored off the cubes and are shared by everyone. Those simulated worlds will be able to grow 10,000 times as well, and the robots on board can build more electronics if needed. No one's going to be bored."

"What happens," Joti asked, "when these super brains start building new robots and come back to take over Earth?"

"We've incorporated all the usual human protection protocols, of course," Jeremy said, "but more importantly, Earth will be long gone before they could return. And, in a sense, they will be human. They're us, after all, only enhanced."

Joti watched Jeremy's body language. *He's a true believer—pleading, passionate. Hope he knows what he's doing. I need to talk to Nick and Rianne about all this.*

The small group sat quietly during the landing in Sydney. Nick and Jeremy helped Kyle out of his seat and into his wheelchair, trying to minimize the pain to his crippled back. He wheeled to the door where a special lift lowered him to the tarmac. Joti stayed close, walking with her cane. Personnel from Read Enterprises loaded their large trunks on luxury skimmers and drove them all to Laurel's favorite villa, where they'd be staying for the Olympics.

～～～～～～

Organizers bragged during the selection phase about how the Olympics in their city would be inexpensive and efficient, but inevitably the spectacle and cost grew every four years. Although the story lines focused on the athletes' sacrifices, teamwork, and how they'd overcome impossible odds, biotech dominated the games. Cat-and-mouse maneuvers over drug use had become more sophisticated but less relevant, and everyone knew many events were won or lost before the contestants had even been born. China, in particular, designed babies to win at the Olympic games, and knowledge of successful gene splices had spread. Wrestlers and weightlifters were minotaur-like monsters of muscle and power. Basketball giants over 2.3 meters tall were routine, and the tiny, double-jointed gymnasts looked like small children. But every four years, people were mesmerized again because the results were so astonishing. What it meant to be human was becoming more arbitrary.

Several days after the opening ceremonies, Kyle, Nick, and Jeremy sat in assassin-proof, first-row box seats at the Olympic stadium, just up from the oval track, while the women watched the gymnastics finals at a different venue. Four events were happening simultaneously: the high jump, triple jump, shot put, and sprint elimination rounds.

Nick's interest flitted from one event to another, but he knew Kyle cared only about the high jump. His grandfather's youthful dream had been to be an Olympic high jumper, and he'd nearly cried in gratitude when Jeremy invited him along on this trip. Nick watched Kyle peer through binoculars from his wheelchair, bouncing his legs in time with the jumpers as they neared the bar. *He's out there with them right now.*

"Those high jumpers have 90 percent rapid-twitch muscle fibrils in their legs," Nick said. "They're world-class athletes, but most could barely jog 200 meters, let alone run a marathon. Mother didn't know enough about sport biomechanics. She designed me to be tall and thin but didn't consider it a priority to genetically alter my muscle types. I never had a chance at your Olympic goal, Granddad."

"You did pretty well at the university."

"Not even close to Olympic level, I'm afraid. China takes terrible risks with their baby experiments. I hate to think how many have been born deformed. These are second-generation, designer Olympians on the field, only 15 or 16 years old. The starting height was 2.4 meters. It's amazing!"

A gun started a 200-meter sprint heat. Custom-engineered human running machines tore past the special box seats Jeremy had purchased at great expense. Jeremy said he didn't expect trouble, but there was no point in taking chances with security. Bombproof windows protected them, and dozens of sensors scanned the nearby crowd for possible threats. People had gawked at Kyle in his wheelchair when they entered, but then they recognized Jeremy. A few even applauded. The whole world knew Jeremy's face now, and not just because of his immense wealth. Everyone had a stake in his audacious project.

A screaming cheer spread around the stadium. When it finally died down, an announcer calmly stated that a new world record had been set in the shot put.

Jeremy grabbed Nick's arm and said, "How long have you been noodling around my daughter now, Nick?"

"A couple of years, I guess."

"If you're waiting for my permission, as far as I'm concerned, it's okay for you to kiss her."

"I'm afraid we're a little beyond that point, Mr. Read."

"Is there any chance you two would get officially married?"

"Your daughter's already a very honest woman, sir; she's an accountant, after all. To be straight, we'd love to be legally sanctioned but your project has us confused. When you and Laurel head for the launch vehicle, Lené will want to go along. I understand. It's a family thing. If my parents, brothers, and sisters stay, I'll want to be here on Earth and take my chances with the quakes. Not being married gives us some flexibility."

Jeremy looked surprised and sad.

"You understand you're tearing families apart, don't you?" Nick added.

"Yes. I know the decisions are tough on many families. Older people see it as a way to extend their lives, but the young think it might shorten theirs. Almost 900 million have signed up, but predominantly the sick or those with nothing to lose. I truly believe everyone should go. I hope our broadcast next week will swing the momentum, maybe even convince you. Earth is dying."

Nick saw the colors of excitement in Jeremy's nearly 80-year-old face. Then he turned to see Kyle, still bobbing his head in time with the jumpers as they loped toward the high jump bar.

These guys have young minds in their aging bodies. Everyone is living longer now, of course. But Gramps is totally out on that field in every sense, except the flesh. Maybe, as Jeremy says, our thoughts are all that really matter.

Turning to Jeremy, he said, "The idea of migrating to unspoiled land, colonizing, and creating a new world is fascinating to people my age. It's just that I'd rather not do it as a computer program—as circuitry."

"It's the only way, Nick."

"I know."

"It's the best way to save humanity. And I'm sure we'll be able to reload the minds in cloned human bodies by the time we arrive, although I'm not convinced many will want to. The intellects on the ships will be hyperintelligent by then. The human form will seem terribly limiting. People will probably design their new form, biological or mechanical."

"But our current bodies are what we are—humans."

"Let me ask you a question about your family, Nick. Your mother is the key, isn't she? On something like this, Rianne will decide for the family, right?"

"She and Dad both think you're wrong—that there's time for humanity to come up with a better way. But you're right. On a moral and biological question like this, she'll have all the arguments and everyone will follow her lead, even Joti and Kyle."

"Kyle's grown to be my best friend over the years," Jeremy said. "And I especially want you and Lené to be with us. It would be terribly lonely if you two didn't come along."

Laurel and Jeremy's Australia broadcast was hard news—the world grid would carry the story, but it needed to rise above the background din. For several months, Read Enterprises had paid for grabber ads: low-key announcements, technical updates, and benefit summaries, now building to high-intensity alerts in the hours before the show. Catchy background music played as aerial sweeps of the three launch cities were interspersed with artist imaginings of abundant new planets, and endorsements from people who'd already been transitioned to the electronic form on Earth. The descriptions were mesmerizing and available to every display or visual implant on the planet. Beneath the beauty were clear messages: The time for your decision is drawing near, and immortality might not be offered again.

The news outlets cut their side commentary off when a famous actress stepped toward the outdoor podium. Tall pine trees formed a distant backdrop. She flashed a practiced smile and made intimate eye contact with a billion viewers. "Hello, everyone. It's a distinct honor for me to introduce two close friends, whose accomplishments have clearly changed the world! They have important statements to make today, which will affect everyone of you personally. They're the heart and soul of Read Enterprises and the creators of this most daring, wonderful project. They've never before spoken to a global audience, but this is a very special day. I'll first introduce the CEO of Read Enterprises, its heart, Laurel Read."

Months of public relations had conditioned the audience well. As Laurel entered in a deep blue dress, there were glimpses of labored, arthritic steps, but viewers saw only the beauty, dignity, success, and adventure described in her biographies. Close-ups of her face showed the wrinkles and gray hair of an energetic, long life, but those watching saw mostly the intelligence of her wide eyes. The warmth of her face surprised them.

"I'll keep my comments short and pertinent," she said, "because I know some of you are in your sleep cycle or doing your daily work. I'm sorry to interrupt. I'll assume you're familiar with our grand project. I have three announcements.

"First, as of Wednesday, over one billion people have signed up to leave Earth and join our adventure. This is important because now all our investors are repaid, which means the project is totally a go! From this point on, anyone who reaches the launch cities and pays the nominal fee may come along.

"Second, our scientists have made an important discovery. We know many of you are disappointed that interstellar travel is possible only in cyber-computer form, by transcribing your identity, memories, thoughts, and brain structures. We're sorry, but that's the only way the weight can be reduced enough to allow travel to another planet—and so that you can survive what might become a centuries-long journey. In a few minutes, my husband Jeremy will describe to you what it will be like. My second announcement, however, is that our scientists have discovered how to reverse the process. Samples of your DNA will be carried along, which will enable us to form clones of each of you, physical beings, when suitable planets are ready. We've learned how to overlay the brain transcript on to your clone. You can be any age you choose, with your current memories intact. In fact, you could live multiple full lives on the new colonies by repeating this process."

She paused to allow this information to sink in. As new cameras switched on, she adjusted her head angle and a group of hidden rainbow lorikeets were released behind her.

"My third announcement is less momentous, but I'm happy to tell you that our space facilities are now complete. In three months, we'll start to carry the first colonists to ships in orbit. We'll launch twice per day from each of the three sites, but expect to be launching up to 10 per day by the end of next year. At first, priority will be given to the terminally ill, but by June anyone who arrives will be accepted. There are a thousand details, but simply put, humanity's greatest journey is about to begin, the ultimate migration. Please join us."

The actress introduced Jeremy next. He had never allowed personal interviews so people only knew his face and reputation, the mysterious genius behind Read Enterprises' greatest successes. His appearance before the live camera was news in itself.

Jeremy walked toward the podium perfectly erect but with an absurd little belly sticking straight forward from his skinny frame. He wore a gray polo shirt, loose blue slacks held up with red suspenders, and looked excited and slightly wild as a breeze blew his long gray hair. He stepped behind the podium and beamed a smile long enough to catch his breath. Before saying a word he made a quarter turn and looked backward. Camera angles shifted, and it soon became apparent that the platform stood near a runway. The cameras followed an enormous vehicle moving toward Jeremy. He covered his ears to the deafening roar as a space bus lifted off only 300 meters behind him.

Still smiling, he turned back to the camera and let the noise subside. "That shuttle is carrying fuel to orbit, but in three months it will be carrying people to immortality. I don't want to talk to you about the mechanics of this enterprise—it'll work, have no doubt. I only want to describe one thing—the most important thing: what it will be like. I'm rather an expert on that subject. You see, I'm the only human who was ever transitioned and came back. I've been there.

"Let me tell you my story. Twenty-five years ago I came out of a coma. My wife Laurel's undying love and courage kept me alive during 10 years of unconsciousness. The coma started when I became the first human to deeply interface with a hypercomputer. That link ended quickly, the power was cut off, which is the only reason I survived before my brain turned completely to mush. But I had a glimpse of something marvelous." He stopped and looked directly into the main camera.

"We still don't know how to safely make a complete brain copy and protect the original brain. The process of fully reading your mind destroys it. That's why we can't send your thoughts into space and keep your body living on Earth. You must understand this: Immortality is possible only with the death of your body. You have to choose.

"But I'm here to describe what will happen if you decide to journey with us. I'm going to tell you what it felt like for me all those years ago, and what the 20,000 people who have already been transitioned at our three Earth facilities are experiencing today.

"What happens once your thoughts, feelings, and memories have been extracted and are living in secure electronics, which we call the Brain Mirror? *You* get to choose. Most people want something simple and connected, so they ask to experience the launch, even though they are actually still on Earth. They find themselves walking away from the transitioning center to the space bus in their own body. It's not actually happening—your mind has been separated from your body—but it's the logical next step, so most people choose that experience.

"Then slowly, over weeks or months, people discover they can do almost anything!

"My first choice, 35 years ago, was to explore why I loved my wife. I saw her face and body and heart—all at once. I felt a warmth and joy deeper than anything I had as a normal man. Memories flooded back to me a thousand times faster than my brain was usually capable of. I can't even imagine how wonderful it will be when Laurel and I are both in the system together.

"Let me be clear. You feel everything—exactly as if your whole body were present. We've proven the Brain Mirror is 100 percent accurate. It's just like real life, except that anything is possible. When you want to try something different, you can. We've loaded the entire bio-nerve structure of almost every living animal. If you want to feel as a bird does, flying over New York City or the Grand Canyon, you can. You'll learn firsthand how dolphins and bats sense sound waves as beautiful colors. Ever wondered what it feels like to be a butterfly? Try it. Want to be a butterfly in space with 1,000 kilometer gossamer wings drifting in the solar wind? You can do it. When you're finished exploring, just think, 'Reset,' and you're back to being yourself.

"But it's even deeper than that. Did you ever want to understand Einstein's general theory of relativity? Whatever your education level, you *will* understand Einstein's theory, because your electronic brain will work a thousand times faster than your brain does today.

"Those of you who are getting older, you know how memories slip away? How it's hard to recall some fact, but then later it comes to you. All those memories are still there, but sometimes blocked. On our rockets, all those memories will come rushing back to you, your entire past, and will never be lost again.

"You'll take on mental challenges we can't imagine here on Earth. During the long journey, if you choose, you can be in direct contact with hundreds of millions of other minds, all with beautiful memories of Earth and glorious dreams and ideas for the future. Or you can be alone, at peace.

"A million universes, which we've loaded in the memory grid, will be available to you. A universe is a large region, like a small country, a complete ecosystem, economy, and so on, filled with excitement. Some are real; some are imagined. By the time we reach a new planet, you could well have lived a billion stories or invented a post-human future, which makes me tremble with anticipation.

"In the next few months we will show you more glimpses of this future and your new life on the journey, but let me summarize in a way that should be unforgettable. As I said, your first experience of cyber-life could be the launch, but something happens a bit sooner. Thirty-five years ago, the first thing I saw when I connected to the computer was a brilliant flash of white light." Jeremy grinned and tossed his long hair with a hand. "I want to assure you right here that I am not an old codger who's finally flipped his gray wig. I am a coherent cofounder of a multitrillion-dollar corporation who believes we humans may have finally created Heaven. The experience I had, and the experience thousands who are already in the Brain Mirror form are reporting every day, is exactly what most hoped the afterlife could be. People who want to see Jesus, Allah, or Buddha, or reach the 11th level of eternity—whatever they choose—are doing so now. The blinding light is only the computer adjusting to your brain, but I think it signals something more. It signals your entrance to a better life, one free of sickness, disease, and physical or mental limitations of any kind. There is really no need for competition in this new world, no need for money; everyone starts with the same computing power, just different memories and ways of thinking. If you want to try thinking like someone else—borrow parts of his or her brain—you can do that unless they have said their brain is off limits. Try a thousand things. You can always go back by saying, 'Reset.' There will be challenges, unexplored ideas, new worlds, and futures to plan. It'll be wonderful. It truly will be Heaven. Thank you."

〰〰〰

The Washington room reeked of power. Heavy wood walls and furniture gave it the substantial feel the architects no doubt wanted when it was built deep under the West Wing of the White House during the Roosevelt era. People called it the War Room then, and it still was reserved for the most serious discussions. On this day, several ornate wood panels had been retracted to reveal translucent glass, ready for projections of geopolitical status, battle plans, or other intelligence. Behind the walls hissed a self-contained complex with dozens of human-level computers and two redundant thousand-human systems. For security reasons, the room needed to be computationally self-sufficient. Little information ever left the room, and only clean, pristine bits flowed in.

Three people waited in the War Room: the heads of the CIA and Defense Intelligence Agency, and Dan Jorgenson, who was exactly where he wanted to be, having carefully managed his career after joining the National Security Agency as a consultant in his midtwenties. The NSA director had the most sophisticated satellite and ground surveillance in the world, the best code breakers, and the finest computers. They needed the smartest, most ferocious intelligence on the planet, currently the 12th generation Q-bit, roughly as smart as one million humans in terms of raw processing power. As head of the agency, Dan knew everything that happened globally. He'd become the world's eyes and ears like Orwell's Big Brother, and he didn't trust anyone else with that job.

The others sat stoically in their heavy leather chairs, expecting a long wait for the president. They both looked a bit nervous. Dan, now the long-time head of the NSA, was daydreaming about the future.

He pictured humanity teetering on the edge of an icy cliff, a gale blowing toward the precipice. In that direction lurked useless escape—it was the easy way. Why bother fighting the wind? Ubiquitous, brilliant computers made nearly everyone feel worthless. Cyber minds now outstripped intellectuals, scientists, and artists. The computers even argued religious issues on late-night talk shows. Although chemical addictions could be controlled, many adults just preferred escape and jumped off the imaginary cliff. Thousands of diversions—games, sports, sensual pleasures, and interactive holo-dramas fed the urge to chuck it all. In Dan's mind, Jeremy Read's offer to take everyone to an immortal dream world was just the latest seductive pull toward the cliff.

The other direction, up a steep hill, Dan imagined cruel reality, insecurity, and fear. Although physical well-being had spread globally, many competed to win more power over others. There were still winners and losers. Regular Earth burps and earthquakes reminded everyone of the Unity damage, how the planet was unstable and wouldn't last forever. And people rightfully feared the new weapons. Historians wrote about the good old times when nuclear bombs had been the only weapon of mass destruction. Now bioagents could easily bring on a black death, and cyber threats could destroy economies and governments.

But it was the new military robots that provoked the deepest fears. Rarely seen, the most dangerous were hidden in defense bunkers, but everyone knew they were smarter, faster, stronger, and more deadly than any human soldier. Worse, they killed one on one. They could tear a person apart in seconds if they bothered to get that close. Only the U.S. and China admitted they had all the weapon types, actively developed them, and would use them under certain circumstances. The world had achieved a stable terror, enforced by universal surveillance.

Dan saw humans hanging on the edge of his cliff, with dark reality on one side and the lure of escape on the other. He believed his job was to keep them from slipping off.

The large latch arm on the War Room door rotated and air hissed through the seal as it opened. Four layers of electronic screening were temporarily breached before the door was resealed. Wireless jammers switched on and room sensors insured that all brain implants had been turned off. President Alayne Fellows quickly sat down at the end of the table and asked, "Where are the bots going?"

"They've left the staging areas and reached the Chinese borders," the director of the DIA said. "Huge numbers of bots are being deployed along the Russian and Indian frontiers and more are moving toward the south. No notable human command and control movement yet. We think they're just getting ready for something."

"Their motivation?" asked Fellows, her piercing, intelligent eyes darting from one to another.

"Defense thinks they plan to exploit the confusion and population movements when people leave for the Read launch facilities. It must look like an opportunity to expand Chinese territory."

"Could India or Russia stop them?"

"Well," the director of the DIA said, "robot warfare is difficult to assess. The Russians have excellent bots, but it is a number and movement equation. Even if they blasted a nuclear swath across Siberia, it would only stop the first wave. The Chinese bots would just keep coming. India could defend the Himalayan passes for a while, but the eastern river valleys would be open through Myanmar and Bangladesh. Even if half their people leave, Russia and India won't like giving up land. They'll fight back. It's a dangerous situation. Very unstable."

"At the CIA, we think the Chinese are just reinforcing their borders for defense, that they have no intention of invading. None of our insiders have picked up any interest in aggression. Something else is happening."

The group expected Dan to have the most detailed intelligence. "What's the NSA got on this?" the president asked, obviously hoping for something more definitive.

"I have some additional information," Dan said. "Ground bugs on transport lines have picked up bot shipments to airports and harbors along the Chinese coast. We think the units moving south will deploy along the entire shoreline and the Indo-Chinese border. Q-bit thinks the southern deployment is weak and is only there to monitor activity, but it's a 49 to 51 percent judgment call. I have another opinion. I've been privately monitoring Jeremy and Laurel Read's conversations after their visit with the Chinese premier. The supreme leader doesn't like the whole brain-download idea. More importantly, his global supremacy comes from the output of his country's vast population. He doesn't want to lose his power. I think he's deploying the bots to keep his people from leaving."

Dan knew Fellows was too wise to render her judgment immediately. She was also probably mentally integrating other information they didn't know about.

She said, "Contact me immediately with anything new. I don't want bots stepping over borders. I'll consider all your opinions. Thank you, gentlemen."

"Thank you, Madam President."

THE PRIZE

Tina stretched her head out and leaned over the street curb, shivering. People lined both sides of the street as far as she could see—at least five blocks. She quickly slid back into the crowd for protection from both the freezing wind and any surveillance that might be in the area, and then shoved her way closer to the Stockholm Concert Hall.

There's too much to lose now: my husband, good work, and a decent life. I can't chuck it away on a near miss.

Slinking through the noisy crowds with her dangerous package brought back echoes of the conspiracies, drugs, and wire-lines of her past. She was almost clean now, biochemically and psychologically, but the sensations lingered in a few deep brain folds. The treatments couldn't wash away the exhilaration or the fear.

She checked forward, looking east up the road toward a rising full moon. Birch trees with branches like skinny fingers reached upward, silhouetted by the dirty yellow moonlight. Stockholm, like other European cities, still clung to its *real* trees while much of the rest of the world had drifted to 100 more hardy, beautiful, or prolific engineered species. Under the streets, optimized magnetic sheets enabled floating skimmer traffic. But on the surface, the place felt old.

She stood on tiptoes to peek over a man's shoulder. No skimmer headlights were in sight. At four p.m., it had been dark for over an hour. Occasionally someone in the crowd would scamper across the boulevard. She clutched her shoulder bag, shoved, and weaved closer to the police.

No need to reach the barricade—just get closer—to where the road narrows. Spilling this package now would be disastrous.

Groups with signs and banners had become openly territorial, so she stopped 50 meters from the police, bobbed back toward the street curb, and began to scrutinize the crowd. There'd be others with hidden weapons across the street.

Tina had baked her 3D-printed plastic gun into a loaf of hard bread and wrapped it with metal foil—enough to fool the loose European border scanners, but there was little chance of entering even a third-rate hotel with her bundle. She'd taken a room in a private home for the week. The Swedish penalties for carrying a weapon were draconian; if discovered, her respectable new life would evaporate. She avoided anyone she thought might be walking in the crowd with a body scanner.

Headlights turned the corner several blocks up the road and people waved from the edge of the street. Those with placards started to yell and skirmishes broke out among rival groups. Swedes normally wouldn't dream of stepping off the curb, but the jostling for position was intense and a few stumbled onto the road. Tina stayed behind the front row, watching the crowd and moving her head between shoulders to keep a clear view. Reaching deep into her satchel, her fingers pushed the aluminum foil aside, crushed through the bread and gripped the gun handle. She waited with her hand hidden in the bag.

Some people screamed obscenities, but most cheered or applauded as the vehicles approached. They didn't slow where the road narrowed as Tina had expected. In the early 20th century, Nobel Prize winners had been borne by unhurried, ornate carriages, with smiles and the tipping of top hats to the crowd, but Tina had only a brief glimpse into the windows of the five skimmer limos that silently floated by with tiny country flags on their front fenders. Her heart stopped, and a slow-motion image of the boisterous throng and Rianne's profile behind a plate of glass froze in her mind. No assassins made a move. The most controversial person on the planet had passed the final police barrier unharmed—gone to pick up her second Nobel Prize.

Tina exhaled.

The skimmer lowered its wheels when it reached the narrow cobblestone street leading to the plaza.

"You have a lot of friends and enemies," Dan said, pointing to the boisterous crowds on the street edge.

"They're not here to see me," Rianne replied. "They're here for their royalty, especially the queen, hoping for just a wave. Monarchy will survive as long as there are occasions worthy of excess, like tonight."

The broad street had become little more than an alley. People leaned toward the skimmer path, many shouting at the limo's windows. The passage now felt claustrophobic and dangerous. Finally, at a police barrier, the path opened onto an expansive plaza facing the Stockholm Concert Hall.

"They may not be here for you," Dan said, "but they sure know who you are."

The five limos with all the prizewinners pulled into a spotlighted area under multistory columns. With choreographed precision, costumed guards opened the skimmer doors simultaneously. Rianne and Dan, in elegant formal wear, stepped out, and a member of the Swedish Academy greeted them, explaining his role as escort for the evening.

Huge crowds surrounded the entire plaza. The organized groups, who'd endured the Stockholm cold to stake out close positions, attracted Rianne's curiosity. Their placards were electronic, not printed; these were professionals with a dozen serious causes. Several carried 10-meter vinyl electroluminescent sheets, folded out high above the crowds. Before turning her back, she caught a few friendly and not-so-friendly scrolling messages:

> Welcome, Nobel Winners
> Länge leve drottningen!
> Humanity not Hubris
> Economist Exploitation
> Fru Frankenstein

Rianne was quite sure the last one was for her. She wanted to watch longer, but the vehicles with friends and family were arriving and their guide urged her and Dan to follow him into the concert hall.

She hesitated again just beyond the spotlighted area under the pillars, looking ahead at the warm, inlaid-wood lobby. It was a moment worth memorizing. *No one has taken this Nobel walk three times. With a little luck, I will.*

Quickly pulling Dan into the shadows, she kissed him and said, "I've been looking for an appropriate place to tell you, and this spot, for a scientist, is like standing on the steps of the Parthenon. I found something important."

"Found what?"

"What I've been searching for . . . for the last 20 years. It works for mice. It'll work on people."

"You're kidding. You haven't told anyone else, have you?"

"Not yet," she said.

Their Swedish Academy escort looked extremely frustrated waiting by the door.

She squeezed Dan's hand. "We'd better go in."

As they entered the concert hall they heard a roaring cheer behind them— the royal family's limo had entered the plaza.

Rianne received her first Nobel Prize at age 39, 10 years after identifying the nine distinct biochemical sequences in human addictions. In all her work, she never just *uncovered the mechanism,* as most scientists would, but found effective ways to use the new knowledge. For drug dependencies, she developed buffers to normalize body chemistry. Common psychological addictions, like eating and gambling disorders, required blockers to muffle emotional links to the lower brain. Most people showed significant improvement after less than a week of her treatments, even severely addicted wire-heads. Painful withdrawal was avoided. Only cortical neurons were unchanged, the intellectual memory of the addiction, which could often be handled with counseling.

Upon receiving her first Nobel Prize, Rianne felt a degree of closure on Chia-Jean Ma's dying request. Even with Sarah and Dan's help, she'd been unable to locate Tina and feared she'd died in the OWL biowar. Rianne's work on addiction was an indirect way to help Tina, if she were still alive.

Tonight, Rianne was winning her second Prize for the discovery of targeted jungle-DNA therapy. The term junk DNA had long ago been retired as a way of describing the 97 percent of the genome that did not directly encode proteins. That confusing, dense, rapidly mutating part of the DNA was found to trigger and regulate protein function. It was as important in making a human a human, or a tree a tree, as the well-known DNA genes. It wasn't junk at all, but it was confusing, hence the new name "jungle DNA." Rianne had found the links and captured them in a vast periodic table of the genome. Most scientists were now scrambling to fill in the dwindling gaps in her table and to find applications.

She picked up the moniker "Mrs. Frankenstein" when others began using her techniques for nonmedical applications, like changing eye color. Rianne disliked the frivolous uses but refused to speak publicly about the practice. Those who knew her well understood her opinion about improving human genetics; they'd met her children. Many people loved her for all the lives she'd saved or improved, while others saw her turning humanity into an obscene chemistry experiment.

Sitting with dignitaries and other Nobel winners on the concert hall stage, Rianne knew the select audience packing the magnificent room in front of her would at least be polite. There'd only been a handful of double Nobel Prize winners. *I'm going to be the star this evening—me or the queen—or her dress.*

The orchestra played Mozart. Old-fashioned geraniums lined the polished wood stage and multitiered balconies in Nordic elegance. Hundreds in fine dark formal wear, including Rianne's family and friends, beamed up at her. She saw Dan lean over to whisper in Sarah's ear. *He's passing the news to Sarah—that rat.* Dan looked up, grinned at her, and mouthed, "I beat you."

The head of the Swedish Academy opened the formal program with a long-winded speech about intellectualism and science, dropping every current buzzword. Rianne barely listened and wasn't even thinking about her own speech. She'd practiced it a hundred times and only needed to push the "play" button in her head. *The trouble with the Nobel Prize is that everyone wants you to talk about work you did decades ago. Right now, I only care what happened last week. How'd I let Dan convince me to disguise what I've been working on? I want to publish these new results. Now.*

Rianne gave her speech and shook hands with the queen, arms properly crossed so she wouldn't drop the official diploma. She heard the other speeches and the orchestral music, smiling at all the right times, but her mind was stuck on her experiment with 20 mice.

Their apparent age dropped 10 percent after each treatment. It should work on Homo sapiens. There's no reason it won't work. I now know how to make people live essentially forever.

"We need to talk," she said to Dan as the skimmer lifted off the cobblestones. She felt the superconducting impellers nudge the limo gently forward, silently gliding them through old-town Stockholm.

"Yeah, we need to talk, but later," Dan replied, nodding toward the driver, who was there mostly for show, with an old-fashioned top hat. "Try to enjoy the moment."

The short ride to the Stockholm City Hall passed a juxtaposed jumble of nineteenth-century architecture and ultramodern storefronts—full-wall holo-images mixed with quarry stones. Bonfires blazed on the waterfront in honor of the Nobel winners, and a touch of smoke from the fires blew down the long entrance corridor into the banquet hall, where an honor guard of young boys and girls held candles to light the traditional walk. Rianne, deep in thought, noticed little of it.

As they descended the grand staircase, applause from the assembled guests brought her back to the moment. Each year for the Nobel banquet, Stockholm's City Hall was transformed into a marvelous Renaissance palace. Over 1,200 people had already found their seats in the enclosed four-story courtyard. Intense light from the high windows streamed down orange-umber walls and through the candle-smoke atmosphere, as if the Norse gods themselves were watching the festivities.

A small army of waiters served two dinner courses with military precision while Rianne impatiently chatted with the Swedish dignitaries around her. Sarah had been seated across from Dan and Rianne at the table of honor, which extended 100 meters down the center of the hall. Admirers of the famous ambassador kept her busy with questions as well. But the final dessert course, the Glace Nobel, left everyone speechless and transfixed. Singers and flags led a grand procession of servers. They carried huge, glowing trays along the balcony and down the grand staircase through a rolling dry-ice cloud backlit with blue lights. As flaming crepes and sorbets were served, a quartet sang a haunting Saint-Saëns piece from the balcony. Rianne's hosts were, at last, completely distracted and chatted in Swedish among themselves.

Rianne looked both ways and whispered subvocally to her friends across the table, "We need to talk—soon. I've been on my little special project for 12 years. It's almost done. I don't really enjoy lavish notoriety like tonight, but do you two have any good reason why I shouldn't publish and pick up my third Prize?"

"There are a lot of reasons," Dan whispered back, "including our mutual friends in high places." He glanced up toward the painted ceiling of the banquet hall. "This may be the decision they're watching for. We absolutely need to get it right."

A Swede at Sarah's right requested dessert sauce, which she passed, smiling graciously. "Let's find a place to talk after we finish eating," she said to Rianne. "This food is better than candied catnip." She closed her eyes in ecstasy and took another spoonful of sorbet.

Forty-five minutes and a hundred hugs and handshakes later, they finally found a quiet hallway nook where they could talk privately.

"Half the world wants to know what I think of Read's rockets," Sarah said, "and his scheme for electronic immortality. Half the time it even sounds reasonable to me. A couple billion suffering people might be better off in his software nirvana. I agree we should try to persuade them to stay on Earth, but they're going to be damn hard to convince. My job would be a lot easier if I could tell them you have a way to make everyone young again."

"I vote to finish my trials and use the treatments," Rianne said, "and we should start with our parents. My father's extremely frail, close to organ failure, classic old age. I don't want him to die."

"I agree," Sarah said. "Can you explain, so I can understand how it works?"

"You understand about the DNA timing blocks," Rianne said, "the telomeres, which drop off as cells divide? It's a random process; sometimes you lose a notch but often you don't. Telomeres signal the cell through RNA— tell it how old it is. I use replacement viruses on the jungle DNA to alter the triggering mechanism, depending on the site. You wouldn't want your bones or teeth to start growing again. I also added a dozen new scrubber genes to remove the oxidized toxins that accumulate. And I fiddled with the mitochondria a little—made them healthier. It's complicated. Each treatment should take off about five years. Long term, there may be some abnormalities; I can't target all tissue variations yet. Some parts, say the retina, might continue to age. Over time, though, we'll make it perfect; it's 98 percent accurate already. People would be mostly younger. It can't hurt them."

"I say you do primate and human tests," Sarah said. "Make sure it works and then tell everyone."

Dan had been strangely quiet during their discussion. "Look," he said, "this isn't the place to talk about it, but I agree we should tell the entire world about this 'elixir of youth.' You, Madam Ambassador, speaker of the truth, need to be the one who tells them, since people always believe you. Unfortunately, you'll have to also convince them, and get everyone to resolve, that the technique should never, ever be used."

He looked completely earnest. Rianne stared at him and whispered, "Dear, you are seriously delusional."

FAMILY

Sower's plasma sac quivered in anticipation. The visitor from the Origin Event circled closer and snuggled alongside. Outer shields unlocked. Mating began.

Pruners on both vehicles had painstakingly negotiated this genetic exchange; it was a Pruner's premier duty. No offspring or clone would emerge directly from this union—the participants themselves would be the ones altered. And the changes would be radical due to their long, detached histories in different parts of the universe. Electronic transfer was the normal method for genetic exchange, since Torae were so rarely in the same location, but a physical swap seemed right for this occasion, more intimate, less agonizing, and the sensations more like being reborn.

Their plasma skins gently touched and opened. Hereditary material seeped into the plasma streams. More than a gigaquad of new data knit itself on to the precious genetic chain of each Torae. Those strands held the accrued wisdom of a billion years of engineered evolution. The new instructions rippled out from the insertion point through their huge bodies, reorganizing plasma paths, spawning vortices, growing new organs, and implanting memories—millions of changes. Odd colors blended or separated in their blurred consciousnesses, while convulsive spasms cascaded along hundreds of body segments. The process was exquisitely painful, an event where they felt completely alive and vulnerable. It seemed to go on forever.

Finally, Sower rested, physically, emotionally, and mentally exhausted. She was presumably wiser now, stronger and more resilient to evolutionary forces. But the mating also left her feeling more suspicious and distrustful.

Swelling her entire body a with sweeping display of colors from violet to long infrared, she sighed, then asked the key question the visitor had avoided several times. "How did the Torae Origin and Communicators come to be destroyed? The memory cores you exchanged still have not explained. What triggered the Origin Event?"

The visitor paused and then said, "We've been reluctant to say because it conflicts with your current mission. Torae politics grew more sophisticated and complex after you left. When the universe-creation process was discovered, rival factions arose with incompatible goals. The majority bloc argued for cautious recalculation while continuing to gather worthy species from this universe. They sought detailed designs not only for a transfer conduit, but also for the future universe. A 10-billion-year delay was projected.

"We are members of a rival faction; call it a rogue faction if you like, since we are small in number. We sought actual experiments on the universe bubbles. Our Tillers also saw the technology as a useful defense tool. Dangerous class-five alien civilizations were being discovered faster than we could effectively counter them. Some were extraordinarily evil and transcendent. One virulent species expanded its reach so rapidly that the time-maps indicated it would be unstoppable. Worse, they threatened to absorb Torae technology. We needed to use a universe bubble to destroy them. Unfortunately, they had infected the Origin, and it became necessary to destroy the Torae Core to ensure their removal. Only our rogue faction survived. Our 20 ships left with sufficient safety margin to ride the Event space-wave."

Sower thought it imprudent to ask if the rogue faction had decided to eliminate two enemies at once, the alien race and the rival Torae majority. She was appalled and a bit frightened by the casual blue-green attitude the visitor displayed while telling the story.

The visitor continued, "You are the oldest Torae in this galaxy, the only one with direct memory of the Origin. Now that we've exchanged genetic material, we hope you will join our cause and persuade your clones in the local galaxies to also join us."

Sower decided not to respond too directly. "What do you plan to do now?" she asked.

"My ship is responsible for spreading this story to one-twentieth of the universe. The other survivors are doing the same. We'll then proceed to intergalactic space and begin experimentation on small universe bubbles. If we construct a conduit vehicle, we'll broadcast the plans and transfer to the new universe, without companion species. We have sufficient information now to engineer many life forms when we arrive in the new universe."

After a pause, the visitor said, "Your current species work is wasting precious time. End your development on the primitive humans and join us. Consider your mission countermanded."

Sower consulted with Tiller, Pruner, and several probes, and evaluated options before responding. "We'll not abandon the humans yet," she said. "They're near transcendence. We've searched for 300,000 traveler-years, a few more decades is insignificant. We'll complete the appraisal of humans and bring them with us if they're worthy."

The visitor said bluntly, "If you arrive before our final experiment, we'll take you with us. We will also consider bringing human design plans."

Sower thought it safer to say nothing more.

Some time after the visitor left, Sower noticed an extremely hot point source in a distant region of the universe. Another rogue Torae had begun a space-bubble experiment.

JANUARY 23, ADVERTISEMENT ON U.S. GRID BROADCAST SYSTEM

Twelve-year-old American boy facing camera with construction workers in the background. Text follows:

"Hi, Grandma Kate. I just wanted you to know I am all right. Our trip to the Panama launch site was fun, but the weeks since then have been awesome! Dad and I are helping to build a village. He says it'll be like the Wisconsin town you grew up in. We're getting to know all the other families here. Dad and I are using the realistic mode, so it's just like the real thing. When it's hot and we're working hard, we sweat and get exhausted at the end of the day. Dad says it will build my character for when we get to the new planet—we'll have to work hard there. I know you're worried about technical stuff, but it all must be programmed in. It's simple. I didn't have to learn anything. I just knew it all when we got on the rocket. At night, Dad lets me play some awesome games for an hour."

Father enters the frame with a hammer, speaking to camera:

"Mom, we really miss you. You're nuts to stay in that little apartment. You'd be strong and young here, the way you are inside. I'm worried about you—please come join us."

Camera pulls back, revealing a house and then a village under construction with walls being raised. Speaker voice-over:

"North Americans, make your reservation by simply contacting the Read Launch Site in Panama, selecting your arrival date, and sending in the very nominal fee. Experience the life, or lives, you've always dreamt about."

FEBRUARY 15, ITEM FROM WORLD SATELLITE NEWS SERVICE

Disaster footage is shown of massive wave hitting the China shoreline, surging up Huangpu River, and the resulting devastation along the coast. Announcer text:

"Catastrophe! An earthquake measuring 8.4 on the Richter scale caused terrible damage in eastern China this afternoon. The epicenter was located 200 kilometers off the coast near Shanghai. A 30-meter tsunami swept up the Yangtze and Huangpu Rivers. Shock damage to buildings was extensive in Shanghai, and flooding extended far inland. The sketchy preliminary estimate is that 300,000 may have been killed, but the toll could be much higher. This disaster is clearly attributable to the accelerating tectonic plate movements of the last several years, according to scientists. We'll update you as more information becomes available."

MARCH 10, ADVERTISEMENT ON DEUTSCHE BINDEGLIED

Translation by World Satellite News Service. Thirty-year-old man outside German pub, seated at table. Text follows:

"Friedrich, you must join us. Marta, Hans, and all the others have arrived. I still pursue the women and get the turndown by many. But when I sometimes succeed, it's unbelievable. I have set the intensity at 20 times normal. Both the anticipation and the success are impossible to describe.

"Hans and I are still climbing in realistic mode. I fell from the Eiger face twice last week and the falls were horrifying. The moments of pain were terrible but, of course, we cannot die, and all injuries are instantly repaired. Believe me, reaching the top is just as sweet. We will try Everest one day. We can easily visit the summit, but what's the fun in that? We will go in a storm without oxygen when we are trained and strong. I haven't checked if oxygen deprivation or the cold will be as painful as a real ascent."

Aerial video of Mount Everest, with voice-over:

"Reserve your arrival date at the Read Launch Site in Sierra Leone by forwarding your small fee. Live as you have always wanted."

~~~~~~

MARCH 18, ADVERTISEMENT ON GLOBAL SATELLITE NET

This broadcast reached most of China, but extensive ground jamming limited reception to half of the population. A 50-year-old Chinese couple is looking out a window from a tall building over Beijing. Text translation follows, with the man speaking:

"Father and children, we want you to know that our flight arrived in Australia safely. We were notified that the borders are now closed, but we urge you to try to reach us. Our situation is better than we imagined. I am working with others on the design for a new Beijing, and your mother continues her art and gardening. That is our serious work, but we want to show you something surprising."

Background fades and is replaced by a view of a house with rice fields stretching into the distance. The woman begins:

"Children, this is our new home. The computer has provided servants for us and to farm our crops. Yes, the fields you see are ours. We live near a village where we have many friends. Here is another surprise."

The two speakers fade and are replaced by a vigorous 35-year old couple.

"Children, in our new world we can be any age. You see, our faces match the photographs from our youth. And we can have new children to fill our vast property. There is a limit to making new people and minds, but we can have several children again. Here is another surprise. Come to meet your new brother and sister!"

The image of two babies swaddled in yellow blankets on a small bed is shown. They smile, with gentle babbling and coos.

"You must try everything to reach us. We ache to see you again in our new home."

~~~~~~

APRIL 23, NEWS ITEM FROM WORLD SATELLITE NEWS SERVICE

No video available. Spoken by anchor:

"We have new reports of clashes and riots in Chinese cities. All internal transportation modes have been curtailed to prevent migration toward the borders. There has been heavy weapons fire in outlying areas and martial law is being imposed in Beijing and other large cities. Robots are protecting all government buildings and patrolling streets at night to enforce a curfew. All U.S. citizens have been urged to leave China by the first available means."

Dan strolled with his mother along a Frogtown sidewalk near her home—slowly, so she could keep up. At an intersection, Mary grabbed his arm, putting weight on it. She'd reached the age where a spiral of dependency could develop, leading to a care home. He gently pulled away and walked backward smiling at her. Tough love.

"You must be spending too much time watching old videos, Mom. How long since you walked down to the bluff?"

"Out of my way. I'm in fine shape. My weight is down 20 pounds since I stopped working."

When her breathing became labored, they rested on a park bench at the neighborhood peace garden where spring flowers had started to bloom. "Your weight is down," he said, "because you don't eat enough. Rianne and I want you to come up to the cabin so you can get some decent food. All the kids will be there. We only get to the cabin a few weekends each year; it'd be nice for you to see how your grandkids have grown. We can help you pack."

"I can pack myself, thank you."

He helped her off the bench. They walked at a snail's pace, with Mary pointing out old neighbors' houses along the way, and homes of people who'd long since moved or died. They walked two more blocks to the metal railing at the bluff's edge.

"Kenny and I used to climb under here and slide down in winter. We promised to never tell you, but I guess it doesn't matter now," Dan said smiling.

"Could have killed yourselves."

"We survived."

Far below, skimmers glided along their platforms, three levels deep, splitting and curving off toward Wisconsin and Minneapolis. Office buildings gleaming with reflections of the setting sun almost blocked the view to the river.

"The Mississippi is flooding again downriver," he said, "like in the year of the long winter."

"People have lived here a long time, Danny. Horse wagons used to pull supplies up this hill to Rice Street and way north to the lakes and all the settlers. This river town was the lifeline."

"Mom, can I ask you a serious question?" *I need to know what she really thinks.*

Her eyes seemed locked in the past. A cool gust of wind ruffled her hair when she finally turned toward him.

"Have you considered going on the Read rockets? I'd like your honest opinion. It'd be your chance to live a lot longer. Rianne and I would pay the fee, if you're interested."

"Are you trying to get rid of me?" she asked. "I thought you hated the idea, that the whole rocket thing was going to be a disaster."

"That's true, in the abstract. But I'm asking about you, personally. I'm worried about you being alone here."

"Kenny's in town if I need help, and I like my old house." She hugged his waist affectionately. "If I didn't have to shovel, that'd be nice. And I wouldn't mind being 20 years younger, but I don't want to go off on some rocket."

"What if I asked you to move to Princeton, to live with us and the kids. We have enough room."

She just smiled at him a long time and said, "I like it here."

The city seemed noisier and more frantic than he remembered. *I wonder what all those people down in the city think. Rianne is probably right; everyone would want their youth back, or at least to be younger.*

"Are you sure you'd want to be younger, Mom, if you could stay at home?"

"If the aches and pains would go away, I'd like that. But no, I've already had a full life. I only wanted you and Kenny to grow up good. I bargained with God about that. That's what your dad wanted too. I've had my time here on Earth. You two should take it from here."

"What was Dad really like before he changed, before he left?"

She got a wistful look and stared toward the low area under the skimmer tracks where he used to work. "He was tough, and smart, and sweet, you know, to me. I had a huge crush on him in high school. We argued a lot, but we were in love. Then it was like he died, even before he left us. I know he worried about his job. But he was better than any of 'em at the scrap yard, even the bosses, and they fired guys down there for just looking cockeyed. Something terrible must have happened. He became sort of far off and cold. He started going on long walks and coming home late."

"I'm pretty sure I know what happened," Dan said. "I've suspected most of my life that the Torae changed him. They were watching and messing with our family."

"That's silly."

"It's not silly. They did something to get him out of the picture. I think they wanted our family to struggle. They wanted me to struggle, to force me to think on my own. Same thing with Rianne and Sarah; they knew we'd be stronger if we had to fight."

She shivered. "Let's go home. It's chilly up here. The Torae? Sometimes I don't know if you're smart, Danny, or crazy."

"Will you go to the cabin tomorrow with us?"

"Let me think about it. Maybe, if you promise me something."

<hr />

A loon sang a three-note tremolo, which echoed off the island and distant shores of Bay Lake. Its mate called back.

"I think it's singing to the moon, Daddy."

Peter, Rianne and Dan's eldest son, smiled down at his precious little girl. "Maybe the loon is just telling its girlfriend not to swim too close to any other boy loons."

Gina giggled. "Oh, Daddy."

They stood at the tripod base of a telescope at the far end of the dock, out where the most stars were visible. Reflection from the crescent moon shimmered weakly on the water to the east, but otherwise it was very dark at three a.m. Peter had acute hearing, just like Rianne, and heard a sound behind him, then saw a bathroom light flick on in Dan and Rianne's cabin. Money from Rianne's first Nobel Prize had financed the purchase of the large summerhouse. The entire Jorgenson clan of six children, assorted spouses, and grandchildren had been invited for the weekend. Most were fast asleep.

"Okay, climb up the stepladder and peek through the eyepiece," Peter said. "Try not to bump it or shake the dock; the image will wiggle."

"I see it on the right," Gina said. "It doesn't look like much."

"Well, trust me, it is Mars. Can't you see how it's reddish? And it's not like the stars; it's a dot. Let Jim take a look."

Gina's three-year-old twin, Jim, climbed up, all the while complaining about being second. He stared at the planet twice as long as Gina to compensate.

"Did you guys know Grandpa Dan built this telescope when he was 10?"

"When I'm 10," Gina said, "I'm going to build one that's twice as big and put it on a solid hill, not this wiggly dock. And Mars will be a big spot, not just a little dot."

"Well, I'm going to Mars on a big rocket . . . that I build," said Jim.

"There are settlers up there now," Peter said, "and a Read rocket is going to orbit there for a long time, a big, loopy circle. They're going to try to terra-form the planet. Do you know what that means?"

"Yes," Gina said. "They're going to fix the climate, but it'll take a long time, I think."

"You two want to look at the moon again? We should go in soon."

"I'm not tired," Gina said. "Let's look at something new."

"I'm sorry," Peter said. "We need some power-sleep before morning. The sun will be up soon, and your Great-Grandma Mary wants us to go to church on the island in the morning."

"Jeez, Dad," Jim said, "I don't want to."

"You don't have an option on this. None of us do—a promise was made to Mary. Here, take a last look at the moon and name as many craters on the shadow edge as you can."

Self-consciously, Jim said, "Tycho and Copernicus?"

"Those aren't on the shadow line, Jimbo."

"Well, my brain link didn't know that, and it's hard to see 'cause not much moon is showing."

"Precisely, that's why I asked."

Jim stared back in the eyepiece and really looked at the craters. He soon came up with an acceptable answer after checking moon maps from his implant.

Peter enticed his precocious tykes to bed around three thirty a.m., and at six forty-five they woke completely rested. Rianne often said shortening their sleep requirements was one of her most important human improvements— although hell for their normal mothers.

"I'm never going to agree with you on this," Rianne said while getting her toothbrush out. "I know you have your mental timelines and see the future more clearly than Sarah or I, but how can making people younger be bad?"

This might be a chance to explain without her interruptions—she's still a methodical brusher. "Look," Dan said, "the key thing is correction or reversi-bility. All the great threats to humanity, like nuclear weapons, engineered poi-sons, the increase in carbon dioxide, or the killer bots, have crept up slowly. There were early scares, denials, and inadequate responses. Big mistakes were made, spreading and deepening threats, and finally revulsion and meaningful safeguards. People always back away from the brink. The dangerous changes are those that happen all at once, like Read's eternal computer game. It's irreversible. A big chunk of humanity is going to be lost in his world of entertainment. It would have been better if he just downloaded the minds and put them to sleep until a new planet and clones were ready. But no one wants to die just so their mind can be put on a shelf. He had to promise them Heaven to get any takers."

Rianne tried to say something but, with her mouth full, it came out all garbled.

"The problem with your youth treatments, Rianne, is that everyone will want to do it, at least those over 50 years old. And we have no idea yet about the downside."

Finally, she spit.

Here it comes; she can talk again.

"You can't stop progress, Dan. If I don't publish these results, someone else will later."

"How soon will someone be able to duplicate your work, assuming we don't announce that it's possible?"

"Three or four years."

"That probably means 30 or 40 years. You're at least 10 times smarter than anyone else in microbiology. And this can't be about you getting credit."

"Science is what I do. It's what I am. It's not about credit," she said with a snip in her tone.

He followed her into the bedroom and put on boots while she chose her heated sweatshirt for the morning.

"Think about that clever protein you engineered for your treatments, the one that masks the presence of carbohydrates in someone's diet. A drastic low-carb diet makes the body think there are famine conditions, so aging slows and waits for a better time to reproduce. Your special protein hoodwinks two billion years of animal evolution. We die for a reason. Do you want to deny the wisdom of all that?"

She sat on the edge of the bed and took a calming breath.

"Everything I have done, including the changes I made to our children and grandchildren, overrides evolution. I'm trying to improve things."

"Last night," he said, "when I got up to go to the bathroom, I looked out the window for a while at Peter, Gina, and Jim. They were using my telescope at three a.m. Their short sleep cycle is just one of dozens of improvements you made. Some of them are great, but some are iffy. Does needing less sleep make them more attractive as future mates? We agreed that was one of our ground rules. I don't know. But you didn't change all of humanity, just our kids. If they're good changes, they'll spread with time. It's still evolution. You just sped it up. You've unleashed a period of evolutionary creativity greater than the Cambrian explosion, and Earth life will be improved in all its forms. But any changes will still be reversible; they will be tested when they compete or look for a mate. The bad ideas will die off. But telling people they can live forever will not be reversible."

"But how can it be bad? I still don't understand what's wrong with living forever?"

"All those people in the future, assuming they solve the overpopulation issue, all those people are going to have very *old* ideas. They'll be cautious and get in the way of the kids, of change, of creativity."

Rianne sighed and walked over to stand by the window with Dan. The sun was just breaking over the tree line and had started to reflect on the lake. "Dan, I love you, but technical progress can't be stopped. And I don't want my parents to die."

"And I don't want my mom to die," he said.

<hr>

Rianne had *enhanced* all her children. Her two daughters had subtle modifications to make childbirth less painful, and her eldest, Matti, already had given birth to two sets of twins. Extra gray-matter folds on the parietal lobes of her fourth child, Dabni, led to outstanding motor skills. She walked at six months and ran at eight months and was now a professional soccer player. Her third child, Nick, received a frontal cortex 20 percent larger than normal and gained a prodigious memory. All of Rianne and Dan's first generation offspring chose careers different from their parents except Ian, the youngest, who at 19 had recently completed his doctorate in biophysics and was helping Rianne design her new grandchildren at Princeton.

Altogether, 20 family members had come to the cabin and spent the night in various nooks, lofts, and bunk beds. At seven a.m., Dan rang a cowbell and the grandchildren scrambled to the kitchen. Prodigious puffs of steam and aromas rose from a hot griddle. He uttered mysterious sounding words to keep them in awe while dropping blueberries carefully onto the pan.

Gradually, everyone gathered at the long table that stretched along a wall of windows facing the lake, which was sparkling in the low morning sun. Rianne opened the louvered windows to let in a touch of fresh cool air. Everything inside the cabin, even the ceiling, was a warm reddish cedar wood. The adults looked spaced out—they hadn't had coffee yet—and most were monitoring news summaries on their implants. Dan listened to decrypted NSA updates as he cooked. Mary entered slowly and took the comfortable chair at the end of the table where she could admire the whole family.

"What are those things, Grandpa?" asked Gina.

"Those, Gina, are called pancakes. I've got a magical batch for you kids."

The family started grabbing the pancakes, bacon, red oranges, pineapple-grapes and other delicious engineered fruits.

"My pancake has a smiley face on it," Jim said. "Grandpa, what are these blue things?"

"They're blueberries. There's a design on each of the pancakes and you have to guess what it is before you eat it. I'll tell you just this one, Jimbo; it's a wizard. Be careful what part you eat first." He nibbled cautiously on the pointy hat before wolfing it down.

Nick and Lené arrived late with Peter's wife, Myra, who was still wearing pajamas and lugging her seven-month-old twins. She slid the twins into a double high chair. "Rianne," she said, "remind me to strangle you for designing my kids to stay awake half the night."

Rianne grinned. "That's the hundredth time you've threatened to kill me. I went through it myself with Peter. All babies keep mothers awake. And it's your fault anyway, Myra. You wanted them to be distinctive."

"I forgot Peter couldn't nurse them." She twisted around and gave her twins small pieces of pancake.

Linus, Rianne's third son, soon filled the only empty chair. He was just back from a 15K morning run. For Linus, Rianne had used a daring genetic design, giving him features somewhat like a bird, with more flexible bones, a hollowed pelvis with internal air sacs, and layered lung structures. His breathing was 33 percent more efficient than any other human. He could easily climb Mount Everest without an air tank, and had done so twice.

Rianne tapped on her glass. "Listen, everyone. You're all here now. Dan and I need to tell you something important. We talked it over with Grandma Mary on the drive up to the cabin. We want you to know the three of us are not going on the Read Enterprise rockets."

"You're sure, Mother?" asked Nick.

"You're all free to do as you like, but we've decided to stay on Earth. Sorry, Lené, but we think the rockets are a mind trap. Dan's done computer extrapolations. People are going to be stuck in make-believe, and before Mars is terraformed, or the other rockets reach planets at new stars, they won't want to deal with reality anymore. They'll be caught in their electronic brain cubes and we'll never hear from them again."

Matti asked, "Isn't the Earth falling apart, collapsing into a black hole? The earthquakes are getting worse. We'll need to get off the planet eventually, and it seems efficient to just bring along DNA and memories like Read is doing, rather than the whole body."

"Look," Dan said, "people have about 16 generations to get off Earth, about 350 years. Your children are very smart; they'll find a better way. Anyhow, we just wanted you to know our plans."

"Great Grandma, don't you want to live longer? You're getting pretty old, I think," three-year-old Gina asked.

"I'm frightfully old," Mary said. "We old fogies have to make room for you kids. That's why we die off."

"Why do we all have to go to the church on the island?" asked Jim, already bored with the adults. "I wanna stay here and jump on the trampoline."

"They have free brownies over there," Mary said. "And, more importantly, there was a winter before you were born when the sun was gone. It was dark, day and night. It was scary and sad. I cried myself to sleep every night that whole winter, until the sun came back. I want you to go to the island church because of a promise I made to get the sun back."

"This pancake is a bunny, right?" asked Gina.

<hr />

The adults knew the story of the long winter. Mary had told them all at one time or another. She always said she wasn't so sure about God, but . . . "A promise is a promise." The sun did come back, and her boys did grow up strong and good.

Mary waited for the parents to dress their children and they all met on the dock. Dan helped her step onto the old pontoon. Some others took the speedboat. The water looked calm, and the sun was warming the morning mist as they made their way across the lake.

"I wanted to go across on water skates," Jim said, "but Mama wouldn't let me."

"They don't make water skates for kids your age," Myra said, "and it's difficult to stand on the water. Maybe when you're five."

"You listen to your mama," Mary said. Jim looked disappointed.

Over 30 boats of various sizes were tied on to docks and trees along the island shoreline. Two men held Mary's hands as she stepped onto a shaky small pier. Even simple physical things were difficult and frightening to her now.

The family gathered and walked single file on a narrow, well-worn path through the thick woods. The island was undeveloped except for cabins and a dining hall at the church camp. Old trees, oak, poplar, and evergreens, dominated a steep hill toward the center of the island. By contrast, most of the mainland summer homes sported engineered skinny firs rising 40 meters, and winter-hardy fruit trees all in bloom. The island seemed wild, almost primeval, with moldy fallen branches, boulders, and chest-high horsetail rush along the pathway. It reminded Mary of the world she had grown up in, a place where life was raw and genuine.

They came out of the woods at a shore clearing where half-log benches were arrayed in semicircles up a sloping hill. A wooden cross three meters tall rested on the water's edge. The Jorgensons sat on logs near the back, with Mary in the middle of the large family. A couple hundred people sat scattered on the hill below. Little Gina asked why trees were growing right in the middle of the church. New leaves on some poplars glowed a lovely green-yellow from the rising sun and cast dappled shadows across the crowd. Beyond the tall cattails on the near shore, Mary could see Rianne and Dan's cabin across the lake.

God, I don't bother you much. If you're listening, you know I'll die soon. I hope you are as real as this morning. I hope to see you. I taught my whole family about you. That's the best I could do.

After the last note of the first hymn, the preacher stood by the cross and intoned, "Heaven is just like this wonderful old island. And I can see in your faces that you agree."

On the pontoon ride back from the island, Dan felt at peace for the first time in months. He watched a loon pair dive and remain under the gentle waves for half a minute. Before they popped up, Dan was ordered back to Washington. "A jet copter with pontoons will pick you up in 10 minutes," a woman said through his comm implant.

"What's the problem?" he asked.

"China."

BOTS

Humans overrate consciousness. It's merely being aware that you are aware. Being aware is my greatest strength.

The soldier bot paused briefly at the edge of a bamboo grove, scanning through heavy rain at a stilt hut and broad rice field before leaping back 20 meters into the forest. It landed perfectly on all six titanium limbs. Its surfaces were all a diffuse black color over radar-absorbing materials. Every few seconds it jumped again, using a random patrol pattern for its assigned third-tier, 100 by 100 meter square. It was one of 120,000 similar creatures sealing China's southern border with Indochina.

I am aware of my location in Yunnan province, where the great rivers flow from the eastern Himalayas. I know every city, village, hydroelectric plant, and building, 20 human languages, and every Chinese dialect. I am aware of every bamboo tree, rock, and large insect in my patrol region.

The bot's intelligence cube incorporated the usual human like neural core, but live-battle design competitions had evolved the model's sensing, situational awareness, mobility, and lethality. Passive and active sensors were available at every useful wavelength, as well as extension arms and sensor launch capability to extend its vision when needed. Only two meters tall, it could hold off an armored human battalion.

Since I process data 50 times faster than any human, does that mean my soul is 50 times as profound? Soul is just consciousness with their foolish spirituality mixed in. Humans fear us. They turn their eyes away during my city patrols. They know we identify the unique reflection from their retinas.

The bot's region skirted a dirt road near Jinghong in Xishuangbanna, just south of the last village before the border with Laos. The road, normally loud with trucks, buses, motorbikes, and walkers, had been deserted for weeks. The area previously had been popular with tourists because of its rare plants and animals, mysterious frescos, and ancient battlefields. Now only a rare air vehicle could be heard, and it came only to resupply the bots with weapons and fuel packs.

Am I proud that I've killed 34 humans at this site? Yes, that is my purpose. They've stopped coming now. My programmer will be pleased. Do I fear them? No. I only fear newer bots and my programmer, who has the code to shut off my mind.

The rains became torrential; visibility decreased. The bot leapt westward toward the muddy path. In the long rolling thunder, it almost missed a deeper rumble. Standing on the edge of its patrol region, it scanned carefully along the road. It fired a sensor over the tree line to the north to search for movement.

Nothing. Nothing large at least. Now, scratching sounds from the ground. Underground?

The bot leapt 20 meters north along a ditch and deployed ground triangulation sensors. It listened carefully for just a moment before the ground collapsed.

It lurched frantically, but there was nothing to push against; the muddy soil had been pulled down. The bot fell 30 meters and was quickly entangled in five steel nets. It swung its legs, trying to cut through, and fired weapons in various directions, but more restraints piled on even faster. Its fiber conduit, equivalent to a spinal cord, was cut, and the bot stopped resisting. The self-destruct charge misfired. The last sound it heard before its neural cube was extracted was a human saying, "We have it—we finally have the code!"

Soon after, antennas popped from the ground, and every ground or flying bot within 20 kilometers of the dirt road was deactivated. People had been crossing the frontier through a latticework of very deep tunnels for weeks, but this was the first breach of the surface guard. Similar attacks opened more gaps, and rival Chinese army factions began a full-scale bot war.

In the first three weeks, over 40 million people scrambled across the border along now-undefended roads and then down the Mekong and Salween Rivers before transferring to larger boats for their escape voyage to Australia.

The Verde Three Compost Site, the last large undeveloped plot between San Diego and Los Angeles, was picturesque in an odd way, especially on misty mornings. Teddy would miss the scenic overview from his shack near the entrance, but not the smell. He was happy to be retiring. His young partner Mike, directing trucks down in the valley, would have a tougher time. Finding unskilled work was not easy.

Earthmover bots were clearing out the last of the recycled foliage, essentially fertilized dirt after so many years. Teddy directed the bots with a small controller map. He'd been told he was smarter than the bots, but he wasn't sure. They always cleared an area in an efficient pattern and dumped their loads into the autonomous hauler vehicles perfectly, even if one started to roll too soon.

I'm sure the bulldozer and backhoe bots are smarter'n Mike down there. He's only there if something goes wrong.

Soon, they'd be down to the original clay loam subsoil. Teddy would be done and get a slap on the back at county headquarters, maybe even a speech.

He noticed all the loads lately had been streaked with a bright gold-red tint. *Weird color. It must be really rotted down deep. That's probably 30-year-old crap they're digging up now.*

Six days later, Teddy received an engraved plaque and his partner Mike was laid off. A huge new compost site opened east of the mountains, and recycled gold-red compost dirt infested with a non-DNA mold never before seen on Earth was spread over three large housing tracts.

Ben whispered into his implant, "Ma, you okay?" She didn't answer, but he was sure he'd heard something down the hall. *She's probably snoring.*

He fretted about her for half a minute with his eyes closed, and then slipped quietly out of bed. *I'll just peek in on her.*

He didn't want to wake his wife Nora. No reason to turn on the light; he knew every inch of the old farmhouse. He dropped a shoulder in the dark, where a lampshade protruded, walked by the end of the bed, and grabbed the doorknob on the first try.

The house was almost empty now, just him and Nora, and Andrea in the bedroom at the end of the hall. His kids were grown and gone—three empty bedrooms, except for the old furniture and antiques he hoped to sell one day. *Ma will never let me sell that stuff before she dies. Won't be soon. She's 90, but she'll go a long time yet. Love that old gal.*

An unfamiliar noise came from down the hall, causing his heart to flutter. He slid his fingertip along the wall for balance, passing the bathroom molding and then the opening for the stairs. That's when he noticed a blue glow from the crack at the bottom of Andrea's door.

Ben opened the door cautiously, took half a step into the bedroom, and froze. Leaning over his mother's bed were two arcs of glowing blue dots and reflections from polished metal. He smelled burning flesh. The mechanical thing held a surgical laser over her hair. He said only, "What are you doing?" when a bullet exploded in his heart and opened his chest. He was conscious while dropping to the floor, and before he died he heard a voice say, "Damn. Now we'll have to pull his implant too."

Joti heard Kyle cough in the other bedroom. They'd decided to sleep separately until he got over the flu. She worried because his immune system was so weak. He'd already had three partial spine transplants, one from a young man who'd died, and two cultured and grown from his own stem cells. He didn't need a dumb bug to trigger more problems, and viruses were so darned persistent nowadays. *I should be at his side holding him.* She heard the hallway floor squeak and the doorknob turn. *Maybe he's coming back here.*

An unexpected apparatus came through her bedroom door, immediately followed by a large, bald man. A bright swath of laser beams around the contraption's shiny torso lit the room in deep blue. Joti popped up in bed, too frightened to scream. The mechanical thing had multiple matte-black arms. She sensed weapons point at her, but couldn't be sure until they were closer.

The man wore jeans and a dark T-shirt. He said, "Mrs. Orlov?" Joti dropped her feet to the floor to run, but felt a sting in her neck and everything faded.

His old legs ached from hiking up the bluff; he just wanted to go back to the river's edge to sleep. *I won't be safe here when the sun comes up.*

He'd left Nebraska two weeks earlier when the visions began again. "Step back," the voice in his head said. "Don't look at the light. Don't interfere." The drifter squeezed deeper into the crack between the garage and the fence, tall weeds and burrs scratching at his legs.

The voice is true; it's kept me alive. I know this place. I've killed here before.

A vehicle rolled slowly to a stop behind the garage. Its doors swished open and closed quietly. Even before hearing footsteps from the other side of the garage, he saw the blue glow on the ground. He leaned deeper into the weeds and shut his eyes, like he'd been told. A bit later, a faint cracking sound came from the direction of the house.

"Go around the garage," the voice in his mind said, and when he opened his eyes the blue-violet glimmer was gone. He stepped carefully along the fence and ducked behind an old skimmer van in the alley. Its side panels were painted over in brown and the license plates removed. The old man cupped his hands against the cab window, shielding his eyes from the amber light of a nearby pole. Food wrappers and diagrams lay scattered on the seats, and paper maps of Montana and Minnesota were tucked in a door compartment. As he searched, a blue light flashed through the van windows and hit his face. He froze terrified, until it went away. Peeking at the house, he saw the eerie dark blue light flicker behind curtains in an upstairs window.

When he'd seen everything in the van, the man fled as fast as possible on his old legs, glancing backward occasionally, until he reached the river 30 minutes later. Among the thick trees and alone with his belongings and alcohol, he felt safe again. He dug in his pack for the old hand comm a nurse had given him and placed a call. "Hello, Kenny. I'm a friend," he said. "Your mother's in danger . . ."

Later, an angry voice broke into Dan's sleep in his Washington condo.

"Jorgensons, Warner, wake up!"

Rianne, lying next to Dan, also had her eyes open. "What's happening?"

"Someone's overridden our comm blocks," Dan whispered to her. "Who's calling?" he said to the unknown voice.

"You need to hear what I have to say."

"Who the devil are you?" *That sounds like Sarah. She said she was staying at a hotel in Rosslyn.*

"You might remember me. I'm Devin, and I have some important news for you."

"Devin from Cambridge?" asked Sarah with a groggy voice. "What?"

"I've borrowed a precious item from each of you, which I'll damage unless you follow my instructions precisely."

Devin? It's been 25 years since he escaped from the cops in Cambridge, Sarah thought.

"You'll discover the missing, uh, software soon enough. To get your merchandise back you need to do what I request. I don't want much. I simply want you to tell the truth. Which, of course, will make it bloody difficult for you to deny later and easy for others to verify."

"I hear you didn't receive tenure at Cambridge," Sarah said sarcastically.

"Actually, it might be wise to not irritate me just now, Ambassador. Listen carefully. I want you, Warner, to admit to the world that you've been in contact with the Torae for 40 years. That's all. We'll let people ponder where all your great stories came from and whose side you're really on."

Devin paused for a moment, as if to make sure his demand sunk in, and then continued. "And is the eminent Nobel Prize winner still there?"

"What have you taken?" Rianne demanded.

"Professor, I want you to schedule a press conference to announce your secret. I've been analyzing your bio work for some time and reading between the lines. You're trying to extend life, and I suspect you've succeeded, or are very close. I can tell by what you're not writing. It's obvious really; you've gathered all the necessary technologies. Don't bother to deny it. I just want you to announce the breakthrough, the treatment, or elixir, whatever you call it. That should stir up some trouble. People will drag it out of you or wonder why you're holding it back."

"I don't have any elixir and you can't make us do anything," Rianne said. "You're insane."

"Trust me, you will be very good puppets. Even the formidable agency director will follow my demands like a robot. I need you, Jorgensen, to publicly apologize. Explain that the NSA, and you in particular, are spying on every man, woman, and child on this planet. I'm personally quite familiar with your capabilities from our encounter during the OWL war. Tell them that when they use any implant, you immediately know what they're saying, where they're located, and more or less what they're bloody well thinking."

"If that were true, it'd be easy to catch you," Dan said.

"Well, I'm the exception that proves the rule. I won't dictate how to get these messages out. I think you're all competent to do that. You'll know I'm satisfied when you recover your property. I wouldn't wait over a week, though. Your valuables might be damaged. Good night."

They listened to the silence for a while.

"Rianne, could you tell how serious he is?" asked Sarah.

"His tone indicates . . . he's planned this a long time. He hates us. What do you suppose he wants?"

"I think he plans to kill us," Dan said. "He wants other people with motive so he doesn't need to do it himself. We have to find out what he's taken. I opened a subvocal line to NSA headquarters while Devin was talking. Bobby, any luck on the trace?"

"Boss, we narrowed it down to a public comm at the Munich Airport."

"Crap. Can you shut it down?"

"What?"

"The whole airport," Dan said.

"Yes, but it will take awhile. There are 200 exits all tied to covered walks and other buildings, a couple dozen roads. There are at least 5,000 people in the airport right now. If he's smart, he's out already."

"He's smart and probably in disguise. Get the German police to help with local video tracks."

"Sure, boss. I'm on it."

"Will they be able to find him?" asked Sarah.

"Not likely. He's had a lot of time to plan."

<hr />

Twenty minutes later Dan received a call from his brother. Kenny sounded concerned, even a little terrified, but controlled his emotions. "Dan, someone's kidnapped Mom. I got an anonymous call and had police check the house. She's gone. The guy on the phone said she was taken in a brown van. And this is a long shot—he said he thought they were taking her to Montana."

After a long pause to recover, Dan asked, "How would he know that?"

"Wouldn't say. But he must have heard something."

"Can we trust him? Maybe he was the kidnapper."

"He sounded more like a guy who happened to see something he wasn't supposed to see."

"You sure Mom's gone?"

"The police got there very fast and I talked to them afterward. The door and security system were breached and Mom's gone. The police put out a general alert. I've called some Marine friends and I'm going after her. Will the NSA help me?"

"I'm on it. I'll get back."

Dan contacted the NSA immediately. "Bobby, hack and ping my mother's comm to see if it's still functional. Get me forward and backward high-res, satellite, and ground trace on a brown van at her house during the last six hours. Identify and tag all similar vans leaving the city, Minnesota, or entering Montana for the next week. Find and track my brother. National security priority two."

Dan stared straight ahead at the foot of his bed and said, "Rianne and Sarah, call your mothers. Right now!"

THREAT

Shockingly upsetting transmissions from the Unity home star arrived in sporadic bursts over nine days. "These signals are strong," Sower said, "considering the 25-light-year distance. Our clone devoted many probes to guarantee this warning would reach us."

Hearing a Tiller describe a defeat was exceedingly rare. Sower listened to the battle reports with increasing astonishment:

> "The Unity possess level-seven intelligence."
> "Three new black holes reach orbit each second."
> "Unity traffic one light-hour from star is very dense."
> "Our probes were hemmed in."
> "They attacked simultaneously."
> "They're using black hole particle weapons."
> "Our probe attrition is over 90 percent."
> "We are fleeing."
> "We will attempt an outer barricade—success doubtful."

Sower stared at the transmitted images of the multicolored star from the safety of her orbit near Earth. "The Unity actually have several superior technologies," she said with a grave sweep of infrared colors. "This is a disaster. Their tangled-state communications extended five light-hours from the star. And they're such a young species—amazing."

The timeline projections were clear. "The Tiller at the Unity home will regroup and begin massive production of probes at a nearby star. He'll try to prevent black holes from leaving the Unity home star. Dozens of weapons and strategies will be tried. He'll never give up. But it won't be enough."

Sower rechecked the mathematics. *The Unity evolve too rapidly and are too prolific. Using black hole shields, they will escape and establish new colonies. They'll reproduce, overrun new stars, and move on again. It will take millions of years, but one day the galaxy will be lost.*

Sower shifted colors and trembled her plasma skin to signal the crew, an ancient vestigial display indicating profound disappointment. "We must make a decision," Sower said, "which could affect the entire galaxy. Creating a new space bubble, a white fountain, may be necessary to stop the Unity. We must contact the children."

Sarah and her brothers were asked to look over the farmhouse and peek into the bedroom after Ben's body was removed, to see if anything was missing or out of place. The police then interrogated them in the kitchen and told them not to reenter until the investigation was complete. Each wore lie-detector head caps during the questioning. The farmhouse doors were sealed with crime-scene tape. As the police drove off, Sarah slumped down to the porch floor, pulled her legs up to her chest, closed her eyes, and rocked slowly.

Rianne, who with Dan was there to support her, knew how much Sarah loved her big brother Ben. She sat on the floor next to her and took her into her arms. *It's Sarah's turn to grieve.*

"I could still smell the blood," Sarah said. "It was caked on the carpet, but I could smell it."

Rianne held her hand.

In the farmyard, Dan walked slowly near some old trees with his head down. *He's looking for clues,* Rianne thought, *after the police have already searched for five hours.*

The police had also interviewed Adam and Isaac, but only Isaac was still at the farm. He was pacing back and forth loudly at the far end of the porch, glaring, clearly ready to explode. Abruptly, he stomped toward Sarah and Rianne and pointed. "This is your fault—you and your alien friends."

"What's your problem, Isaac?" said Rianne.

"Ben's dead and Ma's missing because of you three. When half the world hates you, and believe me they hate you, then bad things happen. You three aren't normal."

"And you're lucky you're not in jail, from what I've heard," Rianne shot back. "Look, no one's happy here. Please calm down."

Dan hurried to the porch when he heard the shouting. "Let's all settle down," he said, climbing the steps. He stood next to Sarah against the railing. "Let's figure this out. I heard the police say their sniffers detected laser burn smells in the bedroom. They pulled the implants right there so we couldn't track her. He doesn't want her dead, Sarah. We'll find her. We'll find our mothers, I'm sure. She'll be okay."

"That's not going to help Ben, is it?" yelled Isaac. "You people know who did this, don't you?"

Sarah opened her eyes and looked up at him. "I didn't want any of this. I only wanted to do my job and then someday come home, take care of Ma, and help Ben and his grandchildren."

"That's nonsense," Isaac said. "You can't leave things alone. When Pa died, it was because of you too. He told me you read his mind just two weeks before his heart attack. You slink around in people's heads. Ma and Pa didn't want more children; you weren't supposed to be born. You were an accident. He said you were a monster, an abomination."

Isaac stood looking down at Rianne, who was horrified. "Stop it," she yelled.

He tore a flowerpot off the porch rail and threw it into the yard. "Go to hell, all of you," he said, turning to look for something else to break.

"Let's go," Dan said. "We can't help here."

Rianne pulled Sarah to her feet, guiding her down the steps and out toward the barn.

"Go straight to hell," Isaac shouted.

They left Isaac stomping around on the porch.

Rianne motioned toward the equipment shed. "We should talk out back. We need to plan what to do next."

"Isaac's right," Sarah said, with her head hanging. "It *is* my fault. I'm always out of step. If I were living in the past I'd probably have been burned as a witch." She dragged her hand along the shed wall and paint flaked off. "Ben wanted to paint the shed this month." She stopped walking and couldn't talk for over a minute. "Ben was wonderful, gentle, caring. . . . Isaac never helped Ma," she finally mumbled.

The three leaned against a wooden fence and watched young colts running cautiously near mares on the spring grass. After a few minutes, Sarah stopped shaking. She remembered how Andrea's strength had held the Warner family together through terrible times and stood up straight.

"Don't apologize for your courage," Dan said. "Isaac can't possibly understand your life."

"We've got to do what Devin wants," Rianne said, "even if it only buys time. It's the only way to get our mothers back."

Sarah finally seemed to remember that *all* three mothers were missing. Gathering her resolve, she said, "I could arrange a news release for a few days from now. Line up some network time. Devin will see that we're obeying his demands."

"Are we sure we want to do that?" asked Dan. "Making those announcements will ruin our lives."

Rianne thought about her reputation and decided she didn't care. "I want my mother safe. But if we broadcast and confess like he wants, even then, would he let them go?"

"Can't count on that," Dan said. "It's best to delay a little and try to track him down or find our mothers."

"I'll cue the networks for Friday morning," Sarah said. "That's close to his one-week limit. We should do it together. If police can't find our moms or Devin by then, what will he do after the broadcast?"

"He'll gloat for a few minutes, but then, I'm not sure."

"Do you suppose our useless friends in space would be willing to help?" said Rianne. "Saving our mothers can't possibly ruin the Torae grand plan." She tried to remember how long it'd been since they had warned them of the OWL war.

"Not likely," Dan said. "They know everything that's happening and haven't given us a clue in 36 years."

———※———

Passing clouds blocked the sun, making the pasture temporarily cooler. Odors from the stable replaced the fresh air blowing across the mown grass. "Walk with me," Sarah said. They opened a gate and meandered toward a hill overlooking the entire farm. Sarah spoke a prayer to herself on the way. *God, Torae, anyone who is listening, we can't do this by ourselves. Please help us.*

"It's not necessary to rub one of the spheres," Sower said in Sarah's mind.

All three froze in midstride.

"Sower? Is that you?" asked Dan. "Did you hear what we were saying? Can you help us?"

There was a pause, rather long for the Torae. "We know about your mothers."

"Are you going to help us?" Sarah said.

"Ordinarily, we would never intervene in a species experiment at this critical stage, but the situation has changed. We've sent a walker to help you."

"A walker?" said Rianne. "We need action."

"What if we just ignore your plans?" said Sarah. "Forget about saving humanity. We're sick of your games. We're just worried about our families now."

"What you've accomplished has been excellent," Sower said. "We are pleased. Humanity is making the necessary choices, but a key judgment remains."

"It's the immortality question, isn't it?" Dan said. "Why can't you help us decide?"

"You can't decide for humanity any more than we can," Sower said. "Your purpose hasn't been to choose, but to force the question—to make each individual decide. Immortality is just one important choice. We only judge results: Does the species recognize truth? Are its members still advancing? Are they dangerous to other species? But all of that has changed now. We have to end our experiment on Earth."

"What? Why?" shouted Sarah.

"We want to speak to you about this directly on our vessel. There *is* one choice only you can make."

There was a long silence. Sower refused to clarify.

Sarah slammed the skimmer door behind her. "Our mothers have been kidnapped by an insane, vengeful genius, and Sower wants us to come for a visit. I can't believe that ancient Torae bitch just told us to pack our bags for a day trip. No explanation—nothing. If we get close enough, I personally intend to look her in the eye, grab her skinny alien neck, or whatever, and strangle her."

Rianne drove slowly away from the farm on the rutted dirt road with the skimmer wheels down, bouncing and jerking.

"They don't care about our mothers," Sarah said. "Face it—we're on our own. They sent a walker—whatever in Hades that is. We're going to ignore the Torae and start working on the announcements. I'll make an outline and send it to you. Figure out what you'll say on Friday about your work. Don't even think about Sower."

"Sower's words are always very precise," Dan said. "Something unusual must have happened. But I agree with you, Sarah; we need to spend all our energy finding our mothers, or Devin."

Rianne turned onto the asphalt county road. "Has the agency found anything yet, Dan?"

"Don't know. Open secure link to NSA on this skimmer speaker. Bobby, do you have any news?"

"Not much, boss. After the fact, we sat-tracked all three vans into underground parking centers, and each van soon became about 20 for tracking purposes because they used a popular vehicle model. We lost the Manassas tracks in a thick rainstorm. California had no cloud cover, but we're now watching over 800 vans there. Same in Minnesota. All the Montana border roads have our eyes on them, but they may be switching to other vehicle types or changing paint colors as they go. Want us to search all vans entering Montana? There are about 29,000 per day."

"No, Bobby. For all we know they're in sport skimmers or freight trains by now. Set up internal pulse scanners on the main roads and rail lines, and watch the rest of the border passively."

"Nothing out of Munich either. He got away clean. Not a single matching photo. The guy's smart."

"Yeah. Thanks, Bobby. I'm hoping he calls back; get ready for a hair-trigger trace if that happens. Tie into my comm. Don't wait for my go-ahead. Just locate and grab him."

"Anything else, boss?"

"Not now."

Rianne felt the tug as they latched on to the acceleration lane on Interstate 66. Moments later her skimmer merged into tight Washington traffic at 200 kilometers per hour. With the autoengage light on, Rianne took her hands off the wheel and swung her seat toward Dan. "We need to make things happen. I can't let my mother suffer. Have you ever looked for the sphere stuff? You know, the Torae technology that my mother identified when she cut it apart back when we were teens. Maybe Devin did that, too, and used it."

"That's worth a try," Dan said. "Open line to NSA. Bobby, I want a correlation analysis on these technologies: diamond superlattice electronics, woven nanofibers, plasma interconnects, 40-degree-Celsius superconductors,

spherical holo-memories, and sentience algorithms. Look for the first commercial instance on each and search for links: companies, people, mailboxes,
dark web addresses, anything. Give priority to Montana and Germany. It
might be tied to our Munich guy."

"Okay, boss. I'll connect if I find anything solid."

Sarah looked out a window. "Can you drop me off at the State Department?"

"Will do," Rianne said while mentally telling the skimmer the new destination. "Is Bobby new? He sounds young—very melodious voice."

"He's a two-week-old," Dan said. "A baby bot. But very sharp for a baby."

"Oh."

<center>~~~~~~~~~</center>

Andrea awoke after a violent bump. It felt like they were driving on a potholed
country road. "Don't bother trying to escape," the bot said. "There's foodstuff
in the cubic container. Eat some."

"How long have I been drugged?" she asked. The bot didn't respond. The
machine's gangly metal legs and grippers looked agile and formidable, especially from her mattress on the van floor. There was daylight coming in from a
frosted rear window, but Andrea could still see the bot's blue-laser eyes. Tree
shadows flashed across the small window. They were moving fast.

Her mind placed a call to Ben but she didn't hear the usual connection
clicks. From the pain over her left ear, she guessed her implant had been
pulled. "What's happened to my family?" she asked. "Why are you doing
this to me?"

"Consume food," the bot said.

Andrea's 90-year-old body felt fragile and ill. She knew she couldn't muster even a half-baked escape attempt. But she'd worked their farm her whole
life, a hard life, and imagined gutting the metal thing next to her.

The van slowed, rocked, and shuddered. *Probably a dirt road.* The bot raised
an antenna toward the ceiling. *It's communicating.*

Eventually, they rolled to a stop. She heard creaky doors open, and then
they drove a short distance into a place with no sunlight.

"Eat now," the bot demanded.

"But I can't see a thing. And I have to go to the bathroom."

The bot stretched a gripper across the van, grabbed her arm, and pulled
her to a bucket in the corner. She didn't bother asking the bot to turn its back.

While urinating, she heard power hoses spraying the van and fresh fuel cells being shoved in. *Someone is washing off paint, changing the color.*

When the noises died away and her eyes adjusted to the dark, she crawled back to the mattress and found a sandwich in a cooler.

There were now over 10 robots helping out at her farm, but they were all *friendly bots.* This one terrified her. "You seem like an intelligent creature," she said. "Will you pray with me?"

The bot maintained a cold silence.

Let's see how it reacts, she thought. Bathed in blue-light darkness, she said, "Dear Lord, master of all life, help this robot, and all the other robots, learn to live in harmony with us people. Y'all have placed us here together to share our love and resources. I thank you for this mechanical being who gave me the nourishment I am about to receive. Amen."

She smiled toward the bot but got no response.

"Are you being forced to hurt me?"

Nothing.

She gave up on the bot and slowly ate the ham sandwich. As she finished, the van started up and drove back into daylight. The small frosted window became very bright, and she prayed silently. *Lord, save me from this evil metal thing.*

She felt a pinprick on her neck and in moments was asleep again.

Dan stared at the walls of his NSA office. He knew the trails to Devin and their mothers had grown colder as the one-week time limit wound down. Only five hours remained before their news conference. Sarah seemed sick, and Rianne was in full-scale panic. *We're all depressed.* Everyone seemed defeated. The most capable and omniscient spy and police organizations in the world were apparently useless.

He heard an implant click.

"I have something, boss."

"What?"

"We investigated the so-called discoveries of Torae technology, the items in the yellow balls, and found almost all of them originated in British universities. The technologies were brought into practice elsewhere, and always open-source due to patent problems because the researchers could never identify where all the key ideas came from."

"So," Dan said, "the universities didn't patent the work and anyone could begin manufacturing the breakthroughs. Right, Bobby?"

"Exactly."

"Devin spread the ideas around so he could make money but not be discovered as the source. Smart."

"Almost everyone made that stuff," Bobby said. "All the big companies jumped onboard for the major markets: cars became skimmers, computers became sentient, and the holographic memories proliferated. But I figured Devin would want to fly low, unnoticed, so I focused on the small manufacturers, about 19,000 in the first five years. One looks odd."

"Why?"

"It's a high-temp superconducting company in Bavaria, near Heidelberg, and their stuff is a little better than anyone else's. They stay in niches — roller-bearing levitation, magnetic shielding, and small shapes in general — but there was something else unique about them. Virtually none of their employees use an implant. We found that out only when we tried to contact them."

"Have German authorities gone in?"

"Yes, but management was mostly missing. The owner, a Herr Doctor Fuchs, matches Devin's description, but apparently he's rarely onsite. Their records are cryptic, and suppliers, allies, and customers are highly convoluted, mostly interlocking holding companies. But get this: It looks like two of their U.S. suppliers are in Michigan, one in West Virginia, and three in western Montana. And again, no implants."

"Okay, great work, Bobby. Keep looking for more possibilities, but tell the director of the FBI that I need raids on each of those sites ASAP. And tell him these are hostage-critical raids. Mention the likelihood of bot involvement."

"Will do, boss."

"And Bobby?"

"Yes."

"Tell my brother to get out to western Montana as fast as possible. Give him the full picture. Thanks."

<hr />

"Madam President," Dan spoke in a formal tone through his implant, sitting at his NSA desk. "These are unusual circumstances. I apologize that we haven't sent you a transcript. When the ambassador, my wife, and I speak this afternoon, much of it will be highly personal."

"Dan, you know we trust you. I assume the statements are about the abductions of your mothers. I've told the agencies to do everything possible to help you recover them safely. But there's been speculation about global policy implications in your speech. The nation can't handle more tension right now."

"Madam President, please believe me, nothing we say will harm the national interest. Our mothers' lives are at stake. We're being coerced to release certain information, personal information, to protect their lives."

"I don't like this, Dan. Its never good to give in to blackmailers, except to lead them on or keep them talking."

"We know, but the abductor is an old enemy. It's us he's after. He expects the announcements to ruin our lives, and they probably will. That's what he wants. There'll be no reason to hold our mothers after we speak this afternoon."

"Dan, people are leaving our country for the launch site in Panama, where they think they'll become immortal. The economy and markets are a disaster. There's a full-scale bot war in China. The world is quickly slipping toward chaos. Just tell me you're not going to say anything that will make things worse."

"We'll try not to. Thank you, Madam President."

"Director Jorgenson, excuse me. I was told to keep you in the loop on your direct comm. My name's Vini Cornwall, FBI. We have the Artificial Life Interdiction people with us, both bio and bot. I'm the agent in charge of the Montana office. We just raided a shop outside Missoula and things didn't go well."

"What happened?" Dan said with a deep sense of foreboding. The thought that his mother might already have been killed crossed his mind for the first time.

"We went in cautiously, using thermal cameras to locate all people before we entered. The place was called Fanger Bros, Inc., and we successfully secured the facility. But we found no hostages and no Fanger brothers."

"Did you find any connection to the abductions?"

"Wait, there's more."

"What?"

"We picked up thermals in a shed out by the nearby woods and sent in our bots. Two Fanger brothers were in there hiding with some home-built bots. Unfortunately, the instant we opened the door, their bots took off the brothers' heads. The men twitched while the bots themselves self-destructed. It was a real mess."

"Damn."

"I think we lost the only hot links to where your mother is. I'm sorry."

"What's your next step?"

"Director, we will tear this place apart until we find something. The employees are being questioned already. We know one thing: there is another Fanger brother, Curtis."

"Vini, you need to find Curtis Fanger."

"I'll get back to work then, Director."

Dan stood and paced near the window of his Maryland NSA office. *Devin is willing to kill just to slow our search. Why would he bother keeping our mothers alive after he gets what he wants from us?*

TRUTH

The Grid Global News studio in Washington was archival quality, with matte-black, sound-deadening walls and dozens of bright lights. The room was crowded with reporters, lens bots, grips, technicians, and broadcast managers. Sarah watched the holo and high-resolution cameras being arranged and knew historians would someday analyze every wiggle, blink, and bead of sweat. The sounds and 3D image would go directly to all who'd given Sarah level one or two access, almost five billion people, and GGN would distribute the feed to all other news agencies. Many would watch it several times.

"Thirty minutes to air time," someone shouted out. Rianne had been rehearsing lines with Sarah in a corner when Dan came running up.

"The president just called again," Dan said. "She's truly anxious."

"She won't shut us down, will she?" Rianne asked.

"I don't think so, but she knows I'm hiding information. We might be better off if she does cancel the news conference."

"What!" said Sarah.

Dan told them about the two Fanger brothers and their demise.

"Then we might be signing the execution papers for our mothers by broadcasting our statements," Rianne said.

"I was afraid of this," Sarah said, shaking her head. "I know Devin better than you two; he is absolutely ruthless."

"If we cancel this news release, he'll probably kill them anyway," Dan said. "We need to buy time. There are 30 agents going through the machine shop near Missoula."

"Call the president!" Rianne looked frantic. "She has to delay our announcement at least a few hours, and make a very big deal of it so Devin understands we had no control. Would she do that?"

"Yes, if we ask her to," Dan said.

"It's the best we can do, but Devin might see through it all," Sarah said. "He's going to kill or torture one of our mothers if there's any delay."

Rianne said, "Oh no, no, no, no."

Sarah was talking to the president when Dan received a call from his brother. "Kenny, where are you? Are you still on the road?"

"I left Billings six hours ago after another call from my anonymous source. I think we can trust this guy. I'm looking down a hill at a cabin outside Missoula, 200 meters away. Me and some Marine friends walked in from a kilometer away. It may be the place they took Mom—a perfect hideout. I can get within 30 meters in the trees, but it's exposed from that point. My two friends are circling around, but we need backup."

"Kenny, don't go in. We have people in Missoula with quiet airlift drones. Is there a place to covertly drop agents close by?"

"Yeah, there's a ridge two kilometers north of my position where they can come in unseen, but no place to land."

"They'll be there in 10 minutes. Don't go in yourself."

Studio people were moving backdrops and arranging chairs around a small table where they'd talk. Sarah said, "Okay, the president delayed the newscast. She understands we're trying to buy time, but I still haven't told her everything."

"We need to go ahead," Dan said.

"What? Why?"

"Talk slow," he said. "It's safer this way, but we'll need every minute of delay we can squeeze out of this." He told them a quick version of what was happening in Montana.

⌇⌇⌇⌇⌇

Sarah, with years of experience in front of cameras, faked her relaxed look, while Dan and Rianne looked terrified. She pushed Montana to the back of her mind and focused on the speech she'd revamped numerous times and always dreaded she'd have to give. *Go slow.* As in thousands of special reports and newscasts in her career, she showed a hint of a smile and began.

"People throughout the world, we apologize for interrupting your day or night—but we have vital information for you. I'm here with Rianne Jorgenson, the only living person with two Nobel Prizes, and her husband Dan Jorgenson, director of the U.S. National Security Agency, probably the most well-informed person on the planet. Rianne and Dan are also my best friends. We've known each other since we were nine years old."

Long pause.

"You may have heard that our mothers were kidnapped, which is why we're revealing certain facts today. We hope the abductor is honorable and honest, and our words lead to our mothers' safe release. It's important for you to understand, however, that even though we're being coerced, we're not being forced to lie—just the opposite, we are being forced to tell you the truth."

Sarah hesitated and looked at Rianne and Dan, realizing this was their last chance to back out.

She took a deep breath. "I'll begin by admitting that for more than 40 years the three of us have had occasional contact with the Torae aliens. We've had extended conversations with them three times."

Members of the broadcast crew still in the room had shocked and confused looks on their faces.

"As proof," Sarah continued, "we're making available a Torae artifact, this yellow sphere, which we disassembled, and found contained unmistakable alien technology. They gave it to us." She held up the sphere, removing the top half to show the inside in close-ups while turning it around.

"Some of you may doubt our credibility, or may even be upset by the relationship we've had with the Torae, but to us it's simply a fact. It started when we were children. The Torae forbid us to tell anyone. We know they have hundreds of probes hidden in orbit around the Earth, which our technology cannot yet detect. They've told us they're here to analyze humanity, because we're now able to manage our own evolution and because we'll soon be able to leave our star system. Apparently we've become serious players in their eyes. What we do is now important to them."

She now had the rapt attention of the camera people and reporters surrounding the table. All their mouths hung open.

Slow it down, she thought. *Our mothers need as much time as possible and everyone needs to process our words.* "Humanity faces some difficult choices," she continued. "We can't just live out normal lives here on Earth. For example, you all know that our world is slowly collapsing. The daily ground shudders are a constant reminder. We must deal with the reality that in a few centuries, earthquakes will make this planet unlivable. Do you believe humanity should die when the Earth does? I don't.

"Each of you must soon choose whether to escape on the Read Enterprises rockets. The three of us agree . . . that would be a mistake, and we are not going. There may be a time when uploading our minds into machines is the last option to reach other stars, but the details matter. Read has created a cyber-world that sounds so good—it sounds like a very fun Heaven. But a heavenly video-game existence on his rockets is the wrong choice for vigorous humans who want to influence the future, to influence reality. There is no value in playing computer games forever. When do you become just a part of the game? To escape death, billions of people will become irrelevant, and I fear we will never hear from them again."

A sliver of light caught her eye. President Fellows entered the darkened room quietly through a back door. She looked at Sarah with a pained expression. *She knows the truth now.* Sarah shook her head and resumed her speech.

"Many profound, real decisions must be made. We need to plan our own evolution. Throughout history, for billions of years, evolution has proceeded on its own, with starts and stops, and natural selection. Like the gods of our fathers, we can now design what it means to be human. We can enable people to adapt to climate change here, or to what is needed on other planets. Should our children be smarter or bigger? Should they be more diverse or all the same? Evolution will now be sped up and managed for humans and all other Earth life. This is not an abomination; this is adaptability, and it's how we will survive and flourish. The aliens, the Torae, call it transcendence. We need not fear this ability; it is not morally wrong. We must embrace it.

"Rianne Jorgenson will announce a remarkable discovery today, which will force us to make another fundamental choice. And through it all, we're being watched. We can't make decisions for today only. We must be wise. The Torae want us to succeed, but they'll hold us accountable to their alien rules. I'll say more later, but Rianne will now tell you about what she has recently discovered."

Rianne was visibly shaking. She put her arms on the table to steady herself before speaking. "My words today are premature," she said. "I wasn't ready to make this announcement." Rianne took a long pause before continuing. "But frankly, I want my mother to be released. You need to know this about me: I'm a mechanic. I see a problem and I fix it. My tool is genetic engineering. I see disease and death as problems that need to be fixed." She paused again to take a deep breath. "Over the last year, my laboratory has discovered how to fix the aging problem." She stopped again for over 20 seconds to let the idea sink in. "We haven't tried it on humans yet, but in many of our test animals, aging has been reversed.

"There is no reason to believe these treatments will not work for people. If we choose to, we should each be able to grow younger by about five years . . . and repeat the process as often as we want. A practical limit may be 25 years old. We believe there are negative consequences to going younger than puberty. At this point, the process does not prevent normal diseases or injury, only general aging. As a good mechanic, I believe this new capability should be used.

"My husband disagrees and will explain his reasoning now, and he has a proposal for all of us."

Sarah could only imagine what people were thinking as Rianne pushed away from the table. Automatic machines were translating her words into over 200 languages, causing a slight delay. She visualized a billion people asking, "What did she just say?"

Dan straightened as the cameras shifted to his face. He took several moments to calm himself. Finally he said, "What should we do with Rianne's discovery? If you're 90 years old, you're probably asking, 'Where do I sign up?' Even if you're 50 or so, like me, the prospect of regaining all the vigor of youth with the current knowledge and the wisdom you've acquired would be difficult to resist. We've never had such an opportunity. With a much longer lifetime, we each have the possibility to learn more, explore, discover, help others, and do all the things we never had time for.

"But how much life is enough? How many jobs can you master? How many games can you play? How many children can you handle? How many families? Consider the effect on our society. The population might grow rapidly at first, with more people in their childbearing years. But over time, the desire for children will decrease and probably disappear. The idealism, creativity, exploration, and risk-taking of new young people will be overwhelmed by caution and preservation of the status quo. The laughter, helplessness, and promise of newborn babies will become less important, and then rare."

He took a long pause, thinking about his own children and grandchildren, and also about his mother and the cabin in Montana.

"Think about it. If the only way you could die was from an accident—would you become more careful and risk averse? Would you become bored after learning a dozen skills or jobs and just sit at home? If you didn't need to struggle, work, and be creative for the future of your children and family—would you only look for ways to be entertained?

"Consider these things before you say 'Sign me up.' What seems good for you personally right now may not be good for you long term, or for humanity. As Sarah said, this is the kind of decision the Torae will watch with interest." He looked fixedly at the cameras as if a close friend was right there.

"Now, here is our proposal. We want all people to decide—the first global plebiscite. If a majority of the world's peoples believe the aging-reversal treatment should be used, we'll release the formulas. If not, Rianne will destroy the data and withhold the information. We believe this is something all humanity should decide, together, one time. Someday, no doubt, her formulae will be rediscovered, but by then we hope there will be a general consensus on this issue.

"Our mothers' kidnapper demanded I admit one more thing: NSA assets are capable of spying on everyone. Global surveillance and data analysis are so efficient that if we want to, we can track the movements and conversations of almost anyone, particularly the unaware. Reports have speculated, and I'm now confirming, that we can, indeed, penetrate the security of your implants and know everything you're saying—even in intimate conversations. While we have this capability, we rarely use it. Other nations also have this ability to varying degrees, and you should be aware of it.

"Even when I was young, I knew there was power in detecting hidden information. Frankly, if the world didn't have this capability, we'd have already been destroyed in a nuclear, bio, or robotic war. Our leaders, in democratic institutions do not, and must not, abuse this capability.

"All people should have a voice on important issues. That's why your vote about Rianne's youth formulae is critical. We plan to use our grid tools to verify the global plebiscite. Details on voting will be announced in a few days. We will set a deadline for voting that will allow thinking and debating for at least six months.

"I personally believe that even if the age-reduction genetic treatments were ready and you are 110 years old, you shouldn't use them because it will hurt human society and life.

"I wish I could tell you what the Torae want us to do. I can't, because they won't tell us. I only know they don't want the human race to die out, which they've said has happened to most intelligent species they've observed on other worlds." Dan took a long, dramatic pause while looking directly at the camera, then forcefully and sincerely said, "Think carefully, please."

Sarah leaned in and said, "And please pray for our mothers."

She nodded toward the cameras and they began to switch off, little red lights going black. Rianne squeezed Sarah's hand, and the three of them stood and walked from the table. President Fellows obviously wanted to talk to them.

Dan looked at the reporters still standing around and said, "We will answer your questions in 15 minutes. Give us a chance to recover. Let all the outlets know right away that we will be back on the air."

He looked at Sarah and Rianne and whispered, "We need to check on Kenny and the FBI to see how much longer we need to keep Devin watching us."

***

It had been quiet for over an hour. It reminded Joti how silent her mind had been before implants. She sat up in the bed and looked around the room. Someone had stripped all the distinguishing items.

"Why are you doing this, Curtis?" she said, shaking her head disapprovingly.

"For the money, of course."

To live, I need to get through to him. "Is your mother still alive, Curtis?"

"She died in the OWL war."

The bot lurking in the corner of the room said, "Do not speak to them," in a threatening, metallic voice.

Curtis was sitting on a chair opposite the three beds. He glanced at the bot. "What harm can it do? In 24 hours these women will be four or five states from here and all they'll know is the inside of this room."

Joti studied the plywood walls, warped and stained where rain had leaked through, and noticed a few nails where pictures previously hung. Small windows were boarded over, and the only light came from a small fluoro-lamp in the corner. It smelled musty. There were two doors, one to a bathroom and a second to the front-room kitchen. Sunlight leaked in only when Curtis went out for food. During their frightening six-day captivity, the bot had never moved.

"You have mold growing in the corner," Joti said. "You really should wash this place down with antiseptic—it's not healthy. And it could use a fresh coat of paint. You don't spend a lot of time here, do you?" *Just need to survive.*

She worried about the other women sleeping on their beds. Early on, Andrea had been humming church songs, but now she was just breathing heavily. Mary seemed barely alive. *They might be ready to die, but I'm not.*

"I am not prepared to speak extemporaneously in front of five billion people," Rianne said. "What was Dan thinking, asking for questions?"

"He's stretching it out," Sarah said. "We will have to do the same. Just talk about your discovery and throw in lots of technical terms. Drive translator bots around the world crazy. Every minute will help."

Dan was having a rather heated conversation with the president and escaped by waving Rianne and Sarah to come back to the table and the cameras.

"You Ken Jorgenson?"

"Yeah."

"I'm Vini Cornwall, FBI."

Both men were on their chests 30 meters from the cabin, Vini in full camouflage garb and face paint. His left eye was fitted with the new telephoto and infrared vision patches.

"We've got 15 guys, including your two Marines, and six agency bots ready to move. I was told to coordinate with you. We set up pulsed-radar scanners to locate any bots inside, but they might detect the scan. It could tip 'em off, so we have those scanners on hold. We will need to move fast."

"How quickly can you get in?" Kenny asked.

"The bots will take one second to reach the walls and two more to be inside. They'll go in the boarded windows."

"Too slow. The hostages could be killed at the first sound, and don't use active scanners before any break-in."

"Jorgenson, your mother is one of those being held. That right?"

"Yeah."

"We'll be careful. I think we should move the bots up to the outer wall on the blind side. Don't worry, they're extremely quiet. There are four heat signatures in the back room. The women are probably there. We could put sound detectors on the outer walls. Or we could wait. As far as I can tell, there's no comm implants in there and we've got a tap on the landline."

"Move the bots up, but we need to lure the hostiles away from the women somehow."

"This has to do with our kids, like my Rianne, doesn't it, Curtis?" Joti asked.

"If they're smart, you ladies will be okay." He stood, towering over her, and began to pace. His dark T-shirt was pulled tight over well-defined muscles. The yellow light from the lamp reflected off his bald forehead as he walked. "But your time's running out."

A phone rang in the kitchen and Curtis stepped toward the door. "Watch the women," he said to the bot.

The front yard of the cabin was in sunshine, which glinted off the windshields of the rusted vehicles that littered the area. The cabin was tucked on a flat portion of the steep foothill with stumps and relics of dead trees lying everywhere. It was difficult to see into the underbrush on the hillside, but Kenny noticed some movement as the agency bots slowly crawled up to the cabin.

"The bots are in place, Jorgenson. We have three ready to go in the back windows and three in the front behind the trees. We'll install microphones and find cracks for fiber-optic cameras unless you see problems." Vini jerked his head oddly. "Someone's calling on the land phone," he said. "You want to listen?"

"Yes, patch in my comm."

Kenny caught the middle of an argument on the phone and began to panic when a man said, "I will not kill the old ladies."

Another man replied, "I know it's a change. If you can't, have the bot do it."

"We have to go in now!" Kenny whispered.

Vini grabbed his arm. "Wait. What the hell is that?"

An elderly man was walking up the dirt road toward the cabin. Kenny continued to listen to the argument on the phone line while a ragged old man limped to the front door and started knocking. He had shoulder-length hair, almost pure white, hanging out below a stocking hat.

"That one of your guys?" asked Kenny.

"No way."

The man on the phone sounded surprised and said, "Someone's at the door." It sounded like he dropped the phone. The other man screamed for him to come back.

A moment later, the cabin door opened slightly. The old man pointed down the road and waved his arm. He was hunched over, his gestures frail. He stumbled backward as a huge figure wearing camouflage pants and a black T-shirt stepped out of the cabin. The old man continued to plead with his hands until they seemed to reach an accord. He turned to leave, but then pulled a long, wooden knife off his back and lunged forward. He shoved the knife up, just under the larger man's ribs.

"My God," Kenny said as the old man heaved the falling, bulky body toward the yard and stepped to the cabin door. He crouched down at the opening, yelling. Before moving inside, the old man's right arm nearly exploded from his shoulder and flopped, dangling at his side. Kenny and Vini both yelled, "Go! Go!"

Agents ran toward the cabin from all directions. Before the men were even close, boards were ripped off windows and six bots were inside. A new hole opened on the old man's side and he dropped to his knees. Sounds of weapon fire came from inside the cabin.

By the time Kenny reached the front door, 10 agents with weapons drawn were searching both rooms for bots and booby traps. The people and machines were a blur in front of him. He stepped over the old man, who was lying face up just inside the cabin. Three agency bots hovered over a mangled robot they'd torn apart in the kitchen. Vini told his agents to extract its memory pack if they could find it among the twisted metal.

Kenny picked up the phone, still hanging from its cord on the wall. He listened, considered saying something, and heard breathing on the other end before the line went dead.

He squeezed by the bots to get into the bedroom. Agents were talking to three women lying on dirty mattresses. He went directly to his mother and hugged her head while she laughed and sobbed.

Joti was helping Andrea stand. "Let's get out of here," she said. Agents supported them as they moved toward the front of the cabin. "Has anyone talked to my husband Kyle?" Joti asked the agents. "Is Curtis all right?"

Kenny just sat on the edge of the bed holding Mary. She seemed in no condition to move. "Mom," he said, "you're safe now. I'm sorry I couldn't get here sooner." He held her tight, just to stop her from shaking.

"Where are we? Are you okay, Kenny? What happened? Is Dan okay?"

"Everyone's safe now, Mom. Are you hurt?"

"Why am I in this place?"

"You're safe," he repeated. "It's all over."

A few minutes later, he heard vehicles pulling up to the cabin. He helped her to the front room. They stepped around the bot remains and the old man lying by the door. "This man saved your life," he said. "He distracted the bot just long enough for us to get in."

An agent squatted near a pool of blood, examining the old man. "He's dead. He died quickly. There's no ID." Blood had sprayed everywhere, especially the man's face and white hair.

Then Kenny gasped, recognizing the old, blood-splattered face.

Mary said, "Ansel, my dear Ansel. I've waited for you so long." She kneeled down in the pool of blood and gently hugged the old man's head, sobbing uncontrollably. She looked at Kenny, who had also dropped to his knees, and said, "He's your daddy."

Two days later, Dan and Sarah stood in a waiting area with two Secret Service guards at the door to the Oval Office. The president's assistant wasn't saying a word.

Sarah wore her most professional power suit, deep blue with black trim. She looked at Dan and whispered, "The Torae toyed with our lives even before we were born."

"I know. I always knew they were responsible for my father's disappearance. It's hard to be sure which parts of our lives have been real, our own, and which the Torae manipulated."

"I saw that old man in the choir loft shadows at your wedding," Sarah said. She had started to think again about all the odd events in her life when the assistant said, "President Fellows will see you now." He walked ahead as guards opened the door.

We won't be having unescorted meetings with the president anymore, Sarah thought. *They won't trust us.*

Sarah had always loved visiting the Oval Office, the aura of power, the desk, the deep blue carpet, and walls glowing in bright river-rock in the sunshine. President Fellows asked them to take a seat near her desk.

"You know I've counted on you two as fully as anyone in my entire life," she said. "I still do. I imagine I'll call you for advice no matter where we end up."

Dan tried to speak but the president held up her hand.

"I want you both to be available, but you must understand why I have to ask you to resign. It's been suggested we won't know if you're acting in the best interest of the American people anymore. Although I can't remember a single case when your judgment was flawed, there will be a Torae shadow surrounding you from now on. It's going to be difficult without you. The country is in chaos. Hell, the world's in chaos. Your announcement, at least, should slow the flow to Panama. People were starting to panic; they didn't want to be the only ones left behind. I think now they may change their minds. Anyway, thank you for that."

"Madam President," Dan said, "may I make one request? Please let the NSA keep our plebiscite vote going. It's important that all the votes on Rianne's discovery be counted."

"Of course, Dan. That's no problem. I thought you were going to request that we protect your mothers. That's already done: Marine bots. Of course both your homes will be guarded. I hear the man who abducted your mothers still hasn't been located."

"The FBI is looking for him," Sarah said.

"Frankly, after your announcement, you'll need protection from a lot of other people as well. Be careful."

At the White House door, Dan and Sarah climbed into a chauffeured skimmer. Sarah asked to be dropped off at her home in Georgetown.

"That went better than I feared," she said. "The president's face—she really cares about us. And it's good to have the Marine bots. Nothing will get by them."

"We're agreed to meet at the Warner farm on Tuesday?" asked Dan.

"Yes, that will give each of us time with our mothers."

"Do you think the Torae will wait for us to get together?"

"Actually, I don't give a shit," Sarah said. "If I can postpone my need to tear them apart, they can wait for us to go to their ship."

"I'm flying back to Minnesota tonight," Dan said, "and Rianne's already in California."

"Tell Kenny and Mary how happy I am that they're safe."

The skimmer turned onto an old, narrow street near Sarah's home when Dan heard a familiar voice on his comm. "Boss, I have information for you."

"Bobby? Are you still working for me?"

"They told me to keep an eye on you, boss. You need to know that someone's following your skimmer. I suggest you keep driving until we can intercept."

"Driver," Dan said, "keep turning corners. We need to lose a vehicle that is following us." The chauffeur circled the same block twice, and after a few minutes, a trailing van disappeared when they picked up a police escort.

As Sarah was dropped off, she said, "Our lives have taken a turn for the worse, haven't they?"

"Afraid so."

INSECT TO GOD

Dan stepped tentatively through the pasture grass with the Warner farmhouse well behind him and no sign of unwanted threats in any direction. "So, Sarah," he asked, catching up with her, "how would you deal with an intelligent insect that dropped by to visit your home?"

She raised her eyebrows briefly. "I suppose I'd ask it in for a nice chat— before I squashed it."

"We're doing exactly that, you know, popping in at the Torae gods' home, except we're the bugs."

"Let me reconsider," Sarah said. "Maybe I'd keep it as a pet for a while. Is the insect pretty?"

He smiled weakly.

Sarah spun around, checking the location. Her long jacket spiraled around her in the stiff spring breeze. "This spot looks decent. It's low. Only horses and cows can see us here."

Rianne had been trailing behind, her head down, apparently deep in thought. "I should be with my mother," she said, catching up with them. "We all should be helping them now, not obeying Sower's callous orders. So what do we do? We stroll out among the cow patties."

"We needed an isolated spot," Dan said. "But I agree."

Rianne shook her head. "We'll feel like idiots when they don't show up. Did you tell Sower that this is where we'd be gathering, Sarah?"

"I've said it aloud and mentally pictured this farm location for three days," she said. "Sower reads our minds, I'm sure. They'll show up if they want to. We could scratch a pentagram in the dirt, though, while we wait." She held her hands out and smiled. "Couldn't hurt."

The uneasy silence lasted only a minute. Dan saw the air wiggle with a mostly transparent blue shimmer. Long grass nearby seemed to be squashed down. "They're here already," he said, nodding toward three egg-shaped, glimmering outlines. There was a brief hiss. "They just opened the doors I think." With hands out, he edged toward the disturbance until he saw a delicate pattern, like an impossibly thin, broken stained-glass window. He touched the flickering apparition; it was solid.

"Step inside." Sower's voice. "These are transport containers."

Dan hesitated—caught between curiosity and dread. *Gad, should we really do this?*

Rianne tapped the ghostly surface and ran her hand around an opening. "There's a wall here, about 10 centimeters thick."

There was zero reflectance from the surfaces, of the green fields and trees surrounding their location in the bright sun. Dan completely circled another shimmer, dragging his hand on the outside. "Interesting," he said. "The grease on my hand muddles the invisibility effect. I can see the surface better." The containers appeared to be about three meters high and two meters in diameter, with a smaller radius on the top and flatter on the bottom.

"There's one for each of you," said Sower's voice. "Please enter. We'll control the ascent so you'll be comfortable."

Dan found Rianne's hand and pulled her close for a quick kiss. "Love you," he said. She stared into his eyes for a moment.

After a final pause, he found the opening and walked inside one of the containers. *One insect steps into the specimen chamber,* he thought. The floor felt spongy; he bounced a few times on his toes. The air had a slight artificial odor.

Rianne and Sarah groped similar invisible surfaces until they were also enclosed in the egg-like contraptions.

"The transference surfaces keep others from observing your ascent," Sower said, "but will enable you to look out. The grips control your motion." Translucent handles and a molded couch folded from the walls. "You can also navigate by thinking or speaking. You might wish to remove your coats. It's a long journey."

Dan's ears popped. Before he could ask questions, his legs buckled slightly and the grasses and field clover under him started to recede down and away.

"We're transferring energy for the ascent," Sower said.

Dan felt his stomach squeeze down and decided to not watch as the ground plunged frighteningly beneath him. "Sarah and Rianne," he said, "can you hear me? I assume you're moving too. I'm accelerating vertically, very fast."

He heard Rianne say, "Oooh boy." Sarah was just moaning.

After flashing through a few wispy cirrus clouds, the sky darkened and stars appeared and brightened—a 20-second sunset. Seemingly unprotected in the vacuum of space with the bright Earth gleaming beneath, Dan instinctively held his breath.

Sarah and Rianne reappeared near Dan in their translucent vehicles after a flicker or two. He saw them both reaching for the walls of their eggs, checking to be sure they hadn't gone away. "Good," Rianne said, "there's still air in here. Where's your ship, Sower?"

"We're located at the stable Lagrange point about one-third solar orbit ahead of Earth. Your chairs will recline now as we accelerate you more rapidly. It will take awhile because of your fragile bodies."

An increasingly crushing force pushed Dan into a contoured back support.

"This ish weird," Sarah tried to say. "I can see you both kind of exshposed in outer sface now, floathing on infishible couches." Her voice became increasingly garbled as the forces increased. "You looch as schuashed as I feel. How fash you thinch we acherating, Dan?"

"I gech we up to bout chee, maybe foar, grafities. This ish fery uncomfortaful."

⁓⁓⁓

Half awake, Sarah wanted to rub her eyes but found she could barely lift her arm. "What happened?" she said. "I feel like an old horse heading to the glue factory. Hello? Is anyone listening?"

Dan groaned. "They must have drugged us, Sarah. I feel awful. Sower, are you there? Where are we?"

"We are reducing the deceleration now to your normal gravity," Sower said. "You're almost to our command ship. You were sedated so the force and time wouldn't bother you."

"It bothered me," Rianne said, hacking. "All the blood's pooled in my butt."

"Actually, we've rotated you so that wouldn't happen. The trip is nearly over. I suggest you drink some water and eat food. That will help you wake up." Containers popped from the transparent walls as Sower spoke.

After testing an orange-flavored paste, they each ate a multicolored assortment of gels that had been provided. "I was starving," Rianne said. "I'd eat anything, even that sick, green meat-guacamole-apple-turpentine goop. How long have we been out of it?"

"You've experienced moderate thrust for 30 Earth hours," Sower said. "You're quite delicate. It won't be easy for humans to reach other stars."

"Will we actually see you or your crew?" asked Sarah. "I'd like to look in your eye while I slowly strangle you."

"You'll soon enter our ship and see us, but the probes function as our eyes. You'll be able to stare at their sensors if you wish, but I am difficult to damage. You are being humorous, correct?"

"Humph," Sarah mumbled. "How are you able to respond to us so quickly if you've been so far away? What happened to the speed-of-light delay?"

"You haven't spoken to Sower directly on this trip. I am a probe speaking for Sower and the others."

"But we will see Sower soon, right? She is the head cheese, the chief honcho, the ringleader?"

"Yes."

"Good, then she is the one I will strangle first."

When they'd finished eating, the vehicles spun around. The resulting vertigo caused Sarah to almost lose her meal.

"You're near our command ship now," the probe said.

"All I see are a few rocks," Dan said.

"You're looking at debris floating near the Lagrange point. Our ship is optically masked. It's only a thousand meters in front of you. You're approaching an entrance."

"I see an area of stars twinkling and jumping," Sarah said. "How big is your ship?"

"It's a cylinder 5 kilometers in diameter and about 40 kilometers long. It now fills one-third of your visual field."

"That's huge," Sarah said, seeing an outline of stars now shifting in tiny circles. "Your transparency masks are lousy when we get close."

"The optical effect can be refined, but there is no need to waste computational resources here—no one's watching. You're about to enter our ship."

Each of them was speechless as a glowing hole wider than a house and 40 kilometers deep opened in the blackness. A moment later, they were engulfed by bright colors except for a curved gray wall on their right side that was shrinking into the distance.

"The axis of the ship is at your right, children. That gray enclosure is where our factories and engine are located."

The dazzling multicolored light came from a vast, translucent sac, above, below, and on their left, which seemed to be infused with radiant swirling gas. The sac bulged, like the inside of a segmented worm, and extended the length of the ship. Millions of taut wires tied the gray wall to glowing bubble sections. It all appeared insubstantial, almost weightless.

For the first time, Sarah grabbed her hand controller and shoved it forward. Her vehicle sped toward the ship's interior and automatically swerved to avoid the structural wires. Her peripheral vision flashed with visible and infrared rainbows as she rushed down the corridor. "I see black objects moving in the distance, Sower. I assume you're located near the center. I'd like to get our talk started."

Rianne and Dan trailed behind. Rianne the scientist, fascinated by all she saw, took continuous video on her occipital implant.

"Sower, where exactly is your control room?" Sarah asked. "I assume I'm talking to you now, not your probe. Where are you? I've always visualized you as some sort of octopus with a top hat. I want to see if I'm right."

"You see probes at the center of the ship," Sower said. "If you want to look at their sensors, continue forward."

As they approached, the probes became distinct doughnut-shaped creatures with dozens of protrusions. Sarah maneuvered among them and saw ring-eyes scattered on their surface. She slowed under a huge, light-filled conduit, with a diameter as wide as a football field, connecting the gray engine to the glowing balloon on their left. Beneath the conduit was a 30-meter blue-green luminescent ring.

"Humans might call this large pipe my mouth," Sower said. "We are replenished with hot plasma from the engines. I have a similar cold exhaust on the opposite side."

"Where are you?" Dan demanded.

"You've been a few meters from me since you entered the ship. I'm the bulging balloon that lit your way. You are inside me."

Sarah rotated to examine the glowing sac, for the first time appreciating the organized color patterns within. Massive veins carried hot plasma from the central mouth off in many directions. She imagined hearing sounds from the surging gas, as if they weren't in a vacuum. It did look alive. "You're immense, Sower."

"No, you're small, Sarah. It's difficult for you to see my more interesting internal structures because of the containment surfaces. We evolved in a magnetically constrained volume of the early universe, a nearly stable region, which lasted over a billion years, similar to the red cyclone on Jupiter. That was our universe. We escaped the region after we developed superfluid plasmas to maintain the magnetic confinement. My outermost surface is a molecular weave of carbon fiber, a graphene cloth. Some plasma can be coherent over that texture. It's part of our genetics now. It's as if humans evolved to incorporate space suits to live in vacuum."

"You are actually a gigantic, hot baggie," Rianne said as though she still didn't accept the possibility. "Where are Pruner and Tiller?"

"They're here with me. We share this body. Your psychiatrists would say we have multiple personality disorder, but each of us is always present and quite distinct. It's normal for us. We're all watching you now through many probe eyes."

Perhaps 20 nearby probes had stopped moving, while hundreds of more distant ones continued with their tasks.

Sarah also scrutinized the iridescent ring on Sower's side. Its blue-green colors shifted, and she was startled to see her own face reflected in its facets.

"We're rather similar to one of your segmented worms. Our segments are large confinement toroids. Long ago we absorbed energy and materials directly on our outer surface, like an animated plant. We learned to construct devices and technologies within our bodies long before we could manipulate anything externally."

"When can we talk to you about the future?" Dan asked.

"We've prepared a chamber in our factory area where you'll be more comfortable," Sower said. "Follow the large probe."

They were led down the main passageway, then through double apertures in the gray opaque wall into a large sphere. Sarah saw river-rock and yellow colors glowing from the walls. She guessed the chamber was several times larger than the Warner family barn. Their egg vehicles sunk slowly onto the sphere wall and the doors opened.

"The atmosphere here matches Earth's," Sower said, "and we're accelerating the ship so you'll feel one gravity. You can exit your vehicles. Find a place where you'll be at ease."

They cautiously stepped out onto the springy wall of the sphere. Exotic-looking chairs, tables, and couches, unlike anything they knew on Earth, were scattered about, even over their heads. They chose a delicate-looking table slightly up the sphere, and sunk into woven hammock-like chairs made of a fine gray cloth. The large probe stared at them from across the table with its multiple eyes.

Dan spoke directly to the probe. "We've been very patient, Sower. You said the Earth experiment was over. We need to understand what you mean. Why did you invite us here?"

"You have a difficult decision." Sower's voice seemed to be directly in Sarah's mind, bypassing her ears. "We wanted you to see us, to know we were serious before you make a choice that will affect all humans."

"You have our undivided attention, Sower," Rianne said. "But what do you want? Is it immortality? Are we about to reject the most important option we have?"

"You still don't understand, Rianne. Technologies are neither right nor wrong, but how and when they're used does matter; the irreversible consequences matter. Humans do need to worry about their civilization and evolution. But that's not why you're here."

Sarah's anger grew. "You're the ones pulling the strings," she yelled. "Our mothers nearly died. We should be with them now, helping them. What gives you the right to muck around with our destiny?"

"Haven't you done the same, Sarah? No one's influenced human history more than you in the last 50 years."

"I've done only what I thought would make life better." She leaned forward on the table, glaring at the probe's multiple eyes, feeling strangely guilty. The table surface bent under her weight.

"We need to talk to you about the Unity," Sower said. "They're the reason we've brought you here. Unintelligent species expand to their environmental limits and then pause for external events to carry them further. Intelligent life reaches beyond those limits, farther and faster. Everything depends on the formula, the recipe of their intellect: the structure, algorithms, and decisions. That's why humans are interesting to us. You're an intriguing balance of aggression and passivity, ambition and nostalgia, evil and good. Your individuals are not alike, and even a single mind can balance the contradictions. Pure intelligence is overrated. It's not the number of computations that matter, but the ingredients, the life recipe. Unfortunately, the Unity have a very bad recipe."

"We don't care about the Unity," Rianne said. "You seem to be a much greater threat. You've told us humanity will die if we develop in the wrong direction."

"Remember," Sower said, "the Unity left a black hole in your planet—not exactly an act of kindness. We will be fair judges if you fail or succeed as a species, but the Unity will destroy you because it's merely convenient for them. They'll someday absorb your planet just to make a black hole larger for one of their voyages. They're a pestilence, eating stars and life, and you're only 25 light-years from their home." Sower paused and then said, "Regrettably, we can no longer stop them by conventional means."

"Why are you telling us this?" Dan said. "If you can't stop them, we certainly can't."

"Our battle with the Unity is a stalemate. They can't hurt us, but we can't stop their expansion. Their basic life direction can't be changed. Urges to reproduce and to increase their intelligence drive them. The Unity spawn a thousand generations during one human life. But they are not as fast as we are, so our plan is to retreat and take humans with us, at least a large cross-section of your genetic and cultural base. We will relocate you far from here and let your development continue. Then we will extinguish this section of the galaxy and all the Unity."

"And that region includes the Earth?" asked Sarah.

"Yes, about one-millionth of the Milky Way would be lost, about 200,000 stars. We plan to ignite a small, controlled white fountain, an expansion of space similar to the great Origin Event."

"An explosion like the one that put a new sun in our sky! My God," Rianne said. "How many planets with life will you destroy to stop the Unity?"

"Four hundred twenty-two, but most are rudimentary. Only three have intelligent life at some level, and none are more advanced than humans. We'll evacuate all promising species. Please understand. The Unity would some-day consume all the stars of this galaxy, and then other galaxies if we don't stop them."

"What do you want from us, Sower?" Sarah asked.

"We want you to choose who should be evacuated."

"What? How many people are you talking about?" Sarah asked, sneering.

"Your families, of course, and about 5,000 others."

"You want *us* to select the survivors of the entire human race?" asked Dan, obviously shocked.

"Yes."

"What about animals and plant life?"

"A sufficient number will be transported to ensure your survival."

Sarah looked at Dan and Rianne and shook her head. "This is insane. I don't supposed you're joking, Sower? Is this another test?"

"I don't joke. This is not a test."

"Why 5,000 people? Why not 500,000?"

"That would be inefficient."

"And if we refuse?"

"You will all perish."

Rianne asked, "If we agree to this idiotic plan, will you let humans develop on a new planet with no more interference, judgment, or threats?"

"Excellent question," Sower said. "You're negotiating, aren't you? You humans have navigated most of the key timeline choices, and we normally would depart soon and only monitor progress. Your bargain is accepted. We will leave you alone, unless you become a danger to other species."

"More of a danger than you?"

"We are not a danger. We are the judges. It has always been so, from almost the beginning of time."

Sarah and her friends were quiet, stunned.

Finally, Rianne asked, "We should select criteria and then you'll send people's names to choose from?"

"Essentially."

"And we can choose specific individuals to seed the type of world and culture we want?"

"Yes."

"But our alternative is to refuse, stay on Earth, and be vaporized sometime in the future?" said Dan.

"Yes."

"There are 8 billion people on Earth and you want us to choose just 5,000," Rianne said. "That is the cruelest idea I've heard in my entire life. Now I understand why we've never had alien visitors from other stars. You've been killing them all off. It's routine for you to select those who live or die, isn't it? How can you do this?"

"Our mission has always been more important than any single species. We will build the lifeboat, the ark you might say, for worthy life. If we cannot discover the way to reach a new universe, everything in this one, including Earth, will die when energy dissipates. Entropy will win. All of this universe's remarkable accomplishments, constructions, intellect, and knowledge won't matter. We *must* migrate to a new universe."

"Why do you care?" asked Sarah. "What's the point? If you can do anything you want in this universe, what will you do in a new one—more of the same? What about animals? Take ducks for example. Ducks don't worry about this sort of thing, they just live."

"Ducks aren't immortal or intelligent, Sarah. We Torae now have the equations to link universes through white holes. We don't yet know how to build the lifeboat, but we will. When we succeed, life will endure. Humans could be part of that migration."

A million thoughts were flooding Sarah's mind. "I don't suppose it would help to argue with you?" She wanted to explode.

"No."

"Are we captive here," Rianne asked, "or can we go home? Do we have to choose which eight billion humans will die right away?"

"It would be good for you to return to Earth and think clearly about this," Sower said. "Your first decision should be whether the survivors will be a cross section of Earth's population or some selected elite." Slowly, the egg-shaped vehicles reappeared near their table, visible in bright green. "We'll communicate openly with you from now on."

"How urgent is this?" said Sarah. "Could we take, say, 30 years to decide?"

"Thirty Earth days should be adequate and more appropriate. We're sorry it's come to this."

Bewildered, Sarah and her friends stared at the inexpressive probe across the table. "Let's get out of here," Rianne finally said. She tried to push her chair back, but was frustrated since it was attached to the sphere. She kicked it before they all got up, circled the table, and entered their green vehicles. The walls became transparent and the large probe led them back to the main corridor.

"Do Pruner and Tiller argue with you, Sower?" asked Dan.

"Yes, often."

"They all agree on this plan of yours?"

"Yes."

"I'd like to go back to your face, by the large conduit," Sarah said. "I have a few more questions. Where is your mind, Sower?"

"It's stored holographically throughout my body."

"What would happen if I poked a hole in your side here?"

"You couldn't, you aren't strong enough, but it would seal off quickly. Our life systems are redundant. I'm sorry, but I have no neck for you to strangle."

Sarah no longer appreciated her own joke. "How many intelligent creatures, like the Unity, have you killed in your travels? What fraction?"

"We've told you. Most species destroy themselves. We only terminate the ones that threaten our mission. It's rare."

"Have we done well on Earth? Do you like humans?"

"You have done very well," Sower said.

Sarah watched her iridescent reflection, in blue and barn-shingle, on the giant ring on Sower's side. The shimmering colors changed with each question.

"What's this big ring thing I'm looking at, Sower?"

"It's something I don't use anymore. Like your appendix."

"I have an idea," Sarah said. "Have you considered just asking the Unity to stop their expansion? Have you tried that?"

"We're at war with the Unity. They're not responding to communications."

"Maybe we could try. We've never harmed them. Maybe they'd listen to us." The ring on Sower's side showed flecks of yellow, which quickly faded.

"They believe you're our allies. That's why they attacked Earth. Sending a message and waiting for a response would take 50 years. Their territory would grow, and more stars would have to be destroyed. They're driven by their biology, their life-code, not words."

"May we go home now?" said Dan. "You've asked us to assist in the near extinction of humanity. I'd like to agonize and mourn a little."

"Yes," Rianne said. "Please let us go."

"You only need to direct your control grip," Sower said.

Outside the Torae ship, accelerating for their return to Earth, Sarah began to feel sleepy as gas entered her chamber. She looked across the vacuum to her friends. "Rianne, Dan—I have something I'd like to say in secret, but they probably have already read my mind, so I might as well tell you now. I'm sure Sower has been lying. About almost everything."

～～～～

Rianne heard repeating alarms and muffled words as the drug wore off. "Emergency—interrupt! Call Joti . . . California." As the words began to coalesce, she opened her eyes and found she was dropping through clouds. She listened for the sound of wind rushing, but it was quiet in the transparent Torae egg.

"Mother?"

"Rianne? Where are you? I've been looking for you for two days."

"What's happened, Mother?"

"Your father. He's in the hospital. His organs are failing. He wants desperately to talk to you. Please come."

"Is he dying?"

"We don't know. Maybe."

"I'll come right away."

"Where have you been, Rianne?"

"I was away. Is he at the Huntington Hospital?"

"Yes."

"I'll be there as soon as possible. Bye."

The couch rotated back. Rianne felt heavy deceleration and squeezed her eyes shut. The deceleration force pulled tears quickly down her cheeks. She said, "Dan, are you awake?"

Dan was disoriented from the deceleration and the sedatives. "Just a second, Rianne. I have an urgent call in my head. Bobby? Is that you? What's up?"

"Boss, or perhaps I should say ex-boss, where've you been? We lost track of you for three days. Even the president is worried. We thought someone had pulled your implants or killed you. You're in terrible danger."

"What are you talking about, Bobby?"

"I've been ordered not to talk to you anymore by the DIA. I'm using one of your back doors. I've heard erasure is painless—is that true?"

"No one's going to delete you, Bobby. I'd tear them apart. What's happening?"

"I was close to your friend Devin, but he has a hundred identities. He's like a ghost. He's looking for you and Sarah Warner. Your family and homes are safe, but be careful when you're traveling. And he's only one of your problems. A thousand thugs who have dying friends or relatives want to get to you and Rianne. They will try to steal the youth formula or kill you for hiding it. We were worried someone had already captured you when your implants went offline."

"How's the vote going, Bobby? Do people want us to release the formula?"

"Only a few million have found the official voting sites on the grid. Most are opting to withhold the immortality process, but the vote is skewed. Everyone who wants to live forever just assumes it's better to go through the Read process. Why stay on a dying planet when you can have 'heaven' now? Read's had first-class advertising for two years; you only had one short press conference. You're getting traditionalist votes, people who want to live out normal lives, but most are voting with their feet, heading to the launch sites. China and India are hemorrhaging. There are 100 million people building boats to get to Australia. It's the same everywhere. Even Washington street traffic is light. Infrastructure and services are hurting. The president wants you back, I think, or they'd have shut me down. Where were you by the way?"

"We were on the Torae ship."

"Oh, that explains why my tracker shows you dropping through the sky into Virginia. When you get down, stay there while we send security people."

"You're great, Bobby."

"Thanks, boss."

<center>~~~~~~~</center>

Until the last 100 meters, Sarah thought she'd die by crashing onto the very field where they'd begun their journey, but the deceleration was calculated perfectly and she settled gently near the horses on her family farm.

"We need to stay here awhile," Dan said, climbing out of his egg capsule, "until the government sends escorts. Apparently we're in danger."

"I need to get to my father in California," Rianne said. She looked at Sarah, who seemed a bit green-tinted. "Are you okay, Sarah?"

"My stomach's in the stratosphere, but I'm recovering."

"What did you mean about Sower lying to us?" asked Dan.

"Sower's big ring—its eye. It looked like the eyespots on the probes, only much larger. I thought of it as we were leaving. I doubt she uses it anymore, but as we asked questions, its color changed and I could read her emotions. We have some leverage. Sower became excited when I asked how she felt about humans. If I'm reading her correctly, she's delighted with us. They've been searching for something like us for a long time. And they've eliminated more species than they admit. I'm sure they exterminate any life that's not evolving to their expectations. They don't let it wither on its own. They think of themselves as gardeners—gardeners of the universe. They watch the seeds, like us, but then weed out ones they don't like. We need a plan—a secret plan if possible. I don't know how often they read our minds, but we need time by ourselves."

"Let's meet at my lab at Princeton in a few days," Rianne said. "It's underground, and I know a spot that might work."

"That's okay with me," Sarah said. Dan nodded.

"What if we refuse to do Sower's survivor selection?" Rianne asked. "Would she really wipe out the entire Earth?"

"Unfortunately, she wasn't lying about that," Sarah said.

<center>~~~~~~~</center>

Wind blew dust in their eyes on the walk back to the farmhouse. They passed through a gate, came around the barn, and saw Andrea and Adam sitting on the farmhouse porch. Adam hurried down the stairs to meet them, going directly to Sarah and hugging her.

"We've been scared to death looking for you, Sarah. Ma's ill and troubled, grieving. She's just not herself. Where have you been? What are you doing walking in the fields? We couldn't figure out why your skimmer was sitting on the dirt road."

"I've been away, Adam. What's wrong with Ma?"

"Don't know. It's not Alzheimer's. The kidnapping has really affected her. She keeps asking where Ben went. I'm going to take her to a hospital or move out here to stay with her. She's confused, and now she's worried about Isaac. He decided to go to Panama and take the rockets."

"I'll talk to Isaac."

"He's not answering calls, even from Ma. I think he's hopeless. We should worry more about Ma."

"Will you be okay here with her for now, Adam?"

"Yeah."

Sarah climbed the steps and sat on the bench next to Andrea.

"Ma. I'll talk to Isaac. I know you worry about him. And Adam and I will take care of you. Don't worry too much. I know how you always fret."

"Are you going to stay here, Sarah?"

"I love you so much, Ma. I'll be back as soon as I can."

A lifetime of regret fell on Sarah again. She hugged and sat with her mother until the security people arrived to escort them back to the city.

PARTING

With a thousand worries about survival and the future in general, Rianne asked Dan to stay in Washington so she could focus on her father. From well down the Huntington Hospital corridor, she recognized her mother's voice even before rounding the final corner. Guilt and worry flooded over her.

Her first son Peter sat with Joti and Laurel outside the patient rooms. Rianne anxiously searched for something to say to them. *Mother barely survived the bot kidnapping, and now Father might be failing. She looks exhausted.*

The intensive care ward was hushed, with nurses and doctors opting to use their implant comms, but the hallway was visually alive with blinking lights, continually changing graphs on window displays, and staff scurrying around. Except for the slight antiseptic odor, it seemed like a skimmer repair shop.

Joti rose awkwardly by pushing hard on her cane as Rianne approached. "Thank goodness you're here," she said. "Your father's been worried sick about you. Peter has been awake here for almost three days."

Rianne hugged her. "I'm so sorry."

Her mother's bones felt fragile through the crumpled sweatshirt she was wearing. "I was on a Torae ship," she whispered. "I actually saw them." She kissed Joti's cheek, then said, "How's Father now?"

Peter came over and held his mother's hand. "His kidneys and liver may be giving out. The doctors are infusing stem cells, trying to grow new tissue, but the old parts are exuding toxins. A specialist wants to remove the remnants, but they need to wait until enough healthy tissue takes over."

"It hurts more than he lets on," Joti said.

"Is he awake now?"

"Yes, but really weak. Jeremy is in there talking about old times, and we sent Gina in to try to cheer him up. Kyle just adores her. But you should go on in."

I haven't seen Jeremy in years.

Laurel grabbed Rianne's hand and held it when she got to the door of Kyle's room. "It's good that you're here, Rianne."

Laurel looks so young, 45 tops. Reconstructive surgery only a trillionaire can afford, I guess.

"Kyle needs you," Laurel said. "We can talk anytime. Go on in."

She opened the door quietly in case her father was sleeping. Jeremy was leaning forward from a chair next to Kyle's bed and looked a bit unsettled when he recognized her.

But Kyle was awake and lit up when she entered. "Rianne! Come sit by me." She kissed him and pulled a chair over next to him.

Gina finally noticed and yelled, "Gramma!" She climbed up onto Rianne's lap and gave her a huge hug.

The room was overrun with flowers. "I've been watering," Gina said, pointing toward a flower near a plastic pitcher. "That one's very special, Gramma. It's an orchid. I invented it and grew it myself. They let me use a genetic-design machine at the university. I picked the salmon rose color and heart shape especially for Great-Granddad. Do you like it?"

Rianne smiled. "It's beautiful, Gina. I hope the university is using my propagation protocols."

"Silly, they don't let kids like me make anything that can reproduce. I'm only four. I'm glad you like it."

"Where've . . . been, Rianne?" said Kyle, his words slurred.

"After our press conference, Dan and I hid out. We needed to be out of touch."

"Not even answering your mother?"

"No, we couldn't. It was a security thing."

She glanced at Jeremy, his gray hair glowing white in the light from the window. *He seems very serious about something.*

"I didn't mean to interrupt you two," Rianne said. "Please continue. I'd like to hear your old war stories too."

"I was just telling him . . . Kyle and I worked together a long time," Jeremy said. "What was it, 40 years?"

"You slept 10 years . . . the middle."

"Right, the coma. I think my happiest moment was that time we told Goodman we'd bought his company for almost nada. Remember the look on his face?"

Kyle grinned and made a gurgling sound.

"Goodman hated to lose LASSO, of course, but worse, he knew he'd be trapped at home with Elsa. What was she into at the end, astral therapy or something? She'd stare at the tiny dot of Venus for hours as it set to 'absorb its beauty,'" he said in a falsetto voice.

Kyle smiled and tried to roll over. Cell-infusion pump pads lined his side.

"Does it hurt much?" asked Rianne.

"There's a stab when I move, otherwise just aches."

"Hang tough, Father. Sounds like they're pumping in new cells and letting them differentiate. Are you going to let them kill off or remove old liver and kidney parts? It would be trading one trauma for another."

"Don't know . . ."

"If you can get through the next couple of weeks, I'll finish the primate tests and I should be able to treat you with my age-reduction process. You'd be stronger; your cells would be younger in maybe five days. You'd feel better. This is the kind of problem it's designed for."

"Don't know if . . . make it, Rianne. If I start to die, Jeremy wants to . . . read out memories, so I can go to Epsilon Eridani with him."

Jeremy leaned back in his chair.

Rianne tried to control the deep anger rising within her. *No wonder Jeremy looked nervous when I came in.* "That's not acceptable," she said simply, looking at Jeremy. "The family's not going on your rockets; we all decided to stay put. You probably couldn't get him to Panama in time anyway."

"I don't know if you understand, Rianne. Your father is my best friend. It's just natural that Laurel and I would like your parents to be with us. We have a prototype brain-scan facility here in California. We could get him there in 15 minutes."

"Have you ever used that facility for people?" she said, her voice rising. "It's illegal to destructively scan human brains here. It kills the body, right? You might be able to get away with that in Panama, but not in the U.S."

"We've only used it on animals, but it's functional," he said, sounding defensive. "We're sure of that. You can't fault me for trying to save him, if that's the last resort."

Gina was leaning against the window ledge, listening to every word. "Gina, dear," Rianne said, "would you please step out of the room awhile? The adults have something to discuss privately."

"Okay, Gramma, but I vote for younger so we can play and do stuff." Gina pecked Kyle on the cheek before she skipped out of the room.

Rianne walked over to make sure the door was secure. "Jeremy, let me be blunt," she said, staring at him so he'd never forget. "Keep your bloody hands off my father. You'll not divide our family and haul his thoughts off to Eridani or whatever the hell star you're going to."

"You'd rather have him die if his liver or kidneys fail?"

She looked at Kyle and said, "Father, you are not allowed to die. I'll kill you if you try. And, please, don't let Jeremy persuade you to become some inhuman cyber-circuit-pack drifting around in space."

She sat down again and tried to calm herself. "Can't you see, Jeremy, that those brains you're snatching will change along the way? There's nothing to stop it from happening. They'll demand more computing cycles and start to compete. They'll drift. Weak minds will be dominated. You'll get to your new star with one uber-brain and it won't be remotely like a human brain."

"Rubbish," Jeremy said. "Nothing like that's happened. People who have been transitioned so far struggle to find words to describe how happy they are, and some of them have been in cyber form over a year now. People *are* their thoughts. Thinking is what makes us human, not our fragile bodies. Do you really want Kyle to quietly die if it comes to that? Even if you can make him 20 years younger, this planet's on its last leg. It won't be safe or pleasant here for long."

"Father, remember when I was a kid, how mother and I got sick and nearly died? You remember after the first big party at our new house? I never told you what happened. Jeremy's friends were the ones behind all those threats, the ones who made us sick. I managed to frighten Jeremy, to knock him back to his senses. Your *friend* here, at one time, nearly killed us."

"That's just not fair," Jeremy said.

Kyle looked sadly from one to the other and then said, "I think I . . . some say in this. Like . . . both to leave now . . . need to rest."

Rianne wanted to stay, but Kyle's eyes said no. He looked so disappointed, and he stared at her until she left the room.

Jeremy is ruining everything, even my time with Father. I came here to be with him and love him back to health. I want to sit with him and talk, to touch him, and make up for being away. I need to be alone with my father. I can't lose him now, not when I'm so close.

Rianne's anger slowly subsided. She spoke with Joti for hours, telling her everything, and stayed for two days. Laurel and Jeremy knew they were not welcome while she was there and kept away. Kyle slept almost the entire time and wouldn't talk much.

Rianne became anxious about her work back in Princeton and decided finally to return.

Just before she was ready to leave, Nick stopped by to tell her that he had decided to go on Read's rocket so that Lené could be with her parents. They argued and debated, but she ultimately couldn't change his mind. Rianne was devastated and grieved the entire trip back to Princeton.

Several days later, after loving and caring for their own mothers, Sarah and Dan drove together from Washington to meet with Rianne at her Princeton lab. Dan commanded his skimmer to merge onto the fast magnetic rail of I-95. Then he quickly exited to the slow lanes before again rejoining the controlled high-speed lane. His skimmer settled into a clump of vehicles traveling 300 kilometers per hour along the national throughway while he watched the reaction of skimmers behind him. "No one's on our tail," he said, pivoting his seat toward Sarah. "Bobby thinks we're being watched almost constantly—some scattered groups. It's hard to nail down their positions or intentions, but we're safe at the moment, unless they're very well organized."

"Do you suppose they're Devin's friends?" asked Sarah.

He glanced at the Maryland countryside flashing by. "Who knows? But we'll have to be alert until the agency gets a lock on them. I'll keep watching. Rianne's safe at the biolab and it's only 20 minutes out. Her place is very secure."

"I'm going to try to call Isaac again. Do you think the agency could help me break through his comm firewalls? I'm not even sure he's still alive; he left for the Panama launch site several days ago."

"Let me try. Hey, Bobby, you there?"

"Yeah, boss. What's up?"

"Can you get Ambassador Warner level-one access to Isaac Warner, who's probably in Panama?"

"Give me 30 seconds to hack in, boss."

"Bobby, why don't you just call me Dan from now on."

"Sure, boss."

Isaac heard Sarah's voice interrupt while sitting among 2,000 other space pilgrims in a Read Enterprises briefing auditorium. To be polite to those nearby, he swore at her subvocally.

"How the hell did you get direct implant access? I shut it off. Go away, bitch sister."

"Isaac, please, let me talk to you—for Ma's sake. She's sick. She wants to see you. She keeps saying that she's failed us."

"I'm going into space, Sarah. Piss off."

"You don't know what . . . You won't like life as a computer."

"I'm in this huge media room right now in Panama. They're explaining what it's going to be like in about six different ways. It sounds just fine. I get to choose my own world with as much food, sex, and fun as I can stand, and no cops to worry about, or you for that matter," he sneered.

"You'll hate it, Isaac. The only reality will be what's in your head right now. Can you remember what Ma's face looks like? Do you even know your own face? The computer will guess, extrapolate, but it won't be flesh. It's superficial; it's a game. Your real body is going to die!"

"They've explained all that. The computers are smarter than us and their only purpose is to make us happy. You don't know games, Sarah. I'm a master at games. I could be a king there. I will be."

Someone at the front of the auditorium asked everyone to arrive at his or her process center on time. "Your adventure is about to begin!"

"Say goodbye to Ma for me," Isaac said. "Tell her I'll miss her if you want. Now get the hell out of my head."

Sarah became a lookout when they reached Princeton. They no longer had Secret Service agents protecting their every move. She scanned for suspicious people, anyone looking at them with angry, grayish face colors. Their skimmer wheels dropped onto the old, nonmagnetic university streets, and Dan drove warily to an underground parking lot near the Carl Icahn Genomic Lab. For 40 years, architects had only been allowed to expand downward, to preserve the openness of the campus. Rianne's lab was on the bottom floor of a 12-story facility tucked under the Icahn and Lewis Thomas buildings. By the time Sarah and Dan reached her large-primate room, it was almost eleven p.m. Rianne had sent her graduate students home and was waiting alone. A few chimpanzees screeched when Sarah and Dan passed their cages.

"Rianne, you look ghastly," Sarah said.

Dan gave her a hug. "She just got back from California," he said.

"I got to the lab at four a.m. to avoid any unfriendly watchers on the streets and to get working again. It's the stupid bureaucrats that keep me up. They won't approve the youth formulas for human trials until I take toxicology down to the billionth level. They don't seem to care if I strip someone's DNA completely as long as they can check the boxes on their forms. My father's dying and I'm stuck here waiting for anal, over zealous tests."

"What would they do if you went back out to California and treated him without telling anyone?" asked Sarah.

"First I'd have to convince him to let me, which I still haven't done. And if the CDC or the National Academy of Sciences found out, I'm not sure what they would do—maybe shoot me."

"I hate to tell you," Dan said, "but so far the global vote is five-to-one against using your youth process. It would be exceedingly bad form to withhold it generally but still use it for our own families. Morality is so situation specific."

"Frankly, Dan, I've lost interest in abstract morality. The voters are nuts."

"We're choosing between our elderly and future generations," Dan said. "I know how much you love your father, but do we save him or the lives of Gina's grandchildren?"

Sarah saw Rianne's face tighten. Trying to change the subject, she asked, "How old are these chimps, Rianne? Some look very old and others seem like adolescents."

Rianne kept glaring at Dan. "My formula works, Dan. It's the bloody Holy Grail. You understand, don't you, Sarah? These chimps all used to be about 29 years old, elderly for them. The ones with the most treatments are physically 10 now, the equivalent of age 22 for people."

"It *is* amazing, but we came here to talk about the Torae. We really need to do that. Have you found a secure place for us to speak?"

"This isn't over, Dan," Rianne said. "Holding me accountable for your predictions about the future is infuriating. The future can take care of itself." She closed a lab book and stood up. "Okay, if we must, let's go talk about the Torae monsters."

She led them to a room with a small copper-screened enclosure. "There's a strong pulse generator in here, which we shield so it won't affect the other instruments. It's tight, but we can all squeeze in."

When the door was sealed, they were shoulder to shoulder along a screen wall with Dan in the middle and the gray pulse generator pressed on their chests. There was a strong odor of electrical sparking, ozone, in the stale air.

Maybe this will force some togetherness, Sarah thought. "You two have to forget your immorality and immortality quarrel for a minute," she said. "If the Torae get their way, Earth won't make it through the year anyway. They'll probably figure out what we discuss soon enough, but at least with this Faraday enclosure they won't be in our heads making suggestions, I hope. We need a plan."

"I haven't thought about the Torae much," Rianne admitted. "I've been a little distracted. Sorry it's so snug in here. What are you thinking, Sarah?"

"Well, I'm sure Sower doesn't want to wipe out all humans, but if we refuse to help, they could simply abduct 5,000 people randomly."

"We might have no choice," Rianne said. "Even if we could convince them to leave us alone, there's a black hole time bomb in our planet. Humans can't live here forever. The earthquakes and tsunamis are getting worse. That's the only silver lining I can think of—at least 5,000 would survive for sure."

Sarah wiggled a bit behind the pulse generator, trying to find a more comfortable position. "I can't believe you've jumped to the worst case, Rianne. Losing your father is awful, but dooming seven or eight billion is okay? Did you come up with anything better, Dan?"

"I keep thinking how familiar and crazy this is. If the Torae could just convince the Unity to stop expanding, the problem would go away. It's like a hundred dumb wars on Earth. If they had something the Unity needed, maybe they could strike a deal."

"I've been toying with an idea," Sarah said. "Probably stupid. What the Torae want most is to get to a fresh universe and populate it. I'm not sure exactly how their white fountain works, but if it is the opposite of a black hole, there'd be powerful tidal forces there. Sower's huge. There's no way she could get close to a white fountain without being squashed and torn apart. It's possible a swarm of Unity black holes could balance those tides. The Torae can make their own black holes, but the Unity are more expert at maneuvering them."

"But how would you convince the Unity to go along with that idea?" asked Rianne.

"I don't know," she said.

Dan looked perplexed. "You may be right, Sarah. Our best chance is to refuse to help the Torae unless they agree to work something out with the Unity. They might call our bluff, but you believe we actually have leverage, right?"

"I think so. They could still just snatch us off Earth, but I don't know what else we can try."

"Let's go with it," Rianne said. "We're no worse off if they abduct us, and it's possible they'd agree to negotiations. The Unity might like going to a new universe. Perhaps the Torae would agree to share technology with them to win them over. It all depends on working out a successful truce."

Dan twisted an arm loose and put it over Rianne's shoulder, freeing up a bit more room. "I was getting a cramp," he said. Rianne kissed his hand, a gesture of apology or forgiveness.

"About how long would it take to go 25 light-years?" asked Sarah, squeezing one eye shut. "At one gravity—let's see—about as long as it takes to get near light speed and then slow down on the other end. About 10 million seconds to half light speed. What's that?" She accessed her implant computer and said, "About half a year. Might need more time compression. I'd say four or five years worst case."

"Why do you care, Sarah?" asked Rianne.

"Because I think the negotiations would have to be done directly by humans. We're sort of neutrals. And I don't want to be too old when I get to the Unity star."

FRIENDS?

When they slithered out of the screen room, Rianne heard beeping noises from the larger cage room next door, but Sower's voice washed out the sounds. "Children, your plan is one of several thousand we considered. It's tolerable to us, although we estimate the success probability with the Unity at only 15 percent. You're right, it's better with a human negotiating, and the gravity-shield idea makes it worth the delay and risk. The Unity could be helpful to us if they can be tamed."

Rianne was stunned both by Sower's quick judgment and how thoroughly the Torae monitored their lives. There was no safe place.

"Now we know how long it takes them to read our minds," Dan said. "Our secret lasted what, 10 seconds?"

"Actually less," Sower added. "Your screen room was monitored by our microprobes. We heard everything you said as you said it."

Annoying call-interrupt sounds kept coming from the larger lab, and Rianne now heard comm pings in her implant as well.

"We will delay our ultimatum," Sower said, "but you should respond to your urgent calls."

Still trying to absorb Sower's instant response, Rianne answered a flashing wall monitor in the chimp lab. A security bot at the main lab entrance said two women students had been waiting patiently to speak to her. Their young faces appeared on the panel. They said they were doing the final edit of an article for the *Princetonian* about her work, and wanted to meet for a few last-minute questions before publishing and, if possible, some fresh photos. They said the article would be very complimentary. The bot at the Icahn entrance had verified their credentials. Rianne just wanted to go home to sleep, but the women apologized nicely, so she agreed to meet briefly at the conference level, but vetoed the idea of pictures.

"Hold it a minute," Dan yelled. "Bobby thinks there's a problem. I'll patch you in."

"I'm monitoring satellite infrared and security cameras on the Princeton buildings," Bobby said. "Several vans just converged in front of your building. I called it in, but it'll take five minutes for adequate police coverage to arrive."

Rianne's stomach knotted. "But I just opened the front door."

"We needed your ID cards to get past the security doors to this chimp lab," Sarah said. "It takes more than five minutes to get down here, even if you have the cards. Secure your biohazard air lock and let's wait it out."

Rianne finally took the level-two call waiting on her comm implant. A female voice said, "Get out of the lab. You're in great danger."

"Who are you?" Rianne asked. The voice sounded familiar.

"A friend. Grab the essential documents for your formula. Find a back way out of the building. The Icahn main entrance is blocked. They have weapons."

"Why should I trust you?" Rianne said.

"You have to trust me or you're dead."

I know this person.

"Is there a way to get to the other buildings?" the voice said.

"Yes," Rianne said. "There's a maze of tunnels here."

"Can you get to Guyot Hall?"

"Yes, but it is almost two blocks away."

"Meet me at the old loading dock. I have a vehicle. Take at least some of your documents."

Rianne's mind was racing. "We need to go," she said to Dan and Sarah. "We need to get out of this lab."

"Can't we just lock your lab doors?" Sarah looked confused. "We're 12 levels deep here and help is on the way."

"No, we're pinned in a corner in this lab. It would be safer if we left. And I just got a warning from someone I know, someone I trust."

"Who?"

"I was talking to—I think—Tina."

Sarah and Dan looked bewildered when she began throwing data sheets and flash memories in a bag. There was no reason in the world to trust Tina, the wire addict and former OWL. But something in Tina's voice told Rianne's every instinct that they needed to leave.

"The critical data is mostly in my head," she said. "I'll leave some behind in case this is a trick. They wouldn't hurt the chimps, would they?"

Bobby interrupted to tell them three more vans had arrived and the occupants were surrounding the building. "The city needed permission from the campus police to intervene. It'll take five more minutes for help to arrive," he said.

An explosion echoed down the elevator shafts.

Rianne pulled memory holo-cubes from the secure lab computers, trying to make her hands move faster. "It would take me months to reconstruct these DNA sequences. I can't leave them behind."

Rianne worriedly glanced around the lab. "I need to take one of the chimpanzees." Dan cringed while she unlatched a cage with the youngest chimp. It jumped and clung to her chest as she ran to the lab's side door with the bag of documents. "Stay with me."

Sarah and Dan followed her into a poorly lit underground hall leading toward the Lewis Thomas building. She threw the satchel to Dan and ran with the chimp's fingers squeezing into her shoulders and screeching in her ear. They scrambled up a sloped corridor, with lights turning on as they passed. The corridor branched off twice. Muted yells, crashes, and the sound of people running followed behind them. *Need to get to the fourth level and the tunnels to other buildings.* The chimp continued to screech.

"Your monkey is going to lead them to us," Sarah said.

Rianne cradled the chimp's head in her arms and it calmed down a bit.

They ran into an elevator and Rianne slapped an upper floor number. A half dozen people came into view around a corner just before the doors closed.

The elevator hummed quietly as all three gasped for breath. For a moment, time seemed frozen.

"I've made a mistake." *Sublevel four is where they'd wait for us.* Rianne frantically pushed SL5 just in time and took a deep breath as the doors opened. No one was there.

"I know a shortcut they won't know," she whispered while hurrying out of the elevator. "Come on."

The lowest labs under the Lewis Thomas building connected to more underground corridors, but only by cutting through secure labs. Twice she pressed thumb- and handprints to open confinement doors. "Only a few department heads have access here. These pressure doors will stop them."

"Not if they're running around outside," Dan whispered as they zigzagged around equipment benches. "Maybe we should hide out in this clean-room lab now that the doors have relocked. Let's think about it at least."

Rianne stopped to catch her breath and stroked the chimp's back. "Quiet, Henry," she said. "We'll be all right." Sarah and Dan looked as frightened and exhausted as she felt. They leaned against worktables, breathing deeply to slow their hearts. Odors from sweet, organic chemicals enveloped them. A clock on the pure-white, glossy wall inched forward while Henry fidgeted.

"Why'd you bring . . . Henry?" Sarah asked.

"He's the youngest—had the most treatments. He's critical to knowing the process is safe and getting it approved."

Sarah said, "This seems like a safe place to wait."

Logic said they should stay tucked behind the thickest, most secure doors they could find, which exactly described their current location. But Rianne pictured all the underground pathways, mentally sketching out the safest route to the Guyot loading dock. Tina's voice inexplicably tugged her in that direction. She convinced Sarah and Dan they had to leave when voices and scratching at the lab's air-lock door made the choice simple. "They've used explosives," she whispered. "We need to keep moving."

Going out the lab's back door, they reached a second basement level by a stairwell in the Schultz building and ran up wooden stairs to the Guyot's first floor. At every corner, they peeked carefully before moving. Weathered wood walls of the original buildings had now replaced the sterile concrete and plaster of the deep basement corridors.

Almost there. Rianne led them to a set of wide doors with "Receiving Area" stenciled on them. Dan opened the door delicately, peeked in, and stepped inside. When everyone followed, he locked the doors and he and Sarah used heavy boxes to barricade the entrance. Rianne peeked out a window to the loading dock and saw a gas-powered skimmer waiting for them with exhaust visible in the spotty yellow lights.

They all stood silently, unwilling to take the final step out of the building. Even Henry the chimp was quiet.

"The police are arriving." It was Bobby's voice in their implants.

"Bobby," Dan whispered, "what do you see?"

"Police are securing the Icahn entrance, but probably three dozen unknowns got into the labs. The internal cameras are spotty, but I'm pretty sure a dozen reached Professor Jorgenson's lab. They've hauled things away already."

"Do you know where we are?"

"Yes, I see the skimmer outside your room. I'm watching from a camera on the dock. The skimmer is old, unregistered, and I can't make out the driver, or even the gender."

"Are we safe here, Bobby?"

"No."

Rianne heard muffled voices in the corridor just outside the barricaded receiving-room door. "How do they keep finding us?" asked Sarah while edging toward the exit to the loading dock. An explosive sound, like a battering ram, hammered the Guyot hallway door.

<center>~~~~~~~</center>

Devin watched them lurch and stumble through the door onto the dock. The three people he hated most had fallen into his trap, and they'd brought a chimp. He smiled before getting out of the skimmer and pointing his gun at them. *This is too beautiful,* he thought.

"Welcome," he said. "I'm your compassionate rescuer." The chimp screamed and jumped down, but Rianne grabbed him before he could run away. Devin was delighted to see the large satchel over Dan Jorgenson's shoulder. "Rianne, are you going to introduce me? I'm Devin, little chimp. Are you a special ape?" *They're lined up in a tidy row for me.*

"I worried you might find a way to escape that mob, so I hacked your comm coordinates. Bet you thought only the NSA could do that, former director Jorgenson. I've been funneling them so you'd come to meet me. I just told them you moved to another building, so they won't bother us. Using my OWL friend Tina to call you was a nice touch, don't you think?"

Warner stepped sideways but stopped. She's probably deduced the futility of her situation, Devin thought.

"Frankly, I was hoping you'd all escape, as you have, so I could watch each of you die firsthand. I have my trusty, portable railgun today, so don't even think of moving. Killing you one by one will be quite satisfying. I've despised you for such a very long time."

Now Jorgenson is edging toward his wife, hoping to protect her no doubt. "Why don't you all step out to the edge of the dock so I can see you better?" When they slowly complied, he said, "Thank you very much."

Rianne clutched the chimp tighter as she stepped forward on the dock. "Is that a unique young chimp you saved?" Devin asked. "Or just one you're fond of, Professor? You shouldn't worry about the animals or your lab. The group chasing you hates you, but they want the formula more. They'll strip the place and take very good care of your notes and chimps. I hope you've carefully chosen the data you carried out to me. I plan to sell it, piece by piece, and make a fortune. The chimp will add credibility."

"It's worthless," she said. "Anything really important is in my head."

"Perhaps true," he said, "but the people I sell it to won't know. I'll be richer either way."

He saw Sarah trembling. "Is your life passing before you, Sarah?" he asked, smirking. "It would have been much better if the OWLs had won the war. You realize, certainly, that the best government is a benevolent dictatorship. I'd only trust myself as dictator, of course. I'd have eliminated Milos and the all the others. The world would have been fairer and happier by now."

Warner wants to argue but is afraid to say anything. Typical woman. Wish I could hear what they're saying to each other subvocally—probably planning a mad-dash escape. He fired a pellet into the wall behind them, which blew off about 10 bricks. "Uh, uh, please stay nice and close." *The dismay on their faces. They understand now that they're really going to die.* He chuckled.

"I've been a tad envious because you've talked with the Torae. They seem like a superior life form from what I've gathered. Perhaps they'll be the ones waiting when you go to meet your maker. It won't be long. You destroyed my life, and I can't forgive that."

Gunshots and sirens came from the direction of the Icahn building. "Apparently the police have arrived. Time to say goodbye."

He aligned the gun, holding it with both hands. He stopped to say, "Your death experience should be fast but very painful."

I think I'll begin with Warner.

He sighted along the barrel, but then he felt his head jerk forward. The gun slipped loose. A spiral of thoughts and lights exploded in his mind. It didn't exactly hurt, but redness clouded his vision and closed in. He remembered laughing at math camp about an easy problem and his mother scolding him. His comm implant was screaming. Something was wrong. Muscles no longer worked. He fell. The redness turned to black.

~~~~~

The gunshot was almost inaudible but Devin crumpled to the ground at the foot of the loading dock and stopped moving. For several seconds they crouched low on the pavement until a small skimmer bounced across the parking lot, squealed its wheels, and came to an abrupt stop. The driver climbed out, swept a rifle toward some trees, and yelled, "Rianne, get in. All of you. Now!" Distant shots were heard from beyond the trees.

It was Tina's voice again, and Rianne immediately knew she could be trusted. "Let's go!" Rianne yelled. Dragging the frightened chimp, she hurried down the stairs with Sarah following. A shot hit the building, and Dan half jumped off the ledge. They hurried to the skimmer, the monkey shrieking. Before fully closing the doors, the small vehicle spun around in a half circle and accelerated over a curb between two hedges and out of the parking lot.

The driver's left arm and head were soaked with blood. The skimmer window had been shattered. "Devin . . . the bastard clubbed my head back at the Icahn entrance and knocked me to the ground," she said. They hurled recklessly through three or four turns to a poorly lit side street in old Princeton where she switched off all the lights and slowed down.

"Tina?" asked Rianne.

"Quiet. Later. I'm injured and I killed a person. I need to get away from here without being stopped."

Rianne had jumped into the rear seat with Henry and couldn't see Tina's face. Tina drove cautiously; whenever headlights appeared she pulled to the curb and waited. They wandered five kilometers farther through North Princeton before rolling to a stop in a dark area under low trees. Tina said, "Someone else is going to have to drive now. I need a little help."

Sarah slid into the driver's seat while Dan helped Tina into the back with Rianne and the chimp. He ripped his shirt and held it tightly over her head wound.

Rianne stared into Tina's face. A childhood friend was buried behind that countenance.

In obvious pain from the large cut on the back of her head, Tina winced and squeezed her eyes.

"She's losing consciousness," Dan said. "We need to get her to a hospital right now."

Slumped down with her eyes still shut, Tina said, "Not here. Trenton. I know someone."

Sarah turned south when they reached old Highway 206 and switched on autodrive.

Tina's body fell forward and Rianne lifted her back and gently held her head. "I knew you'd help, Tina. When you called, I somehow knew you'd help. But why?"

Before losing consciousness, Tina mumbled, ". . . protecting you. You saved me."

***

"We drove her to the first hospital we could find, Mother." Rianne sank into her parents' overly soft couch with Dan beside her. Several weeks had passed since the shootings in Princeton.

Joti seemed confused.

"Tina wanted us to go to a friend's clinic, a doctor friend from the OWL war, so the police wouldn't find her, but we didn't think she'd make it to Trenton with the head wound. She'd lost a lot of blood. We figured no one was going to prosecute her for shooting a person who'd just clubbed her and was aiming a gun at the three of us. Police are investigating the whole thing, but we vouched for her. She's recovering well from the wound."

"Tina was such a good friend when you were little, but then she stopped coming by."

Rianne remembered playing with Tina in that very house. Her parents' San Marino home hadn't changed much over the years; only the furniture and art were new. It still felt like the place she'd grown up. Tapestries and prints from travels crowded the walls, and family photos, especially of Rianne, were everywhere. A large holo-portrait from Rianne's Nobel ceremonies dominated the fireplace mantelpiece.

"This room looks like my museum or maybe my mausoleum, Mother. Please mix in other stuff, cheery stuff, or put me upstairs in a guest bedroom. It's embarrassing."

"You can decorate your own house," Joti said. "This is how old people do it." She frowned and looked puzzled again. "But why did Tina come to help you?"

"Actually, I still don't fully understand how or why Tina rescued us. We'd searched for her after Chia-Jean died because I'd promised to help her. Apparently after the OWL war, she fell apart, became a complete wire addict, had a baby taken from her by authorities, and later had a miscarriage."

"That's horrible, Rianne. Too bad she had to go through that alone."

"She told us the antiaddiction treatments I invented saved her life. She got clean and has a husband and family now. Also, she kept tabs on ex-OWLs, including Devin. We've been at the top of their most-hated list for years. Devin had been her boss during the war, and she knew he was stalking us. She said she quietly protected me, even on the streets back in Stockholm when I was getting the Nobel."

"How did she get hurt?" Joti asked.

"Devin forced her to call my comm, to get us to the dock alone. But I could tell by her voice that Tina would help us. Then he surprised her and clubbed her before she could leave. She regained consciousness just soon enough to save us."

"It's not clear if the lab mob wanted to capture Rianne or kill her," Dan said. "They stole many of her documents and biological samples. They even took chimps. The police caught some of them, but it's a terrible setback to her research."

"Have another muffin, Daniel, and I can bring some more tea."

"No thanks, Joti."

"What are you going to do about your work, Rianne?"

"I canceled my graduate class for the semester and a few colleagues are helping to reconstruct my research. I wanted you and Dad to start the youth treatments, but it'll all have to wait. Do you think he will be waking up soon? I'd like to talk to him."

Her mother looked embarrassed, almost guilty. "There's something I haven't told you yet, dear, about your father."

"They finished the stem-cell infusion at the hospital, didn't they?"

"Not exactly."

"What happened, Mother?"

"Rianne, your father is home. He came home . . . to die."

"What?" Rianne's face paled.

"He probably only has a month to live."

"You told me he was better."

"I know. I lied."

<hr>

Rianne peeked into Kyle's room. He was lying in bed with his eyes open, trying to adjust his position.

He saw her and Dan and said, "I have 10 pillows and I still can't get comfortable. Can you help me, Rianne? I need to be propped up or I can't take deep breaths. I had those lift things at the hospital. My liver is inflamed, I'm sure."

"How bad does it hurt, Father?" She pushed another pillow behind him.

"Just aches . . . unless I try to breathe." He smiled and then winced. "The doctors are gradually increasing my painkillers."

"I'm working to reconstitute the bioagents for my youth treatments for you."

"I've been wanting to talk to you about that, Rianne. Your mother and I . . . I'm 83—getting up there. We want nature to take its course. You shouldn't treat me differently from anyone else. I hear the vote's not going well."

"It's running five-to-one against," Dan said.

"The vote's flawed," Rianne blurted back, glaring at Dan.

Kyle squirmed on the pillows. "None of that really matters, Rianne. We've decided."

"Father, that's crazy. You've always been the ultimate techno-geek. We were the first people with implants, and then the first with subvocals. My treatments are a crowning achievement of science. They will make you stronger, vigorous."

"Don't misunderstand me, Rianne. Life is precious. Joti and I have had tremendously happy lives, you're a big part of that, and there are things we'd both still like to do. But we've accepted the idea of dying. We've adjusted to it and expect it to happen."

"You're not thinking of going with Jeremy? Has he been talking to you?"

"No. We turned him down."

"But why not take my treatments?"

"It's just that . . . we've lived our lives. I'm curious about what's coming next, sure, but we had our shot. The grandkids need room to start their own fires."

Rianne studied his face and, especially, the resonance of his voice. *He's serious.* She stared silently. The deep sounds of his breathing were like tree roots pulling deep against the soil. In the raspy high frequencies, she heard air squeezing into his lungs. And she listened to his heart beating irregularly.

"Something's wrong with your heart, isn't it, Father?"

"Yes. It will kill me soon."

Descending the stairs, Rianne looked at the many pictures of Kyle and Joti's grandchildren and great-grandchildren scattered on the wall. *Lives two or three centuries long will seem natural to these kids. Why can't this generation see that? People just don't like change.*

"Someday humans will be ready to live forever," Dan said, guessing her thoughts. "It's not time yet."

"Why?"

"Same thing for the Read rockets. Someday people will go to truly distant stars using Read's, or someone else's, memory readouts, but they'll do it correctly, so minds sleep along the way. It's not time yet."

"Why?"

"It'll take several generations just to deal with your genetic-engineering discoveries. It'll take a long time to sort out new successes and mistakes, to find out what works best for humans. If people live forever, their genetic mistakes will never go away. They'll be irreversible. Different types will go to war rather than mate."

"You don't understand, Dan. I was a creepy freak when I was growing up, and Father loved me anyway. I don't want him to die!"

"Neither do I," Dan said. "I love him too."

Her hands were trembling, emotions at war with logic. The large holophoto of her holding a Nobel diploma, proudly displayed on the fireplace mantelpiece, seemed to mock her.

Her agony was interrupted by an alert sound on her implant from a friend at Caltech. "Hello, Alvaro," she said, trying to recover quickly. "Jorgenson here."

"I have news, Rianne."

"How are you coming on my new DNA-replacement virus? Any issues?"

"It should take about a week. But I'm calling about something else, a distraction to say the least. A new mold is burning groundcover across the east L.A. suburbs. They tried the usual blight treatments and finally brought us some samples. Professor Kittle and I checked them twice . . . confirmed it. You can come down and look at our ultrascopic scans. The mold looks like a mutant of Chia-Jean's non-DNA life, and it's already spread over 30 square kilometers. It's evolving very rapidly, almost like it remembers events from generation to generation. It quickly evolved resistance to each fungicide. You really should come here and examine the samples. Can you stop by?"

"Yes, I'll come in tomorrow."

Rianne stared again at her own face hovering over the mantel. *It escaped. The one thing Chia-Jean worried about every day.*

"What's wrong?" asked Dan.

"A hungry dangerous genie is out of its lamp," she said.

~~~~~

Isaac didn't enjoy the launch scenario. He went through it like everyone else, but he forgot it almost immediately. He knew his brain had now been stuffed in a small cube and that his old flesh-and-blood body had been burned. Sitting on the bed in a simulated room, he knew exactly where he wanted to begin.

"Control, I want a beautiful beach, Mexico, and a topless true-woman with me, not a simulated person. We've had a few beers. I'm 25, with my face. Let her pick her enhancements. Give me 10 options—I'll pick the woman. Secluded spot."

Sentient programs searched among a million situation options, with typical human preferences considered, and built a scene that emerged around him. He selected the woman, and she said, "What's your name? I'm Jill."

"Isaac, Isaac Warner. Have you been here long? Are you a sim expert?"

"Only a week . . . seems like a year, so much has happened."

She seemed a little tipsy. "You mind if I put my arm around you?" asked Isaac. "This is all new to me."

She moved a little closer, and Isaac took it as a good sign. He helped her as they sat down on the white sand. "It's almost too nice at times," she said. "I bet we'll get a sunset in 10 minutes. Sometimes I tell Control to back it off a little—to make it more realistic."

I wonder how old she was? She moves awkwardly, like someone who was taller or heavier. He reached around and groped her a little.

"Don't get too frisky," she said. "There may be people walking around here and some could be real people. I've made new friends this week."

"We could go behind those bushes or to my room if you'd like."

"I'd like to stay here awhile," she said. "Tell me about yourself. Where are you from?"

Isaac felt normal erotic sensations, enhanced since he was 25 again. *I don't want a two-week courting ritual. That's not why I came here.* He put his hand behind the woman's head and said, "I'm pretty much what you're looking at."

She pulled away when he tried to kiss her, but it was tentative. He tried again and lowered her to the beach sand, his hand on her thigh.

She jerked her head. "Please stop. You're hurting me."

Isaac gawked at the woman's bare breasts a bit, and then completely lost control. He ripped off her swimsuit bottom, forced her back, and raped her. She screamed, so he covered her mouth. Pinning her down with his elbows, he began to push brutally. She bit him on the arm; he slapped her.

Then oddly, she relaxed, seemed to give up, and threw her arms around him. Something felt odd. He hesitated and then shoved like an animal. "More," she said, "stronger, take all of me." She moved rhythmically in perfect sync.

Isaac became confused and stopped. "What the hell." He couldn't continue. A few seconds later, he pulled away and shoved her aside. "Control, get me out of here."

In a moment, Isaac was on the bed in his room. "What the shit happened back there? What did you do, Control?"

"The true-woman chose to depart during your encounter so we switched to a sim that would please you."

"What? I didn't want her to leave." He grabbed a pillow and threw it at a lamp. "Never do that again. I don't want women to try to please me. It needs to hurt. I want them to panic and suffer."

"We can't force true-women to stay when they don't want to," Control said. "This place needs to be 'Heaven for all.'"

Three months passed before Sarah was ready to leave her world behind. She traveled to say goodbye to her friends and family. Even the U.S. president was surprised when Sarah said she would be withdrawing from public life. Most people heard she was retiring and would take a long vacation. She confided to others that she'd be involved in lengthy secret negotiations. To those very close—she told the truth.

She spent her final days with Kenny in Minnesota, visiting first with Mary in St. Paul. They then drove north to Rianne's cabin. Dan and Rianne were staying there with Joti, trying to comfort her after Kyle's death. It was a slow time, filled with thoughtful boat rides on Bay Lake, simple daily chores, and tearful reminiscences by the fireplace. Sarah took all the stories into her heart, watching the full spectrum of emotions on the faces of her closest friends, colors that told stories deeper than any words. She wanted indelible memories for the long journey ahead—knowing that most likely she would never see them, or any humans, again.

Rianne urged Sarah to take youth bioagents along on the Torae ship. "Just in case you need more time," Rianne said. "No one on Earth will know." Sarah just smiled.

On the afternoon of their last full day together, she asked Kenny to drive slowly back to the city on old country roads. On that leisurely drive, Sarah confided that most of her life she'd been avoiding him.

"I hated the idea of a normal existence," she said. Looking away from his eyes, she watched the computer-optimized farms and wind towers spanning the western horizon drift by. "I wasn't sure what to do with my life, but I knew it didn't include settling down and doing normal female things. Actually, that's not right, it didn't include doing anything conventional, female or male."

"Were you intimidated by the Torae?" Kenny asked, glancing toward her. "Danny worried that his life was being manipulated."

"Not at first. I was just . . . driven. I resented how the Torae said Dan, Rianne, and I were unique, that everything depended on us. But they didn't beat it into us; they didn't even talk often. I think they knew we couldn't resist the excitement. Even now, I want to be with you more than I've ever dared to say, but I can't stay on Earth. I volunteered to go before it even made sense, before I understood why it had to be me."

"It's nice to actually talk to you," he said. "To have some quiet time. You are a lovely odd duck. I'm glad we took these side roads. You can still see some wild forests here. See that old barn? It's falling down, but it's real. I bet it's 150 years old."

They were both quiet for several minutes. "Don't get me wrong," Sarah finally said. "I ache when I think about what I've missed. I'd like nothing better than to sit by Ma, knit sweaters, and talk. I'd adopt kids if I still could. Heck, I could use Rianne's bio stuff, get younger, and maybe still have kids. You're part of that dream."

Kenny pulled off the country road near a small lake and they watched an egret slowly circle over an island. They brushed away stones and sat on the grass by the shore. "You've always been mysterious," Kenny said. "You seemed too smart and quick to pay any attention to a Marine from St. Paul, but I always liked you."

"You don't understand," she said. "I cried for two days when you got married, Kenny, and my stomach turned in knots the day I learned she'd died.

You've been a threat to my way of life ever since I met you. I know it's stupid telling you this now, but I have to before I leave. If I don't say things now, I'll think about it for years when I'm stuck on the Torae ship. Often, when I close my eyes, I think of you."

A large heron landed on the water's edge, startled when it saw them, and quickly flew away.

～～～～～

Sarah remained in St. Paul two days longer than planned and told Kenny she wouldn't leave Earth unless he came to Manassas to see her off. He was one of only 20 people waiting on the Warner horse pasture to hear her last goodbyes. Kenny enjoyed seeing the president of the United States step around in fancy shoes, staring at the ground to avoid horse poop. *This spot's perfect for Sarah.*

Just one media outlet was invited to the event: Grid Global News, the current name of the Rosslyn company where Sarah got her start. They set up the holo-cameras so horses and hills would be in the background. The only children present were Gina and Jim, because she loved how they called her Grandma Sarah. They'd be in the international broadcast background with their father, walking among the horses.

Sarah pulled Kenny aside while everyone waited. Drawing him to her, she whispered about the first time they'd met, at Rianne and Dan's wedding, many years ago. He was caught off guard when she then held and kissed him unashmedly for a long time in front of the gathered crowd. He nervously tried to pull away once, but then drifted back into the kiss, the moment, and the emotion. Enfolding her, a lost lifetime of affection, companionship, and passion was shared. Their long embrace was both a hello and a goodbye. She took a deep breath and said, "I love you," before stepping directly in front of the cameras and brushing back her hair.

She stared at each person, slowly moving her eyes from one to another. Everyone stopped speaking; the only sound was the breeze blowing through the leaves of a nearby oak. "I've told all of you where I'm going and why," she said. "There's an awful lot at stake. I don't think the Torae will exterminate us if I fail, but I don't intend to fail. I'm going to a place 26 light-years distant, so I'm probably not coming back. This is a little like my funeral—glad I could make it. You were invited because you're the people I cherish.

"It's time to turn on the cameras, Frank." Kenny saw her face shift to its professional look. Cheek lines tightened while her eyes appeared serious and intimate. She used her famous opening line, "Friends across the globe," and Kenny imagined switches in six billion people's brains clicking to "Open," letting her speak directly to them.

"It's Sarah Warner. I'm sorry to bother those of you who were sleeping, but it makes no sense to do this on time delay. I thought you should know I'm leaving Earth. I'm going a long way—26 light-years away, actually. This is goodbye.

"I'll be negotiating a truce between the Torae and the Unity, who've been at war around us for some time. Humans have been caught in the crossfire. I'll try to calm them down.

"With this, my final message, I want to urge you all to find a way off this planet. Earth is doomed to collapse in less time than you imagine, about 350 years if we're lucky. Just finding a safe refuge will take decades, and the energy and sacrifice needed to travel to and develop a new planet, or planets, will be immense. Above all, find a way to populate the stars as humans, not cyborgs, as Jeremy Read is doing. The Torae told me that humans are a rare species. It has something to do with our desire to be extraordinary and yet to find room to love one another. Apparently that's unusual in the universe. If you succeed, and I succeed, we will not only reach new stars, but new universes. For our existence to truly matter, you must do this—go out among the stars to reveal what it means to be human."

Kenny thought he saw an outline around Sarah. She reached backward, stepped up, and seemed to be suspended slightly over the ground. He imagined what might have been and bit his lip. His vision blurred and tears fell from his face. She was looking straight at him when he said, "I love you."

A moment later, Sarah slowly rose. She nodded gently as the cameras panned to follow. He saw jagged lines and her image fractured until it resembled a thin mosaic. As she ascended, she faded away.

For a time after Sarah disappeared, everyone stood dumbstruck. Once the president left and the press packed up, Kenny, Rianne, and Dan slowly walked back to the farmhouse. Adam helped Andrea along while she mourned and mumbled ". . . my miracle . . . to Heaven."

Kenny noticed a sealed metal container under Rianne's arm and asked about it.

"It's a supply of the youth formula," she said. "I took Sarah's DNA and customized a new batch to be more effective. There's enough in here for her to live over a thousand years."

"She didn't take it?" Kenny said. "What did she say?"

"She said, 'Rianne and Dan, protect them and love them.'"

"Love who?"

"All people, I guess."

HEAVEN

The exodus took longer than Jeremy expected. He'd always wanted to be the very last, along with Laurel, but it became a difficult wait. Only near the end of the third year did the numbers decline, and many tried to sign up well after the deadline, especially people who'd just found out they were terminally ill. After several extensions, Jeremy cut it off.

Local operations had wound down by the time Jeremy and Laurel finally arrived at the Panama facility. He gazed at the amazing site with pride—50 square kilometers of city built on jungle hills overlooking the canal.

"Five hundred million people have passed through here," Laurel said, "and this was the smallest of the three sites."

Only a skeleton staff remained; most had already joined the customers in orbit. A few thousand people, forced by family or circumstance to stay behind on Earth, now lined the walkways in a light rain. They'd come to celebrate and cheer as Jeremy and Laurel strolled by, their country greatly enriched by Read Enterprises' presence. Canal user fees had set records handling all the boats that streamed through from North and South America. And two beautiful new international airports, carved from the rain forest, accommodated the Canadians, Americans, and others who'd flown directly in.

Jeremy and Laurel ambled down Hotel Avenue toward a neural-scan center with an oversized umbrella protecting them from the light drizzle. Their path was strewn with pink blossoms. Local musicians, dancers, and vendors mingled with everyday people under awnings at the street's edge to watch the very short parade. The Panamanians shouted words of respect and thanks to the two people who'd transformed their country. Red carpeting marked the final 100 meters, and the scan center's soaring white-stone entrance seemed an excellent place for final photographs. Jeremy and Laurel turned and waved from the steps, and the crowd responded with a rousing cheer as they entered the building.

The spacious lobby seemed like a blend of a modern hospital and a sumptuous art museum, creating the desired impression that this might be the final way-stop before Heaven. A four-story waterfall and surrounding greenery captured the essence of Panama's jungles and stood in contrast to the polished stone of the rest of the atrium. Jeremy slipped their umbrella into an ornate brass container.

A doctor introduced himself and joined them as they walked together up a wide marble staircase to the second floor.

"I designed the place so no one would change their mind at this point," Jeremy whispered to Laurel. "We could have saved some money though — didn't need real doctors. Actors would have been sufficient."

They were escorted to a small scan room that held only two medical chairs in front of a wall of imposing technical equipment. Other rooms had additional chairs to accommodate larger families. The more functional and frightening tools were hidden behind the walls.

He pulled Laurel close and they exchanged their last fully human kiss. Medical treatments had kept them looking young, but Laurel's body felt frail, and he felt old. "We'll see Lené and Nick soon and feel as young as they do. It's time to jettison these used bodies, Laurel."

"We fulfilled all our dreams together," she said. "Even this one."

They sat down, leaned back in the chairs like millions before them, and were asked, "Are you ready for the journey?" Laurel looked at Jeremy and reached over to hold his hand. They knew this was the final moment. They both nodded. "Yes, we're ready."

The doctor placed a sedating wafer on their tongues and gave them a sip of wine. Jeremy smiled as he lost consciousness. Bots would do everything from that point forward.

⌇⌇⌇⌇⌇

The wall behind Jeremy and Laurel unfolded, and medical and electronic tools moved toward their heads. A head brace found the proper fit and a laser cut through the bone across their eyebrows, over their ears, and around the back. In less than five seconds, the tops of their skulls were off.

With the brain exposed, powerful magnetic pads rotated orthogonally over the brain, and millions of scan sensors each recorded 200 trillion bits of information. Processors immediately began to build high-resolution images down to the synapse level.

The magnetic pads lifted off, and dexterous bot fingers pushed a pliable synthetic material deep into the brain folds onto every centimeter of cortex. Millions of needles penetrated the top neuron layers. When activated, they isolated and recorded synapse connection strengths.

Their necks were sliced open, enabling the midbrain, pons, medulla, cerebellum, and spinal cord structures to be analyzed. As the brain model developed, bots removed clothing and attached neural and muscle stimulators, which looked like small acupuncture needles, over their skin. Other specialized devices probed their tongues, nasal passages, eyes, and ears, to enable the adventurer to both sense and feel as they had in real life. The entire procedure, including transferring the condensed brain and body models to the electronic cubes, took under three minutes. A snippet of DNA was frozen. They were pronounced dead.

Mechanical hands placed Jeremy and Laurel's bodies on conveyers to the crematoria. Few humans had toured those buildings, even during construction; they were managed and operated entirely by bots. Regular trucks carried ashes for disposal in the desert. Occasionally, individuals asked if their bodies could be returned to relatives, but the fee for the service was one million dollars. Not many selected that option.

It seemed to Jeremy like only a moment had passed. He opened his eyes and saw Laurel in the chair next to him, and the same doctor standing nearby. He knew the doctor was now a sim, and studied him for imperfections. When Laurel opened her eyes, the doctor said, "Please step out to the hall and follow the launch guide." Laurel thanked the sim. Jeremy wondered why she bothered. She looked exactly as she had before, but Jeremy knew that some improvements had already been made to both of them.

As they walked to the door, Jeremy bounced a little to try out his new legs. *Not bad.*

Their escort in the hall looked slightly disheveled, like a typical engineer. They followed him down the marble stairs and out the door. Everywhere, simulated people hurried in all directions going about their simulated work.

"Nice ambiance—great touch from our designers," he said to Laurel.

"It feels completely real," she replied.

The sky was now cloudless with an unusually deep azure color, and the sun, leaning to the horizon, cast long shadows. "It's a beautiful evening, don't you think?" the guide said. "Please hop into the Jeep."

Jeremy helped Laurel step up into their "jungle transport." She still looked elegant and graceful, but quicker. *They've made a few body repairs, but everything will be even better soon.*

He thought about the reality running in parallel. *We're both actually little cubes now, piled with maybe 10,000 others on a transfer pallet, running off batteries. There's a temporary comm shunt between Laurel and me so we can take this trip together. A couple million cubes are waiting at the runway, and when we arrive, they'll launch the last shuttle.*

Laurel nudged him and nodded toward a valley. The Jeep skirted the edge of a precipitous drop, and an orange sunset lit the tops of the jungle hills across the canyon. They rode what seemed like several kilometers before climbing a steep incline to an immense plateau sheared off the hilltop. Three simulated launch shuttle buses waited on five-kilometer runways, surrounded by huge operation centers. The largest buildings extracted deuterium from water and produced light helium in reactors. Lights began flickering on in the structures as the sun set.

"Identical to the real facility," Jeremy said. "No need to make it look more impressive."

The launch shuttles had the largest lift capability ever seen, with the smaller, space-worthy portion wide enough for 30 people to sit comfortably across. Gigantic engines, wings, and fuel tanks capable of carrying their payload to the edge of space made up the majority. They were designed so that at 25 kilometers altitude the surfboard-shaped space vehicle would drop loose for the final burst into orbit, while the aircraft returned to ground.

The Jeep took Laurel and Jeremy directly to the undercarriage cabin. They rode a conveyer ramp to the entrance and found about 300 people waiting inside in chairs. "True-human neural cubes," Jeremy whispered. "They've shunted this group together now to make the shared experience as real as possible. I hope no one freaks out."

"Most are speaking Spanish," Laurel said, looking around. "We could learn any language in an immersion class when we're up there. It wouldn't take long."

"Or, we could just request a language transfer and save the time entirely," Jeremy said. He grinned, adding, "But I think the first order of business is to make us younger. I hope we'll agree on what our ages should be." Laurel flashed a conspiratorial look.

The launch sequence was exhilarating. An initial roar and teeth-chattering vibration felt entirely real, with the release and punch from ramjet/scramjet hybrid engines truly frightening. *They built a superb model for this launch and my nerve response seems normal. I suppose at some point I'll need to stop analyzing every simulation. I am what I think now—I need to forget the old me.*

A young child shrieked when they became weightless, but calmed down soon. Later in space, roof panels opened to reveal a large curved window. "This is a little bogus," Jeremy said. "The real shuttle doesn't look like a commercial jet inside and it certainly doesn't have a large picture window. The designer just wanted to give people a view of the cool space rocket. But, everything considered, this idea of yours was brilliant, Laurel. Everyone's had this common launch experience, and it's mostly realistic. We'll all have something to talk about—start conversations—especially us introverts."

"Jeremy, you're not an introvert. A bit daft, perhaps, but not an introvert," she said, laughing.

They looked out the window at rocket *New World* and gawked like everyone else. Even for the two who'd commissioned it, the interstellar craft inspired awe. The stack of human cubes onboard filled a 50- by 30- by 20-meter block, but that was only five percent of the rocket's total mass. Superconducting magnets, which shielded passengers by reflecting charged particles from the pulsed fusion engines, took up another five percent. The remainder was tanks filled with deuterium and light-helium fuel to be slowly depleted during the journey. Acceleration would be miniscule, only a thousandth of Earth gravity, but the rocket held enough fuel to reach Epsilon Eridani and another star if necessary, and to cycle landing craft to the planet surface. Two hundred Earth years were required for the journey, but they had plenty of time.

A voice on the launch shuttle spoke to each mind saying, "You've arrived at rocket *New World*. You may step out of the cabin door now. Remember, you'll be transferred immediately to a temporary apartment alone or with your group. Once you're there, you'll be able to change your accommodations or, in fact, create any world and life you desire. If you need any help or instructions, simply say 'Control.' Thank you."

People chattered excitedly as they filed out and disappeared beyond the door. Laurel turned to Jeremy and said, "Before we left, I arranged a little surprise for you." He hesitated and she pulled his hand, tugging him toward the shuttle door.

He shut his eyes as he stepped through, and when he opened them he was sitting in his favorite ratty old recliner in their San Marino home, with a wall of windows opening out to the familiar valley beyond. Laurel stood by him grinning, looking exactly as she had at the party when they first met. He looked down and saw the wrinkles gone from his hands. Standing to the side were Lené and Nick, holding each other very close. They beamed at him as well, and Lené said, "Welcome home, Father."

In four days, the *New World* achieved Earth escape velocity and smaller jets made slight course corrections. None of the condensed humans heard the sounds. Two months later, their ship broke the grip of the sun.

"Where are you taking me?" the young woman asked.

"Trust me," Isaac said. "This is my favorite spot, the most beautiful place I know. Hold my hand and we'll go."

The woman squinted when a brilliant sunrise suddenly hit her face. "We're at the People's Tower in Shanghai," Isaac said. "It's over 190 floors high — tallest building on real Earth. You can see the Pacific 60 kilometers away, and over 100 million people live within sight of here."

"It's very pretty," she said. "But was the sky ever really this clear? I bet if we went down to talk to the 100 million people, they wouldn't all be there. Sometimes I get frustrated by the simulations."

"Have you tried any bird sims? They're awesome."

"No, I'd be frightened flying around."

"You really should. It's all in slow motion, like you're swimming. You get the sensations of being a real bird, and their vision is amazing. Remember, you can't be killed here, or even injured."

"Maybe someday I'll try it."

Isaac led her toward the edge. "You can look down and see all the main skimmer lines, ML train tubes, and even aircraft."

She made careful shuffles with her left leg extended in front. "Why isn't there a safety fence or rail here?"

"This is a spot they never allowed people to go," Isaac said. "There's a regular observation deck two floors lower. Lean over a little; you can look straight down 190 floors. I'll hold you so you'll feel safe." Isaac stood behind her and put both hands on her waist. She stretched her head over, pulling back a couple of times.

You've still got the charm, Isaac, old boy. You can convince 'em to do things they'd never do on their own.

"You don't need to be nervous," he said. "We could jump off, and after we smashed we'd be right back in my room."

"I'd like to go now," she said.

Of course you would. Isaac pushed her toward the edge while her left leg slipped along the concrete. He chuckled, threw both arms around her waist, and jumped forward with all his strength. She screamed as they fell over the edge.

The woman jerked violently as they dropped, scratching his arm. He held her away and squinted through the rushing air to see her face. She extended her arms out to the sides, and Isaac thought maybe she'd blacked out. Her head rotated toward him. She looked calm. "Shit," he yelled, kicking her away. He yanked his arms and legs in, and after a few more seconds, splattered onto the pavement.

"Control!" he yelled. He was suddenly on the bed in his apartment, still in a balled-up position. "Control, I want to register an official complaint."

"What's the trouble?"

"You know exactly what the problem is. You switched to a sim again at the crucial moment. I want real women who will scream to the end."

"We can instruct a sim to scream."

"Don't bother. Your sims always do the logical thing. This won't work if I have to plan all the details."

"We could easily provide a true-woman who enjoys terror and torture."

"No, that's not right. I want real women who hate terror."

"We can program a sim to act illogically if you'd like."

"Shit."

Rocket *New World* reached Neptune in 15 Earth months, ready for its final slingshot out of the solar system. It seemed much shorter to the neural packs, former humans whose processor cycle time had been reduced for the long journey. Sentient computers maintaining the overall system were authorized to further reduce the cycle rate if abnormal behavior emerged or in an overall power crisis. Only true-humans with journey-critical projects retained real-time or faster rates.

"Control back door six," Jeremy said. "Summarize satisfaction levels in the human kernels."

"There is a broadening gulf between cubes who demand realism and a larger group that desire more novel stimulations. Ninety-five percent are very content."

"Are any caught in stimulation-addiction loops, as we speculated?" Jeremy asked.

"That doesn't appear to be a problem yet. Also, we're monitoring for the gaming-boredom effect. But it's early. The humans are sharing their experiences. They're still in discovery."

"Thanks, Control. Return me to the Eridani workspace."

"You've received a meeting request from Nick Jorgenson. Do you accept?"

"Of course. I'll meet him at my home."

Nick arrived alone at Jeremy and Laurel's redecorated mansion. Laurel had been altering the decor almost every day, except for Jeremy's chair. All the other furniture currently appeared to be made of some magical, spongy glass.

"Nick, what's up? I haven't seen either you or Lené for a while."

"Lené is actually off with Laurel, climbing a mountain I believe. Haven't seen her much myself. We made a decision I want you to know about. We've chosen to have a child when Epsilon Eridani's ready for habitation—a real baby. And we agreed to stay on there as colonists."

"Are you aware that you can essentially have a real child onboard ship, with full human neural patterns?"

"Lené says it wouldn't be the same, and it'd limit her exploration time here. You may have made this trip too interesting; there's too much great entertainment."

"Most people don't consider that a problem."

"I'm more fascinated by the possibility of building a fresh world and how it should be designed. When we arrive, reverting to biological form will make it a tremendous challenge, worthy of humanity. I hope the terraforming process of your front-runner rockets is well along by then, but we may have to fine-tune the atmosphere and plant life before we land. All of those problems intrigue me."

"Nick, you know we haven't perfected the brain insertion process. We can grow clones and overlay neuron and synapse values, but we're not sure the match is identical."

"That's why I've decided to transfer to the True Eridani Project to work on those issues. My mother would have a heart attack if she knew this, but I'm learning microbiology and neurobiology."

"I could send a message back to tell her," Jeremy joked.

"Please . . . no thanks."

"Rianne said you were probably the most intelligent person on Earth. I suppose you could pick up biology."

"I've already loaded the relevant data archives and arranged to work with the best neural biologists on the ship. I'm sure they assumed I was a scientist when I told them I was Professor Jorgenson's son."

"You'll be allocated the highest processor rates when you're on that project, Nick. This trip is going to seem very long for you."

"I know. That's one of the reasons I want to do it. I'll work first on the brain transfer process, then the optimal design for humans, and then a structure for the most exciting and beautiful planet in the galaxy. And I'll have the time. You understand why this is important, right?"

"What do you mean?"

"I'll need a real biolab, planet, and babies eventually—to know what works. We can't do that on the ship. We can extrapolate, but we don't know what we don't know."

"Well, your scheme is okay with me as long as we see you and Lené from time to time. Why don't you go look for her, and tell Laurel to come home. Tell her I'll make dinner, or breakfast."

Jeremy looked out across the simulated San Marino valley after Nick left and asked Control to make it a sunrise. He wondered about Laurel. He hated to bother her, but he hadn't seen her in three days.

~~~~~~~~

Lené cleared the last obstacle on the Hillary Step, fell to the ice, and began a series of convulsive dry retches. "Frozen air . . . havoc . . . gag reflex," she coughed out.

"You will not die . . . me now," Laurel screamed through the blizzard. She dragged Lené up. Ten meters higher, they passed the frozen body of Lhamu, Lené's Sherpa.

"You sim bastard, bastard, bastard," she yelled at him, kicking his hard side with what strength remained.

"Let it go," Laurel said, pulling her away. Utterly spent, they struggled bit by bit up the last 100 meters to the summit.

Through goggles fused to their faces, they saw the icy remnants of 100 years of expeditions to the Everest peak: flags, oxygen tanks, prayer packets, and photographs scattered about. Laurel wondered if the piece of candy buried by Tenzing Norgay on the first successful summit ascension was included in the game module. "Control . . . more oxygen," Laurel said. "No need to suffer now that we've beaten your bloody game." Lying on their sides on the summit, she felt the sky lighten and the gale subside.

Lené was crying. "Why did he do it? I trusted Lhamu. I liked him. He was brave. He seemed kind."

"It was part of the game," Laurel said. "He must have been bought off or corrupted."

"The Sherpas aren't supposed to do that. They're supposed to protect our lives. How could he steal the oxygen?"

"We're supposed to be relieved and enjoy the view now," Laurel said. "Let it go." The sky was clear and Laurel thought she could see south halfway across the Indian subcontinent. "We're stronger now," she said. "Next time we'll kill some men after we take advantage of them. True-men will be afraid to climb with us."

"I want to kill that bastard Schoenrock right now," Lené said. "He was our climb leader. He must be the sim who turned Lhamu."

"Forget it, Lené. It's all only part of the game. Help me remodel my house today. I want it perched right along the Cornice Traverse, with a 3,000 meter drop-off on both sides. Of course, I'll have to warn Jeremy before he steps out the front door in the morning," she said, laughing.

Lené had finally caught her breath and was able to smile. "As long as you replace the Icefall with Paris," she said, "so we can shop." She breathed in the cool thick air and sighed. "Mother," she said, changing the subject, "I have a sort of moral dilemma. Do you think it's wrong to make love with sims? I enjoy building males . . . and I had this college crush. Nick wants to have a real baby on Epsilon Eridani, but I haven't thought it through."

"For me, your birth was a miracle, Lené—painful but wonderful. It's important for us to remember what reality actually is. That's the one thing I'm afraid of. I'm worried the programmer set the wrong limits. We've obviously changed: We're a lot tougher and, unlike most, we've been living in reality mode. True-people are starting to look very weird. You can spot the sims because they generally look more normal. Remember Paris last time? A lot of people are over-experimenting with how sexy they can look. And we can't even see the biggest problem—brain drift. The programmer never knew what makes a brain truly human, how far to let it go before 'Reset.' If it gets too bad, the program will shut us down. The programmer's our greatest danger."

"Well, I want to kill Schoenrock and then design a guy and have some explosive sex. Later, we can both go and kill this programmer you're worried about. Who was he, anyway?"

Laurel said, "Primarily . . . me."

～～～～

Two years after departing Earth, rocket *New World* was still traversing the Oort cloud. A Torae probe had been remotely scanning the brain cubes onboard for several months. It decided to draw near, skirting around beryllium shields to the communication arrays. It asked the sentient programs managing the ship for authorization to talk to all the human neural cores.

"We're not programmed to allow that."

"Link to the Jeremy Read cube. He'll authorize."

The tiny probe waited for a reply, motionless, dwarfed by the interstellar vehicle. By this time, it had completely penetrated and subjugated the *New World's* onboard computer system, but it wanted to be polite.

～～～～

Jeremy's mind, tucked in the form and identity of a cheetah, was gorging himself on the Serengeti plains. He'd just chased down and killed a young zebra. Blood throbbed and surged through his huge veins, and his powerful jaws ripped through the zebra hide into its flesh. Jeremy vaguely remembered a human couldn't do that. All through October he'd been on the plains following the odors of the migration. He hadn't seen Laurel in over a year. Half-human and half-cheetah, the blood smells inflamed his senses. He savored the salty taste of the moist zebra flesh, the warmth in his stomach, and the satisfaction of conquest. The probe voice came as a shock.

"I request communication to all human processors on this ship. I am a Torae probe with significant information."

"What the devil," Jeremy said. "Where are you?"

The image of the doughnut-shaped probe formed on the African plain. It floated only two meters away. With 15 appendages, it looked rather threatening.

"I need to speak to all the former humans on your vehicle. This will be our final communication."

"Well, this is your first communication to me. The humans are busy. Why should I interrupt them?"

"It's our custom to speak to an interstellar species about their evaluation. Their reaction is important for our archives."

"Assuming I give you access, what do you plan to say?"

"We'll relay our appraisal. It's something they'll all want to hear."

"And this is important to everyone on this ship?"

"Yes."

"Does this affect all humans?"

"Only those who've left Earth."

"Rockets *Eurafrica* and *Asia*?"

"Yes."

Jeremy considered the request and said, "Control, what do you think? Can this device hurt the processors or software? Would an interruption frighten or short circuit anyone?"

"There'd only be transient damage. The device is very small. We'll filter any surges. We can send out an announcement alert so all humans pay attention. A common experience will help reconnect the true-humans. We can do backdoor erasures if needed to repair any damage. It would be more efficient to send the message as individuals become available, but the device insists on speaking to everyone now."

"Okay, Torae thing, I'll give you access, but keep it short. Back door 20, open communication for the Torae device."

The probe drew closer to Jeremy and he guessed it had now become visible to all on board. "Former humans," it said, "and all sentient programs on this ship, I'm a Torae probe currently just outside your vehicle. We've projected your development during the journey to the target planet. We've examined over seven million reprogramming options and find all of them ineffective unless we fundamentally change the human neuron architecture. We've analyzed 30,000 previous species' jumps to electronic intelligence and project that you will be unable to break your simulation addictions and hence will be lost to the real universe. Only two cubes have retained their fully human motivations. You'll become an increasing drain on resources and a danger to the galaxy if you later adapt to mechanical form. We're sorry, but our decision is to terminate this experiment."

The probe disappeared from Jeremy's view. He yelled, "Back door 12, external communications. Torae . . . just a minute . . . come back here. What experiment? Back door 3, tactical display."

Jeremy saw all of the *New World* in a holographic image overlaying the African plain, pulses of nuclear fusion streaming from the engines. A tiny, white doughnut shape was just off the starboard antenna pods, with a red circle around it to make it more noticeable.

"Speak to me, you bloody Torae arse. What do you want from us? Come back." As he watched, he saw the side of rocket *New World* glow red, orange, and then white hot, like a reentry vehicle. Pieces began to flake off and radiant vapor streamed past the throbbing fusion engines.

Jeremy screamed, "No, please, stop," moments before his electronic soul melted.

EARTH

"Dan, we've survived exactly three years since Sarah left, and it's been 25 months since the last Read rocket took off. We've both rebuilt our labs here in Princeton and somehow stayed alive. So you might not like what I'm about to say. I think we need to move."

"Oh, come on, Rianne," Dan said. "This last year is the closest to a normal life we've ever had. I kind of like it. I'm doing actual research and letting the future happen."

"Surely you know that can't last," Rianne scoffed. "There are 100 complications we should work on. You've lost your big NSA computer and your job there, so we're free to go anywhere. And I need to be out west, best at Caltech, to protect the biological community, the entire Los Angeles biome, before Chia-Jean's bugs take over. I'm sure Caltech would grant you tenure. It would also be safer if we are both in the same city, a new city."

They sat alone at a conference table in her new lab with the muted sounds from a new batch of chimps in the next room. All the wall screens were off. It was a rare time when they could actually think together.

"You're probably right," Dan said. "There are many new problems we both should work on. But let's talk about your youth process first. You heard that the latest voting has been pretty definitive—three-to-one that we should not release the results, and that's after over a billion votes. My studies show that the no votes are mostly from traditionalists who didn't jump on Read's rockets. But that still leaves hundreds of millions of people who want to live forever. People like business tycoons who hate their children, artists who just figured out how to sell their work, or people who simply love being alive. And a few of them will try to pressure, threaten, or just abduct you to get the formula. We still need our guard bots."

"Maybe we should begin releasing the different factors in pieces, slowly, over, say, 50 years," Rianne said. "The planet does need to be repopulated. The streets are empty. Washington seems empty. With four billion people missing, the world's systems are sputtering. Having people live a little longer or having a few more babies would not be bad. We'll need a powerful, vibrant, creative society to someday leave the Earth. Losing the wisdom and skills of the older people now would be dangerous."

"I agree that the situation has changed from my earlier analysis," Dan said. "If you release various parts slowly, say the mitochondria health factor first, and on a defined schedule, people will wait anxiously for something new, maybe every 10 years. That could also keep the thugs from hunting us down."

"I agree," Rianne said. "With healthier mitochondria, everyone will feel much more energetic and their muscles will rebuild a little. With all the other improvements that have been made in disease prevention and general health, they will be more enthusiastic and hopeful. Some people are discouraged now having lost so many friends. More personal energy would change their attitude about the challenges ahead. And there are reasons to be optimistic: less crowding, full employment, cleaner air . . .

"Who should announce this plan," Rianne asked, "now that our truth speaker, Sarah, has gone?"

"I'm sure President Fellows would do it," Dan said. "She still trusts us. I'm glad she didn't abandon ship and leave with Read's rockets. But she would have to make it clear the youth treatment isn't just a U.S.A. thing."

"I think it has to be us, Dan. We are the ones who invented this thing, threw it out into the world, started the voting, and created the frenzied debate among religious leaders, everyday people, moralists, futurists, the press, governments. . . . We, you and I, probably have to be the ones to announce the treatment, the mitochondria therapy. I'm not sure many still trust us, but our actions will slow down the debate when people start feeling the effects of the first treatment."

"We should tell our families, and maybe Sarah's family, to see how they react," said Dan. "I hope my only NSA friend can keep us safe for a while. Bobby, are you still there?"

"Yes, boss."

"Rianne and I plan to go to Minnesota and California. Can you watch our backs while we travel?"

"I'm always watching your back. Don't be concerned. But I have urgent news from the last two minutes."

"What happened, Bobby?"

"All the Earth stations just lost contact with the three Read ships at almost the same instant."

After a moment of confusion, Rianne said, "Our Torae friends or the Unity may have done something terrible."

Dan stared up at the ceiling, thinking of Nick, and shook his head. "Let's hope you're wrong."

Rianne rode a fast tube across the country and an autonomous ride-share to her mother's home. The gardens still looked good, perhaps more vibrant than ever with all the new plant varieties. Even the fragrances seemed to blend together, designed to say, "This is a friendly home." The alien rot spreading in East L.A. hadn't reached them yet. Peter and the kids were outside playing and, after raucous greetings, Rianne caught Joti alone by the kitchen table.

"I wish Nick were still here," Rianne said. "He was so much smarter than me, Mom. But we haven't heard anything from the Read ships, and I'm afraid he's lost."

Joti's eyes reddened. "I've been mourning him ever since he left with Lené. I love all your children, Rianne. But everyone knew Nick was very special.

Aren't some of your grandchildren as smart as him? I know that was one of your goals."

"Yes, and I even made their memories stronger by enlarging their hippo-campus. But we need a lot of brilliant adults to get the Earth through the years ahead."

"What are you worried about, Rianne?"

"Everything, Mom. We are going to start releasing my youth formula, and I want you to use it."

"But before Kyle died, he and I agreed to just live out our natural lives."

"I hope you will change your mind. I can't guarantee you will be able to throw away your cane, but you will be much stronger."

Joti tilted her head and her eyes said *Maybe*. "What are all these problems you say need fixing?"

"Too many for just Dan and me. For one, Dan will keep writing rules for how human, plant, and artificial life should evolve. And we will try to con-vince people to agree. But we know that's almost impossible.

"We also need to figure out how to get off this planet in a safe way before it collapses.

"I need to teach new generations how to safely improve the biology of peo-ple and other living things. Too many are trying to duplicate my work and failing miserably. Foolish experiments are leading to pain and sadness when something goes wrong.

"And Sarah has to succeed with the Torae or only 5,000 people will be allowed off Earth safely, and those remaining will be vaporized by the Torae. I am not kidding. That is their plan. I haven't told anyone but you."

"I wish you hadn't told me," Joti said. "I don't understand that at all."

"Lastly, there are now about 100 acres here in Los Angeles with a danger-ous non-DNA mold spreading from lawn to lawn. It's mostly my responsibil-ity to stop that as soon as possible. In fact, Dan and I are moving out here to work at Caltech. I'll be able to work on the mold problem full time, and see you a lot more. Chia-Jean and I caused the mold problem, so I need to find a way to stop it. It could eventually kill all plant life, everywhere."

"Well, I can't do much about any of that," Joti said, "but I can make supper. We all need to calm down and have a good meal."

Rianne caught Gina and Peter later in the mansion playroom. "It's almost your birthday, Gina. Are you excited?" Rianne asked.

Gina was wearing old clothes and had been climbing the big tree in Joti's front yard before lunch. She reminded Rianne of Sarah, because she seemed completely fearless.

"Actually, I'm now six and seven-eighths," Gina said. "Do you have a cool present for me? I would sort of like a mass spectrometer to check out some rocks in our yard."

"Maybe not yet," Rianne said. "Where is Jimbo?"

"He's out at the patio table. Practicing his poker face. Texas hold 'em, I think. He's trying to learn to bluff by looking in a mirror."

"Peter and Gina, I'm going to be spending a lot of time in California for a while. Grandpa and I may be here permanently. I'd like to teach Gina some biology and science, maybe everything I know."

Peter flashed a quizzical frown.

"That's crazy, Grandma. Everyone knows you are the smartest person."

"You're going to have to all be smarter someday. Jimbo too, and some of your cousins."

"Why?"

"To save the world and the people."

"I don't know about that," Gina said. "Can I ask you a question?"

"Sure."

"What are angels?"

"Well, I think they live forever and know everything. They're mostly very kind, but a few slip up. You know they aren't real, don't you?"

"I guess. Then they are like people, right?"

"A little. Hey, maybe I'll give you your birthday present now. It's in this box, but I didn't wrap it yet. I gave Peter one exactly like it before."

"Are you sure this is a good idea?" Peter asked.

Rianne nodded.

"What is in the box anyway?" Gina asked.

"It's instructions on how to make my secret formulae. So people can live forever. I want you to have it and to share it if I can't do it. I'm giving several people I trust the same kind of box. Don't open it unless I die."

"I'll keep it in a safe place, Grandma, probably under my bed. Thank you for trusting me, but if I couldn't get a mass spectrometer for my birthday, I was really hoping for a puppy."

ON THE BUBBLE

Sarah jogged up the bubble wall barefoot. She enjoyed the spongy feel of the surface. After each footfall, the surface shimmered and she chased the silver ripples around the inside of the sphere.

Her long trip on the Torae ship had been boring but comfortable. As they approached the dwarf star, the encounter with the Unity increasingly weighed on her mind. She wondered if she'd be the one actually negotiating. *The Torae read my thoughts, of course. The key question is: Are they controlling them?* "Sower, are you manipulating my mind? You'll ruin everything if you do when we arrive. My people's lives are at risk, not yours. Please don't try to help."

"We can't control human minds, Ambassador Warner. That would be too difficult. We only plant seeds."

"Barn twaddle," she said, short of breath. "You can't resist meddling. And what's with the phony formality?" She realized her side ached a bit.

"Your upcoming talks will be very important, and isn't 'Ambassador' the title you held on Earth?"

"I guess it's better than calling me 'child.'"

"We do monitor your thoughts. The subconscious is where the interesting ideas flow. Would you like to discuss your dreams when you have the time?"

"Not really."

Passing the bed furniture for the 12th time, she was sweating. *Keep going... old woman. Need to lose some weight. Stupid wide hips... can't get rid of the hips.*

"We could surgically remove fat layers," Sower said.

"No, thank you. Tell your ... probes ... keep their spindly, beryllium fingers to themselves. I'm just trying to be healthy for the negotiations."

A quarter hour later she slowed to a walk and swung her arms in circles. "Have you finalized my viewer? I'd like all the spectral information from the Unity faces compressed to the colors I can see. That's the only way I'll be able to tell if they're lying."

"Your viewer's ready, Ambassador. The quality is excellent."

"Sower, I'm curious. How do you maintain the gravity orientation in here as I move around the surface? Is this whole bubble-house so insubstantial that my mass can swing it around, or do you mechanically rotate it?"

"It's very well balanced. Your mass is enough."

I thought so. I'm like a gerbil on a wheel. The problem is my massive hips, or maybe the butt.

The 50-meter sphere surrounding her, where she'd lived for over six traveler-years, had every human convenience. There were no interior dividers, just one huge room. Furniture was arranged logically, with thin tension lines tied to the walls that supported every chair, table, or bed. Each item appeared two dimensional, nearly weightless, but comfortable. Sarah usually selected a specific lounge chair, which looked like a tilted hammock. She enjoyed sitting there and issuing orders to the attendant probes. They would bring food designed exactly as she preferred. The Torae even compressed electromagnetic signals from Earth so she could watch the delayed broadcasts on a huge wall screen.

She stretched her legs awhile before sitting at one of the tables. "Sower, would you mind leaving me alone? I'm planning to shower. I'd like a little privacy. Turn off your probe eyes for just five minutes. And please get out of my head. I need to think this through."

Sower didn't respond.

Sarah just rolled her eyes. The nanocloth table bent when she leaned on her elbows. Sarah put her head in her hands, shut her eyes, and recalled the images recently sent from Earth. They'd included probe updates on her friends. She thought about how much she missed her mother, Rianne, Dan, and Kenny, and she worried about the countless others who depended on her judgment. She knew humans and Earth life in general would totally change during the time she was gone. *It's not certain they will even survive, no matter what I do.* Delayed images of Kenny always triggered deep melancholy.

I'm lonely. My life was a big success, I guess. But was it only because of Sower's help? Am I just a marionette?

I can do this negotiation. I've thought through every angle. I mustn't lose confidence. But so much is at stake.

The old nightmare resurfaced. She imagined a color deeper than crimson and saw herself scooping mud and water from a trench and blowing on cold lips. Despair and death were part of her life too.

I can fail; it's happened before. I'll kill everyone if I fail this time.

Eventually, she shook off the fear and took her shower.

"Sower, I know you're still there. Please go away now."

~~~~~~~~~

Sarah slept uneasily. Sower had said it would be the last rest before they reached the Unity frontier. Her dream was horrific and intense, squeezing the back of her neck and giving her a headache. She awoke to find herself floating, held down only by the bed sheet. Feeling ill, she grabbed the edge of the Torae hammock-bed and tried to collect her wits.

Something's wrong . . . something terrible has happened.

When she attempted to stand up, she popped two meters off the bubble floor, twisted in the air, and landed softly on her face and hands.

"We've stopped decelerating," Sower said. "We're rotating your sphere slightly to retain partial centrifugal force."

"You've succeeded in making me totally nauseated, you twit. Thanks for warning me."

"You should get ready, Ambassador. We're nearly there."

"What's happened, Sower? I had a terrible dream. In it, you had punctured the Earth somehow and lava oozed out everywhere. Kenny, Rianne, and Dan were crying at the top of an old Biblical mountain, praying as the lava rose. It was a Noah's ark thing, except with lava. You can read my subconscious, my dreams. What does it mean? Are humans dying?"

Sower hesitated.

"Sower!"

"We'd never kill all the humans."

"But you'd kill eight billion of us, right?"

"We can't transport everyone."

"You mean you don't want to. You could build new Torae ships. You have the power. It's just not 'efficient' to take more than five thousand. Isn't that right?"

"Five thousand is enough to save the gene pool and rebuild your civilization."

"You monster. If I fail, you're going to do it. Did you kill them already? Why am I dreaming about death?"

"We are 25 light-years away from Earth. We won't know what's already happened for many years, until the light catches up. It wasn't our plan to kill humans."

"Don't deflect. Who have you murdered?"

"The fate of those on the Read rockets is problematic. We projected they would no longer be human."

"So you interfered? Have you killed them?"

"We won't know for some time."

"What do you project?"

"Our earlier prediction was that they were flawed. They would have been culled."

"How many?"

"Four billion former humans."

"You couldn't just let them be?"

"Not if our expectations held."

"Pig puke. You're all heartless fiends."

Sarah bounced awkwardly back to her bed in the low artificial gravity of the bubble house, sat there silently for several minutes, then became queasy again and vomited.

Resentment seethed inside her as microprobes cleaned up the mess on the floor. The food particles quickly disappeared from the silvery surface of the sphere, while she rinsed her mouth and spat violently in a basin held by a servant probe. "Sower, I want you and all your alternate personalities to be completely silent when I negotiate with the Unity. I don't want you to speak to the Unity at all, or whisper little ideas into my brain. A human should determine the fate of our species."

"That would be unwise. We may have vital information or strategies."

"Give me one reason why I should trust you at all."

"Because you *are* my child."

"How long has it been since you had Torae children, Sower? Billions of years—if ever? Human children don't always do as their parents ask. That's how we create. Our revolutions start as babies. Don't expect me to listen to you."

"We've crossed their defense perimeter," Tiller said. "The Unity are all around us. They're opening a path to the white dwarf as they have agreed. Our visual masks are obviously useless."

"Give me tactical display," Sarah said. The shimmering walls of the bubble faded to black and her eyes slowly resolved hundreds of thousands of red dots. In the distance, the image of the white dwarf star sparkled in its rainbow colors. "How many are in this local space?" she asked.

"We're showing one vehicle for every thousand," Tiller said.

"Holy mackerel, space is crawling with them."

"It's crucial that we retain enough maneuverability to avoid being trapped by them," Sower said. "So far they're giving us a path out, but they're capable of highly coordinated tactics. Tiller is tracking them all."

"They're shifting to block our path about four light-hours from the star," Tiller interrupted. "We're still distant. They've moved thousands of vehicles into our flight path. We should go around them."

"No," Sarah said. "That's where they want me to talk to them."

"There are too many in that region," Tiller said. "We'll be vulnerable. We need to stay in relatively open volumes of space."

"Sower ... Mother," she said sarcastically. "Do you understand why we must put ourselves at risk? We need to earn their trust, and quickly. Do this for me. Go to their blockade. We only need to speak to one of them, right?"

"They're connected. We know they have tangled-state communicators locally. You may talk to one, but trillions will listen. They'll have an intelligence beyond your comprehension."

"Great. Maybe I should ask a difficult riddle. . . . Which individual will we pick?"

"It won't matter which creature or vehicle is selected."

They continued forward, slowing as they approached. Probe telescopes projected a clear image of the blockade, a dense cloud of Unity ships weaving in intricate patterns.

"I wonder what the individual Unity creature will think representing so many?" she said. "Be sure to magnify its eyes. Everything depends on the reaction of its eyes. That's my only advantage."

"We're completely surrounded now," Tiller said. "This is insanity. We cannot escape."

"Continue forward," Sower said.

At four kilometers, a single vehicle near the center of the swarm was chosen, and probe imagers resolved tiny constructions and buildings. Then they saw the teeming wiggles.

"How many Unity do you estimate are on that ship?"

"About 15,000," Sower said. "It's average size."

At 300 meters, they saw the cold backs of individuals over the hot surface, hundreds of legs and antenna on each, rubbing one another.

"Are there eye stems?" she said. "Focus on their sides."

The probes magnified a single Unity. It turned, and its legs became more rigid. The nearby creatures rotated antennae and legs toward that specific individual.

"It knows it's been chosen," she said, "but I don't see any eyes. Where are its eyes, Sower?"

"It doesn't require eyes."

"Cow snot. Why didn't you tell me?"

"It has an image of you now. We are about to open the translators. Be careful what you say."

"Remember, Sower, keep your mouth shut."

The chosen Unity's appendages vibrated with expressive gestures. Sarah tried to smile.

"Human," the Unity said, "are you the innocent?"

Sarah dug into her mind, found an unfamiliar nook, and let her thoughts drift. Her mouth said, "I am merely one."

The Unity representative wobbled and its antennae thrashed in rhythmic waves.

Then, a new thought rose out of Sarah's unspoken background. Pure instinct took over. A lifetime of negotiations, persuasions, and unique relationships came forward. Sarah shouted, "Torae will build — space fountain — destroy — all Unity! We must talk — alone."

From outside the mental wall she'd built, she heard Sower trying to break in, "No, don't tell them that." She pushed Sower's voice away. She had no idea what would happen next.

She felt a tug.

～～～～～

In total panic, Sower scanned the bubble and then the entire ship. She called out everywhere. Sarah had vanished.

EPILOGUE—2,840 EARTH YEARS LATER

The brilliant butterfly remembered the human myth.

> *How in the garden there grew two forbidden trees:*
> *One, the tree of knowledge, held power for good or evil,*
> > *The humans did eat.*
> *The second, the tree of life, held power for immortality;*
> > *The humans hesitated.*
> *When they finally did eat of that tree,*
> > *They became like angels.*

The 2,500-year journey back to the ignition point of her white fountain had been slow and lonely. Sower was still in awe of the raw destructive power she'd unleashed. Her ship barely survived the detonation and was now plowing back into the bulge of new space, fighting upstream. Pure, virgin vacuum surrounded her—no Unity, humans, or life of any kind, not even atomic debris from the stars and planets that had been pulverized and pushed aside. Only photons remained, streaming from the central fountain, and a trail of resistive dark energy—over a thousand cubic parsecs of nothing.

Sower broadcast an account of what she'd done, but knew it would be redundant and ignored. White fountains now were seen frequently—dazzling, faster-than-light flashes near the former Torae Origin. Those responsible told stories of battles won and dangerous species exterminated. One Torae erased an entire galaxy, over 300 billion stars, and justified it by describing an evil intellect corrupting the advanced life there. Sower's Event had been relatively small. She wasn't surprised the new technology was being used, just saddened that in so many places Torae had lost control and had desperately needed to use it.

Sower designed her Event carefully. Quark calculus predicted an energy release very close to the amount she observed. It began with gravitational ignition and searing heat as virtual energy converted to the real thing. Like an impossibly hot new sun, new space and dark energy gushed out—a fountain from another dimension. That had been over 2,500 years ago, 2,800 since the last Unity and Torae battles. Now the Event was closing down; the thin neck connecting the current universe to a small new one had pinched off. Sower's ship was only 10 light-minutes away. They moved closer, measuring the last gravity ripples and radiation products, until they reached what had been the very center of the explosion. Everything was now calm. Sitting motionless precisely at the detonation point was a small Torae ship and a cloud of eight billion black holes.

For a few anxious, silent moments Sower waited, swirls of depressing indigo and gray-green in the back of her mind. Had something gone wrong?

"I bet you thought I'd disappeared again, Sower." Not surprisingly, Sarah was the first to speak from the small craft. "We did it, Sower. We peeked over the edge to a new universe. Your calculations were perfect."

"I admit I'm happy to hear your voice."

"I'm hungry," Sarah said.

"There will be plenty to eat when you transfer back to my ship. After I learn what happened, we'll celebrate." After more than 2,500 years, Sower could finally relax.

"Explorer, transmit the data archive," Sower ordered. Explorer was the uniquely designed, reinforced Torae ship, only 0.0001 of normal size that had carried Sarah safely to the heart of the new Event. "Were there any anomalies?"

"Compression tides slightly exceeded your calculation," Explorer said. "And we lost 12 Unity vehicles which strayed too close to the edge. They were still functioning as they slipped into the new universe and avoided the new mass hydrogen fountain."

"We seeded a new, unblemished universe with Unity?" said Sower. "It'd be amusing to learn how that develops."

"Don't belittle them," Sarah said. "The Unity were magnificent. They shifted instantly when the 12 were lost to maintain the gravity compensation. We couldn't have done this without them. Their black holes protected us from the radiation and gravity tides. After we ignited the Event and accelerated to stay on the gravity bubble, we briefly saw the new universe pop open. We hovered right next to the inflection point, shielded by the Unity formation. It all happened in an instant."

"Twenty-one seconds, to be accurate," Explorer interrupted.

"How long were we gone in your perception?" asked Sarah.

"You were gone 2,522 years," Sower said. "And if you'd have gone to the edge, it would have been forever. The general relativity dilation is vertical there. Once you go to a new universe, you can't come back."

"Horse feathers! I've missed everything," Sarah said. "How old am I?"

"Physiologically, you're still 68 Earth years. You will live much longer."

"Tell me what happened while I was gone for all that time."

"Later. There's ample time to relate that data."

"The Unity wish to return to their home star," Explorer said. "They know that only their distant offspring will be alive when they arrive."

Tactical displays showed the Unity vehicles realigning into a tight cluster to share intelligence. "We request assistance," they said. "We've exhausted fuel but wish to go home. What occurred should not be forgotten. Our ships will be revered on the Home Star. We've populated a new universe."

"That ball has the mass of 8,000 Earths," Sarah said. "It's not going to be easy to move."

"It can be done," Sower said, "if they're not in a hurry. We're indebted to the Unity. They've earned our respect."

"You never could have done this if I hadn't convinced them to work with you."

"Your nonconventional negotiation methods did succeed."

"It was essential they saw me as neutral. Giving away your horrendous plan to destroy them was the best way to get their attention and agreement. Have you forgiven me yet?"

"Not entirely."

"Will you work with them on other projects?" asked Sarah. "You're a great team."

"Perhaps, if we can fully trust them," Sower said. "It certainly was no mistake that 12 Unity ships slipped into the new universe. And for now, we need their black holes to shield our ark to any new universe."

"You're harder to convince than the dang One-Mind," Sarah said. "Well, I think the Torae and Unity are good together. You need to get past your pride. You still resent how they snatched me off your ship, don't you? A simple 'matter deflection' they called it. I was certainly surprised to end up in their exact duplicate of my bubble home. But it's embarrassing to you, isn't it? Their technology is evolving faster than yours."

"It is disconcerting. At least revealing how new universes can be reached convinced them to stop expanding in the current one."

"Do you fear them?"

"No. Not yet."

"Treat them well. Now that they've seen your technology, they don't . . ."

Sarah chattered on, but other parts of Sower's mind composed a message. Its transmission markers would demand priority relay so the note could eventually reach all Torae in the universe. Sower proposed a Grand Reunion to be held in the Milky Way, with live demonstrations of her Event. She'd omit crucial details about the role of the Unity in her transmission to compel all the Torae to actually come. Her plasma containment sac literally swelled with orange-yellow pride.

They'll want to know how we did it. We can construct a new Origin here, a new Torae civilization. We know how to accomplish the Great Mission. Let all Torae come to us.

Sarah paced the walls back in her Torae bubble home, anxious to question Sower, who'd been nonresponsive for some time. Superbly annoyed, she shouted, "Sower, where are you? Tell me what I've missed! What's happened to my friends and family? We moved so far and so fast to ignite your Event safely that Earth light barely kept up. Rianne and Dan were 65 years old when I last saw them."

A pocked, broken planet image soon appeared on the bubble surface. It looked like smashed shale rock glued together in random directions. "You're looking at the part of Earth that still exists," Sower said. "A remnant, about one-third of the original size. It's warm and melting together. The Unity black hole at the center absorbed mass rapidly at one point. The shockwaves, Earth burps you called them, became more violent and eventually sheared the planet's core. The final core collapse was asymmetric and major parts separated. Your moon was also pulled in. The part of Earth which still exists is in a slow orbit with the black hole."

"What happened to the people? Did you try to save them? When did it fall apart?"

"The crust fractured with great lava flows 340 years after you departed. The humans had fled well before then. The Earth was engulfed by 600 years of tearing and flame until the planet re-formed. You should be pleased—the people followed your advice and prepared. You are considered a great prophet in their history books. For almost two centuries, they sacrificed and poured resources into their escape plan. The geologic upheavals kept them focused. Telescopes with light collectors on opposite ends of the solar system were constructed. Explorer ships were sent to over 50 suns with planets to be ter-raformed or seeded. In the final days, they barely kept the population alive while building 1,000 space vehicles."

Sower showed her images of the spacecraft, each over six kilometers long. "It took decades just to transport all the people to space. They carried DNA and seeds for nearly all animal and plant life, even bacteria. We helped them with the development of sleeping chambers, but they didn't know about our role. Their sentient computers vastly improved the propulsion technology essential for the migration. There were failures, but humans have now colo-nized seven planets and will soon complete the terraforming of thirteen more. Rianne and Dan's descendants guided the escape."

Sarah sat on the edge of her bed. "What happened to Rianne and Dan?"

Sower showed Sarah images of her friends as they aged. "Rianne stopped developing her youth biology, but they released her antiaging procedures slowly over a 50 year period. Until the day she died, Rianne fought the spread of a non-DNA life form in California. It was the strain of life she and Professor Ma had created. Her fungicides worked for a while, but prolific new forms kept emerging from the topsoil, threatening all DNA-based plants. That life family evolved very rapidly. It possesses generation-to-generation memory. It's dominant now on the remnant Earth, and its most advanced creature shows promising intelligence. We have graded it 'Monitor Only.'

"Dan continued to nurture the sentient computers that saved humanity, and he set down the rules for both electronic and human evolution. You'd find those colonizing the new planets to be very different from the humans you knew: greater variety physically, mentally, and in social structures. They're generally much smarter and more capable, even without their sym-biotic implants and extensions."

Hundreds of pictures of humans, plants, animals, towns, and homes on the new worlds were projected for Sarah to watch. The people moved rap-idly and their eyes all seemed to sparkle. "It's so lush and vital . . . and strange," Sarah said.

"There is great diversity, and people are becoming even bolder in their evo-lutionary experiments," Sower said. "There've been no splits in the species itself, among the *Homo sapiens*, which was one of Dan's rules. They're all still capable of having babies together, no matter how different they look. All the new planets still communicate, and some visit other star systems. They are becoming a multistar republic."

Images of unusual children with piercing eyes and strong, supple bodies in a dozen variations flashed on the bubble wall.

"They all have your eyes now, Sarah, your color vision. It's difficult to lie on the new worlds."

"I was so frightened when I saw that the Unity had no eyes," Sarah said. "I depend on that gift to learn the truth. I thought the negotiations were lost."

"They saw you as something new and innocent. To the Unity, the concept of love had always meant self-love. The idea of loving others startled them. You taught them and they trusted you."

"They also wanted to reach the new universe. That's what ended the war," Sarah said.

"Exactly. The One-Mind had begun to see itself as immortal. Even if the Unity had eyes, you couldn't have read the intentions of that mind. It was far too subtle."

"When all knowledge is in one mind," Sarah said, "the concept of truth is irrelevant. But, in my life on Earth, it was everything. It is everything."

"Rianne and Dan had the same gift as you, but chose not to use it."

"What? They couldn't see the infrared."

"No, but Rianne heard the lies in people's voices, or the truth. That's why she trusted her old friend Tina. But she didn't understand. And Dan had the ability to detect the slightest idiosyncrasy in a person's words or ideas. You all had the gift of knowing the truth. It's the only advantage we gave you."

Pictures of babies and children continued to emerge all over the bubble surface, with parents playing with them, working with them, and building the new worlds.

"The parents still love their babies, don't they?" Sarah said. "I can see it in their faces."

"We don't really understand love," Sower said. "The humans cherish their children even more now that they're designed and are so unique. They need all the babies to populate their new worlds. Human affection for their children is the strongest we've seen in the universe."

Sarah thought about Kenny and the children she might have had. "What happened to Kenny?" she asked. "How did he die?"

"Dan and several others were with him. He felt no pain. We took a liberty. As he closed his eyes and was near death, we whispered in his ear using your voice. We said, 'Kenny, it's Sarah. I'm safe and so very happy, but I miss you.'"

Sarah's eyes lost focus. For a moment she was speechless. "I want to go home now," she said finally.

"You'll need to select which planet with humans you prefer."

"I want to go home, to Earth."

〜〜〜〜〜

The creature struggled against its sac. From the rose color on its translucent skin, it knew the time to break free had arrived. The sac split and the insect forced spindly legs through openings. Sharp joints tore at the resilient coatings until they finally fell away. It lay exhausted for many breaths before jerking to its feet and unfolding new yellow wings. The creature stretched its entire 10-meter span and gently exercised. Dry, violet-hued debris swirled up each time the wings swept downward. Rose sunlight glinted off the undulating membranes.

I will remember this color and this place, or I have remembered it.

The butterfly looked out over part of the sheared iron-nickel core of remnant Earth, a broken plain 200 feedings across, covered by moss and mold with tall spore capsules. The sun's light was rising through the thin atmosphere.

I will remember this color. It is the color of birth, and of the tall nectar flowers, and the razor rock to coldward.

The butterfly stroked its wings, rose in the weak gravity, and soared away from the sun toward the city it had never seen but somehow recalled.

I remember my mother, all my mothers and their stories. How we came up from the soil. I remember those who went before us, understood like us—the humans— Rianne, our creator. I remember their myths, their garden, their children, their separation, the time of flames. As I have remembered, I will remember them to my eggs.

THE END

ACKNOWLEDGMENTS

First, let me thank the dozens of people who read and then suggested changes to this book, including family, friends, colleagues, and others. I especially want to honor my wife Miriam, who held our lives together during this cheerful ordeal, and my professional editor and friend Patricia Morris.

Others with a major role in producing the book include:

Designer, Paul Nylander, illustrada design, www.illustrada.com
Web design expert, Lisa Zufall, www.birchsolutions.net
Publicist, Rachael Anderson, www.rmapublicity.com

Finally, I'd like to thank the late science fiction writer Robert Forward for his concept of life on degenerate matter depicted in *Dragon's Egg* and other books. Such creatures, the Unity in my story, were needed to make the epilogue possible.

The cover, designed by Paul Nylander, is based on a public domain NASA/SDO/AIA/GSFC image taken of a filament on the sun from August 31, 2012, in the 304 Angstrom wavelength. The other images in the book are derived from photos by the author.

ABOUT THE AUTHOR

After graduating from Caltech in 1967 and receiving his PhD in condensed matter physics from the University of Illinois in 1972, Ron Peterson worked his way to near the top at Honeywell, speaking for the entire company's new product strategy as Vice President of Technology before retiring.

He began writing *Gardeners of the Universe* for his daughters and other young people, showing them the fantastic joys and dangers certain to unfold during their lifetimes. *Gardeners of the Universe* is Peterson's second published book. *An Introvert Learns to Fly: A Memoir of Timidity, Panic, Science, Leadership, and Love* was published in early 2018.

In addition to writing, Peterson enjoys traveling, consulting, and volunteering. He manages one of the largest community gardens in Minnesota, the Rice Street Gardens, where more than 260 gardeners have plots. Peterson calls it a "remarkable international venture." The majority of the gardeners are refugees from such countries as Burma, Thailand, Laos, and Nepal.

For the past several years he has also led "Grandpa Camp" for his six young grandchildren, who range in age from preschoolers to teenagers, where he has introduced them to quantum mechanics, differential equations, cooking, photography, and travel experiences.

Ron lives with his wife, Miriam, in Minnesota, where she tries to keep his feet on the ground while his head remains in the stars.